# A Girl's Best Friend

Liz Young started writing after a variety of jobs that included being part of an airline cabin crew, modelling for TV commercials in Cyprus and working for the Sultan's Armed Forces in Oman. She lives in Surrey. *A Girl's Best Friend* is her third novel.

D0293243

*Also by Liz Young*

Asking for Trouble
Fair Game

# A Girl's Best Friend

Liz Young

arrow books

Published by Arrow Books 2003

1 3 5 7 9 10 8 6 4 2

First published in the United Kingdom in 2003 by William Heinemann

Arrow Books
The Random House Group Limited
20 Vauxhall Bridge Road, London, SW1V 2SA

Random House Australia (Pty) Limited
20 Alfred Street, Milsons Point,
Sydney, New South Wales 2061, Australia

Random House New Zealand Limited
18 Poland Road, Glenfield,
Auckland 10, New Zealand

Random House (Pty) Limited
Endulini, 5a Jubilee Road, Parktown 2193, South Africa

The Random House Group Limited Reg. No. 954009

www.randomhouse.co.uk

A CIP catalogue record for this book
is available from the British Library

Papers used by Random House are natural,
recyclable products made from wood grown in sustainable forests.
The manufacturing processes conform to the environmental
regulations of the country of origin

ISBN 0 09 946034 3

Typeset by Deltatype Limited, Birkenhead, Merseyside
Printed and bound in the United Kingdom by
Bookmarque Ltd, Croydon, Surrey

*For my daughters, who once said that if they couldn't be vets, they'd like to marry one.*

*And for Bonnie, my beloved little black shadow for fourteen years, who finally had to leave me shortly after I finished writing this book.*

# A Girl's Best Friend

# Chapter 1

Though I say it myself, I made a lovely tart.

From my wardrobe mirror she pouted back at me: Emerald Caprice, slapper with a heart of nine-carat gold plate and very good at games. Naughty schoolgirls with Cabinet ministers, Miss Moneypenny to a bishop's Bond: you name it, Emerald had done it and taken notes. Just now she was about to publish her memoirs, go on chat shows and sell excerpt rights to the Sunday papers.

And get murdered.

'Serve you right, too,' I said in her mother's cockney accent – Emerald had started life as Janice Trotter, a distant relative of Del Boy. 'I always knew you'd come to a bad end. Your dad would turn in his grave, you little trollop. Just look at you – your dumplings is boiling over.'

But possibly not enough. Hitching up my scarlet satin Wonderbra another couple of inches, I gave myself a critical inspection. False eyelashes, perhaps? As I have the reddish-gold hair that often goes with green eyes, my lashes aren't my best feature. False nails would be good, too. Emerald would probably go for those mega-jobs that double as weapons, and woe betide any client who wouldn't pay.

However, the leopard-print top was perfect: two pounds fifty from a charity shop and sprayed on. The trousers were supple black leather, borrowed from my colleague

1

Louise. 'I've only worn them once,' she'd said. 'I was terrified of sitting down in case they split right up the bum.'

They were skin-tight on me, too: one of those size eights that calls itself a twelve. Still, tight was the idea. Much of my stomach was gasping for its life, forced up for air.

After slapping on lipstick in Red Hot Red I went downstairs to show Leo. Flaked out on a beanbag sofa with Henry snoring beside him, he gaped at me. 'Christ, Vera. When you said tarting yourself up, I didn't think you meant it literally.'

My name is actually Isabel, but I won't go into that now. I shot him a flirty pout. 'If that's a gun in your pocket, darling, it's pathetic. Come to Emerald and for fifty quid I'll turn it into an AK 47.'

A grin spread over his face. '*Emerald*? What's all this in aid of?'

'Felicity's party. We're away for the weekend, remember? Her pre-Christmas, getting-in-the-mood bash in Devon?'

This wiped the grin off his face. 'Don't tell me it's fancy dress? Please, not vicars and tarts?'

'Leo, it's a murder party. Didn't I tell you?'

'No!'

His appalled reaction was the reason I'd conveniently forgotten to tell him before. 'Sorry,' I lied. 'I could have sworn I had.' I showed him the invitation, done in scary Gothic script as Felicity liked to do things properly. It said:

### MURDER MOST FOUL
**You are invited to a weekend of treachery, violent death and ham acting at the House of Horror**

Under the date and address she'd written: *Come Fri.*

*night if you can, otherwise Sat. lunch. Bloodstains will be provided. N.B. Do not bring bottles, Bill the Booze gives me a discount.*

Leo was gaping at the address. '*Colditz?*'

'That's what the locals call the house. It's hideous Victorian Gothic, used to belong to her family. I told you she'd rented it for the weekend.'

He was not looking exactly overjoyed at the prospect. 'Is she throwing in the odd vampire as well?'

'No, and there's only going to be one tart, so don't get overexcited. Plus a bishop and a has-been rock star, among others.'

His eyes closed in an '*oh, shit*' fashion. Leo had once told me he had a phobia about anything smelling of fancy dress, ever since his mother had sent him to a party as a tomato sandwich at the age of six. He'd had nightmares about the abject humiliation of it, when every other boy was Batman or Robin Hood, and he'd wet himself because he couldn't get his top slice of bread off.

'Oh, come on,' I coaxed. 'Don't go all boring on me.'

'Who am I, then? Dirty Dick, your pimp?'

'Emerald handles her own career development, thank you very much. You're down as a dodgy City type who's laundering crack money in the Turks and Caicos.'

He groaned. 'I can see it now. Hammed-up Agatha Christie-stroke-*Cluedo*. We'll all be sitting about waiting for dinner when the lights will go out, and somebody'll scream. Then there'll be a body on the carpet and Lady Posh will say, "Dear me, how very tiresome," and we'll all pretend we don't know who dunnit for the sake of form.'

Even this was probably optimistic, culturally speaking. Felicity had asked a friend to dream this murder up, on the grounds that he'd written a panto entitled *Rude Riding Hood* for the Village Players. 'You'll love it,' I soothed.

3

'All you need is some red braces – it'll be a doddle. You're Charles Plonker-fforbes, with two fs.'

'Two effs is about right. I hope this Felicity isn't into cretinous party games as well.'

I couldn't lie, because she was. Killer round the dining table was a favourite, or grown-up Pass the Parcel, with amusing little items from Ann Summers. 'I'm afraid so. Like lining all the girls up on chairs, blindfolding the blokes one by one and getting them to feel all the legs, to identify their own partner. You'll just hate that,' I added, running cunning fingers through his hair. Leo had gorgeous, glossy hair, midway between wavy and curly, and two shades short of black.

At last there was a smile cracking his face, which was a relief. As I hadn't seen Felicity for months, I didn't want a reluctant player in tow. She was one of my best friends and I badly wanted her to like him. Even more, I wanted him to like her, which might be a marginally taller order, at first. My immediate ex, Sulky Simon, had said, Christ, he'd thought those Sloaney pony-club types were extinct, he needed earplugs. Nit-picking Neil (penultimate ex) had said did she have to bounce around like a retriever puppy wanting to play Come and Steal My Squeaky Bone?

I'd been hurt on Felicity's behalf, because although she could seem a trifle bouncy at first, she was one of those people you could phone at three in the morning, knowing she wouldn't say, 'No, it's fine,' while secretly cursing you for being miserable at unsocial hours.

With Emerald's dumplings right under his nose, Leo was finally persuaded. 'All right, Vera. I guess I can do a Plonker for one night.'

Vera was short for Elvira, both strictly between us. I'd told him if he ever used either of them in public I'd call him Snugglebum. On our very first night out, by the river at

Richmond, when I'd been wearing one of those floaty dresses you think might be chilly later, he'd stopped and kissed me on the tow-path. Then he'd said, 'Elvira, I think I have to take you away from here and make violent love to you.'

The effect of this on me had been instant, flooding wooze. 'My name's Isabel,' I'd said. 'But maybe you're muddling me with someone else now it's getting dark.'

'No, I think you're an Elvira. Tell your mother she got it wrong.'

As I'd told someone later, when most men are about as romantic as a pork pie, any wooze-making bullshit is welcome. Vera didn't have quite the same floaty ring to it, but no man can keep pork pies at bay for six months, and I wouldn't trust him if he did.

Leo was still adept at other woozy arts, though. He started playing delicate Erogenous Zones, kissing the inside of my arm. This was guaranteed to get Vera going in seconds, but I was still practising my Emerald. 'If you're after any action, darling, you'd better have the readies,' I said. 'In advance: no cheques, no plastic.'

Halfway between elbow and underarm, he laughed. 'Just out of interest, have you and Plonker had commercial transactions, as it were?'

'Probably. I've been at it with all sorts, and I've just written my memoirs. I've got a massive advance from my publishers, and chat shows all lined up. Which is why I'm going to get murdered.'

'She said it's you?'

'It was an educated guess. Nobody actually knows yet – it'd spoil the fun.'

'Then I'd better make hay before you're on a slab in the morgue.' Turning his attention to my bouncy cleavage, he went on in a drunken Plonker voice, 'Christ, Emerald, you remind me of my old nanny. Knockers like barrage balloons, she had. How much for really kinky stuff?'

'You couldn't afford it, darling.'

A minute later this role-play had warmed up enough for Henry to slink into a corner and pretend to be asleep. Leo said he always looked embarrassed, but as Henry was a very polite sort of animal I put it down to innate good manners. However, just as Leo was growling, 'Todgers of steel, us Plonker-fforbeses – famed for it ever since we came over with the Normans,' his mobile rang.

'Leave it,' I said, but he'd already seen 'home' on the screen.

'Gemma!' he said.

Exit Plonker-fforbes, stage left. Enter Leo Marsh, devoted father.

And Emerald stuffed her left dumpling back into her Wonderbra.

'How are you, sweetie?' he went on. 'How was Brownies?'

Leo was so devoted, he knew that Tuesday was Brownies, Wednesday was ballet and Thursday was being good for the babysitter while Mummy went to the gym.

'Cancelled?' he was saying. 'Why was that then, darling?'

A resigned sort of sigh escaped me. It wasn't that I resented his kids. How can you resent little girls of five and seven who were only sure of seeing their daddy every other weekend? I didn't resent his wife either, as she'd been ex well before I'd met him. Lately, though, it felt as if my share of the Leo-cake was getting ever smaller. I wanted a great big slice for once, slathered with jam and cream and icing.

As he did the doting daddy bit, Henry uncurled himself

from his tactful ball. He sat at my feet with an expression that said, 'Nothing doing after all, then?'

Henry was my other love. He was a Baluchi camel hound, an endangered species since the tribesmen had ditched the camels for Toyota pick-ups. That's what I told people anyway; a few even believed me. Mostly they said, 'Yeah, right,' or made rude remarks about floor mops shagging sheep by mistake.

Personally, I thought Henry had Irish wolfhound somewhere. He had rough, greyish-brown fur and the right sort of legs. The rest of him was a mystery and even his mother would never have entered him for a Bonny Pup competition, which was probably why I loved him all the more.

As he gazed at me with liquid brown devotion, Leo was still at it. From the conversation I gathered that it was Jack's birthday on Thursday and in the background Mummy was telling Leo to be sure to send a card. Jack was one of so many nieces and nephews I don't know how he kept count.

That was the trouble with Leo. One of five siblings, he was crawling with family. He was always having to go home for a birthday, christening or family drama, and home was in Shropshire, while my bijou piece of real estate was in Richmond (Surrey, not Yorkshire or Virginia) and Leo had a flat down the road in Twickenham.

He never invited me along, either. It wasn't that he didn't want to, but it was awkward. Since his ex had the marital home, he usually stayed with his mother, who was still upset that he'd split from the lovely Joanne. ('Like a daughter to me,' was the general tone, according to Leo.)

I hadn't cared, at first. I hadn't minded in the least seeing him only three times a week, and sometimes not even that. After Sulky Simon, Leo had felt like zingy mountain air when you've been stuck in a lift for days. Simon had been so pathetically jealous, he'd thought being glued to the men's singles final meant I was lusting after Pat Rafter. (All right, I was, but what's the point of Wimbledon if you can't lust after hunks in shorts?) After Simon's sulks I'd thought it incredibly grown-up and civilized that Leo never asked what I'd be doing while he was away, who I might be seeing, and who was that on the phone?

The trouble was, I was beginning to wish he would.

Wafting smells reminded me that dinner was in the oven. In my house this was only four paces from the living-room sofa, so half of me was still eavesdropping while I messed with rice and mangetouts. On the fridge door was a poster I was particularly fond of, not least because it bore a photo of Henry. It had been cooked up by my colleagues, shortly after I'd finished with Sulky Simon. At the time I'd been saying things like, 'That's it, and I *mean* it this time.' I'd had it up to here with men who fooled you into thinking they were intelligent, grown-up humans. I hereby gave notice that Isabel Palmer was going celibate. From now on the only male to share my bed would be Henry. He might pong a bit now and then but he never made me cringe by telling my friends, at full volume in the Pitcher and Piano, that I snored like his granny, when it had been a one-off because I had a stinking cold. (Sulky Simon.) Henry never complained that the *gratin Dauphinois* I'd slaved over lacked the *je ne sais quoi* perfection of the one he'd had by Lake Annecy (this was Nit-picking Neil) or said it wasn't much to ask to turn up a pair of trousers, the shop was going to charge ten quid (Tight Tony).

All this had given my dear colleagues the idea. Over the photo of Henry it said:

DOGS ARE BETTER THAN MEN, BECAUSE . . .

Underneath it went on:

1. They never tell you their ex had really nice tits.
2. They do not moan or sulk if you're half an hour late. The later you are, the more dogs are pleased to see you.
3. They never tell you a Brazilian would really turn them on [Sulky Simon again] when certain men we won't mention wouldn't suffer the pain and indignity to turn *you* on for a million pounds. (Not that it would remotely turn you on, but that's not the point.)

And so on: a list of seven, with space left for my own observations.

I'd remained celibate for months, until Leo had walked into the office with a ten-carat smile, asking if we had any purpose-built one-bedroomed flats with assigned parking spaces.

With Christmas coming up, there was another addition I felt like making to that list. It went something like, 'Dogs do not spend Christmas with their kids and make you feel guilty for even secretly wishing there was an alternative.'

Leo was taking the kids to his mother's, where they'd have a brilliant time with all the cousins. His ex, the lovely Joanne, was zooming off to a Goan beach with some Dan she'd been seeing for four months now.

Naturally, I'd fantasized about scenarios that would keep everybody happy, including me. Some really decrepit old relative would die and leave Joanne's mother shed-loads of money. She'd then beg Leo and Joanne to let her take the children to Disney World in Florida as her special Christmas treat. I thought this a very warm and generous solution on my part, even down to the decrepit relative, because he/she would have been in a state of vegetative dementia for years and everyone would say it was a Happy Release.

Off the phone at last, he joined me as I was inspecting my casserole. 'Sorry about that.' Slipping his arms around me from behind, he went on, 'She got two gold stars for some story about a guinea pig. It's going on the wall for Open Day.'

'Brilliant. You always did say she was verbally gifted.' (According to Leo, Gemma was gifted at everything.)

'I said I'd buy her a Tinker Bell outfit,' he went on. 'She wants it for a birthday party next week. Any idea where the nearest Disney shop is?'

'Probably Kingston.'

At this point another man would have started kissing the back of my neck and asking in wheedling tones whether I couldn't nip down in my lunch-hour, could I – he'd never have time, and besides, he'd feel a prat.

Not Leo. However busy he was, Leo would go himself. He wouldn't feel a prat. He'd buy exactly the right outfit in exactly the right size, and a smaller ditto for five-year-old Jodie, because otherwise she'd feel left out. He'd then probably forget to post them until the day before Gemma's party and send them DHL, in case the Post Office cocked up. And once again his daughters would know that Daddy would never let them down. It was one of the things that had always warmed me to Leo. Who'd want a man who couldn't be bothered with his own kids?

But he started nuzzling anyway. 'Leave that. We were playing Emerald and Plonker get dirty.'

'Down, boy. I rather went off the boil, which is more than you can say for this. It's double done.'

Over my shoulder he sniffed appreciatively, at the same time tweaking the overflow round my waist. 'Is that guinea fowl? No wonder I love you. Emerald on the sofa, Delia in the kitchen and Elvira in my dreams.'

It was almost enough to melt me into my sauce *chasseur*. 'You smooth-talking bugger. All you think about is food and sex.'

'It's November, Vera. What else is there to make November fit for humans?'

'Wine. Open that bottle while I drain the rice.'

He drew the cork with a sucky, satisfying plop. 'If you hadn't roped us in for hammed-up murders, we could have spent an entire weekend eating, drinking and embarrassing poor old Henry. And I bet it'll be peeing with rain. It always is, in Devon. Couldn't you say we've both got the pox?'

'No!' I turned to him, brandishing a handy wooden spoon. 'And don't you dare be late. We leave by four on Friday, latest, OK?'

The phone rang shortly after we'd finished eating. As I was in the loo at the time, Leo answered. I came back to find him wearing an expression like that of a very bad actor playing someone about to hang himself.

'Who is it?' I mouthed, half expecting him to say it was my elder sister, Alice, as she could have that effect on me, too.

'Felicity,' he mouthed.

I glared at him, but he was speaking into the phone with a sincerity that would have fooled anyone. 'No, I'm looking forward to it. No, don't worry, we'll bring our thermals. Oh, here's Izzy – I'll pass you over.'

I glared again, while putting a carefree smile into my voice. 'Hi, Fliss. What's up?'

'Nothing whatsoever, unless you count Anita telling me she can't do the food after all, her back's playing up, and the Colditz heating being apparently on strike, and Mike and Daisy saying they can't come after all, her mother's had an accident, and Ian saying why don't we just cancel the whole thing till the spring?'

Mike and Daisy were mutual old friends and Ian was Felicity's beloved. I wasn't acquainted with Anita, but her culinary skills were booked up weeks in advance.

'But I said no way,' she went on. 'It's a terrible shame about Mike and Daisy, though, as he was going to play Medallion Max and she was going to play rich nympho Annabel Plonker-fforbes, so now I'll have to invite another couple, which is a bit awkward at short notice when you hadn't invited them before. Still, that's not my main headache just now. Anita was going to produce a fantastic five-course dinner and you know what my cooking's like – the only things I can guarantee not to mess up are chilli and shepherd's pie.'

'Felicity, the only thing wrong with your cooking is that you get in a tizz about it. I'll give you a hand.'

'I don't want you slaving in the kitchen. It'll have to be chilli, I suppose. As for the heating, I'm trying to sort it out, but if you've got an electric blanket and fleece-lined pyjamas, bring them. I can't guarantee gallons of hot water either, so I do hope it won't kill you if showers are orf.'

No wonder Leo had been making faces. He looked on fifteen minutes of gushing shower twice a day as an inalienable human right. So did I, though at a pinch I'd settle for five minutes, once. 'No problem,' I said nevertheless. 'I love it when Leo smells all rancid and primeval – it really turns me on.'

He made an appalled face, and I stuck my tongue out at him.

'Well, you never know,' Felicity giggled. 'They do say that men's armpits give off pheromerones or something.'

12

'Pheromones,' I said. 'Come-hither chemicals.'

'God, that reminds me. Talking of come-hither, you know I told you Rob had come out of his self-imposed monk-dom at last?'

Rob was another old friend; we both had a special soft spot for him. Feather lined, centrally heated and so on. After months of being cut up over his last relationship, Rob had acquired a new girlfriend back in September. 'Don't tell me it's over already?'

'Far from it. Looks like it's all systems go with Paula.'

'Thank God for that. It's about time.'

'Well, yes. But the thing is . . .' She paused. 'I know it sounds really bitchy, but I don't quite take to her. She seems to have some weird hold over him – it seems to be getting heavy already.'

As Felicity hardly ever took a dislike to anybody, I couldn't dismiss this at once.

'Well, as long as he's happy.'

'Yes, I suppose . . .' She sounded entirely unconvinced. 'But I wish I didn't have a horrible feeling they're going to nip off for a weekend and come back married. I'm sure she's not right for him.'

'What does Ian think?' Felicity's Ian was thoroughly down to earth in all senses, as he dealt in agricultural supplies.

'That it's none of our business, which is perfectly true. But then he said if I wanted to know what he *really* thought, Paula's probably a few years older than Rob, very likely with a string of failed relationships, and she's getting desperate. So of course I said that was an appallingly sexist attitude, he ought to be ashamed of himself, and I agreed absolutely.'

Hmm. 'Apart from all that, what exactly don't you like about her?'

'I can't put my finger on it. She's very attractive, but somehow she makes me think of Cruella de Vil – yes, I know it sounds horrible. Ian says she's got hungry eyes, but then she probably *is* hungry because she only weighs about seven and a half stone. He's worried about Rob getting impaled on her hip-bones. Anyway, I'm so glad you're coming, because she'll be at the murder and you can tell me if I'm just being a bitch.'

'Even if I loathe her on sight, there's not much we can do about it.'

'No,' she sighed. 'I suppose I should just shrug my shoulders and forget it. Only I can't help worrying about Rob.'

This was par for the course. As she had dysfunctional parents she hardly ever saw and no siblings, Felicity's friends *were* her family, and she did worry about them. It was a standing joke that she'd been a mother hen in a previous life; someone had taken her eggs away, and she was still looking for a brood of chicks to cluck over.

'And the thing is, it was me who first introduced them,' she went on. 'At a barbecue back in August, not that she paid much attention to him then. She was too busy chatting up Gordon from the antique shop, but that died a death after three weeks. Ian thinks she probably got heavy and frightened him off, or else it was the hip-bones. But suddenly in September she acquired a very convenient puppy, and it would seem that sparks flew over the primary vaccinations and worm tablets.'

Rob was a vet.

'I mean, she's not even a doggy *type*,' she went on. 'I've got a horrible feeling it was just a ploy.'

'Not a Dalmatian puppy, I hope?'

'God, no – that really would be scary. It's a sweet little

King Charles spaniel called Millie. And talking of dogs, are you bringing Henry?'

'Of course – I've got no one to leave him with.'

'Oh, good – Shep'll be over the moon. They can roll in the mud together. Bring your wellies, by the way – it's like a quagmire round here.'

Later, snuggled under the duvet, I rehashed all this with Leo while Henry snored quietly on the floor. He'd have been beside me, but Leo couldn't hack sharing a bed with an amply-hung hound who licked my feet. He said it made him feel like the kinkier sort of perv.

'Why does this Felicity feel she's got to approve of Rob's girlfriend?' he asked. 'He's a big boy, isn't he? And she's not his mother.'

I didn't quite like the way he said 'this' Felicity. 'She's very fond of him. She helped him through his bad patch, and doesn't want to see him in a state like that again.'

'What happened?' he asked.

'Not enough, evidently. They'd been together for a couple of years, apparently getting on fine, until one day Juliet said, "Rob, this isn't going anywhere, is it?" and walked out forty-eight hours later.'

'It was a rut, then. On her side, anyway.'

'But not on his, poor old Rob.'

There was a moment's silence, while he ran a fingertip lightly over my shoulder. 'Didn't you once tell me you had a bit of a thing about him?'

I distinctly remembered saying this. I'd said it on purpose, to see whether I could arouse even a spark of jealousy in him. 'Only a very mini, embryonic thing. Felicity had a mini-thing about him, too.'

'Ah, now we're coming to it. She's jealous, I bet. Not consciously, perhaps, but that's at the bottom of it.'

15

'Leo, that's rubbish. She's mad about Ian, and she's bombarded Rob with every eligible non-maiden she can dredge up for ten miles.'

'Yes, but they were her choice. She wants to organize him, if you ask me.'

About to scoff, I began to wonder if there couldn't be a tiny grain of truth in this. 'That is rubbish,' I said anyway.

'Maybe.' After a moment he went on, 'Is she a bit of a porker, this Felicity?'

'Leo! How dare you!' I gave him a little punch.

'Well, is she?'

'She's not exactly a stick insect, if that's what you mean. But I certainly wouldn't call her porky.'

'There you are, then.' He gave a satisfied little grunt. 'Poor old Cruella's a stick insect with hip-bones, and she's jealous. If Rob had found himself a porker she wouldn't mind.'

'Leo, that is absolute bollocks. I don't know how you can say things like that when you haven't even met her.'

'I've talked to her. And while I'm on that, you might have told me she sounds like a cross between Oh-yah and *Three Cheers for St Clare's*. Even Princess Di didn't talk like that, for God's sake.'

I was really getting cross now. 'You're just being voice-ist. She's one of the nicest people I've ever met. She hardly ever bitches about anybody.'

'She's got it in for poor old Cruella. With you two ganging up on her, I'm beginning to feel really sorry for her. I might have to treat her to a good dose of my lethal charm, just to even up the score.'

'We're not ganging up!'

'OK, keep your lovely wig on.' Mischievously he went on, 'Tell you what, at this rate we'll be having a good old row in the car on the way down. Then you can go and cry on Rob's shoulder while I check out the sticky-out hip-bones.' He tweaked my own hip. 'Good subcutaneous padding there. No chance of lethal damage from that lot.'

'Oh, bugger off.' I turned on to my side, away from him, but only because I knew he'd follow and make lovely spoons.

And he did. 'I'm beginning to sense a weekend from hell,' he murmured into my hair. 'Undercurrents hurtling about like cruise missiles. It'll turn into a real murder: poor old Cruella shot in the butler's pantry with the blunder-buss. Or bashed on the head in the library with the lead piping.'

'You'll get bashed in the bollocks with the lead piping, if you start exerting your lethal charm on her.'

Chuckling quietly, he kissed my hair. 'Elvira, I do believe you're jealous.'

*Mouth, Isabel! Why did you say that?* 'I just don't want her thinking you'd make a nice Leo-skin coat. You'd look really horrible without your epidermis.'

'OK.' He kissed my hair again. 'As long as you don't go turning embryonic Rob-things into anything more.'

Was this a green-eyed spark at last? Things were really looking up.

'I'm still sensing a weekend from hell, though,' he went on. 'A bloody freezing great house with not enough hot water – is it one of those places where you have to walk three miles to the bathroom in the west wing?'

'Don't be daft.'

'Why did Daddy flog it? To pay for the nice little castle in Tuscany?'

'Oh, shut up. Her grandfather sold it years ago. He couldn't afford to keep it going. Oh, and don't forget to pack your wellies. She said it's like a quagmire.'

There was a resigned groan into my shoulder.

'Stop moaning,' I said. 'And go to sleep.'

'I'll have nightmares,' he murmured. 'I can feel a tomato sandwich coming on.'

That reminded me. 'Why *did* your mother send you as a tomato sandwich? Had you been getting up her nose more than usual?'

He gave a sleepy little chuckle. 'She said it'd be "different". Everybody else would be Batman or Robin Hood.'

'Aah. Poor little Leo. Go to sleep and dream of being Batman.'

He kissed my shoulder. 'Night night, Elvira. Don't have murder nightmares.'

Maybe that was why I did, but my brain often goes wild at night. I dreamt of party games: water-pistols at dinner, one at each place setting, like Christmas crackers. With her bouncy-puppy grin Felicity told us it was her latest version of Killer – we all had to splat each other before coffee or pay a forfeit.

Sitting opposite me, next to Cruella, who'd actually turned out to be a particularly stunning vampire, Leo was muttering that he knew we should have stayed at home, we could have been in a nice hot bath trying out the Rampant Crested Newt position. Mad because he'd been chatting up the vampire, I said, 'Oh, shut up whingeing,' and aimed my water-pistol at him. 'Splat, you're dead.'

But then there was a weird bang, and Leo gaped at me with a startled expression and a neat little hole right between his eyes, before slumping face first into his shepherd's pie. And the vampire said, 'Ooh, yummy blood!' while I gaped at Leo, saying, 'I think I've murdered him!' And Felicity hooted with laughter. 'Izzy, that's the *fun* bit! One of the pistols was real!'

I woke in a sweaty panic with a worried Henry whining

and nosing my face. 'Sshh,' I whispered. 'It's all right, it was just a silly old nightmare.'

Appropriate, though. Before I was very much older, murdering Leo was the least I wanted to do to him.

# Chapter 2

When the alarm went off I wasn't dreaming of anything, let alone murder. I was buried in that deep sleep that might as well be death, the way you feel when you're dragged out of it at six o'clock in winter.

Leo, however, had to be off. Like a caring little zombie I squeezed a fresh carton of orange juice, put coffee on and kissed him goodbye at six forty-five. Needing to be somewhere in Kent by nine, he wanted to miss the rush hour. Leo did something highly specialist in telecoms which I never pretended to understand, but it seemed to provide wodges of cash for maintenance, and, with any luck, a long weekend in Havana he kept promising me.

I left for work at ten past eight, with Henry. It was a twenty-minute walk, which killed the exercise bird for both of us. I shut the gate on my front garden, which measured about four feet from fence to front window, just as my neighbour's front door banged.

'Morning,' I said, as if to a pleasant human being. Having moved in a year previously, Craig Williams had seemed all right at first. Only later had I realized that he was that deadly combination of Who's-a-Pretty-Boy-Then and unadulterated prat.

'Morning, *Ms* Palmer,' he replied, which should give you a fair inkling. 'And if I could take up a moment of your valuable estate-agent time, would you mind not letting that thing you call a dog deposit his steaming turds right outside my gate?'

I'd been waiting for something like this. 'It wasn't Henry. I always clean up after him.' I did. I was meticulous about it.

'Yeah, right. Next time I'll lob it over the fence and see how you like it.'

Arguing would have been a waste of breath, and in any case he was already getting into his car. I carried on past houses like mine: Victorian cottages that not so long ago had been mostly occupied by old people eking out pensions. As I'd done some spectacularly stupid things in my life, buying mine had been the most astute move I'd ever made. Since then prices had rocketed and Christmas Cottage (not my name but I'd fallen in love with it) was now worth nearly three times what the mortgage company had paid for it.

But there was a downside. As the old people had died off or gone into residential care, more like me had moved in. There was always a skip somewhere, filled with ancient baths and sinks, which made the increasing parking problem even more of a pain than Craig.

Still, it was a lovely day for the first of December: sunny and crisp, with only undertones of exhaust fumes. Henry stopped to sniff at number thirty-two's gate. He always did, because he'd once lived there.

I'd inherited Henry from Mrs Denny. Off at the shops one day, she'd found a lanky, half-grown pup running in the street, terrified. When I'd first laid eyes on him, she'd been towelling him after a bath. 'Well, I had to, love,' she'd said. 'He did pong a bit.'

I'd tried to make friends but he'd still been too traumatized to respond. With wet fur, he'd looked even more pathetically thin.

'I'm going to call him Henry,' she'd said. 'Dignified, poor mite. He's got a look of one of those hunting dogs you see in old pictures, don't you think?'

Er, not really. If any historical image came to mind, it was a starving urchin straight out of Dickensian London.

'Someone chucked him out of a car, I bet,' she'd gone on. 'Just look at the state of him. He wolfed down two tins of corned beef and a cheese sandwich.'

I was looking at his paws. A size three would have fitted him nicely but these were seven and a half. 'He's going to be a big boy. He'll eat you out of house and home.'

'I'm not passing him on to the dogs' home, if that's what you're thinking.' Then she'd looked up at me. 'Ron sent him. To stop me being lonely. I know you'll think I'm daft, but I saw him the other night, as plain as I see you now. He said, "Come on, Madge, you've got to stop moping. You've got to get out and about again." '

Ron had died five months previously. They'd been married for fifty-four years.

Having fallen ill two years later and never properly recovered, Mrs Denny had moved into a nursing home. I'd first taken Henry to work with me when she was in hospital. He'd behaved so angelically that Anthea, my boss, had said it was fine with her if he came on a regular basis; if he peed up against that loathsome Rutter man's legs she'd put him on the payroll.

I let myself into Dearling and Dearling, Estates and Lettings. Started by Anthea's grandfather, it was one of the few independents still holding out against the chains. I'd been there four years, having fallen into it almost by accident. Previously I'd been cabin-crewing for a long-haul airline, but had been grounded for an unglamorous medical problem. (All right, recurrent ear trouble.)

Louise was already at her desk, with a coffee and the paper. 'How were those trousers?'

'Brilliant, thanks. And I think Leo's going to make a pretty good Plonker-fforbes.'

'I wish I was going to a murder,' she grumbled. 'I told Todd it's high time we decorated the kitchen, instead of just talking about it and buying dinky little try-me pots of paint from Homebase. Anthea's popping in later, by the way.'

Anthea had hardly been in for ages. Back in August she'd slipped on some wet grass while jogging in Richmond Park. With a broken hip and wrist she'd been taken to hospital where the consultant had informed her that she had the skeleton of a ninety-year-old. Years of eschewing dairy products might have had something to do with it, but it was probably just bad luck and genes. With horrific osteoporosis, she was just forty-four.

In the event I missed Anthea, as I had to do an inventory of a family house before someone from the American University moved in. 'How was she?' I asked when I got back.

'Looking on the bright side, literally,' said Louise. 'She's going to spend the winter recuperating in the sun.'

'In Jamaica,' said Barbara, our receptionist. In her late fifties, she'd been there eighteen years and knew the business almost better than Anthea. 'Some kind friend's lending them his condo.'

'All right for some,' grumbled Ralph, our bright young man with a clipboard, a.k.a. trainee negotiator. 'I wouldn't mind having bones like a fossilized chicken, if I could doss in Jamaica all winter.'

Louise gave the withering look she produced nearly every time Ralph opened his mouth. 'It'll just serve you right if you get them now, you lazy little git.'

'Now, now, you two,' said Barbara.

'How long is Anthea actually going to be away?' I asked.

'At least three months,' said Barbara.

'In that case we're going to need someone else, and not just the odd temp helping out when things are really busy.' Come early spring, when the world and his partner started thinking of nice new nests with room for extensions, we'd be flat out.

'She said she'll sort something out by Christmas,' said Barbara. 'It's all under control.'

'She should have left it up to us,' complained Louise. 'I think we could have managed to recruit someone we could stand working with while she's slobbing by the pool. Personally, I think it's just a bit off.'

I thought it just a bit off, too, but as things suddenly got busy I had no time to think about it. Finally home just before seven, I slumped on the sofa with a bar of Fruit and Nut and watched the news. Beside me on the sofa, Henry watched the chocolate. His eyes focused on it intently, in case it tried to escape.

'There you go.' I gave him the last two squares, just as the doorbell rang. With a sudden conviction that it was Leo, I raced to answer it.

There was nobody there but the wind.

'Present for you,' called a voice. As Craig's front door slammed I looked down to see a massive doggy dump right on my step.

Charging straight round, I yelled through the letter-box. 'You little shit – it – *wasn't* – *Henry*!'

Then another door banged in the wind. Mine.

An hour later, courtesy of the nice human girl next door and *Yellow Pages*, an emergency locksmith turned up.

Locked inside and evidently thinking the man was a burglar, Henry barked ferociously throughout the entire operation.

'Blimey, love,' said the locksmith. 'Sounds as if you've got him trained to go for the nuptials.'

Back inside, still simmering over Craig, I tried Leo. He wasn't answering, but that didn't surprise me if he was still driving home. Leo rarely used his phone in the car. It took only a moment's lack of concentration, he said, and he was damned if he was going to leave his kids fatherless because some impatient sod couldn't wait to talk to him.

It was gone ten when I finally got him.

'Sorry, but the traffic was a bitch,' he said. 'I've only just got in – I'm about to hit the shower. Haven't even eaten yet.'

In that case, my woes could wait. 'Like me to come over? I'll cook you something.'

'Maybe not tonight, Delia. I'd be too knackered to do you justice.'

He didn't mean too knackered to eat. I was about to say, 'We're not obliged to *do* it, you know,' when he went on, 'Anyway, I'm not sure you'll feel like cooking me anything. I've got some bum news, I'm afraid.'

'Not the weekend? Don't tell me you're not coming?'

'I *can't* come. I'm really sorry, but—'

'Oh, don't tell me.' This had happened so often: nearly always some family do he couldn't get out of. 'You have to show your face at your Auntie Mary's budgie's funeral – for God's sake, Leo . . .'

'It's my folks' fortieth anniversary.'

'*What?*'

'Their fortieth,' he repeated. 'Angie's putting on a surprise party – it had gone right out of my head.'

Angie was his sister, who specialized in surprise parties.

According to Leo they invariably included her other speciality: soggy spinach quiche.

'She's invited fifty-odd friends and relations,' he went on. 'If I duck out I'll never hear the last of it.'

'For heaven's sake, how could you forget a thing like that?'

'Because I've been up to my arse,' he said, in the semi-reproachful tones men reserve for such situations. 'You know I have. It only hit me this morning, when Angie phoned to say had I got them a present yet, and if not how about going halves on a trip on the Orient Express?'

'For God's sake, why didn't you put it in your diary?'

'Oh, come on, I'll make it up to you. I've been looking at Havana again – we could maybe fit in a long—'

'Will you shut up about bloody Havana? Nobody in their right mind goes to Havana for a long weekend – it's a ten-hour flight! Felicity's already two players short!'

'Look, I'm really sorry, but—'

Fury was washing the fog from my brain. 'You didn't forget the anniversary, did you? You forgot our weekend, or just couldn't be bothered to remember the dates. Even when I first mentioned it you said it'd be a pain, driving all that way in the Friday night rush. You're glad to get out of it, aren't you? You've made up your mind that the whole thing's going to be a pain – I've had it, Leo. The one time I ask you for an entire weekend with my friends, you let me down. Well, stuff you. Go and play happy families with soggy quiche and see if I care.'

Jabbing 'off', I threw my mobile on the sofa, narrowly missing Henry.

'I've had it,' I fumed. 'If he phones back, I'm not answering.'

Half a minute later he did precisely that and I ignored it.

Or rather, I yelled abuse at my poor little Nokia while pouring myself a large glass of Australian Shiraz.

It was a new experience, being so seethingly furious with Leo that I didn't even trust myself to speak to him. In six months I'd never been mad with him. I'd been the perfect, sweetly undemanding, part-time girlfriend.

Not any more. I was bitterly hurt that he couldn't be bothered to remember the dates of something important to me. Probably it had only hit him when I'd dressed up as Emerald. What kind of fool was I going to look now, telling Felicity he couldn't come?

While I fumed and seethed, the house phone rang. I told that to go and fuck itself too; if he thought I was falling for that he'd got another think coming. Once it stopped I did 1471 just to check that it *was* him, and found it had been Jane.

Another way-back friend who was coming to the murder, Jane was the only one of the party who'd ever met Leo.

'I'm on the scrounge,' she said, when I called her back. 'I'm getting a lift down but I've got a training seminar in London on Monday – you couldn't give me a lift back and a bed, could you? It seems daft to fag all the way home and get the early train down again.'

Jane lived in Leeds, worked in Human Resources and shopped to take her mind off it. After once nodding off for a few seconds on the M1, saved only by violent hooting, she hated driving long distances alone.

'That is, if Leo won't mind,' she went on.

'I doubt it. He's not coming.'

'Izzy! Why not?'

'His bloody family. Again.' But even as the words came out they sounded more wry than furious, and I knew perfectly well why. Jane had liked Leo a lot, even down to telling me with a glint in her eye that if I ever got bored with him . . . If I admitted that he couldn't be bothered to remember something important to me, what did that say about our relationship? So I played it right down. 'Of course I'd never expect him to duck out of a do like that,' I finished, 'but I can't help being a bit hacked off that he didn't remember earlier.'

'A *bit*? I'd have thumped him.'

'Difficult, since he told me over the phone. But he has been unbelievably busy lately,' I added lamely.

'That's no excuse. It'll serve him right if he spends the entire do being wittered at by gross old relatives who smell of wee.'

Next I phoned Felicity. Unlike Jane, she didn't advocate thumping. It was, 'Oh, what a shame,' followed by, 'Still, it's nice that he didn't just make an excuse about going home. Some people would use any excuse to get out of family dos. I mean, they can be a total pain. The last one we had, when I was about sixteen, Mummy got completely pissed – mind you, she was always pissed anyway – and went for Pa with a rounders bat.'

On husband number three, Felicity's mother was drying out in some clinic in Texas. Her father had been a minor diplomat who'd now gone bush in some remote corner of Borneo.

'But don't worry about Plonker-fforbes,' she went on. 'I can do a reshuffle – at least one minor role was expendable in case anyone broke a leg or something.'

Thank God for that.

'And I've already roped in replacements for Mike and Daisy,' she continued. 'Sasha from the Coach and Horses, and Nick who works with Rob – did you meet Nick last time?'

That was five months ago. 'No, but you've mentioned him.'

Nick had been at the vets' practice first. While he was winkling a grass seed out of Shep's ear Felicity had started chatting, as she did with everybody who wasn't stone deaf, and had found out two things. One: Nick and Rob had worked together some years previously, but had lost touch. Two: there was a vacancy coming up.

All this had come in the aftermath of Juliet, when Rob was lower than any of us had ever known him. Added to that, his practice in Bristol had been taken over by someone he just didn't click with. To Felicity, then, colliding with Nick was the kind of Sign Mrs Denny would talk about. Rob was destined for North Devon, sun and roses were just around the corner, and he'd be just around the corner, where she could dish out lots of TLC.

'I'm not sure it's really Nick's sort of thing, but he said he'd give it a go,' she said. 'I've asked him to do Medallion Max.'

'Felicity, just out of interest, who *is* Medallion Max?'

She giggled. 'Rich Aunt Evadne's very personal minder. I'm not sure you'll be the body after all – Auntie's vile relations are probably going to do Max in before he grabs their inheritance. I was going to ask Cruella to do Evadne, but she said she'd rather be the bishop's lady friend – did I tell you Rob was going to be the bishop? I really must stop calling her Cruella, it sounds so bitchy. I'm sure it's just me being horrible because she only weighs about seven and a half stone.'

Leo didn't ring again that evening. I wouldn't have answered if he had, but that didn't stop me getting madder still with him for not trying. Probably he was consulting that Handling Women manual, implanted in most male

29

brains at birth: '*The natural condition of women is to be sweetly reasonable at all times. Any deviation from this norm means that she is an NB (Neurotic Bitch), not to be confused with PMT, which is best dealt with by leaving the country for a few days.*'

In the morning I found he'd emailed me instead. '*I'm sorry – what can I say? I've put my hair shirt on and it's bloody itchy – will that do?*'

Instantly I hit 'reply': '*No, it bloody won't.*'

While Ralph nipped out for a sandwich I had a good old moan to Barbara and Louise.

'Personally, I think it's very nice that he thinks so much of his family,' said Barbara, whose only son lived in Ayrshire and was very remiss about phoning. 'It shows he's got a nice nature.'

'It's not much use having a "nice nature" if she hardly ever sees him, is it?' said Louise.

He didn't phone that evening, and I was damned if I was phoning him. That night, however, the counsel for the defence started arguing in my head.

*You forget things, too. Only last week you forgot your own sister's birthday until the actual day, and posted a card late. Then you phoned to say Happy Birthday, and pretended it was the Post Office's fault it hadn't arrived, and Alice knew perfectly well you'd forgotten and wouldn't admit it. Which is exactly the sort of behaviour you bitch about in other people, if you don't mind my saying so.*

'Oh, shut up.'

*And why the hell did you say, 'I've had it', like that? If you don't call back soon he'll think you meant it. Phone him in the morning and blame it all on Craig. He's got to be good for something.*

By eleven the next day I'd weakened enough to call him.

He wasn't answering, but I left a message: *'Sorry I was such a cow, but Craig had been particularly loathsome, he made me lock myself out so I was already in a foul mood. Give me a call later, lots of love.'*

I set off at four, with Henry in the back. It was a vile drive, dark and full of traffic, and after fifty miles it started raining, too. Around six thirty the traffic ground to a halt. I sat and fumed until fire engines and ambulances screamed down the hard shoulder, when I felt bad for fuming. I thought of anxious relatives saying, 'So-and-so should have been home by now,' and hoped nobody was dead. While we were stalled I fed Henry and phoned Felicity to say I'd be delayed; I'd go straight to the Coach and Horses, where we were eating.

Although I'd been before I still got lost twice in the dark lanes. Felicity's corner of Devon wasn't one of the touristy parts; it was a working, farming area. Anywhere near London the car park of a fourteenth-century pub like the Coach and Horses would have been crammed with expensive cars. Low and rambling, it was like something off an old-fashioned Christmas card.

After I'd run from the car in the rain, it was a cheerful haven. There were blackened beams anyone over six foot would crack their head on, and dozens of pewter mugs hanging from two bars. To the right was the 'public', with dartboard and pool table; to the left was the other, with carpet and a wood fire.

Hearing Felicity's laugh already, I followed it. They were propping up the left hand bar and my first thought was, who's that bloke next to Ian?

Ian saw me first. 'Here she is,' he grinned, and the bloke turned around.

Something socked me in the guts. Meeting a handsome

stranger isn't all it's cracked up to be, not when you're expecting the shaggy bear he was before.

'Hi, Rob!' I said, nevertheless. 'Love the haircut!'

After the kind of hug that lifts you off your feet, I met the woman who'd presumably effected this transformation.

An icicle, was my first impression. A tall, elegant icicle, maybe five foot ten, she exuded an air of glacial fragility. Her skin was very pale, her ash-blonde hair was in an elfin crop. Her eyes were navy blue, like arctic pools. She wore a soft white sweater that looked like cashmere. I couldn't quite see the Cruella connection. She did have beautifully sculpted cheek-bones but they didn't stick out a mile like Ms de Vil's in the cartoon version.

We shook hands politely. 'Hello, Paula,' I said, as nicely as I could. 'If it's you who smartened Rob up, congratulations.'

She gave a pleasant but guarded smile. 'I've heard all about you.'

'God, I hope not,' I said, with the kind of daft laugh you reserve for such occasions. 'Most of it should only be released fifty years after my death. Thanks, Rob, I'll have a white wine,' I added, as he was asking.

'Regular or whopper?'

'Regular – I'm driving.'

'No, I am,' said Felicity. 'I need a clear head in the morning. Leave your car here – we can pick it up tomorrow.'

That's what I call a friend. Rob found me a stool and I sat down and got my breath back. What had she done to shaggy old Rob? His light brown hair was now crisply and fashionably short. He'd lost weight, too, not that I'd ever have thought he needed to. Around six foot three, Rob had always reminded me of a particularly cuddly old teddy. He had lovely blue eyes you knew could never turn cold, even if Genghis Khan was saying, 'Get mean or I'll boil you in oil.'

They hadn't changed. But the clothes!

Rob had always belonged to the colour-blind, 'this'll do', school of fashion, favouring anything that wasn't actually spattered with spag bol. Frequently he'd added the kind of sweater someone else's granny had knitted as a punishment for not eating their greens fifteen years previously. If he'd ever looked halfway stylish, it was because some girlfriend had said, 'If you're going out like that, I'm not with you.'

Any of them would be 'with' him now. It was weird. In the past we'd all despaired over Rob in a fond sort of way, wondering whether any girl would ever sort him out. But now someone had, I wasn't sure I liked it.

But Felicity was talking to me. 'That's Sasha, behind the bar. She's going to do Mrs Plonker-fforbes.'

I saw a dark-haired, attractive girl in her late twenties exchanging banter with a customer who looked like something out of *One Man and His Dog*.

'She was a leading light in the Village Players,' Felicity went on. 'Just finished a Theatre Studies degree, but finding a job's not so easy so she's filling in here. She's matey with Nick – he might be coming later, by the way.'

Seconds later I met Sasha, who struck me as instantly likeable and 'easy'. I wished I could say the same for Paula. During the ensuing chat I began to see why Felicity hadn't taken to her. An open-book person, Felicity got on best with other open books, the types you'd be having a laugh with in two minutes. With Paula, I sensed, you could try for weeks and never get beneath the slightly wary surface.

By nine we were sitting at a dark oak table while Sasha

dished out menus, informing us that the game pie was finished.

'Pity Leo couldn't make it,' said Rob, who was sitting opposite me. 'I gather he was double-booked.'

'It's one of those things.' I tried to give a casual shrug, though I felt neither casual nor shruggy. I'd left that message hours ago – what was he playing at? Letting me sweat?

'Are we ready to order?' asked Ian.

'Not quite.' I'd hardly looked at the menu. There were two types of food: gammon steaks, sausage and mash, and so on. Then there were 'Lighter Bites'. I was dithering over a salad of *lollo rosso* with crispy bacon and warm Brie, when Paula said to Rob, 'Why don't you try that salad with Brie and bacon? Most of the other stuff looks so heavy.'

Before you could say, 'Yes, dear,' Rob had shut his menu with a snap. 'Yes, why not?'

Felicity's eyes met mine, but she was too polite to give any pointed look.

Rob wasn't just tall. He was hefty with it, and had a metabolic rate to match. Having Rob to stay was a bit like that story of *The Tiger Who Came To Tea* and devoured everything in the house, including all the water in the tap. Like me, Felicity knew a salad would never even half-fill Rob and left to himself he'd never have chosen it, except on the side.

Still, a cunning plan had just occurred to me. If I ordered something hot, with bloke appeal, and pretended I couldn't finish it. . . This might mean depriving Henry, but it was in a good cause. Quietly curled under the table, Henry was being a very good boy. He knew that in places like this, Very Good Boys might even get bits of steak.

If only men were as uncomplicated, I thought. A couple

of sausages and dogs loved you for ever. Dogs didn't have forty family dos a year to attend. They didn't make you wait over six hours for a reply to a cringing apology you were stupid enough to make in the first place.

At this point the defence counsel started again. *Maybe he hasn't even checked his messages yet. He's probably still on his way home. Knowing Leo he'll have left late, the traffic'll be a nightmare and it's probably chucking it down, too.*

*Oh, go away.* Thinking of Rob, I was dithering between lamb hotpot and prime local pork sausages with mash and onion gravy.

*He's probably crawling along in coned-off roadworks right this minute. He'll be fretting in case Gemma and Jodie are asleep before he gets there.*

More than likely. He'd probably be staying at Soggy Quiche Angie's, but he nearly always called in to see the kids first, even if only for half an hour.

'What was the hold-up on the way down?' asked Ian, on my right.

Next to Rob, Ian was one of my favourite men in the world. Before I'd first met him Felicity had said, 'Well, he's not exactly drop-dead gorgeous – sort of average height and build, you know, but he's got lovely curly dark hair, usually a bit of a mess, and the sort of face a really squidgy golden retriever would have if he were human, if you know what I mean.'

'There was a bad accident,' I said. 'Ambulances, fire engines, really nasty.'

And that was all it took. In a flash my brain connected those images with my unringing phone.

*Leo.*

My mouth suddenly dry, I tried to call him.

Nothing.

I went cold, as if someone had walked over my grave. I saw Leo, cursing in crawling traffic, his wipers going flat out. I saw the traffic moving again, Leo thinking thank Christ for that . . . I saw cars streaking past on the right, Leo putting his foot down hard at just the wrong moment . . .

'Izzy?' said Ian. 'Have you decided?'

I ordered the sausages, my brain full of nightmare visions. I saw Angie, wondering where on earth he'd got to. I saw two little blonde kids in pyjamas, saying, 'Where's Daddy? I want him to read me a story.' I saw a knock at the door, a policewoman on the step . . .

I don't know how long I was in this nightmare but Rob brought me back.

'Izzy? Are you there?' He was waving a hand, trying to 'find' me.

My brain came back into focus. 'Sorry. I was away with the fairies.'

'You were away with something. Izzy, this is Nick. Nick Trent.'

I'd just registered him. Waiting to sit down, he was about six foot two of jeans, navy sweatshirt and an air of mildly bemused patience. Was the creature coming to life at last?

'Oh,' I said, like an idiot. 'Hello.'

*My God, she speaks*! 'Hi, Izzy.' After a brief handshake, he sat at the end of the table, at right angles to me. 'They must have been some fairies.'

I could hardly say I'd been at Leo's funeral, wishing to God I'd never told him to go and play happy families and see if I cared. *Get a grip, Izzy. Imagining disasters like that – you're getting as bad as Mum.* 'I'm afraid I was miles away.'

'If you ask me,' Rob said to Nick, 'she was thumping her boyfriend. Did I tell you he ducked out at the last minute?'

'He couldn't help it!' It came out more prickly than I'd intended, and Rob looked slightly taken aback. 'It was a family do he'd forgotten,' I explained to Nick.

'Maybe you should have been thumping him, then. Hasn't he got a diary?'

I did not need this. People I've only just met are not supposed to come out with blunt, cut-the-crap questions. They're supposed to come out with platitudes like, 'Tell me about it,' 'Don't we all?' and so on.

'He's been very busy,' I said, because I couldn't think of anything less pathetic.

'Oh, dear.'

I didn't need this, either. 'Politely cryptic' might describe his tone, if that covers 'thinking something scathing but refraining from saying it'. He had dark hazel eyes, of the hyper-intelligent type that sum you up in an instant, can tell you're making feeble excuses for someone who's let you down, and move instantly to the person on your right. 'Ian, sling me a menu, will you?'

Ian slung.

'You should get him a palmtop for Christmas,' said Paula. 'I couldn't live without mine.'

Leo had one. He had a state-of-the-art thing that could probably tell you exactly where to find Starbucks in downtown Okinawa and how to compose sonnets in Sanskrit. Obviously it was far too cerebral to be bothered with what you were supposed to be doing next weekend.

But I didn't say so. Not to her, and certainly not to non-platitude Nick, whose attention was now on what he was going to stuff himself with. Not designer salad, I bet. A T-bone steak, more like. With a baked potato, big enough to make poor old Rob – er, hang on . . .

37

Suddenly I was getting a weird feeling of déjà vu, as if he reminded me of somebody. It was fuzzier than the echo of a distant chord, but at the same time I was getting vaguely uncomfortable vibes I couldn't begin to put my finger on.

*Maybe he looks like some awkward passenger, way back. On one of those nightmare flights when the tonics ran out and you had to divert to Manchester because of fog.*

*Maybe he was an awkward passenger. But at least he's not that prat you were dying to spill coffee over on purpose, pretending it was the turbulence. And certainly not that man you did spill water over on purpose, just so you could mop him up and thus provide him with a brilliant opportunity for asking for your phone number. 'I shall have to exact an exceedingly stiff penalty for this,' he said, a smile playing about that mock-mad expression on his virile yet somehow tender mouth. 'Dinner, at the very least, followed three weeks later by a proposal of marriage on a Caribbean beach.'*

*And what a misery he turned out to be. Served you right for having adolescent fantasies when you were supposed to be dishing out chicken or fish.*

Snapping his menu shut, Nick turned to me. 'How was your drive?' Mixed with a hint of West Country was the crisp, polite tone he might he might have used to a friend of his mother's.

'Horrible, thank you.'

'Probably inevitable, on a Friday night in the rain.'

'Probably.'

After this scintillating exchange he started talking to Rob about something work related. At the same time Ian and Felicity were talking to Paula, and out of the blue I began to experience that leaden feeling I got about once a year for no apparent reason. At some social gathering I'd suddenly realize that no power on earth could get me in the mood; if my life depended on it I wouldn't be able to make any remotely sparkly conversation; I didn't want to play any more.

In a short black skirt, Sasha appeared at my left elbow. 'Made up your mind yet, Nickel-arse? They'll be closing the kitchen soon.'

'I'll have the game pie,' he said.

'No, you won't, sunshine. It's finished.' To the entire table she went on, 'He's going to be pretty crap tomorrow night, I'm afraid. I offered to coach him, but he wasn't having it. I said, "look, if the last acting you did was second ass in the nativity play when you were four, you need a bit of help." '

Nick looked up from the menu. 'I shall be crap in my own sweet way.'

'But at least he's letting me sort out his wardrobe and special effects,' she went on. 'About a gallon of hair gel, for starters. And baby oil, slathered all over his muscles.'

'Christ, I hope he's not coming in a thong,' said Ian.

'No, but the toyboy would want to show off as much of his body beautiful as possible, wouldn't he? I wanted to wax his chest hair, too, but he chickened out. Said he'd pass out with the agony.'

'Dear God, how she betrays me,' Nick tutted. 'After all I've done for her.' Snapping his menu shut, he handed it to her. 'Get thee to the kitchen, wench, and bring me a lamb hotpot.' He added a slap on her bottom that made her squeak.

'You wait,' she flashed, but still went off giggling as if he'd made her day.

No wonder Felicity had said they were 'matey'. I looked

at Rob. 'Is he always like this?' I asked, in a jokey tone that didn't quite come off.

But it was Nick who replied. 'Like what?' he asked, with an air of detached amusement that got up my nose even more than the fact that I couldn't think of a snappy answer. 'Like a bit of a sexist prat' was what I'd meant, as he knew perfectly well, but I could hardly say it when Sasha obviously didn't object.

'Ignore him, Izzy,' grinned Rob. 'He's just winding you up.'

'Well, feel free,' I said, as lightly as I could. 'There's probably a key in my back – no wonder I couldn't get comfortable on the way down.'

Nick's mouth flickered, in that way that says someone's laughing at you inside, and that social-death feeling came on me worse than before. I still hadn't a clue who he reminded me of, either. On top of all that something else about him was niggling me, but I couldn't put my finger on it.

Actually, that's a lie; I could. Virtually every other friend of Rob's I'd ever met had been particularly nice to me from the word go. Some had flirted a bit, in that gentle, non-cringe way that just makes you feel good and special. And now, when I'd had a long, weary drive; when I was dying to ring Leo just to make sure he wasn't dead after all; when I felt bereft, and leaden social death was upon me; when I could have done with some feel-good treatment, I wasn't getting it.

Not that I cared. For a start, he wasn't remotely my type. Facially he made me think of 'Join the Army' posters: blokes in berets messing with tanks or staring in a macho way into desert wastes, eyes screwed up against the sun. His hair was even shorter than Rob's, mid-brown with a hint of copper, and I had enough copper of my own. Quite apart from all that, he just didn't conform to my idea of a vet. Vets had no business looking like 'Join the Army' posters; they should be sweet and cuddly, like Rob, or that lovely man on *Animal Hospital* who splints a hamster's broken leg as if it were a prize racehorse. Somehow I couldn't see Nick Trent splinting hamsters. I could see him whacking them over the head while the owners' backs were turned: 'Oh dear, looks like Cuddles has had a heart attack, never mind, plenty more in the shop, next please.'

This was when I remembered his alias for tomorrow night. 'I gather you're going to be Medallion Max.'

'So I'm told.'

Whacking Cuddles was one thing; this was quite another. Without conscious thought I pictured a five-star, nightmare version of Craig: smirk, swagger, massive gold coin on a chain. 'I can't quite see it, somehow.'

His mouth flickered again. 'I'm not sure I can see you as Emerald, either. The tart with a – Jesus!'

He started as if he'd been electrocuted. Or, indeed, as if Emerald had just whipped a pair of tasselled knockers out.

And for the first time that evening, I laughed.

# Chapter 3

So did everybody else, once they realized what was going on.

'It's only Henry,' I said.

'You might have told me there was lurking livestock. It's not funny, getting a nose in your crotch when you're not expecting it.'

'You should count yourself lucky. Emerald usually charges extra for that particular service.' I was pleased with this, as it was the kind of thing I'd usually think of twenty minutes later.

Unaware that he was the object of ribald mirth, poor Henry was anxious to make friends. 'Well, good Lord,' said Nick, as Henry poked his head between his lap and the table. 'What have we here?'

Here we go, I thought. Any second he was going to make the usual crack about Shetland ponies shagging sheep by mistake. Someone once said Henry probably had a touch of Bedlington terrier, but since they look much like woolly lambs it was just a kinder way of saying the same thing.

'A pick-and-mix,' I said, as he'd never buy the Baluchi camel hound bit.

'Yes, I think I worked that one out.' Fondling Henry's ears, he was observing with a professional air. 'Eyesight problems,' he mused. 'I'd put money on it.'

*What*? 'His vision's perfect! He can spot a cat at three hundred paces!'

'I'm not saying he's directly affected. I was referring to a genetic defect, probably way back.'

'How on earth can you tell?' Crossly I appealed to Rob. 'How can he possibly tell a thing like that, just by looking at him?'

Before he could reply, Nick did. 'Of course I could be wrong, but it looks to me as if one of his ancestors had sufficiently defective vision to mount a sheep by mistake.'

A gale of mirth hit the table, except from me. 'Sorry to tell you, but I must have heard fifty-nine variations on that.'

'Personally I think he's got a *sweet* little face,' said Felicity.

'Izzy loves him,' said Rob. 'Insult her baby at your peril.'

'Look, I'm sorry,' said Nick, in soothing tones.

'No, you're not, you prat. Personally I think it's pathetic, trying to be funny at a dumb animal's expense.'

Not that I actually said it. I was trying to think of something marginally less rude when Sasha appeared with plates of food. 'There you go, Izzy. I hope you can manage all that.'

I looked down at four fat sausages and a mountain of mash in a sea of onion gravy. Then I glanced up. Rob's was a mountain, too. A mountain of lettuce and air, with morsels of Brie and bacon that wouldn't have made a mouthful for Henry.

There was a rueful glance at my plate but he said not a word. Felicity did, however. 'Dear me, Rob. That's not going to keep you alive very long, is it?'

'Looks great to me,' said Rob, in a hearty voice I knew was put on.

'He's re-educating his palate,' said Paula, in a voice that

managed to be tinged with frost and defensive at the same time.

'About time, too,' said Nick. 'He was turning into a fat bastard.'

He said it in semi-jokey, male-banter tones, but that didn't stop me bristling. Henry, Rob – who was he going to take a crack at next?

Even Paula's dinner would have provided Rob with a bit more sustenance: plain grilled sole with salad, but nothing else. As they ate I noticed discreet eye contact and touching, the odd word between them alone. And I saw what Ian had meant by 'hungry eyes', though it wasn't the sexual hunger I'd expected. He was tender with her in a way that had once caused a tiny ache in my heart, because it wasn't for me. At the same time her manner towards him almost reminded me of an overprotective parent. I saw her brush a minute speck from his sweatshirt with a little frown, like a mother checking that her child's school uniform was pristine.

It was a weird combination.

Once I'd demolished half my mountain and slipped a bit of sausage to Henry it was time for my Cunning Plan. 'I have to admit defeat – anyone want to be dustbin?'

'Get a doggy bag,' said Nick. 'You've already given him half of it.'

'He's had quite enough. Too much human food upsets his tummy.' This was a massive lie, of course. I wasn't going to ask Rob straight out, even though I saw him waver longingly.

But for just a moment too long. 'Pass it over, then,' said Nick briskly. 'I don't suppose you've got anything catching.' Before I could say, 'Pig,' he'd swapped our plates in a businesslike fashion.

After that massive plate of hotpot Rob would have

loved, I could have thumped him, but my phone was ringing at last.

Hallelujah. 'Hi,' I said. 'How's the hair shirt?'

'Nearly as bad as the hair Calvin's. I've been scratching my balls all day.'

Flooded with feel-good, I laughed. With an 'Excuse me' I departed for the ladies where I could talk to him in peace.

'I was crying into my beer last night, thinking you'd cast me off for ever,' he said.

'I very nearly did.' I perched on the vanity counter in the ladies, next to a little vase of obviously artificial flowers. 'Where are you?'

'At Angie's, via the kids. I hope you passed my apologies to Felicity,' he went on. 'How's it going?'

'Fine, except that the bloke who's playing Medallion Max just made the usual pathetic crack about Henry looking like a sheep.'

'Tosser,' he said. 'Sorry I'm not there to duff him up.'

Mellow and forgiving though I was, I didn't want him thinking I couldn't have a great time without him. 'Oh, he's not that bad. And the heating's been fixed, so I won't be freezing to death without you, after all.'

After we'd said lovey-dovey goodbyes, I gave myself a long overdue tart-up in the mirror. My hair, twisted into a hasty 'up' hours ago, had been escaping in messy coppery wisps ever since. Whatever make-up I'd put on first thing had long worn off. I was wearing an old pair of jeans (I hadn't planned on impressing anybody) and a fitted, pale blue roll-neck sweater that had been expensive. However, the label said 'Dry-clean Only', which I'd ignored after the first month. Now half a size smaller, it was adorned with pretty little bobbles.

I was still taming my wisps when Felicity came in. 'I had

to come anyway,' she explained, as if I'd thought she was planning on eavesdropping. 'Was that Leo?'

'However did you guess?'

'Thank God for that.' From inside a cubicle she went on, 'I was in a tizz in case you'd rowed with him on my account.'

Thank God I hadn't told her. 'As if. I was upset when he first told me, but it was one of those things.'

She came out and washed her hands. In a half-whisper, as there were other people in there, she said, 'Talking of "upset", I thought you were going to wallop Nick when he pinched Rob's sausages.'

'Greedy bugger. I could easily have finished them myself. I was just being noble.'

'Well, it *was* a bit obvious. And I didn't help, saying that salad wasn't going to keep him alive long. I'm sure Nick already thinks I'm a terrible mother hen where Rob's concerned.'

This sharpened me right up. 'Why? Has he said something?'

'Oh, no, I just get a feeling. After all, I *have* been a bit of a mother hen,' she went on, running a comb through her hair. 'Inviting him for shepherd's pie and barbies, trying to pair him off with every Trish, Di and Sally – never mind getting him down here in the first place . . .'

'You were only trying to help! And how dare he call Rob a fat bastard?'

'Well, he *was* putting a bit of weight on. Letting himself go with the oven chips.'

'Even if he was, it's better than being a rude bastard who insults people's dogs.'

She laughed. 'Poor Izzy – it was very naughty of him.' But her face creased with concern. 'You're not getting a thing about him? Please, Izzy, don't get one of your "things" – I'm already having nightmares about everything going wrong tomorrow night.'

If there's one thing guaranteed to pull me up, it's someone pointing out my obnoxious personality traits, especially when I'd always kidded myself they didn't show. 'I'm not getting a "thing"!'

'Thank God for that. He's actually very nice, you know. Nick, I mean. Just a bit spoke-outen, as Ian calls it.' Inspecting herself in the mirror that ran across three washbasins, she went on, 'Talking of fat bastards, I'm turning into Lard-arse Lil. I really must start going to Weight Watchers after Christmas.'

Felicity was invariably about to start a diet, but never did. She'd always hovered around a size fourteen. Now it was probably verging on a fifteen, but she was five foot eight against my five six and carried it well, especially in tailored brown trousers and a cream shirt. She had smooth, fair, shoulder-length hair that had always been much the same, and a face her beautiful bitch of a mother had once told her was too wholesomely English to ever be properly pretty.

'You look exactly the same to me,' I told her. 'Which is more than you can say for Rob. You might have told me she'd given him a makeover.'

'It wasn't an overnight thing. And even you have to admit it's an improvement.'

*It won't be much of an improvement if he gets sticky-out hip-bones, too.* I thought back to the way she'd flicked that speck off his sweatshirt. Control-freak tendencies, if I wasn't mistaken. But I didn't say it, as Felicity would only fret. 'Still, as long as he's happy.'

She lowered her voice again. 'I know it doesn't sound very nice, but I've come to the conclusion that one of the reasons I can't get on with her is that she's one of those women who just don't care for other women. Or at least, like men a whole lot better.'

I saw the cool little smile again, the guarded manner. Usually you could spot the type at fifty paces; the narrowed eyes, the instant sizing-up of any possible rival. Your antennae went into red alert instantly, especially once they started oozing honey to any passable man on your arm. And the men always fell for it. They said things like, 'Lovely girl, that Tasha,' while you gritted your teeth and said, 'Yes, isn't she?'

But I didn't think Paula fell into this category. It had been wariness in her eyes, rather than Essence of Classic Bitch. 'She strikes me as very reserved, that's all.'

'Maybe. Heaven knows I've tried hard enough, but it's as if she's put up a sign saying, "That's far enough, thank you." '

'Don't let it get to you,' I soothed. 'Rob will never let her distance him from you, if that's what you're worried about.'

'Now you're making me sound like a jealous mother-in-law. Still, better get back . . .' She made a suddenly appalled face. 'God, I hope Paula doesn't think we're talking about her!'

That was entirely possible, and I knew how I'd feel. 'You go, then. Say I'm still nattering to Leo – I'll come in two minutes.'

She gave a guilty little laugh. 'Izzy, how devious. Why didn't I think of that?'

Because, unlike me, she wasn't a devious cow. Was that another obnoxious trait I should keep an eye on? From now on I was going to be a Better Person. I would be charitable and forbearing, and not get 'things' about people just because they had really annoying hair (the woman at the dry-cleaner's), or merely irritated the shit out of me (that weather presenter who said 'spits and spots' and had a weird neck), or anyone I'd only just met in the Coach and Horses.

After a minute I followed, via a detour to the bar. Rob and Nick were propping it up and if they were ordering another round it was my turn. Knowing Rob, he might even be settling the food bill on the quiet. With their backs to me they didn't see me coming, so I paused a couple of paces away, delving in my bag for no-arguments cash.

Their voices were low but I have very acute hearing.

'I know,' Rob was saying, 'but it's just her way.'

'Rob, if she wants something to mother, she should have a baby. Sasha!' Nick called, at higher volume. 'Any danger of some service here?'

In mid-chat with another customer, Sasha waltzed over with a pertly mischievous expression. 'Certainly, *mein Führer, Sieg Heil* and kiss your bottom, what is your pleasure?' But then she saw me hovering and flashed me a grin. 'Sorry, Nick, ladies first. What can I get you, Izzy?'

Rob and Nick turned as one.

I flatter myself I acted brilliantly here. 'Another round, if that's what these two are after.' I put a twenty-pound note on the counter. 'And if you were about to get the bill,' I added to Rob, 'that's my share.'

'We weren't,' he said. 'It's all going on the tab, so hang on to it for now.' He tucked the note in the pocket of my jeans, Sasha dished out a bottle of water and pudding menus, and we returned to the table.

'From the way your face lit up like a little pink sunbeam, I gather that was Leo on the phone,' Rob said, as we sat down.

'Yes, bless his little heart. He'd have made a brilliant Plonker-fforbes, but there you go.'

Nick passed me a menu. 'I can recommend the apricot

49

crumble and the double chocolate mousse. But I guess you're too full, since you couldn't manage your sausages.'

He looked me right in the eye, as if to say, not very subtle, was it? But it was lightly done, like an invitation to some mild verbal sparring, and I was very tempted. However, after that snippet at the bar I wasn't sure I could keep my 'thing' safely under wraps. I knew it was Felicity he'd been referring to – how dare he talk about her like that? He'd only known her since the summer – what did he know about what made her tick? After she'd said he was 'very nice', too. That was what really galled me.

But if he thought I was going to forgo pudding just to save face, he'd got another think coming. 'Oh, I don't know,' I said. 'I've always got room for something sweet and gooey.' I added an airy smile, but I wasn't sure it quite came off. A minute flicker in his eyes said he could smell 'things' the way Henry smelt cubic millimetres of farm-house Cheddar, and this one was amusing him in a cynical sort of way. Well, feel free, I thought. As a new Better Person I wouldn't dream of depriving you.

From Sasha I ordered apricot crumble with cream *and* ice-cream. At Nick's elbow with her order pad she was saying not double chocolate mousse again, honestly, he was such a pig.

How true, I thought.

The others, meanwhile, were talking murder. 'You'll get sealed envelopes tomorrow, with instructions and all your guilty secrets,' Felicity was saying. 'Which you are not to open until just before kick-off, and there's to be absolutely no conferring.'

'I take it we'll get a cast list?' said Paula. 'I have absolutely no idea who anybody's supposed to be. Who's Emerald, for a start?'

'The tart with a heart,' said Nick. 'As I was about to say before I got a nose in my crotch.'

I shot him a pitying look. 'No heart. It's such a cliché.'

'But she's very high-class,' grinned Ian.

'Oh, no, darling,' I said, in my Emerald voice. 'That wouldn't be any fun. I'm a low-down filthy little floozy with attitude. But I'm very expensive, and I only do members of the Establishment.'

'Talking of the Establishment, Rob's going to make a lovely bishop,' said Felicity. 'He used to be a choirboy, you know.'

Nick nearly choked on his mousse. 'You didn't, did you?'

Rob put on a solemn, pious voice. 'I will ignore that crass aspersion on my spirituality. Emerald knows the true nature of my calling.'

'You bet I do,' I said.

Rob was doing his damnedest not to laugh. 'Come to me after Evensong, my child, and though you are but a harlot and full of sin, I will pray for your soul and lay hands upon you.'

'You dirty old git, you'll get defrocked,' said Nick.

'I should think so, too,' said Paula. 'And who are you?' she asked Felicity.

'Betsy Blob, the dopey poor relation who's just come out of an institution. I found a fantastically frumpy frock in a charity shop, but when I asked Ian what he thought, he said, "Yes, you look gorgeous." He actually thought I was going to wear it *out*!'

'Can't do anything right,' said Ian. 'I didn't think it did anything for her, but I didn't like to say.'

Felicity's voice turned plaintive. 'Ian, you say, "Yes, you look gorgeous," whatever I wear. Sometimes I think you

51

wouldn't notice if I went out topless with my nipples painted green.'

'I think I would, Eff,' he said. 'As long as I'd got my contacts in.'

'Who are you playing?' I asked him.

'Ricky Rock, the has-been rock star,' he said. 'I've got some great purple flares, last aired at a cheesy seventies night.'

Paula wore the faintly bemused expression of someone who wouldn't be seen dead within fourteen light years of cheesy seventies nights. 'It seems a rather ill-assorted cast. I don't quite see why they'd all be assembled in the same place.'

That was when someone called, 'Anyone got a blue, T-reg Peugeot 206?'

From behind the bar a man with a rubicund-landlord air was looking round inquiringly.

'Yes, me,' I called. 'Don't tell me I left my lights on?'

'Even better, my love – you've got a flat. Front nearside.'

'Oh, great.' I gave a resigned sigh.

'Never mind, Izz,' said Rob. 'I'll change it.'

'Rob, I'm perfectly capable of changing wheels.'

'Bravo,' said Nick in firm, approving tones, as if I'd actually meant that to be the end of it. As if Rob was now going to say, 'Please yourself,' and let me curse at jacks and get my hands filthy for the sake of feminist principle.

But nobody called my bluff twice in one night. 'I was obliged to say that for the sake of form,' I told him, with a mock-earnest air I thought was rather good. 'You say it as if messing about with jacks is no big deal, while secretly hoping and praying that whoever made the noble offer will come back with—'

'That's what ugly great sods like me are for,' Rob cut in, with a grin. 'Ignore him, Izzy. He's just winding you up.'

'You did say there was a key in your back.' Nick raised mock-apologetic eyebrows. 'I was just checking.'

We left shortly afterwards, but only Felicity, Ian and I were staying at Colditz that night. I left my keys with Rob. He'd do the tyre around eleven tomorrow, he said, and leave the keys with whoever was behind the bar.

Felicity's black and white collie cross, Shep, was in the back of her estate car. She'd left him there as smells of steak made him dribble. He was delighted to see Henry as they'd met several times and got on fine as long as no bones were involved.

'I'm beginning to get an awful feeling about tomorrow night,' Felicity said, as she turned in to the lane. 'Did you hear Paula? She can't seem to understand that it doesn't *have* to make sense. It's just supposed to be a laugh.'

'If you ask me,' said Ian, 'she was off at the shops when sense of humour was being dished out.'

'Yes, but it's not just her. Even Ellie groaned just a bit when I said we were doing a murder – she pretended it was a joke, of course, but I'm not so sure. What if Adam feels the same?'

Adam and Ellie were another pair of old friends, due tomorrow.

'If people don't enter into the spirit of it, it'll be a disaster,' she went on. 'I'm beginning to see everybody just going through the motions and feeling ridiculous.'

I made up my mind there and then that Emerald was going to be an over-the-top triumph. An icon among tarts. 'Well, I won't.'

'Nor will I,' said Ian. 'Stop worrying, Eff. It'll be fine.'

'I do wish you wouldn't call me Eff,' she said plaintively. 'It sounds fat. And what if the actual murder turns out to be a damp squib?' As the screen was misting up she wiped it with what looked like a dead rabbit. In fact, it was a soft toy she'd given Shep for his first Christmas. It was the only one he hadn't chewed up; he still carried it around like a toddler with a comfort blanket. 'What if it's really obvious?' she went on. 'If everybody gets it straight off there won't be any point. Jim was dying to tell me the whole plot, but I said that would spoil the fun for me, too.'

'It'll be brilliant,' I said firmly. 'It'll go down in the annals, you'll see.'

'Yes – the annals of disaster. Ian was right, I should have called it off. Only I did want poor old Colditz to go out with a bang.'

I frowned. 'What do you mean?'

Ian half turned to me. 'She wasn't going to tell anybody. It's going to be demolished.'

'You're kidding!'

'It's about to change hands,' he went on. 'With planning permission to cram thirty-odd houses on to the site. There's a new industrial estate going up not far away.'

I couldn't believe it. 'I'd have thought a place like Colditz would be listed!'

'It is,' said Ian. 'Listed under "too bloody hideous to be preserved".'

'Ian, must you?' said Felicity.

Feeling awful for Felicity, I sat back. When she was a child, Colditz was the only real home she'd known. With her parents moving from one minor embassy to another, Felicity had been packed off to boarding-school at the age of six. This had horrified me, but she'd told me blithely that she'd loved it. In the holidays she'd nearly always gone to her grandparents at Colditz. Her parents had blown in and out now and then, but never for long and she hadn't much minded. Even if it hadn't come to rounders bats, there had always been tension between them.

Colditz was about five miles from the Coach and Horses. I'd seen it before, but never from the inside. Built by a many-great-grandfather who Felicity cheerfully admitted had been mad, it was a particularly unlovely example of Victorian Gothic in grey stone. Mini-turrets and twisty bits were stuck on for no reason other than to scare off the peasantry. In a pretty county stuffed with pretty houses, it wasn't surprising nobody had slapped a preservation order on it.

Once we were inside I realized that all those twisty turrets made it look a lot bigger than it was. The hall had a stone floor with an impressive staircase, and the walls were largely panelled in wood.

'They'll be ripping that lot out,' Ian said. 'Worth a bomb in scrap.'

Off the hall was an oak-panelled study with a wood-burning stove Ian had lit earlier. With heavy velvet curtains drawn, it was surprisingly cosy. Over Gaelic coffees Felicity showed me her Master List for tomorrow. 'Have a quick look and see if you think I've forgotten anything. If you come shopping with me in the morning we can pick your car up on the way back.'

Sitting at her feet, Shep gave a pathetic little whimper.

'Oh, buggeration,' said Felicity. 'I left Bunny in the car.'

The room she eventually showed me to was on a chilly landing with a bathroom four doors away. On the doors, in carefully penned Gothic, were signs with all the players' names. Inside my room there were flowers on a dressing-table of ponderous Victorian mahogany.

'I'm afraid the furniture's horrible,' she said, wrinkling her nose. 'Much of it's the original, sold with the house. Granny always said Grandpa's ancestors had all the taste of a lugworm, but the buyer thought it "went". He was only planning to let it, anyway. Or rather, sit tight until he could flog it off to a developer.'

On the bedside table was a bottle of Highland Spring, a couple of Bonios, and a white envelope saying 'Emerald Caprice' in the same black Gothic. She picked this up. 'You're not supposed to open it till tomorrow, but I won't tell if you do.' She paused. 'Only, if it sounds like damp squibs waiting to happen, please don't tell me.'

'It'll be fine!'

Just as she was leaving I said, 'Felicity, does Nick remind you of anybody?'

'Like who?'

'I don't know like *who*, that's why I'm asking.'

'Can't think of anybody.' At the door she paused. 'But now I come to think of it, my hairdresser said he reminded her of someone who used to be on the television. She's got a Westie called Trixie – poor little thing had a terrible allergy to cat fleas. Night night, then.'

That was very helpful: the field narrowed to everything in *TV Quick* for possibly the past five years. Still, it might come to me.

Although the heating had been fixed the room was still none too warm. Sliding into a double bed that felt like a football pitch in February, I was glad I'd brought warm, non-glam pyjamas. As Henry curled up beside me, I opened my envelope with a horrible feeling that Felicity might be right. What if it turned out to be a corny, utterly obvious embarrassment? If it was just us, the old crowd, we'd have a laugh anyway, but it wasn't. What if Paula stood about with a fixed smile, pointedly failing to get the joke? As for Nick, I could see him wearing a look of private amusement at Felicity's expense, as she realized we might as well pack it in and play *Twister*.

From my envelope I took four typed sheets. The first was headed:

## MURDER IN MIND

*A game of lies, treachery and violent death,*
*devised by Jim Dangerfield of the Village Players*
*(book your tickets now for our*
*Christmas pantomime).*
*The action takes place at the home of Evadne*
*Midas-Browne, at a family gathering.*

### Dramatis Personae

**Evadne Midas-Browne**, obscenely wealthy unmarried woman of a certain age. [This was Ellie, due tomorrow, and I wasn't at all sure she'd like playing a toyboyed old bag.]

**'Medallion' Max Carver**, her resident personal trainer and masseur. [Nick, with yucky baby oil.]

Evadne's four nephews and their consorts:

**James St John ('Call me Sinjun, my dear') Plonker-fforbes**, Cabinet minister with expensive tastes, well known for thundering speeches on Family Values. Engaged to rich exotic socialite Ivanetta Trompinka, St John recently arranged a gagging order on a Sunday paper's allegations of his high jinks with low women. Plays golf with High Court judges. [This was Alastair, who was giving Jane a lift down. I could see him relishing this one, so maybe things were looking up.]

**Ivanetta Trompinka, fiancée of St John, above,** precise origin unknown, but probably former Eastern European Republic of Wurzo-Slavinia. Loaded, but wealth also of unknown origin, very likely dubious.

[Even better. Rich, dodgy and exotic would be just up Jane's street.]

*Charles Plonker-fforbes*, City type under investigation by Drug Squad for suspected money laundering and connections with organized crime. Recently observed with head down toilet on realizing he'd lost ten million dollars in dodgy currency deal, now imagining Mafiosi hit men with chain-saws around every corner. [This was Adam, Ellie's husband and a bit of a smart-arse. Probably wouldn't act at all, in case he turned out hammer than a sandwich.]

*Annabel Plonker-fforbes*, nympho and independently wealthy wife of Charles. Currently desperate for vigorous younger model, has visited dear Aunt Evadne on many occasions, purely out of concern for her welfare, of course. [Sasha. Yes, this boded well. Could definitely see her with designs on Auntie's toyboy.]

*Hugo Plonker-fforbes*, a.k.a. the Bishop of Upchester. Has undergone prolonged psychotherapy for guilt complex of unknown origin. [Rob, of course – but guilty of what? Nothing to do with choirboys, I hoped.]

*Lavender Freud*, his former therapist and companion. [Paula, couldn't see her as a therapist but never mind.]

*Richard 'Ricky Rock' Plonker-fforbes*, youngest brother and former rock star living on faded glories and proceeds of two massive hits in the eighties. Was wild rebellious youth, rejecting Establishment family. Still despises three brothers, above. [Ian, who did a really dreadful Rod Stewart if let anywhere near a karaoke.]

*Bettina 'Betsy' Blob*, feeble-minded stepsister of

Plonker-fforbes brothers. Put in institution at seven-teen, recently rescued by Evadne thirty years later. [Felicity, in frumpy frock.]

*Emerald Caprice, formerly Janice Trotter*, Purveyor of Special Services to the Quality, soon to publish memoirs entitled *Boys Just Want to Have Fun*. Acquaintance of Ricky Rock, brought along by him solely to outrage snotty family. [Then I'd do my best.]

N.B. These details are not necessarily complete and may be deliberately misleading.

Sheet two was headed:

*For Emerald's Eyes Only.*
*On pain of death, no detail shall be divulged before the denouement, except as instructed.*
*And remember, there are villains in our midst who will stop at nothing. Trust nobody!*

God help us, I thought. 'Over the top' wasn't in it. My CV ran to an entire A4 sheet.

The next page was headed:

*Specific instructions and timings. Please synchronize watches.*

As this also ran to an entire page it was a while before I'd taken it all in, by which time my feelings were wildly mixed. On the one hand, there was rather more to Emerald than met the eye. The squib was looking a good deal less damp than I'd expected.

On the other, I had a partner in crime. At ten past eight we had an appointment with murder. At eleven we had to be entwined in a steamed-up clinch in my room, where a person or persons unknown were presumably going to catch us in the act.

'N.B.,' said the instructions, '*actual snogging need obviously not take place, especially if either party has been eating garlic, but please try to look for half a minute as if the entire North Devon Fire Brigade couldn't put your flames out.*'

Talk about Sod's Law. Why couldn't it have been Rob? An oiled Nick clinched up to my dumplings was probably more than even a Better Person could stomach.

On the other hand they'd be Emerald's dumplings, and Emerald was not a Better Person. She was a devious little cow, and growing on me by the second.

'I think Emerald's going to snog him whether he likes it or not,' I said to Henry. 'I do like to do things properly. Artistic integrity, and all that. As for garlic, a couple of cloves will do nicely. Big fat ones, eaten raw.'

His tail wagged sleepily and he gave a deep sigh.

'Exactly,' I said. 'That'll teach him.'

# Chapter 4

Unfortunately, like a lot of ideas that come to me last thing, this one didn't look quite so brilliant in the morning. First, it would entail secreting the garlic about my person, peeling and chewing at the last minute. Second, he might just think I was some weird garlic addict with secret hots for him.

Nice thought, though.

After scrambled eggs cooked by Ian in a vast kitchen with the statutory Aga, Felicity and I departed for dog-walking, shopping, and picking up my car. In rain-washed sunshine she drove half a mile to a favourite spot, and after tramping through two fields and half a wood, we reloaded two dogs and half a ton of mud into the tailgate.

By now Felicity had found something else to worry about. 'Oh, buggeration – Ian's mobile's off and I forgot to remind him to go to the Graystocks.'

They were their neighbours. 'What for?'

'To borrow their old rocking-chair and a doll. Betsy Blob's supposed to sit with a doll in her lap, rocking herself and looking vacant. Don't ask me why,' she added, seeing my face. 'I haven't cheated and read my own CV yet.'

The nearest town was about four miles away, largely through high-banked lanes where we saw more pheasants than other traffic. She parked in the pretty market square, where they were probably selling mangel-wurzels when Henry the Eighth was but a twinkle in his old dad's eye. There were still horse troughs, crammed with winter pansies now. There was an old inn, with a coach entrance, but there was also Safeway's, and an up-market deli. Masses of Saturday shoppers thronged the square, and cars were parked anywhere it was allowed. In front of the ancient Market House was a tall, lit-up Christmas tree, and across the house was a banner saying, 'US BE PLAIZED TO ZEE EE!'

'What's that in aid of?' I asked.

'A leftover from the autumn fair – nobody's got round to taking it down. If you ask me, they should put up a translation for foreign tourists. They can have enough trouble with spoken Devonish, let alone written. That's the Butchery,' she added, pointing across the square.

As she was apparently indicating a house, I suppose I looked blank.

'That's what Rob and Nick call their place of work,' she added. 'Terrible, isn't it? I just hope they never let any of their patients' humans hear.'

'Highly irreverent.' It was a period house, probably Queen Anne. Stone steps led up to a blue front door and two stone dogs stood guard on either side.

'The owner's been there since the year dot,' she went on, as we crossed the square. 'Old Mr Markham. He was on the point of retiring when he had a stroke, a few weeks ago. It was a terrible shame. Nick had had an agreement with him that he was going to buy the practice, so I think he was a bit browned off.'

'Browned *off*? I don't suppose the poor man was too thrilled about it, either.'

'Oh, I don't mean *that*. Old Mr Markham fully intended for Nick to buy the practice, only there was nothing in writing. And now he's in a bad way his son's got power of attorney, and he told Nick that as far as he was concerned, verbal agreements counted for nothing. I suppose I shouldn't say it, but he's not very nice, Mr Markham's son.'

Felicity knew just about everyone for ten miles. If she didn't know them directly, she knew of them.

'Because Nick was just going to buy the practice, not the premises,' she went on. 'But now Markham junior wants to offload them as a package, which'll mean a lot more money. So since they get on pretty well, Rob and Nick have decided to go for it together. I knew it was the right thing, getting Rob down here,' she added. 'I just had a sort of feeling.'

Outside shops, tubs of fuchsias were still blooming. Felicity headed for a covered market for free-range bacon and eggs. Next she headed back to the square, for just-out-of-the-oven bread. The queue stretched into the street, so while she was waiting I looked in the estate agent's window next door, purely from professional habit. Compared with south-west London, prices were a joke. A Devon-white version of Christmas Cottage was less than half the price.

On our return to the car, the dogs greeted us with flattering ecstasy. 'I swear he thinks the wolves and bears are going to get me,' Felicity said, as Shep went mad. 'I keep telling him I'm only going hunting in Safeway's, but he doesn't believe me.'

'Separation anxiety,' I said. 'And no wonder, if he's with you all day.'

Like me, Felicity took her dog to work every day, but work was Ian's office, which she'd been running for five years now. It had started as a temporary thing, when someone had left him in the lurch. Formerly his father's agricultural-supplies business, it was an informal set-up, and being Ian he probably wouldn't have objected to a Vietnamese pot-bellied pig snoring by the photocopier. As Felicity sometimes said, it didn't exactly make much use of a geography degree, but neither had her previous job in London, organizing events.

Since we were heading for the Coach and Horses, she took a slightly different route on the way back. As we passed the umpteenth pheasant in a bank, I thought that the local Mr Fox would have no trouble finding gourmet dinners. The lane rose gently to the breast of a hill, and for a moment I wondered why I chose to live in urban choke-dom, where plagues of *homo parkingspaceus* drove me crackers. A panorama of green tranquillity stretched before us, dotted with clumps of winter-skeleton trees. Sheep grazed on steeply rising fields, the odd hamlet nestled in a dip. Part of the sky was still a milky pale blue, but dark grey clouds were scudding towards us.

'I'll pop into the pub while we're there,' said Felicity, as we approached. 'I've roped in Ted and Maggie's daughter to do maid duty – I just want a little word . . .'

Ted was the rubicund landlord, Maggie his wife and co-licensee.

By the time we reached the Coach and Horses the clouds had caught up with us; a few fat drops were spattering the windscreen. My car was exactly where I'd left it, and *homo wheelchangeus* was getting stuck in. Only it wasn't Rob.

'*Nick?*' frowned Felicity, as she drew alongside. 'What happened to Rob?'

Which is exactly what I asked a moment later, amid a cacophony of dogs dying to be let out.

Spanner in hand, he straightened up. 'Paula was in a panic. Her pup had something stuck in her throat – he's taken her to the Butchery to sort her out.'

'Oh, poor little Millie,' said Felicity. 'Still, that's puppies for you. I'm just popping inside – won't be a tick . . .'

I was left with Nick. He wore navy jogging bottoms, trainers and a grey T-shirt, already spattered with raindrops. 'There was no need for you to do it! If Rob was tied up, he should have let me know.'

Aware that this had come out sounding ungracious, I tried to sound more like a Better Person. 'I'm sure you've got other things to do, and I wasn't kidding when I said I was perfectly capable.'

'I wouldn't bet on it,' he said. 'I think I've got my fair share of brute force and ignorance, but I was still having a hell of a job with one of those nuts half a minute ago.' His eyes suddenly switched to somewhere over my left shoulder. 'Alex! I told you to stay in the car!'

Two small boys were emerging from an estate car nearly as mud-spattered as Felicity's. One was blond and clutching a football, the other was darker. 'I'm fed up of *wait*ing!' complained the blond one. 'Will you please hurry *up*?'

'Alex—'

'Please, Daddy!'

*Daddy*?

'You said five *min*utes,' the child went on accusingly, 'and now I s'pose you're going to start talking and *talk*ing –' here he shot a look at me – 'and we'll be here for *hours*.'

I bit my lip. 'No, you won't – I was just telling your daddy I can finish it myself.'

'But he won't let you, I bet,' said the child, with an air of roughly six-year-old resignation. 'Because I said, "Oh, *no*," when Rob phoned, just as we were off to the common, but Dad said it wouldn't kill him, 'specially as he was a bit nockshus to you last night.'

'What's that mean, anyway?' asked the other child.

Blond Alex raised his eyes to heaven. 'Didn't you hear my dad? It means being a *bit* of a *prat*.'

How I didn't explode with laughter I'll never know.

'The word is *ob*noxious, Alex,' Nick said, in terse tones. 'Will you two please get back in the car?'

'What for?' demanded Alex.

'Because this is a car park, cars are coming in, and squashed kid makes a hell of a mess. *Now*,' he added, as a BMW swept in.

As the pair of them returned to the car, I turned back to Nockshus Nick. 'Am I looking at a father of twins?'

'God, no. Just Alex.'

Which was more than enough, by the looks of it. 'How old is he?'

'Six and a half.'

'Then I should congratulate you,' I said, deadpan. 'His verbal skills would seem to be highly developed for his age.'

This brought a very wry smile to Nick's face that almost made me think he wasn't so nockshus after all. 'He's a cheeky little sod, you mean. Unfortunately, I don't have him often enough to do much about it.' He paused. 'Look, I think maybe we got off on the wrong foot last night. If it was that stupid crack about your dog, I'm sorry.'

Being a gracious Better Person, I said nothing about sausages or slagging off my friend. 'Forget it – I over-reacted. But please, don't let me keep you from your football. I really can finish it myself.'

'No, it's fine. It's nearly done, anyway.'

It wasn't. He still had to un-jack it and put the spare back, but as Louise often said, you have to let them feel useful now and then. At least the rain had stopped; the cloud had passed over. Watching him work with tense, purposeful energy, I wondered why his daddy status had startled me. Felicity hadn't said anything about kids. 'Will you be bringing Alex to the murder?'

'God, no.' He was tightening nuts so hard, the muscles in his forearms stood out. 'He's staying over with Jamie, the other one. He only lives two doors away – they get on pretty well. It wasn't my official weekend to have him, but his mother and her husband had a last-minute invitation to an NBK do in Wales.'

'Would that be No Bloody Kids?'

'It would. No non-bloody kids, either.' Hefting the flat back into the boot, he went on, 'You'll have to get your skates on if you're going to get this fixed for tomorrow night. There's a place called Granger's on the other side of town – Felicity'll know it. If they can't do it today, I'm pretty sure they're open on Sunday mornings.'

'Thank you.' As he banged the boot shut I took a packet of wet wipes from the glove compartment and handed him a couple.

'Thanks.' Having wiped his mucky hands, he looked me up and down. 'How long's it going to take you to turn that lot into the filthy little floozy?'

'That lot' was the perfect kit for country walks. Real country walks, not the type they portray in *Idyllic Country Lifestyle*. I was wearing a manky old jacket bearing the odd artistic splatter of mud. My wellies were generously caked with a ripe mix of mud, muck and green slime of unknown origin. Round my neck I wore some designer jewellery in steel and leather, a.k.a. Henry's lead, clipped together at the ends. From my pockets bulged Henry's ball and a stick he'd taken a fancy to.

'Oh, an hour should do it,' I said. 'I shall be floozing for England.'

'I can't compete with that. Maxing for North Devon, maybe.'

I still couldn't see it. Fleetingly, I wondered what on earth he'd think when he read his own instructions for tonight, and I suppose it showed.

'Something funny?' he asked.

'Just nockshus.' Just as well I hadn't bought any garlic; it would have been a non-starter now he'd so nobly changed my wheel. What's more, he was doing that little smile again. 'But I was probably just a bit nockshus, too. Thanks again, for the wheel.'

'No problem. See you later.'

Just as he headed off, Felicity came back. 'Oh, has he gone?'

'Only just. You might have told me he had a kid – I nearly had a fit when a little boy got out of the car telling his daddy to get a move on.'

'Oh, *Alex*. I suppose I didn't think – I've never even seen him. What's he like?'

'In his father's own words, a cheeky little sod.'

'Well, that figures. Between you and me, Rob says he's a little bugger.'

'Is he divorced?'

'Oh, no – they were never married. Not that Rob's ever told me much, but I gather it was rather messy. She lives near Exeter, I think. With husband and baby on the way.'

That was enough of his CV. 'He said there's some Flats "R" Us place on the other side of town – can you give me directions?'

'It's a bit complicated from here – I'll take you.'

So I lugged the flat into her boot, in case my spare came out in sympathy. 'Rob should have phoned,' I said, as we drove off. 'It seems a bit of a nerve, asking Nick to change my tyre when I hardly know him.'

'Oh, stuff it. It's nothing to what Sasha gets him to do, believe me. The other week she had him lugging a massive old fridge to the tip when her mother got a new one. She's staying with her mother for now, trying to pay off a massive student debt. She's after a job in Scotland, but there's nothing doing at the moment.'

'Why Scotland?'

'Her boyfriend's up there, at some RAF base practically at the North Pole. She only sees him about once in three weeks, and sometimes not even that, because he's off on sweaty exercises in Saudi Arabia or somewhere. Mind you, she's being strictly faithful by all accounts, as long as you don't count this flirty thing with Nick. That's dangerously close to eruption if you ask me – poor old RAF'll die the death through sheer distance. Ian's expecting the funeral before Christmas. He says it stands to reason. Nick's a vet – he's got cupboards full of stuff for putting dying things out of their misery.'

This murder was seriously miscast, I thought. If Sasha were playing Emerald, no garlic-flavoured thoughts would have entered her head. Then, gazing at placidly grazing sheep, I wondered what Leo was up to. Not football, anyway. If he was home on a Saturday morning he usually took the kids swimming. Besides being little blonde angels, they were baby dolphins in the water.

'. . . and she's been here about eight months now,' Felicity was saying. 'Lived in London before. Fulham, I think.'

I realized it was Paula she was talking about now. 'What does she do?'

'Journalism. She went freelance recently, so she can live where she likes. She writes pieces for magazines and the Sunday papers – lifestyle and all that.'

Maybe she was doing a 'lifestyle' piece on Rob, I thought. Before and after photos, as if he were some junk-shop chest of drawers that was nevertheless made of sound timber with proper, dovetail joints. 'From Shaggy Scruff to Hunk – How I Fulhamized My Man.' But I didn't say it. It smacked of what my mother called Not Very Nice, which was her term for Bitchy as Hell. And suddenly I wondered what Paula would have thought if she'd heard us talking about her last night. Or some friend had heard us, just as I'd overheard Nick.

I dropped the tyre at Granger's, where a nice man said it'd be ready in the morning, only I'd better come by twelve thirty, or they'd be closed. Back at Colditz, the others all arrived within fifteen minutes of each other. Almost immediately Rob turned up, and suddenly the kitchen was full of people saying, 'Christ, what a drive,' and, 'Honestly, Fliss, if you think *you've* put on weight . . .'

Shep greeted everybody with warm wags and Bunny in his mouth. Henry was far too macho for such wussy behaviour, but still liked offering gifts. At home it was any shoe that happened to be lying around, but here he made do with that stick he'd found earlier.

There followed a minor panic as Felicity realized she'd forgotten to bring a corkscrew and no amount of ransacking kitchen drawers could reveal one. 'Well, this is an *utter* cock-up, and all your fault,' Ian told Felicity, with mock severity. 'If we can't open any of the wine we'll have to make do with beer, or really slum it with the Moët.'

Ian was the only local at this gathering. The rest of us dated back to our first year at university. In my case this had been my only year, but more of that later. Felicity had known Ian since one summer when she was eleven, when Ian had scored a lot of points by telling her graphically exactly what her grandfather meant when he referred to someone in the village as a 'pansy'. For years she hadn't seen Ian at all; their relationship had only blossomed six years ago, when her grandfather had fallen ill and her grandmother had been getting very frail.

'What's all this about Leo?' asked a wide-eyed Ellie, as I washed the rocket we'd forgotten to put in the salad. Married eighteen months, she and Adam lived near Oxford, with a massive mortgage and a hot tub. Nearly as tall as Paula, Ellie was willowy rather than thin, with a mass of dark hair and large brown eyes with a slightly exotic slant, a legacy from a Russian grandmother. 'Something about double-booking? I'd have slaughtered him.'

'I very nearly did.' Adding the rocket, I put the salad on the table with baguettes, bread and cheese.

'Personally, I don't believe a word of it,' said Jane, with the wicked glint she often wore. 'Izzy just didn't want to inflict us lot on him, in case we put him off for life. It's a great personal tragedy for me, though. I was looking forward to seeing Luscious Leo again and indulging in some outrageous flirting.'

'You'd frighten him to death,' retorted Ellie.

She went to talk to Rob, and I was left with Jane. Roughly my height, she had exactly the same tendency to thigh saddle-bags as me, which was one reason we'd always got on. She had blonde hair in a shaggy-chic crop, and grey eyes with an air of permanently hovering mischief. 'If it wasn't for Felicity, God knows when we'd all see each other,' she said. 'She's a bit like my mother, getting the "family" together. I'd never get round to organizing anything like this in a million years.'

'Neither would I.' We were all chipping in with the money, but that wasn't the point.

She nodded towards Rob. 'I can't get over what Paula's done to him. What's she like?'

'Tall, blonde and sylphlike.'

'Izzy, I know all that from Fliss. I mean, what is she *like*?'

'Reserved,' I said, as it was only the truth. 'Not a bundle of laughs after five minutes, but obviously keen on Rob.'

'Well, it's about time someone appreciated him.' Then she turned back to me. 'Just wait till you see what I'm wearing tonight. Think Las Vegas meets Blackpool with shoulder-pads – it's right up Ivanetta's street.'

We were interrupted by hoots of laughter from the other side of the kitchen. 'Come and look,' called Felicity. 'You'll never believe what I dug out the other day.'

It was old photos. 'God, those were the days,' grinned Rob. 'Permanently broke and a thirty-two-inch waist.'

They were holiday shots from aeons ago. Turkey. All of us on the beach, or crowded round a table at night in one of those restaurants where you could order something local for about fifty pence and fill up on the free bread. I had my own set at home, in some album I hadn't looked at in years. But one shot still stood out, filling me with nostalgia.

We were standing on a jetty. I was in Rob's arms, we were laughing, and he was about to chuck me in the sea. I was a size ten then, not a thirteen pretending it was a twelve. I was delicately tanned, with golden glints in my hair. Add some particular angle and a magical fluke of light, and that shot had turned into the best of my entire life. So much so that my mother had said, 'I'd hardly have known it was you, dear. Who's the boy?'

The photos were soon put away, but I couldn't forget them. That holiday had been a milestone. One of the spectacularly stupid things I mentioned earlier was getting kicked out of university for failing five out of seven of my first-year exams. I could have done resits, but that would

72

have meant spending the whole summer revising, or rather doing the work I hadn't done in the first place. And with a summer job lined up, to pay for that holiday eight of us had booked, I'd thought what the hell. Life was too short when you were nineteen, a little bit in love, and October was never going to come.

I hadn't told my parents for months. As we'd all planned to share a house I'd gone back anyway and got a job. Only after the second year had I actually left and joined the airline. I'd gone back to see the old crowd often, usually with a tan and clanking with duty-frees, with a nice little car outside and money for treating them to a meal at the Bombay Nights. I don't think they'd ever realized I'd regretted what I'd done, because I'd hardly admitted it even to myself.

'Lunch' continued until four thirty, when we all started disappearing upstairs. With kick-off at six thirty we needed time to change and absorb our roles. By six I'd made an interesting discovery. Namely, that when you pick up a set of false nails in Boots, thinking they'll be a doddle to stick on in around half an hour, you are suffering from an appalling case of self-delusion.

I'm not referring to tasteful little fakes here. I mean those things that extend about half a mile and render previously adequate fingertips utterly useless. Why don't they tell you on the packet that you need three hands? Have these people ever actually tried picking up a false nail with digits like something out of *Edward Scissorhands*? Let alone applying glue with any degree of accuracy, or painting the whole lot with Scarlet Vamp afterwards. I swore a good deal. Poor Henry retreated to a safe distance and watched me warily, his head on his paws.

Still, the finished nails could have been murder weapons in themselves: ten scarlet daggers at my fingertips. Entirely suitable for Emerald, then, and from head to toe, she was a triumph. Fluffed-up hair, in big rollered waves. Fake-tan foundation and lots of it. Half a ton of blusher and eye make-up, false eyelashes, a pouty-red porn-star mouth glistening with gloss. Pushed-together dumplings that defied the laws of gravity, bared almost to the nipples, with golden-shimmer dust brushed across them. Dangly gold hoops in my ears, and a few gold chains I'd once bought at the gold souk in Dubai, because it had seemed like a good idea at the time.

The leather trousers were brilliant, except that the zip was sticking badly on the way up and I seemed to have put on six pounds since trying them on. With them I wore the sprayed-on leopard-skin top and a pair of black patent sandals I had called my slut heels ever since a kerb-crawler had pulled up, asking if I had 'the time'.

I made a kissy pout at the mirror. 'You look gorgeous, luv. Shall we go?'

# Chapter 5

The hall was deserted as Henry and I descended the carved staircase. They were all in the drawing-room, behind double doors so hefty I heard only faint party sounds. As we got to the bottom of the stairs, the jangly, old-fashioned doorbell rang. Instantly, a blonde girl of about sixteen came scooting from the kitchen. The Coach and Horses daughter, I realized, in a black dress and frilly apron. On seeing me she put a hand to her mouth and stifled an explosive giggle.

'I dunno what you're laughing at,' I said, in my Emerald voice. 'Show some respect, you little skivvy. Answer that door.'

'Yes, madam.' On opening the impressive oak door she erupted anyway.

'Not bad, is he?' said Sasha's voice. 'I've got half a mind to take a picture and send it off to *Blind Date*. A really good sleazebag always livens it up.'

Sasha might have stepped straight out of my dream, when Leo was chatting up the vampire. Her hair hung in straight, dark curtains. Her skin was perfect pale cream. Her mouth was deep plum, almost exactly matching a low-cut velvet dress. She looked stunning in a predatory sort of way, as befitted Annabel Plonker-fforbes, hungry for a more vigorous model than husband Charles.

More vigorous 'Max' was right beside her. I couldn't

believe what she'd done to him. He might have been the owner of one of those clubs the Vice Squad are always trying to shut down, but never quite get the evidence for doing so.

Sasha evidently felt the same about me. Open-mouthed for half a second, she then burst out laughing.

Nick didn't even have the courtesy to look gobsmacked. 'Hi, babes,' he said, in a 'new' lazy voice tinged perfectly with East End and sleaze. 'Long time no see. How's business?'

If this was the 'crap' he'd been talking about, I was Indiana Jones. Time for a bit of attitude, then. Hand on tilted hip, feisty little toss of the head. 'Great. How's yourself?'

Sasha slipped instantly into her part. With cut-glass tones to match, she gave me a look of sniffy disdain. 'Max, are you acquainted with this "person"?'

'Way back, Annabel,' he said easily. 'We were at Tesco Road Comprehensive together.'

He'd absorbed his own notes, then.

'Annabel' gave me another 'riff-raff' look. 'I was under the impression, Max, that you were trying to leave your low origins behind.' So saying, she swept across the hall. 'Come along, we're late already.'

'Snotty cow,' I muttered to 'Max', as we followed. 'Who does she fink she is?'

He was Maxing beautifully, even down to the aren't-I-gorgeous swagger. 'Don't let it get to you, babes. Stay cool until we're out of here.' In his normal voice he added, 'You said floozing for England, not the entire Western Hemisphere. Are you sure those trousers are legal?'

I didn't get a chance to reply. We were making an entrance to gales of mirth.

It had never occurred to me how quickly I'd get into it.

Twenty minutes later I almost *was* Emerald, hyped and excitedly nervous. Could we really pull off this foul murder without anyone sussing us out?

Childhood sweethearts, Max and Emerald went back a long way, not just to Tesco Road Comprehensive, but to a certain magistrates' court where they'd both been done at twelve for pickpocketing tourists in Oxford Street. Let off with a caution, they'd made damn sure they never got caught again. Unless of course you counted ten days later, when they'd been caught by Emerald's mum, at it on the front room rug.

Her parents had been horrified, for the Trotters were respectable people. They were not, however, her natural parents. Adopted as a baby, Emerald had only lately bothered to trace her real mother. Who knew, she might be someone rich who'd pay to keep an embarrassing daughter out of her life.

No such luck. Quite by chance, however, when a client had been unburdening himself, Emerald had discovered who her father was.

It had been a revelation. A whole world of possibilities had opened up. And by lucky coincidence, Max just happened to be employed by a member of this man's well-connected family. Max was minder and toyboy to Evadne, who was loaded, and infatuated with him. By further lucky coincidence, the guests at the birthday party which she was throwing for herself included Evadne's nephew Ricky Rock, who just happened to frequent the same D-list parties as Emerald.

Given all this, Emerald and Max had put their scheming heads together.

I went to join Jane, who was flicking cigarette ash into a huge fireplace where Ian had persuaded some apple logs to burn. The room was high-ceilinged, but there was no baronial oak here. The walls were yellow, with panels of decorative plaster. There were a couple of chandeliers, two formal armchairs, and a *chaise longue*, upholstered in faded, slippery brocade – the other seating would probably end up on the tip once the bulldozers moved in.

As Ivanetta, fiancée of St John Plonker-fforbes, Jane was nearly as over-the-top as Emerald. Covered with multi-coloured sequins, her top had shoulder-pads straight out of *Dynasty*. She had 'big' eighties hair to match, gold stilettos, and a holder for the fags she'd never quite given up. 'I've worked it out already,' she grinned. 'Evadne's changed her will, I bet. She's leaving all her money to Max and the horrible nephews are going to do him in. Or else St John's going to do *you* in before you're signing your memoirs in Waterstone's and exposing him.'

So far, so good, then. 'Serve him right,' I said. 'Tight sod even asked me for a discount.'

'Well, poor old St John's strapped for cash, isn't he? He's only marrying me for my money.'

'So what do you get out of it?'

Jane put on an accent full of husky, Wurzo-Slavinian disdain. 'Use your brains, darrleeng. He promise me title. He said he get knighthood in Birthday Honours. He said I will be Lady Ivanetta, and everyone suck up to me in Harrods.'

I almost wished she wouldn't make me laugh. My trousers were practically cutting me in half; I had to keep my stomach permanently sucked in. 'You won't get no title if he's banged up for murder.'

'Exactly, darrleeng. I don't make pre-nuptial agreement with jailbird. Maybe I say fock him and run off with Medallion Max.'

Her eyes were already on Max, who was a couple of yards away. 'Are he and Sasha an item?'

'Not officially. She's got a boyfriend in Scotland.'

'Oh, good, then I can flirt a bit. I'd never say so to Fliss, but even a murder's not much fun if there aren't any spare men.'

'You're welcome to him. How on earth can you fancy anything in that shirt?'

She lowered her voice to a wicked whisper. 'I always did have a secret little thing about glammed-up sleazy rough.'

That summed up Nick's alias perfectly, I thought. He was wearing black trousers and a loose shirt of sheeny black silk, open virtually to the waist. The medallion wasn't a whopper, but looked like twenty-two carat. There was enough fuzz on his chest to make me realize why waxing would make him shudder. His hair was gelled and spiky, but not overdone. However, what really made Max was the total change in his demeanour. The smirk and swagger were understated, but that only made them more believable.

Jane was still giving him the twice-over. 'What's he like when he's not Max?'

'Extremely rude. He said Henry looked like a sheep.'

She giggled. 'Well, he does just a bit, bless him. Did you thump him?'

'Of course not. I was behaving myself.'

'Izzy. How unbelievably boring.'

Possibly sensing our scrutiny, Nick turned around.

He acted exactly as if we were two girls in a club, saying, 'Phwoar, he's pretty fit – I bet you I pull him.' He raised an eyebrow. He gave a little 'looking for me, girls?' smirk. It was magnetically loathsome, especially when Jane giggled.

Evidently enjoying the reaction, he sauntered over.

Still, the glammed-up sleaze could have been worse. 'What happened to the baby oil, then?' I asked.

'He wouldn't have it,' pouted Sasha, who'd followed him over. 'We had a trial run but he put his foot down.'

'It was gross,' he said, in a decidedly Nick voice. 'Made me feel like a piece of marinated chicken. If that's what babies have to put up with, no wonder they puke all over you.'

Sasha gave a mischievous little grin. 'Oh, come on. I bet you'd just *lurve* to have baby oil smoothed all over your little nappy bits. Maybe Emerald even does it as a special.'

'Yeah, nice little warm-up,' I said. 'Only forty quid extra.'

My Emerald brought pure Max back. 'Great,' he said, with a lazy look from my eyes to my shimmering cleavage and back again. 'If you're the kind of sad tosser who has to pay for his warm-ups.'

This line of conversation got no further, as Felicity, Rob and Paula had just joined us. 'We really have to get going properly soon,' Felicity said anxiously. 'I do hope everybody's not getting too pissed to remember what they're supposed to be doing.'

It was typical of Felicity, I thought, to pick the least glamorous role. Her 'Betsy' frock was high-necked with a lace collar, in that peculiar shade of old-ladies' mauvey-blue. It made her look like a loosely belted sack. To increase the effect she'd even left her bra off. 'Saggy bosoms, I think,' she'd said earlier. 'Betsy would have really saggy bosoms, wouldn't she?' She'd done her hair with a side parting, and somehow managed to make it look like a photo of someone's granny when she was at school.

'We should have had an official prompt,' she went on.

'Only it's a bit difficult when nobody's got the whole picture.'

'Calm yourself, my child,' soothed Rob. Whatever bishops wore on their nights off he looked perfect: sober dark grey jacket, dog-collar, plain silver cross on his chest. With a side parting his hair had been turned halfway traditional, too. 'Have another drink and put your faith in the Lord,' he added.

Jane gave a hoot of laughter. 'Rob, you missed your vocation. You could make a bomb as one of those televangelists who get people to phone in with their credit cards.'

'I did actually think of being a priest once,' he grinned. 'When I was about seven, and someone told me animals didn't go to heaven. I thought, right, I'd fix that. I'd be a sort of neo-St Francis and pray so hard for the lot of them, God would have a rethink and at least take Sooty.'

Who else but dear old Rob?

'Who was Sooty?' asked Paula.

'His rabbit,' I said, as he'd told me about poor mangled Sooty years ago.

'Bloody cat next door got him,' said Rob.

'Would the bloody cat have to go to hell, then?' asked Nick. 'Or didn't your theological argument go that far?'

'Oh, leave him alone,' I tutted. 'He was only little.'

But Paula's smile had tightened, and I didn't altogether blame her. Whoever wants some other woman coming out with private little heartaches he hasn't shared with you? 'How's your little dog?' I asked.

Her expression relaxed. 'She'd got hold of a wooden spoon, can you believe, and a little bit had got stuck in her throat. Rob was marvellous.' Already holding his arm, she squeezed it. 'So calm and reassuring – I was in such a state ... You make a brilliant Emerald,' she went on, evidently trying to be nice in return. 'Everybody else has made such an effort, I feel terribly underdressed.'

I wouldn't have called her underdressed, but she didn't look much like my idea of a psychotherapist called Lavender, either. She wore a white shift dress in what looked like raw silk. Utterly simple and screaming expensive, it made me feel fat, cheap, and blowzy. The fact that I'd intended to look cheap and blowzy was beside the point.

Ian chose that moment to join us. As Ricky Rock he'd teamed those purple flares with a curly seventies wig and a black velvet jacket. 'Izzy, your back view's been playing havoc with my animal lusts. Your bottom looks like two leather balloons, about to burst.'

'For heaven's sake have a little grope, then,' said Felicity. 'I don't suppose she'll slap you.'

'No, just charge you forty quid,' said Nick. In his Max voice he went on, 'So how's your dear old mum, Emerald? Still working down the chippy?'

Except for Annabel the others all looked startled. 'Do you two already know each other?' asked Jane.

'Unfortunately, yes,' said Annabel, in her cut-glass voice. 'Apparently she and Max were at school together.'

'Aha!' said Jane, with a glint in her eye. 'Methinks maybe the plot thickens here.'

Oh, Lord. If Jane had smelt a rat, we were probably doomed already.

'*Such* an unfortunate coincidence that Ricky had to bring her,' Annabel went on sniffily. 'Though why he'd bring such an un*speak*ably common creature to his aunt's birthday party I can't imagine.'

As Emerald would never have stood for this, I didn't. 'Excuse *me*, you toffee-nosed bitch, who are you calling common?'

Everybody but Max cracked up. 'Cool it, Emerald,' he soothed. 'Excuse us, folks, she's not used to polite company.' Taking my arm, he drew me aside.

'Thought I told you to keep cool,' he said, like a Max beginning to be dangerously narked.

*Cool?* Emerald was incandescent. 'What d'you expect?' I flashed. 'Who does she fink she is, talking to me like that?'

'*Think*, Emerald. You're not down Shepherd Market now, for thuck's sake.'

He was laughing underneath, which made me realize that he was enjoying this much more than he'd expected to. 'It's your own fault,' he went on. 'You ain't on the job now – you should have dressed a bit more classy.' In his normal voice he added, 'Is that actually gold dust on your cleavage?'

'It's Desert Shimmer. And you can talk.' I eyed that shirt, open virtually to the waist. 'Undo any more buttons and you'll be done for flashing.'

'The old girl likes it.' He shot a look at the back view of Ellie, who was playing Aunt Evadne. 'Her birthday, innit?'

'Deathday, more like.'

'You said it.' He lowered his voice. 'Have you got the stuff?'

'The stuff' being surgical gloves and a lethal overdose of painkiller I'd blackmailed someone to nick. 'Course I have. In my room.'

'Then be there at ten past eight, OK?'

'OK.' Over my shoulder I saw Sasha suppressing giggles as she gave us mock-suspicious looks. Well, her Annabel would, and Emerald's antennae would be instantly alerted. 'That snotty cow fancies you, if you ask me.'

He gave a truly wonderful smirk. 'Can't help that, can I? Got to keep her sweet. Dangle a little promise under her nose, see?'

Art imitating Life, I thought. 'Is that real?' I asked, eyeing what looked like a gold Rolex on his wrist.

'Bangkok fake,' he said, in his normal voice. 'Sasha borrowed it. Come on.' With a little pat on my waist, he nodded at Felicity, who was trying to get everyone's attention. 'Looks as if kick-off's coming up.'

It was. We were all rounded up and told to shut up for a bit. Aunt Evadne, in whose honour we were all invited, was going to make an announcement. 'But fill your glasses first,' said Felicity. 'Birthday toasts, and all that.'

As the maid filled my glass, Alastair sidled up beside me. He lived in York, which was why it had been easy for him to pick up Jane on the way down. About six foot one, he had dark-toffee hair like Leo's. I think he'd once had a little thing about Jane, and she'd often said she wished she could fancy him, because it was a terrible waste when he was such a good laugh and not gay.

He made a lovely St John, if 'lovely' is the right word. He was smartly suited, his hair slicked back in a way I associated with spin doctors and the posher type of sleaze. In a voice to match, he said, 'I want a word with you, Emerald.'

I had a job not to laugh. 'Sod off, you dirty old git.'

'Come, come, my dear.' He was hopeless at keeping a straight voice, but doing his best. 'I'm being entirely reasonable here. If you go ahead with publishing your so-called memoirs, which are nothing but scurrilous libel, of course, I shall have no option but to call on my friends in high places.'

'They're going ahead,' I said. 'So up yours. Anyway, I've got friends in high places, too. Half of them are my clients.'

'Then I shall call on friends in low places. You should be careful, my dear, living by yourself. There are a lot of deranged people about. With knives and acid, and so on.

We wouldn't want anything happening to that pretty face, now would we? Acid attacks can even be fatal.'

At this point Ricky Rock (Ian) appeared at my side. 'Is my brother threatening you?' he demanded, with a broad grin that completely wrecked the effect.

'Certainly not,' said St John huffily. 'She's one of my constituents. I was merely warning her about the dangers of crime in the area.'

'Yeah, right. Like you give a toss.'

Evidently as instructed, St John gave a black look and left us.

Ian dropped his Ricky act. 'That was the evidence, then,' he grinned. 'My witness statement for when he does you in.'

'Will you all *please* shut up?' called Felicity. 'Curtain up, Act One.'

Playing Aunt Evadne, Ellie sat facing us all, in a formal armchair like a throne. As Betsy Blob, Felicity plonked herself in that rocking-chair, with a hideous doll I'd have left in the cabbage patch. With the prescribed vacant look she started rocking, but the creaking woke Shep, who was napping by the fire. He trotted up to her with a worried expression and Bunny in his mouth.

Ian shook his head. 'I wonder about that dog sometimes. Anyone would think he was having a permanent phantom pregnancy.'

'I wouldn't,' said Nick. 'He's just a furry great jessie.'

'Nick!' said Felicity crossly. 'How dare you? He had a deprived puppyhood, poor little boy.'

'Look, are we doing this murder or not?' demanded Ellie. 'Where's my toyboy? Max, come here. You're supposed to be hovering at my elbow like a devoted slave.'

'Sorry.' Max oiled up to Ellie's version of loaded, face-lifted Evadne. She'd done it very well, in a severely elegant black dress with long sleeves. Her hair was scraped back tightly, like a ballerina. From a distance you could just about imagine a rich woman with a first-rate plastic surgeon and perfect taste, except when it came to gigolos.

Coming to stand just behind her 'throne', Max put his hands on her shoulders. 'I *am* your devoted slave, Evadne,' he said, with cringe-making 'sincerity'. 'Body and soul.'

'Christ, just look at him,' grinned Rob. 'The sleazy sod's really coming out of the woodwork.'

'Rob!' said Felicity. 'Shut up and just act your role for five minutes, will you? And don't say "Christ" – you're supposed to be a bishop. Get on with it, Ellie, or we'll never get any dinner tonight.'

Ellie began her Aunt Evadne. 'It was very good of you all to come and help me celebrate my birthday. It gives me great pleasure to see my nephews and their wives and companions, especially as none of you could be bothered to come last year.'

Her pause for effect was wrecked by Adam. Just audibly he murmured to Rob, 'I don't know about you, but I haven't a clue what the fuck's going on here.'

Ellie's eyes flashed. 'Well, what a surprise. If you'd spent more than half a minute skimming your notes before falling asleep—'

'*I* was bloody driving!' retorted Adam. 'You were sleeping all down the M5!'

'Oh, for heaven's *sake*!' This was Felicity, as exasperated as I'd ever seen her. With a jerk she rose from her rocking-chair. 'Just listen, will you? *St John* is a sleazy bastard of a Cabinet minister, she pointed to Alastair, 'who is engaged to dodgy, loaded *Ivanetta*,' and she pointed to Jane. '*Ricky* is a has-been rock star,' she pointed to Ian, 'and *he*,' she pointed to Rob, 'is a psychologically damaged bishop.

86

*You*,' she pointed to Adam, 'are dodgy financier Charles, and *you – are – all – brothers*. OK?'

After a breath she went on, '*I* am your mentally challenged stepsister, and *she*,' she pointed to Ellie, 'is your filthy-rich Aunt Evadne. *She*,' she pointed to Sasha, 'is your posh nympho wife Annabel, who fancies the pants off *him*,' she pointed to Nick, 'who is Evadne's slimy little bugger of a toyboy. And *Izzy*,' she pointed to me, 'is a dirty little tart who's come with Ricky. OK? Got it now?'

'Just about,' said Adam. 'No need to blow a gasket.'

'He was snoring, too,' said Ellie. 'I could see his uvula-thing vibrating over his tonsils. It made me feel quite ill.'

'Don't you start,' said Adam darkly. 'Or I'll tell them about your—'

'Come on, you two,' soothed Rob, as the rest of us laughed. 'Save it for later, will you?'

Ellie resumed her Aunt Evadne. 'As I was *say*ing, before I was so rudely interrupted by Snoring Pig, it's my birthday. The fact that you've all turned up this year has, I know, nothing to do with the letter I included with the invitations. The one informing you that I'm suffering from a heart condition that might carry me off at any moment. None of you, of course, came purely to ingratiate yourself, so that I might leave you a bit more in my will.'

'Really, Aunt, I must protest,' blustered St John. 'To suggest that I, of all people—'

'Be quiet, St John.' She glared at him so hard, a wave of suppressed laughter went round the room. 'And as for you . . .' She shot an equally contemptuous glare at Adam/Charles. 'Do you think I'm an imbecile? Sending your wife to ingratiate herself on your behalf – I know why Annabel really comes, and it's not to see me. She sniffs around my devoted Max like, well, I'm far too much of a lady to say a bitch on heat.'

'Well, *really*,' said Annabel.

Max only gave a pious little smirk.

'Do you think I'm stupid?' Evadne went on. With an expression of contempt, she surveyed us all. 'I brought you here to tell you that whether I last a month or another twenty years, none of you are getting a penny. I despise the lot of you, always have. As for your poor stepsister . . .' She cast a glance at Betsy, still rocking. 'The way you treated her was shameful.'

'My baby,' said Betsy vacantly, right on cue. 'I love my baby. *I* won't throw her away.' Having said that, she did just that, chucking the doll on the floor.

'Poor, tragic creature,' said bishop Rob, shaking his head sadly, while a wave of mirth went round everybody except Felicity.

'Shep, *no!*' He was giving the doll a good exploratory licking. 'Ian, take it away – he'll eat it and I've got to give it back. Sorry, Ellie,' she added. 'Do go on.'

Ellie's Evadne resumed that expression, as if we were some virulent strain of flesh-eating bacteria. 'If not for me, poor Betsy would still be languishing in that institution. If I die next week, what will happen to her?'

She was doing it so well, everybody had gone quiet. 'I will tell you.' She put up a hand to Max's, still lying on her shoulder. 'I am pleased to tell you that very soon, my dear Max and I are going to be married.'

We all gave gasps of collective fake shock.

'He will therefore be the sole beneficiary of my will and legal guardian of Betsy,' she went on. 'And I know the dear boy will care for her just as he cares for me.'

A little buzz went round the room.

'However, I have every intention of living several more years,' she went on. 'With my beloved Max at my side.' She looked up at him with an expression of simpering devotion; he made a besotted kissy face that made us all crack up.

Evadne glared at us. 'And that concludes what I have to say. I am now going upstairs for a nap before dinner, which I shall take on a tray in my room. I have no wish to look at any of you over the dining table – I hope your dinner chokes you. But thank you all so much for coming – seeing your faces has made my day.' She stood up. 'Max, come with me. I should like a little massage to get me off to sleep.'

Just before he exited, Max shot the guests a lazy little smile that should have got him an Oscar. It said, 'Up yours. I've shafted the lot of you, and there's nothing you can do.'

As the door closed, Evadne's guests stared at each other with suitably outraged expressions.

'Wasn't Ellie brilliant?' Felicity beamed. 'And so kind to rescue me from the nut-house before my bosoms hit my knees.'

'What about Nick?' demanded Sasha. 'Pretending he couldn't act for toffee – if you ask me he's been practising in the mirror.'

'If you ask me, Max is for the chop,' said Adam. 'Pretty bloody obvious, isn't it?'

As I said, Adam was a bit of a smart-arse. He and Ellie had married a year ago, after being an on-and-off item ever since they'd met. They rowed a lot, but I had a feeling much of it was on purpose. Ellie had once told me that screaming and throwing things turned her on.

Just now I could have thrown something at Adam; his 'pretty obvious' remark had deflated Felicity instantly. 'At least my little recap gave you a clue what the fuck *is* going on,' she said. 'Excuse me, everyone, I've got to see to the dinner.'

As the door closed behind her, Sasha said, 'I suppose poor Betsy had a baby. Would that be why they had her put away? To cover up?'

'*Betsy*? Who ze hell care about her?' This was Jane, doing Ivanetta with bells on. In her best Wurzo-Slavinian accent she addressed her fiancé, St John. 'Iz disgosting, your aunt having jig-a-jig with man so young. In my country ze male relatives would feed iz testicles to ze pigs before he get her money. You Eenglish, you have no testicles.'

'In this country, my dear girl, we have laws,' said St John pompously.

'Fock laws. You let him fock old woman and take her money? In my country old women cook and knit shrouds for old men. In any case, iz terrible waste, young man wiz good body focking old woman. Geev me anozzer drink, you piece of Eenglish sheet.'

With everybody cracking up, this seemed like a good time to slip off. My assignation with Max was coming up and I needed to disappear anyway. Those trousers were so tight, two glasses of fizz felt like a couple of gallons.

Teetering along in slut heels that were killing me already, I made a detour to my room first to check my phone in case Leo had been trying to get me.

The screen said 'Message, 1'.

It then said 'Mum'.

'*Nothing urgent, dear, but I've tried three times since last night – do hope everything's all right. Speak to you soon.*'

I hadn't called for ten days, but she'd have to wait. Bulletins from expat Spain, where my folks had been spending most of their time for the past six years, took at least twenty minutes, and preferably not at mobile rates.

When I finally hit the loo a major disaster manifested

itself, but not even Felicity had imagined this one. First, getting hold of a minute zip tab with Edward Scissorhand fingers was not easy. Second, once I'd grasped it the bloody thing would only descend three inches. And of course, once that happened my moderate urge turned into Niagara Falls hanging on by a whisker.

'Please, come *on* . . .' The zip had been sticking before, but nothing like this.

*Calm down, Izzy. Gently does it – don't try to force it* . . .

Gently didn't do it. Ditto non-gently.

Emergency assistance was called for. I was on the first stair down when a low but compelling voice called, 'Emerald! Where d'you think you're going?'

'Sorry, Nick – I have to see someone on an urgent matter.'

In a couple of strides he was beside me. 'You up to something, Emerald? We're in this together. We had a deal.'

'Nick, I'm not playing for a minute, all right? I really do have to see someone.'

He dropped the act. 'Look, it's no skin off my nose, but we're supposed to stick to timings or the whole thing's stuffed. What's so urgent, anyway?'

'If you really must know, I'm desperate for the loo, I can't get my zip undone, and if I have to murder anyone like this I'll wet myself, all right?'

With evident effort, he restrained a split-arse grin. 'And you were going to see who on this urgent matter?'

Suddenly I wanted Leo so badly. It took a lot to embarrass me, but this was just a tad *personal*. 'Rob. At least he won't laugh,' I added, with feeling.

'Am I laughing?'

'Yes!'

'Oh, come here . . .' Taking my wrist, he half pulled me back to the landing. 'Right, keep still – my God, who poured you into these?'

Maybe Nockshus Nick had a piquant ring to it, after all. 'I don't need a running commentary, all right?'

'Then stop talking and hold your stomach in.'

He gave a hefty tug. 'Hmm. Stubborn little bastard. Brace yourself – I'm going in on six cylinders here.'

This time he yanked harder. 'Christ. Are you sure this isn't a built-in chastity belt?'

'Just get on with it, will you? Use some of that brute force and ignorance you were bragging about.'

'I'll rip them apart, if that's what you want.'

'I don't! They're not even mine!'

'Come on, then. Up against the wall.'

Braced against the wall, sucking my stomach right in, I felt his fingers against my skin, getting a firm grip. 'Hold tight, then . . .'

There was an almighty yank and suddenly my stomach was rebounding as the zip shot down. 'Oh, my God, thanks – back in a tick . . .' I charged back to the bathroom, and the bliss of release. This was followed swiftly by the realization that he must have got an eyeful of that filmy black thong I'd thought would be right up Emerald's street.

Tough. Needs must when you're desperate. The zip even went up again without much argument.

He was waiting on the landing. 'Any more little problems?'

'No, I think you frightened the life out of it.'

'Come on, then – we should have been co-murdering three minutes ago.'

The room was at the far end of the landing, the door set in a little alcove. Lying on the bed reading *OK!*, Ellie sat up with a start. '*You* two? I was half expecting a poisoned dinner.'

'No such luck,' said Nick. 'So lie down and behave yourself while we call in your life insurance.'

'I thought you might,' she said, in resigned tones. 'But I never thought you'd be in on it,' she added, to me.

'Sorry, love, but Max and I were childhood sweethearts, and you'll only spend all your money on boob lifts and Botox.'

'Well, I must say it's most ungrateful behaviour,' she said crossly. 'After I gave him a Porsche and a gold Rolex, too.' Tossing *OK!* aside, she lay down. 'Get on with it, then. I'm getting really bored up here.' Having closed her eyes, she opened them again. 'I hope you're not going to suffocate me? I've got a thing about suffocation.'

'Relax,' Nick soothed. 'You won't feel a thing.' Holding up an imaginary hypodermic, he pretended to flick at it as if he did it every day, which I suppose he did. Having 'injected' half the dose, while Ellie stifled most un-deathly giggles, he 'passed' it to me and I completed the operation.

'Right,' Nick said briskly. 'Sit tight and be a good little corpse until someone finds you won't be needing that dinner, after all.'

She opened an eye. 'You'll get caught.'

'No chance,' said Nick. 'We're wearing surgical gloves.'

'They'll have your fingerprints on.'

'Not after I've shoved them in the Aga, they won't,' I said.

'What about the hypodermic?'

'Take a wild guess,' said Nick. 'See you later.'

He shut the door quietly. I was on my way when he caught my wrist, and drew me back into that little alcove. From there he took a quick look on to the landing. 'The coast's clear. Told you it'd be a breeze, didn't I? Another few weeks and we'll be tucked up in Miami.'

'Yeah,' I said, as we were due to fly off to Florida once all this was over. 'Sun, sea, and chilling.'

'Stuff chilling,' he said. 'I could start a nice little business with the old girl's cash. Nice white powder from Colombia. Illegals from Cuba. We'll make millions, princess. We'll be drowning in dollars.'

*Princess*? I hadn't expected him to take it this far. Still less had I expected him to pin me gently to the wall, gaze down into my eyes and brush a hairsprayed wisp from my cheek.

I was bursting to laugh. He could have been a bad soap actor, doing the 'about to snog her' bit. He did a surprisingly good line in fake, melt-you eyes that had a fair bit of green in them, close up. Sasha would have lapped it up.

As for me, I was getting another glimpse of that elusive déjà vu. 'You know what?' I said. 'You vaguely remind me of somebody.'

'I know, princess. That hunky sex god who haunts your dreams.'

I suppressed a volcanic giggle. His voice was pure, God's-gift sleaze. 'Sorry to disillusion you, but it's probably someone on the television.'

*Cut!* 'Not you, too,' he said. 'The last time anyone told me that, I was doing something unmentionable to her poodle.' He put on an anxious, old-biddy voice: '. . . oh, dear, he does so hate being interfered with – keep *still*, Binkie, for Mother – by the way, dear, you remind me a little bit of What's-his-name who used to be in What-d'you-call-it on the telly. The one who turned out to be a bit of a baddy and got blown up.'

It was such a wicked impression, I couldn't help

laughing. 'You are a baddy now, so it serves you right. What are you going to do with that pretend hypodermic concealed about your person?'

'Plant it in St John's socks – what d'you think?' He made another check down the landing. 'Off you go, while the coast's still clear. And don't forget our little date later, will you?' He went right back to Max, sleazy smirk and all. 'Leave the door open, princess, and I'll come and kiss you good-night.'

'I'll try not to fall asleep first. Who d'you think's going to catch us *in flagrante snoggio*?'

'Nobody, princess. Trust me.'

Scheming little floozy that she was, I almost felt sorry for Emerald. 'That'll be a great comfort when I'm in the dock because we blew it for the sake of a snog.'

As I turned to go he said, 'Oh, just one little word of advice . . .'

I turned around. 'Yes?'

'Watch how you sit down in those trousers. From behind they've got a look of the poor old NHS.'

'Sorry?'

'Dangerously overstretched,' he said, not quite deadpan enough. 'I should lay off the gooey puds tonight, if I were you.'

# Chapter 6

I gave him the best 'nice try' look I could manage. 'Oh, didn't you know? Bursting out of my trousers is already on the agenda. Part of the after-dinner cabaret, when I get up and dance on the table.' A passable response, except that I only thought of it five seconds later, halfway down the landing.

Still, I would heed the warning. I was visualizing this nightmare in cellulite when I collided with Alastair. 'I'm supposed to be hunting you down and issuing more dire threats but I forgot the time,' he said. 'Felicity was looking for you, by the way. In a tizz about the food, I think.'

I headed for the kitchen, where the maid was arranging starters on plates and Felicity was tizzing for England. 'It's all Ian's fault – he said I never put enough chilli in it, so I slung some more in and now I swear we'll need fire extinguishers. And did you hear Adam saying it was bloody obvious? I told you it was going to be a disaster, didn't I?'

'Everyone's having a great time,' I soothed. 'And of course it won't be obvious – Jim's just chucked in lots of red herrings.'

'*I* think it's all brilliant,' said the maid, dear girl that she was. 'What *is* this, by the way?'

'Smoked trout pâté,' said Felicity. 'Oh, Lord, it looks a bit grey and unappetizing – I knew I should have got something else. And that rice is taking ages to boil, everybody'll be starving.'

'Relax,' I soothed. 'There's no rush. And you were a brilliant Betsy.' I sidled up to the Aga, as if suddenly fascinated with household appliances. 'This is solid fuel, isn't it?'

'No, electric. Why?'

'Just wondered.' How was I supposed to incinerate imaginary evidence in it, then? Hadn't Village Players Jim checked these minor little details?

'Please, go back to the party,' she went on. 'Take these, will you?' She passed me a platter of party nibbles. 'And if anyone's saying trust Felicity to organize a really stupid murder, please don't tell me.'

'They won't be!'

They weren't exactly. As I offered nibbles, I heard Adam say *sotto voce* to Rob, 'There's a pool table, you know. Let's hope we're allowed a session once this circus is over.'

'I wouldn't bank on it,' I said. 'You might well be skewered to it, with a cue through your guts. Have a nibble,' I added sweetly.

Rob winked at me as he speared a spicy prawn on a cocktail stick.

Nick speared two. 'I hope neither of you is on call or anything,' I said. 'Bit awkward if you've just been murdered.'

'No, the local animals have strict instructions,' said Nick. 'They don't go sick when we're out swilling booze.'

'What he means *is*,' said Sasha, 'they have a rota with a couple of other practices for after hours. And don't tell anybody, but Nick's been known to pretend he's on call when he wants to get out of something.'

'Giving away my trade secrets,' he tutted. 'I'll sort you out later.'

'Promises, promises,' she giggled.

Honestly. Still, she was so open about it, you couldn't help liking her.

Soon afterwards I was in a quiet corner with Jane. 'I still can't believe what Paula's done to Rob,' she said. 'She's turned him into a bit of a catch.'

'I always did think he was a bit of a catch.'

'Oh, yes.' She gave a mischievous little smile. 'You used to have a little thing about him, didn't you?'

'Only very little.'

'I know.' Her eyes were back on Rob and Paula. 'She'll be good for his ego, what was left of it after Juliet walked out. Can you imagine Juliet hanging on to him like that? Never in a million years.'

I hadn't known Juliet that well, but the last time I'd seen her was at Adam and Ellie's wedding. Far from hanging on to Rob, she'd been flirting mildly with sundry morning suits. Nobody had read anything into it, though, least of all Rob, as this had been pretty standard behaviour for Juliet. 'Maybe Paula's finding us lot a bit of a strain. Meeting anybody's "lot" can be daunting.'

'I wouldn't call us lot particularly daunting, but I take your point. I think it's more than that, anyway. If you ask me she's colossally insecure.'

'*Insecure*? How the hell do you work that one out?'

'The way she's hanging on to him like a security blanket, for a start.'

This conversation was cut short by the door bursting open and a shriek. 'Somebody come quick! I can't wake her up!'

It was the maid, hamming it up through volcanic giggles. 'It's Miss Evadne! I took up her dinner, and I can't wake her up! I think she's – [gasp] – dead!'

Right behind her came Felicity. 'OK, everybody, end of

Act One. If anyone's starving enough to risk it, dinner's ready.'

Unlike the drawing-room, the dining-room was done in pure fake-feudal style. Baron of Beef style, I'd call it, half panelled in wood, with dusty deer heads on the walls and a fireplace big enough to roast any peasant who forgot to warm up Sir Peveril's codpiece. The table was reproduction Tudor, installed by the current owners to 'go' with the room, and there was no expensive china or glass, either. Since the place had only been used for holiday lets for the past couple of years, most of it looked like car-boot dynasty, but nobody cared.

I found myself sitting opposite Sasha. Nick was on her left, looking remarkably cool for someone who was going to be arrested for Evadnicide before he was much older. Much to Felicity's relief, speculation was buzzing around the table.

A couple of hours were supposed to have elapsed by then. In theory, the doctor had been called. She'd pronounced Evadne dead, probably of heart failure, but there'd have to be a post-mortem.

'And we're supposed to think the Old Bill are going to turn up, telling us it was murder,' Adam said, over starters. 'But maybe it's a bluff. Maybe it *was* natural causes. In which case slimy St John's going to do Max in, to stop him getting the money.'

'Will you listen to him?' said Ellie. 'An hour ago he hadn't a clue – now he's Inspector sodding Morse.'

'Why St John, anyway?' I bluffed. 'Charles is desperate for money, too. He's got the Mafia on his back. Maybe they'll murder Max together.'

'That wouldn't do them much good if she'd already changed her will,' Jane pointed out.

'Oh, come on,' said Nick. 'Those two wouldn't let a little thing like a will get in their way. They'd bribe some shrink to say she was of unsound mind and have it declared invalid.'

It went on like this for at least ten minutes. Nobody was acting any more. It had turned into a game of bluff or spot-the-bluff, according to status. The non-guilty were determined to suss it out now, in order to prove that a mere Village Players amateur couldn't possibly outwit them.

As Rob had brought a corkscrew, we were no longer having to force down champagne. Instead I was managing to swallow some sublime New Zealand white, sitting up very straight to lessen the pressure on my waistband.

'I must say, I think you're all horribly unfeeling,' pouted Ellie. 'Nobody's expressed the slightest regret at my tragic death.'

'Sorry,' said Nick. 'I'd have been only too pleased to weep and wail over your body, but dinner was calling.'

'As if we'd believe any weeping and wailing,' said Jane. 'You were probably planning to roger poor old Evadne to death on your honeymoon – I bet you had a supply of paper bags for the purpose.'

'Do you mind?' said Ellie. 'I was in remarkably good nick for a woman of my age. Anyway, I always used to make him do it with the lights off. I had a very repressed upbringing, you know. The nuns at my convent even told us never to wear patent shoes in case they reflected our knickers and inflamed men's vile lusts.'

Ian grinned. 'Do they really? Have I been missing something all these years?'

'I don't see how a convent education would make her repressed,' said Paula. 'All the ex-convent girls I ever knew had A levels in inflaming lusts. Particularly a so-called friend of mine who ran off with my husband three weeks after the wedding.'

Her voice fell on sudden, crashing silence. In fact, it was a conversation stopper *par excellence,* as she realized too late. Seeing her flush slightly, evidently wishing she could evaporate, I felt sorry for her.

Typically, it was Felicity who spoke first, with genuine sympathy. 'You poor thing. How *aw*ful.'

Paula gave an awkward little shrug. 'I was only twenty-two. It was probably doomed anyway.'

Rob said nothing, but I saw him reach for her hand under the table. In return she shot him a quick look of gratitude that made me think Jane was probably right. Under that glacially groomed perfection there lurked just another poor mortal who said stupid, inappropriate things and felt an idiot. Who needed a rock to reassure her that it didn't matter, he was there.

'Anyway, let's assume it *wasn't* natural causes,' said Rob. 'In which case, who did it? Who slipped out of the room? Come to that, where was Max after he massaged the old girl off to sleep?'

Max lied beautifully. 'In my room, catching the football highlights. Why would I want to murder her, anyway? She'd have given me anything I wanted. Walking cash machine, she was.'

'You're still a suspect,' said Ian. 'Who else was gone for long enough?'

'St John,' said Jane. 'And Emerald.'

Adam shot me a suspicious look. 'Yes, Emerald. Where were you?'

'Havin' – ay – slash,' I said, with dignity. 'Not that it's any of your business. Why would I want to do the old cow in, anyway? What would I get out of it?'

A gleam came back to Jane's eye. 'Nothing, but Max

would, wouldn't he? And you and he just happen to be already acquainted.'

*Oh, Lord.* 'That was years ago!' I scoffed. 'I ain't hardly seen the tosser since.'

This brought Max back, albeit with a fleeting grin first. 'Who are you calling a tosser?'

'You,' I retorted. 'You always did go for old birds. Even when you was fifteen you was shagging the netball teacher at Tesco Road.'

This made Sasha resume her sniffy Annabel. 'Would you kindly watch your language? There is a bishop present.'

Everybody laughed, except Max. 'She can't help it. Just look at her.' He shot me a look of conspiratorial relish, but his voice was pure contempt. 'Always was common as muck.'

As bluff it was very effective, but I had a feeling even Emerald might have been wounded here. Even Ricky wasn't sticking up for me, and he was supposed to have brought me to this do. 'Are you going to let them talk to me like that?' I demanded. 'I'm supposed to be your guest!'

'Sorry, Emerald,' said Ian apologetically, 'but Ricky only brought you to wind his snotty family up, and I'm afraid he's deriving malicious pleasure out of it.'

I put on a plaintive tone. 'Nobody loves poor Emerald. I'm going down the garden to eat worms.'

'Then for heaven's sake put your wellies on first,' said Felicity. 'You'll ruin those shoes.'

Rob shot me a wink. 'Jesus loves you, my child.'

'Bugger off.' Draining my glass, I held it out for a refill, and that was when the maid came in, trying not to giggle, as always.

'A policeman's just come, madam. Shall I show him through?'

Lurking in the doorway was an Inspector Frost look-alike, complete with scruffy raincoat. Wearing a moustache and a barely suppressed grin, he just had to be Village Players Jim.

Stepping into the room, he said in ponderous tones, 'Chief Inspector Slammer. I'm sorry to have to inform you that the post-mortem has revealed suspicious circumstances. To put it another way, I am now conducting a murder inquiry. I shall have to ask you all not to leave this house for at least another twenty-four hours.'

This was enough to get Jane right back into Ivanetta. 'Out of ze question,' she said. 'I have hair appointment tomorrow.'

He fixed her with a perfect, unfazed policeman's gaze. 'I'm afraid, madam, that your hair will have to wait.'

'*Wait*? Appointment wiz Nicky Clarke and you tell me wait?' She turned to her fiancé. 'St John, fix him. In my country policemens know their place. They take bribe and drink wodka. My fiancé is very important man,' she added contemptuously to Chief Inspector Slammer. 'Only last week he sack junior minister who refuse to lie to newspapers. You want to end up in salt-mines?'

'Ignore her, my good fellow,' said St John hastily, while everybody else cracked up. 'She's from Wurzo-Slavinia, you know.'


Ten minutes later the chilli was finally on the table, speculation was buzzing, and Felicity wore that look of profound relief only seen on hostesses when they've finally realized the party is going fine.

Jane said, 'What about Betsy? This doll business can't be just a red herring. If she did have a baby, who's the father?'

'Oh my God, I'm forgetting my act,' said Felicity. Putting her ladle down, she resumed her vacant Betsy expression. 'Where's my baby? I want my baby!'

'Well, you can't have it,' said Annabel, with beautiful contempt. 'It's quite ridiculous, a grown woman carrying a doll around, even if she is retarded.'

'Oh, leave her alone,' said Max. 'Let the poor cow have her doll. Where have you put it, anyway?'

'In the Aga,' said Annabel. 'So tough.'

I neglected to say it was electric.

'You what?' He was really getting worked up. 'What d'you want to do that for? What did she ever do to you, poor cow?'

I was touched. If I was going to be tried for murder, at least my co-defendant was a nice bloke at heart.

Annabel was not touched in the least. 'Max, you're being ridiculously sentimental. Why Evadne didn't leave her in that institution I'll never know. If you've got any sense you'll send her straight back.'

'She wasn't always like this,' said bishop Rob, in sorrowful tones. 'The poor creature was never quite Oxbridge material, but she wasn't a sandwich short of a picnic, either. She was driven out of her mind by cruelty.'

St John glared at him. 'Shut up, you pious oaf.'

This was it, then, I thought, trying to remember my notes. Skeletons were about to emerge from murky closets.

Jane was hot on the trail now. 'OK, she obviously did have a baby, so who *was* the father?'

Annabel shrugged. 'Probably some ghastly unwashed yokel. It was adopted. She made the most colossal fuss when they told her she couldn't possibly keep it, so they had her sedated and told her it was dead.'

'They threw her away,' said Betsy pathetically. 'They threw my baby away.' She began to cry in a positively piteous fashion.

So did bishop Rob. He actually did it rather well, putting his hands to his face, his shoulders shaking with pent-up emotion. 'I can't bear it any longer,' he sobbed. 'I have carried the guilt too long. I have prayed to the Lord to forgive me, but it's a stain of sin on my heart.'

'My God, it wasn't *you*?' said Jane. 'Was he the father?' She looked at Paula, the unlikely Lavender Freud. 'Come on – you were his therapist – surely he must have told you?'

'I couldn't possibly divulge any such thing,' said Paula apologetically. 'Haven't you ever heard of patient confidentiality?'

This was where my notes told Emerald to chip in. 'Some therapist she was,' I said. 'It was me he told, poor sod. It took him three visits to tell me his little Miss Moneypenny fantasy, but he still couldn't do it, could he? All he ever did was talk.'

Rob was still pretending to sob as if he'd never stop, Lavender trying to soothe him.

Ivanetta put a cigarette in a holder. 'My God, you Eenglish,' she said contemptuously. 'Iz pathetic. In my country ze priests get dronk and have sex wiz ozzer people's wives.'

St John tried to glare at her, but it was rather spoilt by laughter. Then, as I was about to go on, he shot me a look that was supposed to be murderous. 'Emerald, be very careful what you say.'

'Don't you threaten me, you filthy git.' I looked round at the assembled guests. 'It was him. Pretended he loved the poor cow, and she believed him. His own stepsister. But they couldn't have the scandal, could they? Not in a posh family like that. So they had her put away before she blabbed. Him and the bishop – he was only twenty-two and scared stiff of St John. They shut her up with a load of nutters and got some shrink to say she was suffering from delusions.'

Everybody went quiet. The atmosphere was suddenly filled with an expectant hush, like a theatre as the curtain goes up.

St John gave a short laugh. 'You're not going to believe *that*? I'm a government minister, for God's sake. I've spent weekends at Chequers. Look at her – who's going to believe a cheap little tart like that?'

'What about your brother?' said Jane, looking at the still-pretending-to-sob Rob. 'They'll believe a bishop.'

'Believe *him*?' St John gave a lovely little snort. 'He's pathetic. Always was inadequate – couldn't even play a decent game of cricket. Besides, he's been seeing quack therapists for years – they've probably planted him with False Memory Syndrome. Just look at him – he's cracking up already.'

Rob looked up at last. 'St John, I beg you to confess,' he said, in anguished tones. 'For the sake of your immortal soul.'

'Immortal bullshit,' snorted St John. 'I'm untouchable. Anyway, you've got no proof.'

Cue me again. 'Oh, no?' I said. 'What about that poor little baby you couldn't give a stuff about?'

I paused a moment, just for effect. 'It's me, Daddy. That cheap little tart you paid two hundred quid for a special. Didn't have a clue who you were, did I? Not then.' I paused again. 'And that's in my memoirs, too. The Sunday papers are going to love it.'

For the rest of the meal speculation hurtled around the table like balls on a squash court. Rob said St John was now going to do Emerald in, to shut her up. Don't talk rubbish, I said, her memoirs would come out anyway. A murdered author was a marketing hook to die for. Jane said Emerald might do St John in, out of pure hatred for a man who'd paid his own daughter for sex. Nick said it wouldn't surprise him if Betsy suddenly showed psychopathic tendencies. She might well take a carving knife to Annabel for putting her baby in the Aga.

All this was accompanied by tropical fruit meringue and Muscat. Although I'd never fancied dessert wine I had some anyway and found out what I'd been missing. Nectar, tasting of fat, sweet raisins. It was the perfect anaesthetic for the increasing agony of my trousers cutting into a full stomach.

Everyone else was perfectly relaxed. By now even Paula was smiling and laughing properly, especially at Rob's jokes. I watched Sasha, doing her mischievous-flirt bit with Nick, and wondered whether the RAF boyfriend had a clue what was going on here. Still, given the nature of the beast, maybe he was doing exactly the same up in the frozen North. Maybe even worse, in which case good on her.

'. . . and I've got a good mind to come and wax your chest hair anyway, when you're asleep,' she was saying, with a mischievous little pout. 'Serve you right for pretending you couldn't act your way out of a paper bag.'

'I didn't pretend anything,' Nick said, in the half-teasing tone a man only uses when a woman's looking at him like that. 'You made an assumption based on one fact: namely, that I played second ass when I was four.'

'Now I come to think of it, he used to do some good take-offs,' said Rob. 'Used to do a hilarious Postman Pat in the style of Laurence Olivier doing Othello.'

'He deceived me.' Already Sasha was looking as if she might have a terrible head tomorrow, or even be yacking up tonight. Flushed and giggly, she put her chin on her hand, looking Nick right in the eye in a pure come-and-get-me fashion. 'You deceived me on purpose, you deceivious bugger. It'll serve you right if you do get murdered tonight. Maybe it'll even be me doing the murdering, because you spurned me for that old bag. Hell hath no fury like a woman – hic – spurned for an old bag, you know. Have you got an Oedipus complex or something?'

'No, a rich-old-bag complex. She gave me a Porsche.'

She giggled. 'Annabel might give you a Ferrari.'

'Annabel would just give me trouble.'

At this point he shot me another conspiratorial little wink, but this time Jane caught it. 'Aha! I knew you two were in cahoots! Max just winked at Emerald,' she added to everybody else.

'I wink at all the girls, Jane,' he said. 'Force of habit, when you're Max. You like to spread a little sunshine, give them all a little spark of hope.'

'Nice try.' Raising her glass, she looked at me with a wicked little gleam. 'I'm on to you two. I think you're up to no good.'

I could have thumped Nick. Still, too late now.

By ten thirty I was watching the clock. My assignation with Max was coming up, and others were glancing at their watches, as if we all had prearranged timings to think of. I slipped off fifteen minutes early, as the trouser situation was getting desperate and I wanted to check my phone in case Mum was really panicking.

The only message was from my sister Alice. '*Mum's been trying to get you. I told her you've probably gone away for the weekend and forgotten your mobile, but please give her a call. She was basically ringing to tell you Marisa's having a baby in February. Pigs will fly next. Still, I suppose babies have turned into some sort of designer accessory – I expect she'll call the poor little thing Cosmo or something. Don't forget to give Mum a ring, will you?*'

Well, that gave me something to think about as I peeled those trousers off. Nick had certainly scared the pants off that zip; it barely argued at all.

Marisa, having a baby! She who used to nip off to film festivals and Grands Prix in boyfriends' Learjets! Don't get me wrong, I was very fond of Marisa, who was my cousin. When I was about four I'd adored her, because she'd let me play with her vast collection of Barbies. At fourteen I'd adored her even more, because she'd let me experiment with her even vaster collection of make-up and even done my maths homework on one memorable occasion. (*'Have you had help with this? See me.'*) However, I just couldn't see her in Baby Gap. Mind you, I'd never imagined her getting married, either, yet there she was, eighteen months ago, saying 'I do' to the last man anyone would have thought of.

Still, good luck to her. What was wrong with Cosmo, anyway? Alice could be so niggly.

I stripped my bra off, too, and replaced it with the common-or-garden one.

Oh, bliss. I lay on the bed in my pyjamas. The top was navy fleece, with a big Winnie-the-Pooh. The bottoms had little Tiggers all over them. I glanced at my watch. Ten minutes to go, always assuming I was still awake. Maybe that Muscat had been a mistake . . .

I didn't even hear him come in. The thing that roused me was Henry's tail, wagging against my thigh. I opened my eyes with a start to see him sitting on the edge of the bed.

'God, I'm sorry, I must have nodded off . . .' I heaved myself to a sitting position.

He shook his head. 'Some act this is. You're supposed to be slavering in anticipation of our clandestine clinch.'

'I was just taking a little break. And I'm sorry, but I really do draw the line at slavering.'

He nodded at my pyjamas. 'Not quite Emerald, but I like the Tiggers.'

'I had to get out of those trousers,' I confessed. 'They were killing me.'

'I'm surprised you didn't get out of them before. They were above and beyond the call of duty.'

'Well, if I do a thing, I like to do it properly.' I inspected my left set of scarlet-dagger fingertips. 'These were a bit too much of a good thing, though.'

'Pretty gruesome,' he agreed.

'You said it. I wish I could take them off, but I haven't got the right stuff.'

'Can't help you there, I'm afraid. Sticky zips, OK.'

'Yes, I'll know where to come next time I have a little plumbing emergency. Mind you, Devon's probably a bit far away if I'm desperate in Richmond.'

'Just a bit.' He smiled, and two things hit me. Or rather, sort of trickled into me. One, even if he was vaguely nockshus now and then, I wouldn't necessarily hold it against him. When he smiled properly he didn't even look like a 'Join the Army' poster any more.

Two, any minute now we were supposed to be entwined in a pretend, steamy clinch. Obviously it *would* be pretend; I would not be required to perform any messy tongue stuff with a man I hardly knew.

And just as well. I hadn't brushed my teeth for hours. 'Why did you wink at me like that, you dope? We were going really well till then. I was hoping to pull off a stunning denouement and have everyone say I should get an Oscar.'

'There won't be any denouement at this rate.' He glanced at his watch. 'Come on – time to get our act together.'

'Oh, dear.' I sat up properly, tucking my legs sideways

on the bedspread. 'We're about to be caught. Exposed for the scheming co-villains we are.'

'Didn't you hear me before? Max has no intention of getting caught.'

'Of course he hasn't. Max is the cocky little sod to end them all, so he's probably done something really stupid, like leaving a fingerprint on that hypodermic he's planted in St John's socks.'

'No, but he's nicked something. From the old girl's jewellery safe.'

'Might have known. If it's diamonds, I hope they're for Emerald.'

He patted his trouser pocket. 'Of course.' He went right back to Max, with a cocky little smirk to match. 'Close your eyes, princess. I've got a little surprise for you.'

I only half closed them. I saw him take a string of what looked like pink plastic beads from his pocket. 'Not exactly Tiffany,' I said. 'More like Christmas cracker.'

'Use your imagination, can't you? And stop cheating. Close your eyes.'

'Yes, *sir*.' So much for Florida. About to be caught mid-snog, with Evadne's diamonds round my neck, I could feel the handcuffs already.

He put on his best Max voice yet. 'You'll really look like a princess in these, babes.'

I had a job not to laugh. 'Get on with it, you smarmy little toad.'

'Come on, Izzy,' he tutted. 'I'm doing my best here. Think Emerald, with twenty thousand quids' worth of sparklers coming up.'

So I thought Emerald. Actually, it wasn't that difficult. With my eyes closed it somehow increased the anticipation as he laid the beads lightly against my neck.

'Get your hair out of the way, will you? Please, babes,'

he added, in a voice like Max trying to be seductive. 'Lift that mass of golden gorgeousness off your pretty little neck.'

Really wanting to laugh now, I held it up with my left hand. He was so close, his cheek just brushed my ear. Funnily enough, it was quite nice. On balance, perhaps I could handle a five-second clinch after all. On the sensitive side of my neck, the touch of his fingertips was rather nice, too.

So naturally, there just had to be a catch.

'Sorry, babes,' he said. 'I'm really gutted to have to do this, but you've got to go.'

# Chapter 7

I don't know when I've ever opened my eyes so fast. 'You bastard!' I pushed him away, hard. 'You were going to strangle me!'

'Actually, the deed is done.' Already he was pocketing the beads. 'Quick and painless, I hope.'

Almost as shocked as if his fingers had actually started to close around it, I touched my throat. Talk about a sitting duck – how could I have been so stupid? 'Why?'

'I'm off to Miami with Annabel. You'd have been so wild with jealousy, you'd have grassed me up about the other little business.'

'You're swanning off to Miami with that toffee-nosed cow?'

'Sorry, babes, but I always did like a bird with class.'

Adding insult to strangulation now. 'You're a slimy, lying little reptile,' I retorted. 'I shall laugh from beyond the grave when you're in Wormwood Scrubs. I hope you get beaten up and have extremely unpleasant things done to you by very large inmates who aren't too fussy about gender.'

His mouth flickered. 'I honestly thought you'd have worked it out. If you trusted a slimeball like that—'

But Henry's ears were pricking up. He was looking at the door.

'Shit.' Nick glanced at his watch. 'I should have been out

of here by now.' Whipping his shoes off, he padded silently to the side of the door, where he'd be concealed when it opened.

We heard footsteps on the landing, a tap at the door. 'Emerald?'

It was Alastair, or rather, St John. As I was dead I could hardly utter a cheery 'Come in' so I just closed my eyes and waited.

By the time I opened my eyes, my dastardly killer had slipped out and my unloving father was standing over me. 'I like your 'jamas,' he grinned.

'Hi, Daddy. I hope you haven't come to murder me.'

'God, no. Just to appeal to your better nature, beg you to forgive me and so on. Failing that, to ask how you'd like being beaten to death by a few heavies with baseball bats.'

'Too late, I'm afraid. I've been strangled.'

'You're kidding! Who did it?'

'Alastair, I'm dead. Including my vocal cords, I'm afraid.'

'Shit, they're going to pin this on me, aren't they? Sorry, but I'd better leg it.'

Unmourned even by my own father, I was left to wonder at my own stupidity. '*These details may be deliberately misleading . . .*'

*You don't say.* To think how I'd even lifted up my own hair, like a lamb to the whatsit. 'Some best friend you are,' I said to Henry, flaked out beside me. 'Couldn't you have smelt his evil designs?'

For a couple of minutes I gazed up at the ceiling, wondering how long I'd have to lie there, my body going cold. It wouldn't take long; the room was none too warm. Still, at least there'd be a denouement for Village Players Jim to be proud of. Nobody had worked it out, I was sure.

Felicity would be delighted, so on balance I didn't mind being both dead and as gullible as they come. All that 'princess' stuff, never mind that pre-snog bit just after we'd murdered Ellie; he really was the most devious beast. Still, I'd have a good laugh when they clapped him in handcuffs and led him off to 'durance vile'. Pity we didn't have rat-infested dungeons any more, but there you go.

But Henry's ears pricked up again and I heard footsteps. In half a second I turned myself into a proper violent death: eyes wide open in a scary-corpse fashion.

The door creaked open. 'Christ,' said a voice. 'Can I give you the kiss of life?'

I swear I thought I was hearing things. I sat up so fast I felt dizzy, but there he was, in familiar navy cords and black polo-neck, armed with a bunch of flowers. 'Leo! What on earth . . . ?'

'Hi,' he grinned. 'Better late than never.'

Then he was kissing me, and I stopped thinking he was an illusion. 'Don't tell me you ducked out of the soggy spinach quiche?'

'No, I did my dutiful bit. Hello, hound,' he added to Henry, who had to be included in any cuddly reunion. 'It was officially a lunch thing because of all the kids. In our family they usually drag on for ever, but by six most of even the hardened old bores had gone and I thought, fuck it, I might just be in time to mop up the bloodstains. And . . .' Brushing my hair aside, he murmured into my ear, 'I had to come and make sure your mini-Rob-thing wasn't getting any bigger.'

I knew he didn't really mean it, but a little pink glow washed over me anyway. 'Consumed with jealousy, were you?' I teased.

'Agonized.' With a teasing little smile back, he kissed me again.

'Why didn't you phone?'

'I was going to, on the way, but I'd left my mobile on and the bloody thing was dead.'

'I can't believe you remembered where to come.' He'd surely only had the briefest look at the invitation.

'It was the name that stuck in my head. Even so, I had to stop at a pub and ask if anyone knew a house called Colditz. I was half expecting them to call the funny farm.' He nodded at the flowers, dumped on the bed. 'Peace offering for Felicity. I hope she won't set the dogs on me.'

'Shep'll set himself on you, and probably lick you to death.' I saw his point, though. A lot of hostesses would be seriously put out if someone who'd dropped out at the last minute then turned up unexpectedly. 'And if I know Felicity, she'll be killing the fatted leftovers. I take it the maid let you in?'

'If that's the giggly girl who opened the door. She said to go on up, you'd all retired to your Act Three beds.'

'I think it's nearly time for the final curtain. I was the second victim.'

'Poor little Vera.' He took my hand and kissed it. 'I had a premonition that you needed me.'

'I needed you a few hours ago,' I said, with feeling. 'Can you believe the zip on those leather trousers—'

The door opened again. It was Nick, and the sight of Leo stopped him in his tracks. After his foul treachery I rather enjoyed it.

As for Leo, he sat up with a start.

'Leo, meet my killer,' I said. 'Nick, this is Leo.'

For a second Nick took him in. 'Not-coming Leo, I take it?' His tone was pleasant enough, but you didn't have to be very bright to detect the subtext. It was '*Now* he turns up?', more or less.

Leo didn't rise easily, but I could tell he was very slightly rattled. 'Made-it-after-all Leo,' he said, and you didn't have to be very bright to detect his subtext, either. This time it was 'Do you have a problem with that?', more or less.

'Last-minute window,' I explained.

That seemed to dilute incipient atmospheres. Nick said, 'Oh, right. Sorry I've landed you with a corpse.' Stepping forward, he extended a hand. 'Hi. Nick Trent.'

Leo took it like a good, well-behaved boy. 'How did you murder her, just out of interest?'

'Strangulation,' I said. 'After a most cruel and devious deception, I might add.' I turned to Nick. 'I hope you know you're making a classic error here? Coming back to gloat at the scene of the crime is what gets scum like you convicted.'

'Izzy, give me credit for a little intelligence. I've come to apologize for wounding your feelings over dinner.'

'Are there no depths to which you won't sink?' I turned to Leo. 'He called me common as muck – I was bitterly hurt when we were supposed to be lovers. And now I suppose you're going to "discover" my body and go into agonies of fake grief,' I added to Nick.

'Spot on. If you'll excuse us,' he said to Leo, 'we have a little role-play to finish here.'

I shot Leo an apologetic look. 'Sorry, but you came at a rather crucial point.'

'Carry on, then. I'll sit in the front row.' Folding his arms, Leo tried to look like an amused spectator. It didn't quite come off. He looked more like a man who'd driven for hours for a lovey-dovey reunion, had found he was temporarily surplus to requirements, and wasn't quite a happy little bunny.

Still, it couldn't be helped. 'OK, you treacherous piece of slime,' I said to Nick. 'Get on with it.'

117

'You make a lovely little corpse.' He patted my cheek. 'Ups-a-daisy, then . . .'

I wasn't prepared for this. I certainly hadn't expected him to scoop my lifeless body into his arms with a 'Hmm, not quite such a dead weight as I thought'.

'What are you doing?' I demanded. 'You're disturbing the scene of the crime!'

'I'm too overcome with fake shock to think straight. Keep quiet and pretend I'm Tarzan. Leo, could you open the door?'

Only then did I think of the others. 'Oh, Lord, Leo, you'd better stay here for now. If I have to start introducing you it'll rather destroy the dramatic tension.'

'God forbid,' he said. 'I can see it's *King Lear* meets *Shallow Grave* – let me know when it's safe to come out.'

He said it lightly enough, but as we exited I saw his face.

God help me, a spark of jealousy had actually hit him at last. He didn't care for this. He didn't like seeing me in the arms of a man who'd rattled him, who'd told me to pretend he was Tarzan. Simultaneously, something else dawned. Nick had made the Tarzan crack for precisely this reason. He'd thought Leo had a bloody nerve to turn up like this. He'd thought a little wind-up was in order.

Not that I was complaining. After all this time, the thought of Leo being even remotely jealous gave me a little pink glow. It added an edge to the sensation of being swept off like a seven-stone sylph. Having rather missed out on such politically incorrect girlie pleasures, I might as well make the most of it.

On the landing Max stopped and uttered an anguished cry. 'Help me, somebody! Call an ambulance!'

'What the hell for?' I muttered.

'Just to make it look good. And it may have escaped

your notice, but death invariably results in total loss of speech.'

'Smart-arse.' That sheeny silk might look gross, but with a hefty shoulder underneath it felt quite nice against my cheek. 'It's a great pity this country's abolished the death penalty. It really grieves me to think of the taxpayer shelling out for your keep. And this is a really poofy shirt, you know. Are you sure Max isn't a closet gay?'

'Keep quiet or I'll drop you on purpose. Help!' he yelled again, louder this time.

There wasn't much dramatic tension in the next couple of minutes. There was a cacophony of talk and extremely callous laughter.

'You OK there, Izzy?' grinned Rob. 'Sorry I wasn't there to administer the last rites.'

'Why did she change out of her tarty things?' asked Paula.

'Her trousers were killing her,' said Nick, and everybody laughed.

'I hate to tell you, Izzy, but I think one of your false eyelashes is coming off,' said Jane.

'At least it didn't fall in my dinner.' As there wasn't much dramatic tension left, I thought there was no harm in Leo making an entrance now. 'If you could all just shut up a minute, I've got a little surprise for you.'

If anybody but Nick thought Leo had a nerve, they covered it. Felicity was only delighted that he could make it after all, touched by the flowers and full of solicitude. Poor Leo, he must be ex*haus*ted, had he eaten, she could put some chilli in the microwave in two ticks. Ian was much the same, great to see you, mate, no, for God's sake don't apologize, come down and have a beer.

And whatever his state of mind only minutes previously, Leo displayed none of it. Instead, he was full of exactly the right degree of apologetic charm, sorry to be a pain, yes, he'd love some chilli, but please don't let him interrupt the murder . . .

It warmed me to see how they took to him. It warmed me to see how he came across: nothing to make even the often critical Ellie say, 'Yes, he's OK, but . . .' Above all, it warmed me to think of Leo driving all that way – and being just a little bit jealous at the end of it.

The final curtain took place in the drawing-room, where I was instructed to lie on that slippery *chaise longue* and look deceased again for two minutes.

'Poor Betsy,' said Felicity. 'Her baby's really dead now, and she didn't even utter a fond farewell.'

'What about poor me?' I demanded. 'Why isn't some-body calling the police?'

Inspector Slammer came in a moment later, still with that deceptively thick look TV detectives often go in for. 'Hello hello hello – what have we here?'

'Another body,' said Annabel, in her best cut-glass tones. 'It really is most inconvenient. Such a low class of corpse.'

'Thank you, madam, that will do. I must ask you all not to leave this room. My lads are already searching the premises.'

'You don't have to search to find who did this one,' grinned Ricky. 'I heard my brother threaten her earlier.' He nodded at St John. 'She was going to expose him.'

'Now look here!' blustered St John.

Chief Inspector Slammer gave him a look of mild inquiry. 'Expose you for what, sir?'

'Nothing! It's quite preposterous. My brother's always had it in for me, officer. Jealous of my first-class brain, poor lad.'

Leo wasn't pretending to be amused any more. Nursing a can of Bud, he was quietly cracking up.

This was when Max spoke up. Like someone coming out of shock he said, 'I saw him.'

'Saw who, sir?'

'Him.' He nodded at St John. 'Going into her room. I was going to see her, to say sorry for slagging her off earlier, but I went away, see? Thought I'd leave it ten minutes.'

Racked with fake grief, the callous devil put his hands to his face. 'I only wanted to make up – we were mates all those years ago – but it was too late . . .'

It was intensely frustrating, having to maintain dead silence through a sickening display like this.

St John had really got the wind up now. 'He's lying! It's utterly preposterous. He was my aunt's gigolo, for God's sake.'

However, someone in a fake policeman's helmet had just come in, presumably one of the village players. 'We found this, sir,' he told Slammer. 'Concealed among socks in the room of Mr St John Plonker-fforbes.' He held up a plastic bag containing a real empty phial and a hypodermic.

Alastair did a fair job of looking horrified, which he probably was. Until then he'd probably thought he was a mere red herring. 'I've never seen those before in my life!'

'Really, sir?' said Slammer. 'Why don't you tell me about it down the station? You're nicked.'

Ten minutes later, with evidence against him and motives for both murders, St John was banged up and exceedingly put out about it. Especially when Village Players Jim revealed who the real guilty parties were.

'Are you telling me that bloody gigolo got away with it?'

he demanded. 'While I got double life? Whatever happened to good old British justice?'

'Ah. I was coming to that,' said Jim. 'Max took off for Miami with Annabel, of course, and enjoyed a successful criminal career for ten years. However, as one can in America when popping to the shops, one day he encountered an angelic-looking blonde who asked if he would let love into his life. He didn't realize she meant the love of Jesus, but within a week he was born again and desperate to cleanse his soul. I am happy to inform you that he is now locked up awaiting trial, and you are about to be released after an appeal.'

'But I served ten years!' said Alastair.

'Serves you right, too,' I said. 'And if you don't shed tears in the dock over my callous murder,' I added to Nick, 'I shall be extremely upset.'

He patted my fleece-clad shoulder. 'It's been haunting me ever since, but I know we'll meet in heaven. I expect you'll beat the shit out of me, but I shall smile kindly and forgive you.'

I appealed to Inspector Slammer. 'What sort of useless policeman are you? He stole Evadne's diamonds – why haven't you nicked him for that?'

'Because I put them back,' said Nick. 'They'd served their purpose – a little treat for your last seconds on this earth. Not to mention the perfect way to get my hands round your unsuspecting little neck.'

It was too much. 'I really don't know what Emerald ever saw in him,' I said to Leo. 'It'll serve him right if she comes back and haunts him.'

After photo shoots were over, I found myself alone with Leo in the kitchen.

He ripped the ring-pull off a second beer. 'So who's the one who said Henry looked like a sheep?'

I was shoving a few glasses in the dishwasher. 'Nick.'

'Oh, right. I should have guessed.'

It was lovely to hear his faintly sardonic tone. It told me that spark of jealousy hadn't been wishful thinking. 'Don't you like him?' I asked, all innocent.

He shrugged. 'He's all right.'

*Bingo.* 'He's actually rather nice,' I said, as casually as you like. 'Anyway, I've forgiven him the insult. I was in dire straits earlier, and he charged to the rescue.'

'What dire straits?'

I told him about the trousers.

Leo pretended to be amused, but I could tell I'd stirred up his antipathy very nicely. 'Are you telling me he ripped your trousers off?'

'Not *ripped*, Leo. He just applied some hefty muscle to a desperate situation.' His expression barely changed, but I thought I'd gone far enough. Any more and he'd realize what I was up to. While casually wiping the worktop I changed the subject. 'Weren't the kids expecting to see you tomorrow?'

Leo took a suck from his can. 'No, they've got riding lessons first thing, and then Jo and Desperate Dan are taking them out for the day. Some Christmas show, McDonald's, you name it.'

Funny how one little piece of information can deflate you. 'Lucky kids. Do you fancy a game of pool?'

By then everybody had adjourned to the games-room, which Felicity said had once been an unused morning-room smelling of dead aspidistras. With holiday lets and wet summers in mind, the current owner had installed not only a pool table, but table football, table tennis and a dartboard. In case these weren't enough, in the corner was a tongue-and-groove pine bar that looked as if it had come in a cut-price flat pack. Felicity said Grandpa would have had a blue fit.

I think she'd been hoping for some raucous charades, or that game where you hold a ten-pence piece between your clenched buttocks, walk with it across the room and drop it into a saucepan, or pay a forfeit. Such games of skill were customary in the more drunken stages of Felicity's dos but it was a forlorn hope this time. Raucous games of darts were played instead, cheats' table tennis, and table football that turned into a Girls v. Boys World Cup. Jane and I thrashed Ian and Rob in the final and were told we had shattered their egos for ever, but if we went and fetched a few more beers they'd find it in their hearts to forgive us.

Magnanimous in victory, we went to raid the fridge in the kitchen. 'I still can't get over Leo showing up,' said Jane. 'How sweet of him to drive all that way. Unless he was just escaping the wee-smelling wrinklies, of course.'

It was a joke, but suddenly I wasn't laughing. I told her what he'd said about the kids. 'If they weren't out all day tomorrow, I bet he wouldn't have come. It was a case of, well, if I can't see the little loves of my life, there's always Izzy.'

'Oh, come on.'

OK, I know it sounds horrible, but from being over the moon that he'd made the effort, I sagged in the middle. I was a sort of lesser option to the kids, but better than a cosy family evening with his mum saying, 'Goodness me, I thought old Bert was looking pretty good for ninety-two.'

'You always said that was one of the things you liked about him, that he dotes on his kids.'

'It is. Only I just wish I could be number one now and then.'

We took half a dozen beers out of the fridge. 'How old was he when they got married?' said Jane.

'Twenty-two. They'd been together since they were seventeen.'

She made a face. 'Just imagine. No wonder it died of boredom.'

That had been one reason for the split; realizing they'd both missed out on being young was the other. He'd had an affair and she'd found out, but far from going mad she'd told him she'd had one, too. Eventually they'd agreed that they'd be better apart, but would stay friends for the kids' sake.

'But I suppose it's nice that they get on,' Jane added.

*Was it*? 'I know it sounds awful, but now and then I wish he'd slag her off, call her a neurotic bitch, like they're supposed to. He doesn't like this bloke Joanne's going away for Christmas with, either. Calls him Desperate Dan, or the Humanoid. From the sounds of it Joanne's pretty keen – sometimes I think Leo's just a bit jealous and won't admit it.'

'If the kids like him, he's bound to be. He might be looking at a potential stepfather.'

And Leo would hate that. Another, permanent father figure in his kids' lives. He'd probably move back, to be near them. He'd only moved away in the first place because he'd been offered a much better-paid job and he didn't want the kids to suffer because he was forking out for two establishments.

Back in the games room I found Leo playing Nick at pool. It was all very chilled on the surface, but I'd seen Leo play before and something in the way he handled the cue told me this was different. It was the old male thing: a duel of honour. This silk-shirted Tarzan who'd muscled my trousers off had to be put in his place.

The little glow this should have given me was tarnished by Nick. Now and then a flicker in his eyes or at the corner of his mouth said he knew exactly what Leo was up to and was amused by it, in a detached, cynical sort of way. When Leo finally beat him Nick seemed not in the least put out. In fact, as our eyes met briefly he might have been saying, 'There you go. He'll be happy now.'

It was intensely irritating, but I was irritated with Leo, too, for starting duels at all. Then again I was irritated with Nick, for starting the whole stupid thing by rattling Leo in the first place.

By three o'clock Sasha was so seriously pissed she was turning into a danger at the dartboard, and Nick said he was going to put her to bed before she passed out. Shortly after that Leo said he was knackered, he was going too, was I coming?

'You go – I'll be up in ten minutes.' The only thing detaining me was sudden acute dehydration brought on by Felicity saying she could murder a cup of tea. She, Jane and I repaired to the kitchen, where we also devoured an entire packet of Jaffa Cakes and indulged in forty minutes of the kind of girlie natter we'd enjoyed in the old days.

By the time Henry and I finally went upstairs, Leo was out for the count.

It took me ages to get to sleep. Things were zooming round my head like demented bluebottles. Even after I drifted off they were still at it. I dreamt that I was back in my kitchen at home when Leo said he was off to the Disney shop again because Gemma and Jodie wanted a couple of Little Mermaid bridesmaids' dresses for the wedding. I said, what wedding? And he said, oh, didn't I tell you? Joanne's and mine. I shot Desperate Dan – he supported Everton, you know.

I woke with such a start, I nearly woke Leo.

Phew.

But the bluebottles hadn't finished. I dreamt that Marisa had her baby. I dreamt I went to see her with a nice little present from Baby Gap, but she said she'd gone off babies, she'd given it away and got a dog instead. Oh, I said. Was it called Cosmo? Oh, no, he was called Henry, just like mine. She'd found him in the street. That was when I realized I'd lost my own Henry; I hadn't seen him for ages. Maybe her Henry *was* mine. In a panic I asked to see him, but Marisa said the nanny was taking him for a walk. Only when the nanny came back, it was Max. I thought this very weird, but Marisa said it was unbelievably chic to have a male nanny nowadays. But there was no Henry on the lead, just a little King Charles spaniel. I said, where's Henry? And Max shrugged and said he'd got rid of him, he looked like a sheep.

Really panicking now, I said, 'Where is he? What have you done with him?'

'Oh, I slung him in the Aga,' he said. 'This one's got a lot more class.'

I woke with a panicky start, screams echoing in my head. '*Murderer! Murderer!*'

And that was all it took. As my heartbeat calmed down, something in my head went 'ping'. Finally, out of billions of brain cells, out of all the mountains of junk lurking in my memory, emerged that one, elusive thing.

Oh, God, I thought. Not *that* Nick. It can't be.

But I knew it was. Nick from that far-off summer, when I'd done a very bad thing.

# Chapter 8

When I woke again, the clock said nine forty. Rousing in sympathy, Henry stuck a friendly nose in my face. 'Hi, it's me!' Slurp. 'And guess what? It's morning!'

'Sshh,' I murmured, as Leo was still flat out. 'Go back to sleep.'

'Oh, OK, then.'

Flop.

I was nodding off again when I remembered that tyre. *Oh, bum. Better not nod off again, then. Better get up. Henry's bladder, too. And mine. Feel a bit rough, actually. Mouth like cat litter. Stomach bloated like long-dead animal. All that booze and chilli. Possible vast emission of foul gases any minute. Lovely erotic waker-upper for Leo. Will definitely get up in one more minute.*

It was probably more like ten. I slipped back into those Tigger pyjamas and Leo's discarded socks, as I couldn't be bothered to put my trainers on. I tiptoed out, shushing Henry's excitement, because he always found mornings a source of great joy. New smells in the garden! Hedgehog! Fox! Postmen to terrify! Breakfast! God, life was good.

Except for his claws clicking on the stone-flagged hall floor, the house was quieter than a graveyard at midnight, and nearly as cold. The kitchen was warmer, but full of the frustrations you find in a strange house. The garden door had umpteen locks and bolts and it took me five minutes to

128

find the keys. Next, after I'd let Henry out, the wretched taps turned the wrong way, i.e. not like mine at home.

After putting coffee on, I slipped into Ian's huge, manky old trainers, which were conveniently by the back door, and went out to see what Henry was up to. As the kitchen door opened on to a neglected kitchen garden, I followed a paved path to the back. For the beginning of December it was unbelievably mild, with a watery sun trying to shine.

At the end of what I'd describe as 'extensive, mature gardens', Henry was sniffing at the trunk of a large beech tree. It was all a bit depressing in daylight. The paved terrace where I stood had weeds growing in the cracks, the lawn was rough and patchy, and dead leaves were everywhere.

'I'm impressed,' said a voice to my left. 'Not only up, but you've put the coffee on, too.'

It was Nick. 'I'm not sure I'm talking to you,' I said, in only half-jokey tones. I hadn't planned on anyone catching me like this: unwashed and wearing Ian's trainers. 'It's very upsetting, being strangled. What are you doing up, anyway? I thought everybody'd be snoring for hours.'

'Guilty conscience,' he said. 'Visions of Alex up since six, creating havoc, and Jamie's folks cursing so-called quality-time dads. In any case, I have to take Sasha home – she's got some family lunch thing. What's your excuse?'

'Henry's bladder.' He was now digging enthusiastically in what had once been a herbaceous border.

Nick was standing only about three feet away, and I rather wished he wouldn't. I hadn't so much as brushed my teeth, and as for cleanse, tone and moisturize last night, forget it. Still, he didn't exactly look like Mr Shining Morning Face, either. He had yet to shave or shower; there was still gel on his hair. Now I was minus slut heels he seemed about three inches taller. He was wearing just a sweatshirt, white boxers, and a pair of well-worn leather deck shoes. Minus trousers, his legs were respectably robust, but not faded-tan olive, like Leo's. They were faded weather-beaten, fuzzed with light brown. 'Leo still asleep?' he asked.

'Flat out. How about Sasha?'

'Presumably, and if she doesn't feel like worst-case shit when she wakes up, I'm Little Bo-Peep.' He nodded towards the garden. 'Bloody mess, isn't it?'

I thought of bulldozers ripping the whole lot up. 'It must upset Felicity to see it like this.'

'I'm sure. What would upset me is to think of her grandfather selling it for relative peanuts. And then to think of what it just fetched, with planning permission thrown in.'

'He needed the money. It was far too big for an old couple, anyway.'

During this little exchange I had naturally been recalling my nightmare and that very bad thing. He obviously had no notion that it was me, which hardly surprised me, but I knew now why it had come back to me. Marisa had been the key. Until Alice's message I probably hadn't given her a thought for weeks.

I was suddenly aware that Nick was deriving innocent amusement from my footwear.

'Ian's,' I explained. 'Easy to slip into at this time of the morning.'

'They look good on you,' he said, deadpan.

A sudden, cool breeze made me shiver. 'I'm going in. I'm getting cold and that coffee'll be ready.'

He followed me back. Roasty-toasty smells were filling the kitchen, but as I opened the fridge something else really made my mouth water. Next to the milk lurked litres of proper orange juice. If anything could dissolve cat litter, that would.

The bottle had one of those caps with a strip seal and a little tab you have to pull hard. With my killer nails this wasn't easy. As the first pull didn't break the seal I gave an almighty yank.

'*Ow*!' The bottle fell to the floor as I doubled up, clasping my thumb in my left hand.

'What the hell . . .?' He came up smartly to investigate.

*Just a Gestapo torture* . . . 'These sodding nails – I caught my thumbnail on the cap – it must have bent right back . . .'

'Let's have a look, then.'

'Look, it's fine.' As there was no blood, I felt an idiot for behaving as if my entire hand had been severed. I retrieved the plastic bottle. 'Here, you open it.'

As the first liquid sunshine hit my taste buds I felt almost human again.

He perched on the kitchen table. 'Is it still hurting?'

'A bit. I can't wait to get these things off.' I inspected my left set of nails. 'Quite apart from potential passing agony, it's so difficult getting hold of anything.'

'If you can't get them off, why don't you just cut them?'

Why the hell hadn't I thought of that myself? 'Don't you think I hadn't thought of that? I didn't bring any nail scissors.'

'It doesn't take nail scissors.' Before I could utter a word he was checking drawers. 'How about these?' He held up what looked like a more lethal pair of the kitchen variety.

'Don't you come near me with those things! After last night I wouldn't trust you with a wooden spoon.'

'Very wise. Still, they might do.'

One Gestapo torture was enough for anybody. 'Pass them over, then.'

131

The nails were unbelievably tough, but I managed half. However, with right-handed scissors in my left, the other hand wasn't such a doddle.

'Here, let me,' he said. 'I'm a dab hand at clipping claws.'

I was tempted to bare my fangs and give a little snarl. 'I'm not sure I like the look of you. I think I might bite you.'

'You'd better not.' He took my right hand in a firm grip. 'Hold still and I'll give you a nice meaty chew afterwards.'

A little laugh escaped me. 'Do you give all your patients nice meaty chews?'

'No, rabbits and budgies aren't too keen.' *Snip*. 'Just the mutts, especially any nasty-looking customers.'

I was thinking he had nice hands, firm and capable. Capable of anything from lugging tyres to much more delicate tasks. Surgery, for example. Tying off tiny blood vessels. Fastening necklaces round unsuspecting little necks . . .

*Snip*. 'God, what are these things made of?' *Snip*.

'Don't ask me. Industrial acrylic?'

'Industrial something.' *Snip*. 'Do you want me to do this thumb, or is it still tender?'

'I think I can stand the agony.'

In fact I was expecting it to hurt, as the tough acrylic curve was briefly straightened, pulling my own bruised nail-bed with it. Evidently foreseeing this, however, he pressed down gently and I hardly felt a thing.

'God, what a relief.' They hardly even needed an emery board. I looked up at a pair of amused hazel eyes. 'Thank you.'

'Don't mention it. Would you like rabbit flavour, or beef?'

I laughed. On a sudden impulse I said, 'Actually, I've realized who you remind me of. Only it's not "reminding", exactly. I think we've met before.'

He gave a little frown. 'I must have been very drunk. I don't remember.'

*You soon will.* 'Do you remember a summer in Cornwall in, oh, about eighty-five?'

'I spent all my summers in Cornwall. It was where I lived.'

I tried again. 'Do you remember a girl called Marisa?'

'*Marisa*?' he frowned. 'Now that rings a vague little bell somewhere . . .'

'How about a seagull? A very sick seagull, and a very upset kid who wanted to take it to the vet's?'

That was when light dawned. It was a very incredulous light at first. 'Jesus,' he said at last. 'Don't tell me that was you?'

'I'm afraid so.'

'My God.' A slow smile spread across his face. 'You've changed just a bit.'

'I should hope so. I was only about thirteen. The "brat from hell" was the term you used, I think.'

'Oh, come on. I'm sure I was a lot ruder than that.'

This conversation got no further, as Sasha chose that moment to come in. Half hunched, in a knee-length blue T-shirt thing with a teddy on it, she trod gingerly in bare feet. 'Don't anybody say anything. I think I'm about to die.'

Nick pulled a chair out for her. 'Morning, Sasha. I can see you're full of the joys of spring.'

Sitting with extreme care, she put her face in her hands. 'If you dare say "I told you so", I'll kill you.'

133

'I told you no such thing. You'd have told me to mind my own business.'

'You should have told me, anyway.' She sat white-faced and huddled, smudged mascara round her eyes. 'Do I look as shit as I feel?'

He pretended to give her a critical inspection. 'Probably worse. You look as if you've had a heavy night with Count Dracula.'

'Thanks a lot.' She looked at me. 'He can be really horrible, you know. I threw up last night, and he laughed.'

'I did not,' Nick tutted. 'I gave you a glass of water and asked if there was much more where that came from.'

'You were still laughing, you arse.' Elbows on the table, she put her face in her hands again. 'God, I'd give anything just to go back to bed.'

Nick glanced at his watch, which was no longer the Bangkok fake. 'You could, for half an hour. Then I'll come and shove you under a cold shower. Guaranteed shock treatment for drooping bushy tails.'

It was a measure of how rough she felt that this offer produced barely a flicker. 'Might have known I wouldn't get any sympathy from you. A three-course nightmare coming up and all you can suggest is inhuman torture.'

'You'll probably feel better in a couple of hours,' I said.

'It'll still be a nightmare,' Nick explained. 'Her mother's invited a pair of poisonous toads for lunch. Roasted grasshoppers, is it, Sash? Stuffed with lightly sautéed maggots and—'

'Nick, *please*!'

She looked so fragile, and he slipped an arm around her shoulders and gave her a little squeeze. 'Sorry.'

'I really absolutely *hate* you sometimes,' she said, with no conviction whatever. To me she added, 'My dear

134

Auntie Jean and Uncle Frank are coming. Mum loathes them even more than I do.'

'Then why did she invite them?'

'Duty.' She took a sip of Nick's orange juice. 'They tided Mum over when she was really broke after Dad walked out. They were actually delighted he left, as they'd been telling her ever since she met him that he was no good. So every time they come we get a smug, "Well, we told you time and time *again* not to marry him," and poor Mum smiles brightly and says, "Well, it's all water under the bridge now," and wishes she had the nerve to tell them to sod off.'

'Tell her to spit in the gravy,' said Nick. 'It might give her a small measure of satisfaction.'

'She'd never do that. I might, though.' She turned a wan face to him. 'Do you think a cup of tea would make me throw up?'

'Possibly, but I'll get you one anyway.'

Huddling her shoulders, Sasha shivered. 'It's freezing in here.'

It wasn't, but she was suffering from exacerbating conditions.

Nick yanked his sweatshirt over his head and tossed it to her. 'Shove that on.'

She looked at the mere pair of boxers, now taking kettle to sink. 'I'm not sure it's the done thing, making cups of tea on a Sunday morning in only your pants. Izzy might be very easily nauseated, you know.'

'I'll find her a sick bag.'

'And you'll freeze your bollocks off.'

'Never mind, I'll have a good bitch at you afterwards.'

'Oh, all right . . .' Evidently thankful that her objections had been rebuffed, she pulled the sweatshirt on. 'He does

135

have his non-horrible moments,' she added, as her head emerged. 'I really almost like him sometimes.'

*You don't say*. Henry chose that moment to scratch at the door. Nick opened it and he bounded in, all excitement and muddy paws.

After I'd given the floor a perfunctory wipe, it was time to go. 'Right, I've got a tyre to collect,' I said. 'Good luck with your poisonous toads, Sasha, if I don't see you.'

Leo was still out for the count. After a quick shower I saw nobody as I left the house. Once in the car, with Henry in the back watching for wildlife, I thought there was something to be said for the country, even in its winter undress. For a start, no traffic lights for miles. No 'keep clear' boxes, with prats blocking them at junctions. No fumes. The banks were pretty bare, but a couple of months would fix that. When I'd come last March they'd been covered with primroses and the wooded hill where we'd walked the dogs had been carpeted with wild violets. Of course, there was no twenty-four-hour shop, either, which could be a total pain if you ran out of loo rolls at three in the morning.

I was glad I'd confessed to Nick. It would have been silly not to, especially with that apology long overdue. Not that I'd actually made one, now I came to think of it. If he now told everybody else, at least it'd give them a laugh.

That holiday had marked the end of an era. My folks and Marisa's had often taken a seaside house together, as Marisa was an only child and Mum and her mother were sisters. With only eighteen months between us, they'd thought we'd be company for each other. Alice was five years older than me, my brother William two years older still. By then he'd long stopped coming on holiday with us; family was just too embarrassing.

136

The trouble was, that summer when I was thirteen, Marisa had just hit fifteen. No longer did she want to mess about on boogie boards or inflatable crocodiles – not with me, anyway. All she'd wanted to do was hang around with girls of the same age, all constantly flicking their hair and pretending they didn't want the boys gawping at them.

At that awkward, in-between age, barely filling even a trainer bra, I'd felt miserable and left out. What did anyone see in boys, anyway? They had spots and put their slobbery tongues in your mouth. I'd tried to ignore the part of me that was beginning to say it might just be exciting. What was the point, when none of them ever even looked at me? Or at least, only to check that I had boobs like sparrows' eggs and was therefore unworthy of notice.

Alice was no company either, just lying on the beach with *The Seven Habits of Highly Successful Would-Be Entrants to Dental School*. At eighteen, that was all Alice had cared about. Our parents had gone out most days, to look at the lovely scenery we didn't give a toss about, Mum asking Alice to please keep an eye on me, and make sure I didn't Do Anything Silly.

Nick had been one of that group of boys hanging round the beach. All aged around fifteen or sixteen, they'd got on my nerves. When they weren't showing off on surfboards and trying to look cool, they were eyeing the girls, obviously making remarks full of new testosterone and sniggers. There hadn't seemed to be anyone spare, of my age, wanting to do pre-hormonal things.

I'd found the seagull while wandering alone to the far end of the beach. It was scruffy and miserable, and I'd known at once it was very sick or I'd never have caught it. It had barely even tried to peck me as I'd carried it up the beach, distraught.

Marisa had been with two other girls and a bother of boys. I'd particularly disliked one of the girls, a blonde with lilac toenails. Any fool could see she was jealous of Marisa, because even I could tell it was Marisa all the boys would cherry-pick, given a choice. Lilac Toenails in particular had made a face as I'd come up with the seagull, saying could we please take the poor thing to the vet's this minute, if somebody'd lend me the money I'd pay them straight back.

After some fruitless discussion – it probably had some horrible disease, where was the vet's anyway – Nick had taken it from me. He'd said not to worry, he knew where the vet's was, it'd be fine.

Until then I'd only noticed Nick because Marisa et al. had designated him number two in the Who We Wouldn't Mind Snogging league. Should I come too? I'd asked anxiously. No, it was a long walk – maybe Marisa would come with him.

About two hours later, seeing them back on the beach, I'd run up to ask how it was. Should be fine, Nick had said. They were sending it to the wildlife rescue. No charge.

'Oh, what a relief!' I'd said. 'I thought they might put it to sleep!'

And I thought that was it, until the following evening.

Marisa and I were supposed to be going to the cinema, but she had other ideas. The beach boys and hair-flickers had planned a beach party, but her folks had ummed and eventually put their feet down. All sorts might go on in the sand-dunes. There might be druggies turning up. The fact that she was on the beach all *day* was entirely beside the point. At night it was different – please don't argue, it just *is*.

So I was her cover, and I didn't like it. Not because of

deceiving parents, I hasten to add, but because I knew I'd feel awkward and left out. 'Oh, come on,' she said, as we took the beach path rather than the one signposted 'Town Centre'. 'It'll be wicked.'

'Can't I just go back? I'll say I felt sick.'

'Are you kidding? Mum and Dad aren't completely stupid.'

On one of those rare, sultry evenings we headed for the dunes at the far end of the beach. Someone had brought a ghetto-blaster; others had brought bottles of scrumpy and plastic cups. It was amazing how quickly I took to scrumpy. It made you enjoy yourself after all. Instead of feeling like a self-conscious prat, you got up and danced like Olivia Newton-John. As for your conversation, it made everything you said positively hilarious. Some boy called Chris even talked to me as if I were at least fourteen. I had nice hair, he said, would I like some more scrumpy? You bet I would. How about a fag? Well, why not? Boy, I was really living at last.

I don't remember much else until it was dark. Suddenly alone with Chris in the dunes, I was getting my first lesson in French kissing. At least, I supposed that was what you called a hot, slobbery mouth trying to eat you. I wasn't sure I liked it. In fact, it was starting to make me feel sick, but I didn't like to say so. Not until hot, damp hands started groping at my sparrows' eggs.

'Get off!' Pushing him away, I wiped my slobbery mouth with my hand.

'What's up with you?' Undaunted, he launched himself again, but I pushed him away, harder.

'I don't want to, OK?' I felt funny, and anyway, that coarse grass that grows in the dunes was prickling my back.

'You frigid or something?'

139

Was I? How awful. 'No! I just want to go home.'

I rose unsteadily to my feet. My head felt funny, sort of dizzy and whirly.

'I bet you're a lezzie,' he taunted.

God, what if I was? Mum would cry her eyes out. 'I am not!' Stumbling off, I came across Lilac Toenails and a couple of others. 'Have you seen Marisa?'

'Over there.' She nodded towards a couple sitting twenty yards away in the sand. 'Talk about cootchy-coo ickle lovebirds.'

The previous evening Marisa and Nick had turned into an embryonic item, which was one reason she'd been dying to come. I knew Lilac Toenails didn't like this; in fact, she was pretty pissed off about it. 'There's no need to be like that, just because he likes her better than you.'

That really got up her nose, which was the general idea. 'You think *I* want him? I don't even like him.'

'Well, *I* do. He took my seagull to the vet's.'

She sniggered, in that bitchy, pitying way. In fact, they all sniggered.

'God, you're so thick,' said Lilac Toenails. 'Do you really think he could be bothered to take it all the way to the vet's?'

My head was feeling seriously weird. 'What do you mean?'

'He killed it, thicko. The minute you were out of sight he broke its neck. *Snap.*' She even did the action. 'OK?'

For a moment I gaped at her, appalled. Then, with fury and betrayal rising like a hot wave, I ran like a missile to where Nick and Marisa were sitting on the sand.

He must have wondered what the hell had hit him. 'Murderer!' I bashed him, hit his back and shoulders, while he tried to fend me off. How could he? Murderer! I hated him, he was a lying saddist . . .

140

Of course, Marisa had screamed at me to get off, and Nick had restrained my flailing arms. He was sorry, but anyone could see it was very sick – will you *stop* trying to kick me? – the vet would only have put it to sleep, anyway. It hadn't felt a thing; it had been instantaneous, OK?

As he'd finally released me, Marisa had glared. I was just so unbe*liev*ably embarrassing; she was never taking me anywhere ever again.

It was so unfair. 'You made me come!' I burst out. 'So you could snog *him*!'

I think she could have killed me, but instead she looked daggers as she took Nick's arm. 'Come on, let's go down the beach, I'll have to go soon, anyway.'

I watched them turn away. Over his shoulder Nick said, 'It's pronounced saydist, not saddist, all right? And I'm not.'

That did it. 'You *are*! I hate you!' I rushed at his retreating back, but he anticipated me. Intending to fend me off, he turned around fast. So fast, the kick I aimed at his backside landed somewhere else entirely.

For weeks, the next couple of minutes might have been burnt into my brain. They came to haunt me when I woke in the small hours, scorching my cheeks as I buried my face in the pillow. They came to me on the bus, even when singing, 'O God our help in ages past,' in school assembly.

If I'd intended to do it, I could hardly have managed it better. Instantly, he was doubled up on the sand, too agonized even to swear at me.

Falling on her knees beside him, Marisa had screamed at me. 'What the hell did you do that for? Just wait till I tell Auntie Jenny!'

Who was, of course, my mother. As everybody came running up, I could have died. I wanted to say, look, I'm

141

sorry, I didn't mean to, but it never came out. My head was spinning; suddenly I felt really ill.

'I feel sick,' I mumbled, swayed and fell forward. And as I did so, about a pint of scrumpy, plus the fish and chips I'd had earlier, saw daylight again. The whole, stinking gutful projected itself neatly on to Nick's back as he clutched himself on the sand.

And Lilac Toenails laughed.

# Chapter 9

As Nick eventually staggered to his feet and sluiced himself in the sea, I prayed quite seriously to die. A furious Marisa took me home, saying how *could* I? Showing her up like that, and if I dared say *one word* to her mum and dad . . .

As if.

There were only three days of holiday left, which was just as well. My mother said, 'Have you and Marisa fallen out, dear?' and I said no, I was just fed up with the beach, could I go out with them, instead? For two days I was dragged into mouldery old churches and antique shops, where Mum bought things like cracked Victorian chamber-pots. I was grossed out. 'Eeugh! Dead people have weed in it!'

'Don't be silly, dear,' she tutted. 'Only eleven pounds – it'll just do for my spider plant.'

Almost worse than the thought of everybody sniggering on the beach, was falling out with Marisa. By the evening of the second day, though, she said, look, I know it wasn't *all* your fault, Nick probably won't actually kill you if you come to the beach tomorrow.

So I'd gone back. Moody and embarrassed I'd sat alone on the sand, wondering how on earth I could go up and say sorry when he was in a crowd who'd all laugh at me. Lying on my stomach, I read Marisa's *Teen* instead. I was engrossed in the agony column (*'My boyfriend says you only have to put condoms on at the last minute*') when someone tapped me on the shoulder.

'Here you go. Probably better than scrumpy.'

It was Nick. In just a pair of faded denim shorts, he was offering an ice-cream cone with a flake in it.

I went hot pink. What if he'd seen what I was reading? Surely '*ROLL CAREFULLY ON TO A FULLY ERECT PENIS*' was screaming from the page. 'Um, thanks,' I mumbled.

'I'm sorry about the seagull. I didn't like doing it, you know.'

Even then I couldn't find the words. All I could mumble was, 'It's OK.'

'Right, then. Don't drip that ice-cream down your front.'

As I drove back, all this replayed in my mind. Funny how I could laugh about it now. How old would Nick have been? Fifteen? Sixteen? Certainly no more.

With Henry's head hanging out of the window, I slowed down on the way back and enjoyed pootling through the lanes. The sun was making a valiant effort and the only scents wafting through the window were fresh and earthy, from rain-washed woods and fields. I was miles away, back on that Cornish beach, when I became aware of someone flashing impatiently behind me.

'Prat,' I muttered. There was barely room to overtake, even if we hadn't been rounding a blind bend. But then the prat tooted as well, and stirrings of road rage hit me. What did he expect me to do? Take off like Herbie? At the next clear stretch I slowed right down, yelling, 'Prat!' as he finally overtook – and I saw his face.

*Nick*? Oh, God, was my exhaust hanging off or something?

Already nearly at a standstill, I stopped and got out.

Twenty yards further on, so did he. He came towards me with that expression men are so good at when you've just done something they're going to amuse other men with later. 'Didn't you see me? I must have been flashing you for half a mile!'

'What the hell for?' Unless I was going blind, no bits of Peugeot had dropped off. 'I thought something was wrong with the car!'

'There was. It was going in the wrong direction.'

Oh. That shut me up.

'You took the right fork back there, instead of the left,' he went on.

So what if I had? Getting lost in these lanes was a fact of life for 'foreigners'. 'But that junction can be very confusing,' he added.

This was obviously supposed to mollify me, in case I thought he was having a silent laugh at innate female lack of direction. 'I was just having a little pootle round the lanes! I don't often get the chance to pootle round country lanes on a Sunday morning, you know.'

That wiped the silent laugh off his face. 'Oh. Sorry.'

Then I felt bad. 'But I'm sorry for calling you a prat.' *Thank God it wasn't 'wanker'*. 'I thought you were some road-rage idiot.'

'Just as well I'm not. You might have got more than you bargained for.'

'I doubt it. Henry has a pretty scary woof when he puts his mind to it.'

'Yes, I can see he'd terrify the daylights out of anybody.' He put out a hand to Henry, whose head was still hanging out of the window. His tongue was dangling from his mouth, his back end wagging for Dogdom.

Nick had rather more on than the last time I'd seen him.

He was wearing sand-coloured chinos and a soft shirt in a sludgy shade of olive. Like me, he wore no jacket. I wore a black sweater with a floppy polo-neck and my seventy-nine-pound jeans. In positively spring-like weather they were quite enough. The sun felt almost warm on my face, and in the nearby bank a robin was singing his little head off.

'Have you just dropped off Sasha?' I asked, as she wasn't in his car.

'Twenty minutes ago. I was on my way back from offering apologies to Felicity – that's how I saw you at that junction. I was just coming from the right fork. Or the left, the way you were looking at it.'

As a car was coming, we moved in slightly. A middle-aged couple passed, the woman giving a smile and wave as they went. Nick acknowledged her likewise, and I thought how weird it was after London. 'I sometimes feel like an alien here. People are so entirely different, waving at total strangers.'

'She wasn't a total stranger. The face was vaguely familiar – I've probably dosed her overweight cat for fleas. But to get back to those apologies . . .'

I could guess. 'You'll be diluting poisonous toads instead of brunching?'

'That's the idea. Sasha's mother said she could do with reinforcements, and I didn't think Felicity would mind. Plus there's Alex. He can be a bit of a pain at NBK dos.'

Felicity wasn't an NBK person, but I took his point. Anyone else feeling rough would probably be that way inclined. 'I'm surprised you can't manage both. Given your previous form, a pound or two of bacon and sausage would still leave plenty of room for roasted grasshoppers.'

'Tell Rob he can have my sausages.' He gave me a little

up-and-down look. 'I still can't believe that was you. I hope you never took up kick-boxing.'

'Afraid not. Salsa classes are more my line.'

'Thank God for that. So what's Marisa doing these days?'

'Oh, nothing much. Highly successful in PR, married to Peter the banker, expecting first baby in the New Year. Pretty boring, really. Still, I'd better get moving.' I nodded down the lane. 'Is there anywhere to turn around for the next five miles?'

'There's a farm entrance not far down. You've had enough pootling, then?'

As he'd clipped my tender claw so gently, I came clean. 'All right, I *had* taken the wrong fork. I was away with those fairies again.'

He laughed. 'Izzy, I'm getting seriously worried about you. Two confessions in one morning is serious stuff.'

'Well, I had a near-death experience last night. It changes you, you know. Still, it was nice doing murder with you. Enjoy your grasshoppers.' Although it felt over-formal, I held out a hand. I didn't want him thinking I was expecting a kiss.

With a hint of amusement, he took it. 'Take care.'

'You, too.'

I don't know why I checked myself in the mirror the instant I was back in the car. Latent masochism? Certainly nobody would have used me in a feature on Achieving that Artfully Radiant Glow on your Idyllic Country Weekend. Except for a slick of mango-flavour Born Lippy I wore no make-up. My half-dried hair was hastily twisted into a scrunchie. As for my un-mascaraed eyes, they might have been peering out of a morning-after sty.

God, it was horrible.

*

Back at Colditz, everybody else was up. Bacon and sausages were already on, Felicity was wondering how much cream to put in the scrambled eggs and whether to add the smoked salmon or serve it separately. Coffee and warming bread were scenting the kitchen.

Showered and dressed, Leo drew me on to his lap. 'Why didn't you tell me about the tyre? I wondered where you'd got to.'

'I forgot,' I said. 'You rather put minor matters out of my head.'

'Nick said to say goodbye to you,' said Felicity. 'Sasha's mum invited him and Alex for roast beef and horrible relatives – I think he feels a bit sorry for Sasha's mum.'

'Just as well,' said Ellie, who looked less glowing than usual. 'I don't think I could have faced some whingy little pain of a kid.'

'Oh, I don't know,' said Adam. 'I'm rather fond of kids, as long as they're done with plenty of garlic butter.'

'Adam!' said Felicity. 'Leo's got children, you know.'

Leo only laughed. 'On purpose, too.'

Leaning against the dresser with a coffee, Rob said, 'Alex doesn't whinge. He's just a little bugger.'

Ian was putting mushrooms under the grill. 'Mind you, roasts with Mum are getting serious. I foresee a "dear RAF" letter before the year is out.'

'Oh, come on,' said Rob. 'If you ask me, it's just a bit of fun on both sides.'

'Maybe,' said Felicity. 'But you know what they say about absence making the heart grow fonder – of someone else. Ian, turn those sausages over, will you?'

'She really is the most terrible flirt,' said Paula, somewhat primly. 'Still, at least *he's* not attached.'

'Nick never is attached,' said Felicity. 'Not that I hear of, anyway. Although didn't he see What's-her-name from the riding stables a couple of times?'

'Don't ask me,' said Rob. 'I don't interrogate him about his nights out.'

'Honestly, men are *hope*less,' Felicity tutted. 'You are, anyway. Ian's a proper old woman when it comes to gossip.'

'Do you mind?' said Ian. 'I call it keeping myself informed on community issues.'

As we were finally eating Felicity said to me, 'So what are you two doing for Christmas?'

'I'll probably go to Alice's,' I said. 'Leo's spending Christmas with his kids.'

'Why don't you go to Spain, to your mum?' asked Rob.

'She'd have to put Henry in kennels,' Felicity said. 'Where Father Christmas might not know how to find him.'

I fed Henry about his ninth morsel of smoked salmon. 'And they wouldn't give him a proper Christmas dinner.'

Ellie gave a little snort. 'Honestly, you two are *mad*.'

'How about New Year?' Felicity asked. 'Anything planned? Because if not, why don't you come down here?' In the middle of pouring coffee, she had that 'idea!' face.

'Ian, how about that ball at the Tawton House? I bet there are still a few tickets.'

Ian groaned. '*Please*, Eff, not that. I'd have to ponce myself up in a penguin suit.'

'Oh, come on. Masses of people are going. It's for charity. The children's hospice.' She appealed to Rob. 'You wouldn't mind putting on a penguin suit for charity, would you? We could get a table together. It'd be fun.'

Rob raised an eyebrow at Paula. 'If you like,' she said. 'I think you'd look rather dashing in a dinner jacket.'

Felicity turned to me. 'How about you and Leo?'

As I hadn't even discussed New Year with him, I wasn't sure Leo would want to be put on the spot. But he answered, 'Fine with me.'

About to say, '*Sure*? No birthdays stroke christenings stroke wakes in the pipeline?' I swallowed it. 'Put us down for two, then.'

Adam and Ellie were already booked, however, and so was Alastair.

Felicity turned to Jane. 'How about you? I could find you a nice blind date.'

'Maybe not, thanks.' Jane made a face. 'One thing I've learnt in this life is that any spare men I end up on blind dates with are spare for very good reasons.'

We sat over brunch for two hours. As if she'd got an ordeal over, Paula had relaxed still more since last night. She wore a soft pink sweater and a little glow to match, of the type that often comes from lovely Sunday-morning shenanigans. Maybe that was why Rob was allowed a sausage and two rashers of bacon. Compared with their almost honeymoon air, Ian and Felicity seemed like an old married couple, but then they always did.

Shortly before we left, I had a moment alone with Rob. 'Paula seems nice,' I said. 'I hope she wasn't dreading meeting us lot.'

'Funny you should say that. She's actually rather shy, underneath. And she had a bit of a rough time before moving down here.'

I didn't ask what kind of 'rough'. Some miserable relationship, I could bet. 'A bit like you.'

'Well, that's history now. Pastures new, and all that.'

'Not to mention, "image new". It was high time somebody gave you a trim 'n' edge. And you've lost weight.'

'I needed to. Too many pies, chips and beers. It was a wonder she even looked at me.'

I could see exactly how it had happened. Still in the slough of despond, he'd let himself go. To anyone who didn't know, though, he'd still have appeared kind and cheerful. I could just see him calling, 'Millie!' to the waiting-room, and a probably anxious Paula coming in with her pup. She'd have seen a shaggy bear with lovely blue eyes, a reassuring manner and strong, gentle hands: it was Mills and Boon made flesh. 'Oh, come on, Rob. Nice men like you are even more of an endangered species than Baluchi camel hounds. I could almost fancy you myself now she's tarted you up.'

He gave a half-guilty little laugh. 'Don't let her hear you make jokes like that, for God's sake. It wasn't just her husband, you know. Keep it to yourself, but her own sister waltzed off with someone else about three years later.'

I'd like to say here that I kept it to myself, but I'm only human. While Jane was packing I ran Felicity to earth. Standing on the terrace, she was gazing at the garden, and her face said she was thinking of the bulldozers.

'Poor Felicity,' I said. 'It's a terrible shame.'

She tried to shrug. 'I don't mind so much about the house, even Granny never really liked it, but the apple trees at the end, and that horse chestnut . . .' With obvious effort, she brisked herself up. 'Still, it's people that matter, isn't it? If you offered me this, on my own, or a cowshed for two, there'd be no contest.'

Rather wistfully, she added, 'I do wish you'd come here for Christmas. I'd give Henry a brilliant Christmas dinner.'

'I know, but even Alice does her best. Won't Jack be back by then?' Jack was Ian's younger brother, who lived with them on and off. Just now it was 'off' as he'd left about a year previously for the Australia/Far East trail.

151

'He should have been, but he's met some Pippa in Thailand and she wants to stay a bit longer. I'd have asked Rob and Paula, but she's planning a cosy little dinner *à deux*. In any case, he's going to be on call. He volunteered ages ago, thinking Nick might want to spend the day with Alex.'

I told her what Rob had said about Paula.

'Well, that explains a lot,' she said. 'Poor Paula, though. And I've just realized why she made me think of Cruella. It was that pink jumper she had on this morning.'

'Sorry?'

'The fact that it was *pink*,' she explained. 'Practically every time I've seen her she's been in white, and always absolutely simple. The very first time I met her she was wearing an *absolutely simple* white linen dress like the white cloak in the book – did you ever read the book? *The Hundred and One Dalmatians*, I mean?'

'No, I only ever saw the film.'

'Well, I must have read it hundreds of times. Cruella always wore an *absolutely simple* white mink cloak, you see. Don't ever tell anybody, will you? I feel really bad now.'

I kissed Leo goodbye at half past three, and ten minutes later Jane and I followed.

Of course, I told her about Paula, too.

'Told you,' she said, as we passed ploughed fields in fast-falling dusk. 'Insecure, and clingy with it. I hope poor old Rob knows what he's got into.'

'Oh, come on. You said yourself she'll be good for his ego.'

'Yes, but for how long? And you know Rob – if it goes sour he'll agonize for ever before ending it. Why the hell can't he find someone nice and normal who'll just appreciate him?'

'Yes, why doesn't he? It's so dead easy, finding the right person.'

She gave a rueful little laugh. 'OK, I know. I haven't met anyone I'd prefer to a pot of Nutella in months.'

The run-up to Christmas went even faster than usual, starting with a phone call from Alice. Was I coming? I'd said probably, but that was back in October.

'Sorry, I should have phoned before. Yes, please.'

'Oh, lovely. Ben and Sarah will be so pleased.'

Ben was eight, Sarah just five. Bright and lovable, they were always flatteringly delighted to see me, but possibly even more delighted to see Henry, as theirs was a pet-free house. This was only partly because Alice never felt quite comfortable around anything that didn't shower on a daily basis and pee tidily in a loo. Ben and Sarah were far too young to look after even a goldfish properly, she explained, and she herself just didn't have time.

However, whenever I went, Henry was banished to the utility room at night. 'Would you mind if Henry slept upstairs this time? I'll bring my own duvet, if that's what's worrying you.'

'You never minded him sleeping in the utility room before!'

'I did, Alice. I just didn't say so.'

'Oh, really, Isabel! If you weren't happy, you only had to say. As for bringing duvets, I never heard anything so ridiculous. I can always get it cleaned.' After a pause she went on, 'So what *is* Leo doing?'

'His mum's, with the kids. The ex is going away.'

'Oh, well. When a man's got baggage, I suppose you're always going to have to share him.'

As if I didn't know.

*

I saw more of Leo than usual in the next couple of weeks. He came with me to a few of the usual round of parties and we did some Christmas shopping together. We went ice-skating at that seasonal rink at Somerset House, zipping round hand in hand and laughing as we fell over. It felt almost like our first weeks all over again. I felt like number one love.

As Joanne and Desperate Dan were leaving for Goa on the twenty-third, he was off home early the same day. I had a work bash on the evening of the twenty-second: dinner at an expensive restaurant, courtesy of Anthea. Leo was coming round afterwards, for our last night before the holiday. However, I woke up on the morning of the twenty-second with those shivery aches and pricking throat that presage flu. Proper flu, not just a cold.

When I phoned work to say I wouldn't be in, I knew they were relieved that I wasn't doing the nobly-soldiering-on bit. Nobody wanted me passing on flu just before Christmas, especially not Barbara, who had twelve descending for dinner. And Anthea certainly wouldn't want flu when she was off to Jamaica on Christmas Eve.

And then there was Leo. What if he got it? What if he passed it on to all the sundry relatives flocking to his mother's? I began to realize just how those plague victims felt, shutting themselves away to die alone so that others might live. Trying not to sound too much like a martyr, I told him maybe we should pass on tonight. 'I'll feel a whole lot worse if your entire family goes down like flies. If I don't feel better, I won't even go to Alice's.'

There was a long pause. 'I hate the thought of you being on your own.'

'It won't kill me.' Like the nobler type of martyr, tossing merry quips as she went to the stake, I added, 'I wouldn't want you coming tonight, anyway. All I can face is bed and a gallon of hot Ribena. In any case, I'm not on my own. I've got Henry.'

'Try to sleep it off, then.' He made a kissy noise into the phone. 'I'll call you tomorrow.'

I was doing my damnedest to sleep it off when the phone rang at ten past eleven.

It was Louise. 'Sorry, I know it's late – how are you feeling?'

'Pretty awful.' My eyes felt hot and scratchy. 'How was the dinner?'

'That's why I'm phoning. It wasn't just a nice little dinner, to say thank you for holding the fort for bloody months. It was so she could drop a bombshell in public and no one could throw a fit.'

Even before she said it, I knew. 'She's done it, hasn't she?'

'How did you guess? After saying, "Over my dead body," about a million times.'

Anthea had sold out, then. To one of the chains who'd been just waiting to gobble us up. 'Who is it?'

'Moving On.'

One of the biggest. 'Might have known.'

'The consultant says she's got to take it easy,' Louise went on. 'She's thinking of actually moving to Jamaica, or somewhere else hot where she and What's-his-name can amble round golf courses. And she said that if she's ever going to do it, now's the right time. She thinks there's going to be a recession.'

'She might well be right.' Anthea often was.

'I know, but I'm just so hacked off. She said it won't make much difference, just a new name over the door, but it will. They'll be bringing in their own manager, for starters. Barbara says if they make her answer the phone like a singsong bimbo, as in, "Good-morning-Moving-On-Barbara-speaking-how-may-I-help-you," she's leaving.'

Barbara had a bit of a thing about singsong bimbos.

'*And*,' Louise went on, really steamed up now, 'it'll be the end of Henry in the office.'

'What?'

'Litigation, Izzy. In lawyer-think, dogs at work equal possible biting of clients, which equals massive suing of corporate arses.'

If I'd had time to think about it, I'd have expected this. Even if I produced a cast-iron guarantee that Henry had no teeth, they'd come up with 'hygiene', or some other excuse. 'We should have seen this coming. She might have told us before, though.'

By the time Louise hung up it was half past eleven. After dosing myself with paracetamol and about fourteen times the RDA of vitamin C, I turned the light off.

By some miracle I felt ten times better in the morning. Slightly wobbly, but no aches, no shivers, no swallowing through a throat full of cactus spines.

I tried Leo at ten to nine, when he'd almost certainly be awake but still at home. After five rings a sleepy female voice said, 'Hello?'

'Oh, sorry – I must have got the wrong number . . .'

'Er, probably not – if you want Leo he's just gone in the shower. Is that Joanne?'

# Chapter 10

I jabbed 'off' like a reflex. Like the way you jerk your hand away from the iron before the burn reaches your pain centre.

This took rather longer. Slowly, like warmed-up frost-bite, shock was replaced by the sick, horrible pain of betrayal.

And the questions.

How could he do this to me?

Who was she?

What would she have thought when I hung up like that? Would she have stormed straight to the shower? 'Leo, what the hell's going on? Some woman just phoned for you and hung up!' Or would she have shrugged, merely assumed I was a wrong number after all?

*Who was she?*

One thing was clear; she wasn't a one-night stand. For starters, 'Is that Joanne?' indicated familiarity with his circumstances. Maybe she even knew that Joanne was going away that day. Leo could well have said she might call, with some instruction like, 'And for heaven's sake don't let your mother stuff them with sweets. You know they make Jodie hyperactive.'

Pacing and fidgeting, I asked myself endless questions. If she'd confronted him, surely he'd phone me? Or would he? What if she'd thrown him out, with only a floral shower cap for a fig-leaf? How long had he been seeing her? What about that night he'd been 'too knackered'?

By nine forty I couldn't stand it any longer. I called him, instead.

He answered after three rings. 'I was just about to call – how are you feeling?'

*O smooth-tongued treachery, thy name is man.* 'Much better, thank you. I tried to call you earlier, but some woman who evidently thought I was Joanne said you'd just gone in the shower.'

There was a long pause that said it all.

How I kept cool I'll never know. My voice came out in neat, iced mouthfuls. 'Like to tell me who she was, Leo? Your cleaning lady, doing an early shift?'

I heard his tense exhalation. 'Look, I'm sorry. I feel terrible.'

'Oh, good. Do go on.'

'I feel like shit, all right? I know how it looks, but it's not quite what you—'

'*Think*? I'll tell you what I think. I think you were in bed with someone who answered your phone while you were in the shower. Who was she?'

There was a resigned pause. 'Laura.'

'Right. Lovely. Did you sleep with her? Sorry, I'll rephrase that. Did you see her last night while I was ill and have sex with her?'

I heard his 'this is it' sigh. 'Yes. But if you'll just—'

'Fuck off.'

I cut him off with trembling fingers. I knew he'd phone back, and he did. The phone rang in my hand until he gave up.

When it rang twenty minutes later it was Anthea, and how I managed to sound like someone merely suffering from flu I'll never know. She was really sorry she'd missed

158

me. She felt bad about selling out, she'd never have done it if she were fit, but the offer really couldn't have come at a better time. Yes, of course, she must do what she thought best, blah-blah, have a lovely time in Jamaica, yes, Happy Christmas to you, too, will you please just *go*?

But when she had it was almost worse.

Compared with this, the previous day had been a picnic. No amount of Panadol would shift this cold sickness in my stomach. No amount of hot Ribena would soothe my miserable anger. I could think of nothing else, settle down to nothing, do nothing but think of it. The only thing I did was walk Henry. I'd felt too ill the day before and he was patiently dying for exercise. Still physically wobbly, I tramped wet pavements seeing nothing but Leo with Her. Talking to her. Laughing with her.

Desiring her.

Bastard. Bastardbastardbastardbastard*bastard* . . .

Only when some passing woman looked askance did I realize I'd muttered it aloud. And you can sod off, too, I thought savagely. You and your silly face and stupid velvet hat – what the hell do you know about anything?

How could this have happened to me? It was the kind of thing that happened to other people. Stupid people. Behind their backs their friends said, 'Poor cow, she phoned him and he was in bed with someone else. Classic or what?'

I was never telling anyone, ever.

Not a soul.

No one round here, anyway.

At twenty to eight I phoned Jane.

'Hi, Izz! How's it going?'

From the background noise I could tell she was in a bar. 'Look, if you're in the middle of getting hammered, it'll keep.'

'I was just about to leave – are you all right?'

That was all it took. The river of misery I'd kept back all day burst its banks. She said, 'Oh, Izzy . . .' about fifty times, and 'Arsehole,' and 'I'd honestly never have thought it of him.' The one thing she didn't say was, 'You're better off without him.' Friends like Jane knew it didn't help.

Eventually, as I wiped my nose on the tenth soggy tissue, she said, 'If you've bought him some incredibly expensive Christmas present I hope you kept the receipt.'

'I've got a good mind to use it myself. I got him a boy-racer session at Brands Hatch.' *Happy Christmas, Leo – a hundred and fifty quids' worth from a mug who actually thought you were worth it.* 'Jane, I know it sounds stupid, but please don't tell anyone else – I feel such a fool. I'll leave it a bit and then say I dumped him after he let me down once too often.'

'You'll have to tell Felicity. That New Year ball, remember?'

'OK, but I'm not telling her the truth. Knowing Felicity she'd drive straight up with the *Bridget Jones* video and a gallon of Häagen-Dazs.'

'My lips are zipped. And personally, I think you did ex*act*ly the right thing, dumping him after he told you he couldn't make that Christmas party after all.'

Good old Jane. 'The one I didn't even want to go to.'

'But were obliged to. Especially when you'd told him you particularly needed him there to fend off some revolting old lech with ginger hairs in his ears.'

I spent the evening slumped miserably on the sofa. With unwrapped presents lying on the table, I watched rubbish TV and ate microwave chow mein straight from the plastic dish. Over about the seventh glass of wine I wondered how the hell I was going to get through the loathsome jollity of Christmas, and whether to tell Alice I had flu after all.

Henry lay with his head in my lap, licking my arm now and then. Like some telepathic radar, he invariably picked up my mood. He even licked the chow mein dish as if it were merely a tedious duty.

'Bastard,' I said to him. 'I hope his balls drop off.'

He looked up at me with melting brown love. 'I bet she's some trollopy old hag of a nympho. *I* love you, anyway.'

Lovely, ever-faithful Henry. I'd never appreciated him more.

I didn't make excuses to Alice. If nothing else, Ben and Sarah would be disappointed not to get their presents. On the way, I called in on Mrs Denny. She was in a nursing home three miles away, and I tried to see her every couple of weeks. I always took Henry, as she missed him a lot more than she admitted and the other old dears loved giving him biscuits. I took her a large box of chocolates that said 'With love and licks from Henry' on the label, some early daffodils, and half a dozen bottles of Guinness.

Mrs Denny was getting frailer, but assured me that a drop of Guinness would perk her up. 'You should have one yourself, love. You're looking a bit peaky.'

You couldn't win. I'd put on blusher specially, and *Touche Eclat* to cover my miserable rings. 'Too many late nights,' I told her. 'Three Christmas parties on the trot.'

'Well, what it is to be young. Dear me, is he still wearing this old thing?' she added, fingering Henry's collar. 'It's looking just like me – a bit past it. I should have asked one of the girls to get him a new one for me, for Christmas.' Having belonged to her old dog, the collar was rather past its wear-by date.

'I'm sure he'd rather have a bag of treats. I'll get him a new one after Christmas.'

'But don't throw away the old one, will you? I know I'm

daft, but it's a little bit of Rusty.' She looked up at me. 'And how's your young man?'

'Oh, fine,' I said brightly. 'Spending Christmas with his kids, though, so I'm off to Alice's right after leaving here. That's a pretty jumper – is it new?'

When I finally kissed her goodbye she took my hand and held it tight. 'Plenty more fish in the sea, love,' she whispered. 'Better ones than ever came out of it.'

And she'd smelt this particular fish all right. *Pisces multishaggus*: apt to go stinking rotten when you least expect it. I don't know why I'd tried to fool her, except that I hadn't wanted her upset on my behalf. 'Maybe, but I never seem to pick them, unless they come with chips.'

'I'll have a word with Ron, love. I'm talking to him a lot lately. He beats some of this lot,' she added in a wicked whisper – several of the residents had dementia.

For this reason I hated seeing her there, though there was no alternative. Her only son lived in Vancouver, and she always said that even if he didn't she'd never have burdened him. In a horrible way, though, it was therapeutic going to that home. Seeing those withered old things, who hadn't a clue what year it was, being wheeled off to have their incontinence pads changed, made me realize life could just be marginally worse.

Alice lived in Hertfordshire, in the sort of house I could have sold in a week. Twenty-five years old, neo-Georgian, pristine decor right out of the more countrified end of *Homes and Gardens*.

I got on with her a million times better than when we were kids. On my last visit she'd even moaned about her husband, David, who was also a dentist, and far too lax with the children. Left to babysit on a Saturday he'd let them watch videos all day. At the rate he let Sarah watch

Disney's *Cinderella* it'd be worn out soon, and just as well. The child was addicted to it.

So I'd had no problem choosing a present for Sarah.

After slapping a layer of jollity on with the blusher, I got through Christmas Day without the cracks showing. I said not a word about Leo, because I knew exactly what Alice would say. 'To be perfectly frank, Isabel, when a man's got a failed marriage behind him, you have to ask yourself why.'

Another couple with children much the same age came for dinner. Patted and petted non-stop, with a proper, human turkey dinner, too, Henry was in doggy heaven.

My only feel-good came from dishing out the kids' presents. For Ben I'd bought a twelve-inch electronic dinosaur. Whenever anyone approached its eyes glowed red and evil and it gave off fearsome growls. He was equally delighted with a remote-controlled fart machine I'd nearly put back, in case Alice had a fit.

For Sarah I'd bought a Cinderella dress from the Disney shop, complete with tiara, and a set of kids' sparkly nail polishes. I knew Alice would disapprove of these (so tacky, seeing little girls in nail polish) but it was just tough. Ecstatic, Sarah insisted on putting the dress on at once.

'Well,' said the other mum, when she was twirling in it. 'You really look like a princess in that.'

'I know,' she said, with the air of Posh Spice being told she was famous. 'I'm going to be a princess when I grow up.'

Alice raised her eyes to heaven. 'I knew that wretched video had gone to her head. You can't really *be* a princess, darling.'

Oh, leave her alone, I thought. She'd enter the real world soon enough.

Sarah was not easily put off, however. 'Yes, I can.' She

twirled again. 'You said I can be anyfing I want. I shall marry a prince and live wiv him in his castle.'

Alice fought this subversive attitude with another tack. 'I didn't mean that sort of being something, darling. I meant *do*ing something. Like being a doctor.'

'Being a doctor's yuck,' said Ben, who'd already made up his mind that he was going to make world history by doing Jurassic Park for real. 'You have to look at old people's wrinkly smelly old bottoms.'

'Ben!' said Alice, but everybody else was laughing.

'*Ack*shully,' said Sarah, still twirling, 'I fink I might have a hopsicle in ve castle.'

'*Hos*pital, darling,' said Alice. 'Well, that would be lovely.'

'But only for kittens,' said Sarah. 'And puppies.'

'You could be a vet, then,' said Alice brightly.

'Auntie Izzy wanted to be a vet,' said Ben. 'Didn't you, Auntie Izzy?'

'So what happened?' asked the other mum.

'Oh, I went off it by the time I was about sixteen,' I said. 'When it dawned on me that it was a non-starter.'

'She didn't work hard enough at school,' said Ben. 'Mum said—'

Suddenly realizing that things had gone quiet, he shut up, but only for a moment. 'Well, you *did*,' he went on defensively, as Alice was giving him just-you-wait looks. 'You said that's why I've got to work really hard, if I want to be a palaeontologist.'

Alice looked so awkward, I almost felt sorry for her.

'It wasn't really Auntie Izzy's fault, Ben,' she explained. 'She just wasn't quite good enough at science. She was good at other things, though.'

Ben gave her an accusing look. 'You told me you can do anything if you try hard enough!'

164

Trust me to be the means of undoing years of careful training. 'That's perfectly true for lots of things, Ben. Especially being a palaeontologist.' Because I couldn't resist it I added, 'But try asking Mummy to sing in tune.'

David gave a hoot of laughter, for which I was profoundly grateful.

Alice wasn't. 'Oh, come on. That *is* rather different.'

'No, it's not,' I said. 'You were born tone-deaf – I was born with rubbish-at-maths-and-science genes. And I'd rather have been tone-deaf, I can tell you.'

'*Any*way,' said Sarah, adjusting her tiara, 'I fink I might have baby rabbits in my hopsicle as well. And Auntie Izzy can come and help me look after vem.'

'Thank you, darling,' I said. 'I will.'

She smiled kindly. 'You'll be really really *old* by ven, but never mind.'


When I got home late on Boxing Day, there was a message from Leo on the house phone.

'I didn't try your mobile – I knew you'd only cut me off.' Look . . .' He paused. 'I'm not going to make excuses, but I have to explain. I'll come round on the twenty-eighth. Bye.'

Oh, will you? I thought savagely. Then I shall be out.

But that was before I remembered his jacket. The one he'd spilt a cappuccino over and left behind by mistake. And I, doting mug that I was, had taken it to the cleaners and forgotten to give it back to him. If you look hard enough, there's always a crumb of comfort somewhere.


I phoned Felicity on the twenty-seventh, and I think I lied magnificently.

'Oh, Izzy, what a shame! I thought you were really keen!'

165

'I was, but he messed me about once too often. It was only ever going to be part-time, anyway. But I'm really sorry about New Year – I'll pay for the tickets.'

'Oh, don't worry – I'm sure I'll find another couple.'

Until Leo actually turned up, I knew exactly how I was going to play it. With luck, I could even persuade his ego that all he'd have got from me for Christmas was a pair of tacky musical socks. This illusion might be shattered when he found my little crumb of comfort, but as I wouldn't be there I didn't care.

On the step it was different. He didn't even wear the please-forgive-me little smile I'd almost wanted, so I could despise him for it. Suddenly the sick, empty ache in my stomach consumed me. Part of me would have taken him back whatever he'd done; the rest knew I could never trust him again.

'Well?' I said. 'Had time to dream up a nice little story? No, don't tell me. Some confused tooth fairy thinking you were still six?'

'Izzy, please . . .'

I flared up like a Roman candle. 'Don't you "please" me! You lying reptile. I suppose you're going to tell me she hypnotized you into it – forced you to shag her senseless while I was feeling like death—'

The only thing that shut me up was the click of next door's gate. It was Craig, looming out of the dark like the sneakier kind of shark. 'Evening,' he said, with a smirk that said he'd heard my outburst. 'Lovely night for romance. Just look at the stars.'

'Piss off,' said Leo, and pushed me inside.

Afraid of weakening, I let him in anyway. Whatever he was going to come up with, I had to hear it or be wondering for ever after.

Arms folded, I stood and faced him in the living-room. This chilly reception was diluted by Henry coming to greet him, but I couldn't help that.

'Can't we at least sit down?'

Unwilling to do even that, I perched on an arm.

Leo sat on the beanbag sofa, and I knew he was glad of Henry. He gave him something to focus on besides my face. 'I knew her for years, back in Shropshire. We were seeing each other for a few months, but it was over before I met you. She got a promotion and came south. I'd hardly thought of her in ages.'

That was a great comfort.

'Out of the blue I got a phone call, a couple of weeks ago,' he went on. 'She'd heard that I was in roughly the same area, and thought she'd give me a ring.'

'Just for old times' sake, of course.'

He ran a hand over the back of his neck. 'All right, it occurred to me that maybe it was more than that. She suggested meeting up for a couple of drinks.'

'And you forced yourself.'

Only then did he look up at me. 'I told her I was tied up, OK?' He paused. 'But I said maybe I could manage a couple of hours before Christmas. I could tell she was lonely,' he went on, before I could say anything. 'She didn't say as much, but I could tell. So that night you were supposed to be out with the office, I said I'd see her in the Dog and Fox.'

In Wimbledon Village. Where we'd once gone on a warm night after an evening at the tennis, watching Tim Henman go to five sets on the screen on the hill.

'I knew after half an hour I shouldn't have gone,' he went on. 'She was as down as they come and trying to pretend she wasn't. Her dad had recently died, she'd just hit her thirty-fifth birthday, and she was living in a poxy little flat in Raynes Park. We ended up eating as well, and as she'd come by cab I took her home.'

I saw it all. A bit pissed, she'd invited him in, and one thing had led to another.

'All right, I shouldn't have gone,' he went on. 'But it just happened. I felt sorry for her.'

How very noble. 'Are there any more, just out of interest? Any more poor desperate spinsters tucked away in Tooting?'

He had the grace to wince.

'Did you tell her about me?'

'No.' With crushing honesty he added, 'She wouldn't have wanted to know.'

'Why didn't you tell me you'd arranged to see her that night?'

He looked me in the eye. 'Would you have wanted to know?'

About to say, 'Yes!' I bit it back. 'Just a couple of drinks with an old flame' wasn't the kind of thing anyone wanted to hear. 'You're getting careless, Leo. For future reference perhaps you should remember to switch off your mobile during unscheduled stopovers.'

'I had!' But realizing how it sounded, he looked ashamed. 'Her neighbour's car alarm went off around five. It's always going – the only way she can get him to turn it off is by ringing him. My phone was nearest – she must have forgotten to switch it off.'

It was so nice to know. 'Then please ask her to pass my thanks to her neighbour. Otherwise, I'd still be labouring under the naive delusion that I could trust you. I take it you will be seeing her again?'

'No.' He paused and looked away. 'Not like that, anyway.'

He didn't have to spell it out. After he'd spent the night

168

with her, Laura was now going to hope the relationship might be up and running again. And he was going to have to tell her that it was a one-off because he'd felt sorry for her. He would not add that he'd been unable to resist something offered up on a plate; she'd deduce that for herself.

'Well, congratulations,' I said. 'I'm sure she's going to feel a hell of a lot less depressed afterwards. On top of the world, I'll bet.'

'I'm not proud of myself, all right?' He paused. 'I gather this is it?'

'You gather correct. I expect it's very quaint and old-fashioned, but I prefer a man I can trust.'

He rose to his feet. It was weird. He'd behaved nothing like I'd expected. He seemed tired and diminished, as if someone had taken half his stuffing out. 'I think I'd better go.'

'I think you had.' En route to the door I said, 'You know the biggest laugh? If it was going to be anybody, I thought it would be Joanne. I actually thought you might get back together with the mother of your children. Hysterical, isn't it?'

'Hysterical.'

'Oh, hang on a tick . . .' I ran upstairs for his plastic-swathed jacket. If I'd left it downstairs Henry would have given the game away. 'Don't forget this.'

He produced a very small, very wry smile. 'Thanks for not cutting the sleeves off. What do I owe you?'

In that instant, I was a heartbeat from melting. 'Nothing, Leo. Have it on me.' I opened the door.

As he gazed at me, I thought for a moment that he was going to take me in his arms after all. 'Look, if you'll just give me another chance . . .' But he didn't. He didn't even come out with one of those male-crap lines like, 'I think you always did want more than I could give.' He kissed me lightly on the cheek. 'I'm sorry,' he said. 'Be happy.'

As the door closed behind him, I burst into tears.

The following evening, Jane called. 'I just had Fliss on the phone. She was having trouble getting rid of your tickets after all, and now Paula can't make it either, her mother's ill and she's had to go to her. Then Rob said maybe he wouldn't bother after all, and Fliss started her famous organizing. Roughly, if Rob and Nick take Rob's tickets, you and I can take yours.'

The enforced jollity of New Year's Eve was all I needed. 'Look, Jane, I'm sorry, but—'

'You can't face it. I *know*, Izzy. You're miserable and you're going to make the most of it. A red-hot date with egg on toast and a couple of videos, I bet.'

'I'm just not in the mood! Anyway, don't tell me you didn't have anything planned?'

'Nothing I can't get out of. Two invites, but they're both with people from work. I won't be able to let my hair down, not in the same way.'

Well, yes. Jane loved New Year. She liked doing things like dancing a flamenco with a wilted carnation in her teeth, and falling into a swimming-pool with her clothes on.

'Oh, go on,' she urged. 'I bet you anything it'll be a really cheesy laugh. They'll play corny old stuff and nobody'll feel obliged to pretend they're too cool to like it. And it's for charity,' she added cunningly. 'We'll be morally obliged to drink vast amounts – they're probably donating half the bar profits.'

About to say, Jane, I'm really not in the mood, I stopped. Was I going to let him do this? Turn me into a miserable wreck, slumped on the sofa with *Sleepless in Seattle*? 'Oh, go on, then.'

'Brilliant. It'll perk you right up. And even if it doesn't, how about this? I've got a week's leave in February – do you fancy a little girlie jolly somewhere?'

'Tignes again?' We'd had a week's skiing last February.

'I was thinking more of sun. Proper sun, like the Caribbean.'

'Expensive.'

'We could get a cheapie off Last Minute dot com. I'm just dying for some sun, and you know what they say about vitamin C.'

'Sorry?'

'S-E-A. As in gorgeous and warm, with palm trees round the edges.'

With a glance out of my window, at winter-grey drizzle, I didn't have to think long. 'OK, I'll force myself. As long as you promise not to go on some vicious diet first and show me up.'


She took the train down on New Year's Eve. After picking her up at King's Cross, we headed south-west.

As we hit the Westway she said, 'I gave Fliss a quick call last night, and guess what? She's lost eleven pounds on vile milkshakes and vegetable soup. I said that in that case we weren't speaking to her. We were going to bitch about her all night and say her face has gone all haggard.'

'Felicity never goes on diets!'

'Well, she has now.'

'I'll give it three weeks. She'll get Mars-bar withdrawal symptoms.'

She shot me a sideways glance. 'Talking of withdrawal symptoms, if you want to slag off a certain person I shall listen sympathetically and agree with everything you say.'

I didn't need encouraging. 'I know it sounds stupid when I'd never have taken him back, but I was still shattered when he didn't even ask. It was almost as if he was secretly relieved. I was half expecting him to come out with that, "You always did deserve better" crap.'

'Probably thought you'd thump him.'

We were still on the Westway, the hideous concrete flyover leading to the M4, the golden prettiness of the Cotswolds, and thence to the M5 and the West Country. All around, beneath thick grey cloud, lay that urban mishmash of leftover Dickensian, drab sixties concrete, and nineties mirrored glass, crammed together wherever a spare square metre would bring returns to developers.

'But I know he was telling the truth,' I went on. 'He *did* feel sorry for her. I know he didn't just think, fuck it, this is the easiest bit on the side I'm ever going to get.'

'Izzy! If you dare start making excuses for him . . .'

'I'm not! I just wish he could be an unadulterated arsehole, so I could get on and hate him. And why couldn't she have been some slaggy little cow he'd picked up in a bar, so I could just get on and hate *her*?'

Until then I hadn't mentioned his jacket, or how he'd thanked me for not cutting the sleeves off. I told her now.

'You should have,' she retorted.

'Far too obvious. I unpicked a little bit of lining, instead. Stitched a few defrosted prawns into the cuffs.'

She exploded into fits. And although it was a wry and creaky effort, I found myself joining in. 'Poor Henry thought it was a terrible waste of prawns. I wonder how long it'll take him to realize where the stink's coming from?'

'A month, with any luck. Tell you what, you could join my little club. I call it The Determinedly Single Until After Valentine's Day Club, no matter what the inducement.'

'Why Valentine's Day?'
'Oh, Izzy, why d'you think?'

Later, as dusk fell on wintry fields, she got back to that Caribbean sun. 'I've been checking out Internet deals but it's still arms and legs unless you settle for two-star "unspecified" accommodation. Which is bound to mean miles from the beach and no pool. And I've been doing some pretty serious spending lately – I'm not sure I can manage arms and legs. Still, how about Morocco? Or Tunisia?'

'Even North Africa can be chilly in February.'

'Probably sunny, though. We could go camel riding and learn how to say, "Two double vodkas, my good man," in Arabic.'

With Jane, even Bognor in November would be a laugh. 'Jane, I'll go anywhere you like.'

Then I told her about Moving On, which at least took my mind off Leo for five minutes. But the closer we got to Devon, the more I thought I should have stuck with *Sleepless in Seattle* after all. Watching a hundred couples kissing each other at midnight, dancing to the smoochy songs, was hardly ideal therapy. Having made my New Year bed, however, I'd lie on it with a smile. According to Dr Jane, tarting myself up to the nines and dancing my feet off was the only prescription. 'And lots of outrageous flirtation, of course,' she said. 'You can't beat a bit of flirt-therapy. Even if it's only with the waiters.'

Felicity's face had got slightly thinner, but that wasn't what made our jaws drop.

'God help me,' said Jane. 'First Rob, now you – I'm not sure I can take much more of this.'

I was almost speechless. 'You look fantastic.' Her hair,

173

straight and shoulder-length for almost as long as I'd known her, had been attacked by a magician. Cropped, layered and highlighted, it had transformed her.

'Well, it was about time.' She led us into the sitting-room of a house that had once been two farm cottages. It had belonged to Ian's parents, who'd died within eighteen months of each other not long before Felicity and Ian had got together. Over the years, Felicity had partly revamped it, replacing chintz with warm, earthy tones and naturals.

'You're going to be lumbered with Jack's room,' she said, as Shep and Henry woofed with excitement. 'His Pip's come for New Year, so they've got the spare double, and the bed in the little room's so old it's collapsed. So it's Jack's creaky bunk-beds, I'm afraid.'

Jane and I looked at each other. 'Well, *really*,' said Jane. 'I don't know about you, but I was expecting at least a personal suite with Jacuzzi.'

Later, as we sat over cups of tea (pacing ourselves), Felicity produced a photo. 'That's what sparked me into making my New Year's resolutions a month early.'

It was a group shot, taken by Village Players Jim just after the murder was wrapped up. I'll admit it didn't flatter her. A belted lavender sack, with institution hair.

'But Fliss, you *meant* to look like that,' said Jane.

'Yes, but I didn't have to try very hard, did I? Saggy-bosoms Betsy, the big fat blob. And look at you two.'

Jane's sequined top glittered in the flash, and they'd made me put my tart outfit back on for that shot. I stood with my stomach sucked in and that cheesy, please-hurry-up grin. Between me and Sasha stood Nick, with a non-Max smile and an arm around each of our shoulders.

'I'm surprised Nick hasn't cried off tonight,' said Felicity. 'Rob gave fair warning that he might have to partner Jane for that terrifying tango she's liable to do when she's pissed.'

Jane made a mock-hurt face. 'I always thought it was rather good, myself.'

'But he said no problem, he'll remember to wear his surgical truss. Oh, and he said he'd save one particular dance for Izzy. "No prizes for guessing." '

My face was probably as blank as my brain. 'Maybe I'm thick, but I can't.'

'Well, don't look at me,' she said. 'That's all he said, "no prizes for guessing." I thought maybe you two had some private joke.'

'Well, we didn't!'

Jane tucked her feet up on a terracotta sofa. 'You never know, maybe there's some jolly Kicked-in-the-Balls polka we've never heard of.'

I'd only told her about this on the way down, but it was news to Felicity, who gaped at me. 'What?'

I'd expected it to be common knowledge by now. Nick would have told Rob, who'd have told Felicity . . . So I had to explain it again, and Felicity was predictably hurt because I hadn't told her before.

'Still, this dance business is all very intriguing,' she said eventually.

'Intriguing?' Jane echoed. 'It's bloody infuriating. We must suss it out before we go. We can't have him thinking we're too dense to work it out.'

'Oh, and he did say he hoped you'd be appropriately dressed,' said Felicity.

'In what?' I gaped.

'To be honest, Izzy, I didn't quite like to ask.'

# Chapter 11

Jack's room was decorated with pictures of racing dinghies and Page Three girls. One of these had been taped to a dartboard, where judging from the little holes all over her 38DDs, her nipples had provided double bull's-eyes.

'I can't get over Felicity,' said Jane, once the rustic latched door was shut behind us. 'Who's going to be next for a makeover, I wonder? And fancy not asking what Nick meant by "appropriately dressed".'

'Jane, it'll be some stupid joke.'

While we got ready, Henry checked out the bottom bunk for fit and comfort. 'How about The Dance of the Seven Veils?' Jane asked. 'Did you tell him about your belly-dancing class?'

I was easing on the kind of filmy tights you've only got to look at to ladder. 'No! In any case, I only ever went four times. No one else had a belly.'

'Think, then. It's really bugging me.'

It was beginning to bug me that she was going on about it. The thought of Nick was making me vaguely uncomfortable. I could still see his face over that pool table, the eyes that said, 'He'll be happy now.' I imagined myself saying casually, 'Oh, yes, we split up just before Christmas,' and receiving another dose of that unnerving perception. 'I see. *Can't say I'm surprised.*'

Still, more immediate matters were on my mind. My

dress had been an impulse buy, and I still couldn't decide whether a) I absolutely loved it, or b) I should have taken it straight back. It was sleek and slinky, but the top was asymmetrical, with a strap over only one shoulder. This meant a strapless bra and they never do quite such an uplifting job. 'Never mind Betsy – just look at saggy-tits Izzy,' I said.

'Oh, rubbish. They're just discreetly voluptuous.'

'They'd have looked less discreetly bloody voluptuous in black.'

'Everybody'll be in black – it's so boring. That colour really suits you. And I love your hair like that.'

The dress was dark emerald, and I'd put my hair up. That is, I'd twisted it into a knot that was supposed to look as if the wispy bits already drifting loose were artfully contrived. Any riotous cavortings would probably have the whole lot falling apart, but then letting my hair down was the general idea.

Jane wore a slinky scarlet dress that went brilliantly with blonde and the sparkle in her eyes. She was determined to have a wild time, and when Jane was firing on all party-animal cylinders it was infectious. Already I was beginning to feel as if the past week was elsewhere: shoved in a cupboard where I couldn't see it for now. 'I call it very cruel of you to force me down here to enjoy myself,' I told her, as we added the final touches. 'I'd much rather have been miserable at home on my own.'

'I know. I'm nasty like that.'

I misted my hair with Kenzo Flower, she sprayed Romance up her skirt. 'The night is young,' she grinned. 'And you never know your luck.'

As Ian had been out earlier we didn't see him till we were

about to leave. 'I feel like a stuffed turkey in this thing,' he grumbled, adjusting his collar.

Felicity raised her eyes to the ceiling. 'Penguin suits, turkeys – can't you at least make up your mind which species of whingey bird you are?'

Ian put on his hurt-spaniel look. 'It's all right for you! You don't have to truss yourself up in bow-ties.'

'Take it off, then!' she retorted. 'Put your old cords on and bugger off to the Coach and Horses!' To Jane and me she went on, 'We practically *live* at the bloody Coach and Horses – wouldn't you think that just once, he could get dressed up without moaning? It's for charity, for heaven's sake!'

Ian put on a face suspiciously like that of a small boy turning mutinous. 'Right, I'm shutting up. I'm not saying another word until next year.'

All this was so unlike them, Jane and I exchanged taken-aback looks. 'Come on, you two,' I soothed. 'You both look gorgeous.' Felicity wore a black dress, cut like nothing I'd ever seen her in before, or maybe the 'new' hair just made it look like that. She'd taken a lot more trouble than usual with her make-up, too. Even her eyes looked two sizes bigger. 'You're making *me* feel like Betsy Blob,' I added.

'As for him . . .' Jane gave Ian the once-over. Like most nice-looking men when forced into a dinner jacket, he looked like a different animal. 'Remind me not to have any smoochy dances with you, Ian. I might forget myself and give you a little grope.'

'I'll try not to scream,' he grinned. 'I shall stiffen my upper lip and take it like a man.'

Looking twitchy, Felicity was checking her watch. 'For heaven's sake, where's that cab?'

It arrived half a minute later, to whisk us off to the

Tawton House Hotel. About three miles away, it was plonked in the middle of what would be beautiful rural views in daylight. The kind of place you'd find in the three-star section of Weekend Breaks brochures, it was a pretty, white-painted country house dating from the seventeen-hundreds. Inside there was a lot of old oak, thick new carpet and the quieter type of chintz.

We headed for the Wisteria Room, which wasn't quite grand enough for a ballroom but probably hosted lots of wedding receptions. Felicity and Ian instantly collided with two couples they knew and once we'd done the polite-chat bit, Jane and I moved discreetly aside.

'What's got into her?' Jane asked, *sotto voce*. 'I've hardly ever seen her like that. Certainly not with Ian.'

'Maybe it's just low blood sugar.' Sipping a champagne cocktail (one included with the ticket) I was thinking they'd been pleasantly heavy-handed with the brandy. 'Still, she's stopped twitching for now.'

About ten feet away, Felicity seemed even more ani-mated than usual. Already there was a cacophony of talk all around us; the room was filling fast. At one end was a buffet table, and round, white-clothed tables lined the sides. To every dining chair, upholstered in blue velvet, was fastened a blue helium balloon saying 'Happy New Year'. In a side room just behind us, a five-deep crush was fighting its way to the bar.

Like me, Jane was sizing up the guests. 'Not quite as muddy-welly-ish as I thought,' she said. 'I hope they're not all going to be as well-behaved as they look.'

I don't know what on earth she was expecting. They could have been from anywhere, except perhaps the type of London club where they only let you in if you've been featured in *Hello!* Ages ranged from teens to sixties, but the vast majority were probably in their twenties and thirties, which didn't surprise me in an area where cool alternative venues were not exactly ten a penny.

'I was hoping for some disgustingly bucolic lack of decorum,' she went on.

'Some really pagan debauchery might be fun,' I agreed. 'Anything particular in mind?'

The voice came from behind us. And because I connected it with a wolf in Max clothing it was a bit of a shock to see it coming from a dinner jacket. 'Oh, nothing special,' I said. 'An excuse-me orgy, human sacrifice of the worst male dancer – that sort of thing.'

He shook his head. 'Izzy, you're not very clued-up on human sacrifice. The general idea was to appease the gods of whatever with the best. Not the worst.'

'That'd be a sinful waste when most men are so rubbish at dancing.'

'Well, that told you,' grinned Jane. 'Nice to see you, Nick.'

'You, too.' He kissed her cheek, followed by mine. 'How's it going, Izzy?'

'Brilliant. How were those roasted grasshoppers?'

'Not bad with Yorkshire pudding. It was the poisonous toads that stuck in my gullet.'

As Jane was looking blank, I had to explain. 'Those horrible relatives Sasha's mum had for Sunday lunch, remember?'

'Oh.' Her face cleared. 'I thought maybe you two had some private joke, after all.'

Nick raised an eyebrow. 'After all what?'

It was too late to give Jane a shut-up nudge. Now she'd make him think we'd been indulging in girlie speculation about what that 'particular' dance could be. God forbid, he might even think I'd been mildly fluttered at the mere thought. Still, he was a vast improvement on Max: living

180

reinforcement of my theory that a dinner jacket gives a man a distinctly unfair advantage. His dress shirt was snowy crisp and the tie looked like a proper one, not one of those elasticized jobs.

'That particular dance you were saving for Izzy,' Jane explained. 'Felicity was thinking it was some kind of private joke, but Izzy said she wasn't in the habit of making private jokes with men who strangled her when she wasn't expecting it.'

'I should hope not.' He nodded over my shoulder. 'Izzy, you're blocking the stampede from the water-hole.' With a light hand on my waist, he moved me a little to the right as a horde came through bearing drinks. 'I wouldn't want you trampled to death. Once as a corpse was more than enough.'

Given his unfair advantage, I'd almost enjoyed that little touch until he said that. 'Thanks, Nick. How very gallant.'

'Don't mention it.' He looked down at my nearly empty glass, and thence to Jane's. 'Can I get you a refill?'

'You bet,' said Jane. 'After you've enlightened us about this particular dance.'

'Jane, it was just a crack. Forget it.' He looked at me. 'And I can guarantee they won't be playing our tune.'

It was all very well to say, 'Forget it,' when he'd just baited an infuriating hook like that. 'And I'm afraid you're not dressed for the occasion,' he added.

Jane rose beautifully. Or to put it another way, she was lapping it up. 'Nick, how would you like the pair of us to thump it out of you?'

She said it in an almost Sasha-type manner, as if some rough-and-tumble with a man who could probably manage both of us with one hand tied behind his back would spice up her evening considerably. When she'd made up her mind to have a bloody good laugh, Jane could occasionally be a liability.

The idea seemed to amuse him, anyway. 'I'm not sure I should answer that – you'd probably thump me in any case.'

Cut the crap, I thought. 'All right, so what *was* I supposed to be wearing?'

'Black.' He looked me right in the eye. 'But it wouldn't suit you. Far too macabre with your dancing shoes.'

With a clue like that on a plate, my brain went 'ping'. 'Not the *"Danse Macabre"*?'

He had the grace to look slightly apologetic. 'I did say it was only a crack.'

No wonder they wouldn't be playing our tune.

Jane was looking blank. 'I don't know it.'

'Yes, you do.' Going down the scale, I sang a few spooky, minor-key bars. 'De *dah*, de *dah,* de *dah,* de *dah* . . .'

'That's the theme tune from *Jonathan Creek*!'

'Also known as "The Dance of Death",' I said.

'Nick!' Under a show of outrage, she was laughing. 'And there was me thinking it might be "The Last Waltz", after the way you finished her off.' Her eyes shifted to somewhere over his shoulder. 'Rob!'

'Hello, my lovely scarlet woman.' Bearing two beers, Rob gave her the best kiss he could manage. 'Christ, it's like a bun fight in there.' Passing a beer to Nick, he then kissed me. 'Izzy, you're looking gorgeous, too.'

'So are you.' I hadn't seen him in a dinner jacket for years, and then it was a borrowed one with trousers that were too short. 'I hope Paula's considered the dangers of letting you loose like that.'

'We'll take it in turns to chaperone you,' said Jane. 'Izzy and I can ward off predatory nymphos with a mere glance.

182

Rob, did you know Nick was planning on doing "The Dance of Death" with Izzy? We're seriously upset with him.'

Rob winked at me. 'Nick can be a nasty bastard. I should tread on his toes, if I were you.'

We were interrupted by a brisk woman in a blue dress, bearing a bucket of money. 'Hands in pockets, please!' she said. 'Raffle tickets, for the hospice. A pound each, or eleven for a tenner.'

After stumping up at least a tenner each, we stuffed tickets into bags and pockets. 'That woman,' said Nick, as she departed, 'should run for Prime Minister.'

'Twenty quid!' said Jane, looking at him. 'Were you feeling lucky?'

'Just shortening the odds.'

'And she never even told us what the prizes were!'

As far as I was concerned it was immaterial. I never even managed to win that cheap bottle of wine they invariably drew last.

Fifteen minutes later, armed with another champagne cocktail courtesy of Nick, I found myself talking to a friend of Felicity's; a girl called Chloe with glossy dark hair. The place was buzzing by then, seething with black ties and posh frocks. As Jane had predicted, masses were black, so that the odd electric blue or silver really stood out. Chat and laughter were growing in decibels by the minute, with a background of the kind of music you only notice when it stops.

'Isn't Felicity looking great?' enthused Chloe. 'Almost like a different person.'

Acting like one, too. Not far away, she was talking to some penguin suit in a way I hadn't seen in years. To be blunt, she was flirting. It was subtle, but written all over her body language. Ian was nowhere to be seen, which didn't surprise me. Given their earlier spat, he was probably propping up the bar with a pint of Old Peculier.

What had got into those two?

Then I saw something that really made my heart miss a beat. My breath caught in my throat – and the man turned around. My God, I thought, did you have to do that to me? From the back he'd looked exactly like Leo. For a crazy moment I'd actually thought it was him. Why did you only ever see people like that when wounds were still bleeding?

Nick chose that moment to appear at my right shoulder. 'Did Felicity get a fairy godmother for Christmas?' he murmured. 'She's looking incredible. Quite a change of image.'

'Not quite so much of the fussing old hen, you mean. The one who needs something to mother.'

I hadn't meant to say it, but it was too late. For an instant he looked blank, before his eyes closed in an 'oh, shit' fashion.

'Sorry, but I couldn't help overhearing,' I added.

He looked down at me with an expression I had to concede was genuine. 'If it's any use saying it now, I'm sorry. It was out of order.'

By now I was wishing I'd kept my mouth shut. 'Forget it. I shouldn't have said anything.'

'You didn't tell her?'

That almost made me do my Roman candle bit. 'Of course not! What on earth do you think I am?'

'Sorry.' His eyebrows gave an apologetic little lift. 'But thanks. I'd have felt like seven kinds of shit.'

'I should hope so.' On the other hand, I knew how I'd feel if a supposedly private remark were thrown back at me. Who but pain-in-the-bum saints only say things that bear repeating worldwide? Moving a little apart from the others, I lowered my voice. 'Look, I know how she can come across, but Rob's like family to her. In case you didn't know, her own family might as well be orbiting Mars. Her mother could never be bothered with her, and her father's round the twist.'

'I didn't know. At least, Rob did say something, but I didn't realize it was that bad.'

He did now, so maybe I'd achieved something tonight. Not quite what Jane had in mind, I thought, hearing her laugh through the increasingly noisy hum. A few yards away she was talking to about six foot four of unfair advantage. Golden-blond and hunky, I could see he was spicing up Jane's evening very nicely.

As I turned back to Nick, his eyebrows gave another apologetic little lift. 'I knew I'd hacked you off. It wasn't just Henry and the sausages, then?'

'They were just the undercoats. The other put the gloss on it.' But I said it as if it was a joke, and he smiled.

'I should have stayed at home that night,' he said. 'I wasn't at my milk-of-human-kindness best. In fact, I felt like kicking something. I only went because I was famished and there was sod all in the fridge.'

Funny how it had never occurred to me that maybe he'd just had a bad day. 'Why did you want to kick something, or shouldn't I ask?'

He hesitated, if only because some girl in a gold dress was brushing past, shrieking, 'Jilly! Where's Tad got to?'

Once she'd moved on he said, 'Did you know Rob and I were hoping to take over the practice?'

'Felicity mentioned something. Only the old man's ill and his son's calling the shots. Has he decided not to sell after all?'

'God, no. He's desperate for money – lost a stack in

some dot-com thing. He just doesn't want to sell to us. He's going for the big boys. A chain.'

'A chain?' I couldn't believe this. 'A chain of *vets*?'

He seemed almost amused. 'It's business, Izzy. Units of potential profit coming through the door.'

The cynical note didn't escape me.

'The old man had an offer before, but he told them to shove it,' he went on. 'But that night of sod all in the fridge, Markham junior told me the deal was un-shoved. Back on the table, and looking very good from his bank manager's point of view.'

'So he's just going over your heads?'

'That was the gist. "So up yours."' But he smiled. 'Sorry, it's very tedious. Can I get you another drink?'

'I think I'd better eat first.' As I said, the champagne cocktails were heavily laced with brandy and I'd nearly finished my second. Through the crowd I saw Felicity again, still acting more like Jane on the pull than herself. Trying to sound casual, I nodded towards her. 'Who's that man Felicity's talking to?'

'Luke Archer. I think she used to work for him when she first moved down.'

Around forty, Luke Archer was tall, dark, and undeniably good-looking in a heavy sort of way. He also possessed that air of overt sexual arrogance you could spot at twenty paces, that a lot of women find magnetic.

I drained the last of my cocktail. 'I don't think I like the look of him.'

'Irrational prejudice,' he said, looking down at me with amused eyes. 'You've never even met him.'

'Oh, I don't let little things like that bother me. I can take irrational dislikes to people I've never met with no trouble at all.'

But I said it lightly, and his mouth flickered. 'I'm pretty

good at taking irrational dislikes to people I *have* met,' I added. 'But I do sometimes feel a bit bad afterwards, when I find out they'd had very bad days and should have stayed at home kicking something. Though not the cat, I hope.'

'Christ, no. That really would be nockshus.'

He was trying not to laugh as he said this, which brought home to me two inescapable facts. One, when men are trying not to laugh it goes into their eyes. Two, this kind of behaviour can compound the dinner-jacket effect alarmingly.

But I laughed, and he laughed back, which compounded it even further. In fact, I was almost beginning to understand a certain person's behaviour. 'I don't see Sasha,' I said, looking around.

'That's because she's not here.'

Why had I assumed she would be? 'Manning the bar at the Coach and Horses?'

'No, she's in Scotland. And at this moment, probably all dressed up in the Officers' Mess, being introduced to Andy's Squadron Leader.'

So much for Ian's 'Dead by Christmas' theory, then. 'Of course, she'd want to be there for Hogmanay. But it's a hell of a hike from here. Where did she meet him?'

'In an Edinburgh club, last summer. She was doing the Festival.'

For a student of theatre studies, that figured.

A peal of laughter took my attention back to Felicity, who was still talking to Luke Archer. 'I don't care if it is irrational, I still don't like the look of him,' I murmured.

He lowered his voice. 'To tell the truth, I don't much care for him myself.'

Hmm. 'What does he do?'

'Fingers in several local pies, and owns a few of them. Not so long ago he bought up a load of land from a farmer who'd gone to the wall. Every spring he puts down ten thousand pheasant chicks, feeds them up till they're almost too fat to get airborne, and flies in rich Arabs to shoot them. It's a nice little earner.'

'I bet it is.' Taking my eyes off Felicity, I changed the subject. 'Did you see Alex over Christmas?'

'Yes, on the twenty-seventh. I took him to see *Harry Potter* for the second time and tried to persuade him to let me take the stabilizers off his bike.'

'And did you succeed?'

'No chance. Mummy had said to tell me *on no account* to take the little wheels off. Mummy's just a tad overprotective,' he added.

There was enough 'dry' in his tone to hint of hostilities, but I certainly wasn't going to ask nosy questions. Like, 'Whose fault was it that you split up? Do you get on with/despise/still love her?' I'm just not the nosy type, and naturally I wasn't remotely interested. 'How did you like *Harry Potter*?' I asked.

'Better than I expected to.' Then he changed the subject. 'Good Christmas?'

*Bright smile here, please.* 'Brilliant, thanks.'

'Friends or folks?'

'My sister's. She's got two kids, so I can stop pretending I don't believe in Father Christmas. We left out one carrot each for the reindeer, a malt whisky and two mince pies. And do you know, they were all gone in the morning? How about you?' I added, as he laughed.

'Friends,' he said. 'By the coast in Dorset. On Christmas Day we tramped two miles through fields of sheep shit, took one look at the sea off Dancing Ledge, and promptly repaired to a nice warm pub.'

I laughed. 'I hope you wiped your feet.' Feeling slightly

nosy I added, 'No family sulking that you were shunning them, then?'

'Doubtful. I have one brother who loathes Christmas and takes off every year somewhere hot. Then I have two sisters with five kids between them, who were inundated with parents, in-laws and those hangers-on who wouldn't have anywhere else to go. So I don't think anyone missed me.' He paused. 'Oh, Christ . . .'

This last was a mutter I wasn't supposed to hear. His eyes were fixed somewhere in the distance and for a moment his expression might have belonged to a man who's just realized he's about to be boiled alive by cannibals.

'What's the matter?' I asked.

He'd already snapped out of it. 'Nothing.'

'You could have fooled me. You looked as if you'd just realized you'd left the gas on and a naked flame.'

'No, just a vision of doom. On second thoughts, Izzy . . .' His eyes shot to whatever it was again. 'Could you do me a little favour? Be "with" me for a couple of minutes?'

'Sorry?'

I caught his drift too late. A woman in a silver tube of a dress, with hair like a brown silk cap, was bearing down on him. Tall and attractive, she nevertheless wore the kind of smile that makes you think of particularly determined steel. '*Nick*.' Saying it in that peculiarly proprietary way, she kissed him on both cheeks. 'I wasn't expecting to see you here.'

'It was a last-minute thing. How are you, Tamara?'

I had to hand it to him. He greeted her with every appearance of pleasure, as if doom was now inevitable and he'd resolved to die like an Englishman.

'Wonderful.' Linking her arm in his, in that supposedly

casual way, she looked me up and down. 'And who's this?' she asked, in a brisk and pleasant enough manner.

Slim but strongly built, she exuded 'no shit' and that arm had a definitely claim-staking air, in case anyone else was getting ideas. It tickled me, but I wasn't impressed with Nick's tactics. If he'd wanted me to be 'with' him, why hadn't he slipped a proprietary arm around me while he still had time?

But I smiled nicely and shook hands. 'Izzy's a friend of Felicity's, from London,' he added. 'Tamara and her mother run the local riding stables.'

A bell rang in my head. If this was the 'What's-her-name' Felicity had mentioned, and Nick had 'seen her a couple of times', presumably on purpose, on his own head be it.

'Do you ride?' Tamara asked, in an incisive voice that had little of the West Country about it.

Since I'd come to this do for a laugh, there was no time like the present. 'Ooh, no,' I said, with a little shudder. 'I'm absolutely *terr*ified of horses.'

'How sad,' she said, with a satisfied expression, as if she'd ascertained that I might as well be limp lettuce, unfit even to wash the socks of any man she had her eye on.

This seemed a good time to leave Nick to be boiled alive. 'Excuse me,' I said, in the best limp-lettuce voice I could do at short notice. 'Must just pop off for a tinkle.' Just to keep the cannibal guessing, though, I pecked Nick's cheek. 'See you later, Nicky. Don't forget our little dance, will you?'

Waiting to see their faces would have spoilt it. However, I heard her incredulous '*Nicky*?', which gave me a laugh until I found Jane.

She was still in a group that included Golden Boy. Called Rufus, he was even hunkier close up, so it took a few minutes to ease her away.

'Did you see Felicity earlier?' I whispered. 'She was positively flirting with some bloke who looks like an oversexed gorilla, and Ian's disappeared. I'm getting seriously worried about those two.'

'Smells like some festering row to me.' She peered in the direction of the oversexed gorilla. 'Still, she's not flirting with him now.'

'Maybe she's in the loo. Come on.'

We found Felicity repairing her lipstick. Her face was slightly flushed, but in a purely attractive way.

'Oh, there you are,' said the devious Jane. 'I was going to ask you to introduce me to that bloke you were nattering to. He looks like the rampant-testosterone type I have primitive yearnings for.'

'Lots of people have primitive yearnings for Luke.' Having done her lipstick, she flicked a mini-brush at her hair. 'I worked for him for a couple of months when I first came down. Of course, he was still married then.' She put her brush back in her bag. 'Has anyone seen Ian?'

'Probably in the bar,' I said.

'Might have known. I don't know why I didn't just let him go to the Coach and Horses.' Licking a fingertip, she ran it over newly plucked eyebrows.

Since at least three other women were in there I had to lower my voice to almost nothing. 'Felicity, what's up with you two?'

'Nothing! It's just that he can be so unbelievably, well . . .'

'Well, what?' I demanded.

'Boring! OK?' She picked up her bag. 'Still, if he's in the bar at least he can get us another drink. Shall I see you there?'

# Chapter 12

Before we joined her, Jane and I found an ear-free corner in the main foyer.

'For heaven's sake, did you hear her?' Jane lit one of her last cigarettes before midnight and exhaled sharply. ' "Of course, he was still married then . . ." She's got six-year itch, or I'm a banana.'

'I'd never have thought she was getting bored with Ian. They always seemed so, well . . .'

'Like an old married couple, Izzy. You've said it yourself. We've all said it.'

I was looking at the Christmas tree in the corner. A red bauble had fallen off and a child in a velvet party dress was trying to put it back. 'But surely she can't fancy that Luke? He's got the look of one of those men who head straight for the red-light district on business trips.'

'And his hair's too black to be true.'

'Just For Men, I bet.'

'Yes, but if you fancy that sort of thing at least he'd be exciting.'

'She'll catch something. And Ian's going to be devastated.'

'If they don't split up first. Still, there's not much we can do about it for now.' She put her cigarette out, barely smoked. 'So don't you dare let it wreck your evening. How

A Girl's Best Friend

did you like Rufus?' she added wickedly. 'He's actually come with his *sister*, can you believe? Ideal therapy.'

'You have him. Maybe I'll target Red-light Luke and divert him from Felicity.'

'God, Izzy, he'll never do. The first requirement of flirt therapy is that the bugger at least doesn't make you want to puke.'

When we finally made it to the bar, Ian wasn't crying into his ale. He'd been waylaid by some rather older Ted he did business with.

'I don't know what you've done to her, but she's looking gorgeous,' said Ted, looking at Felicity.

'She always looks gorgeous to me,' said poor old Ian.

Back in the Wisteria Room ten minutes later, I was half listening to a conversation when someone materialized at my right shoulder. 'Oh, hi, Nicky,' I said, not quite deadpan. 'You're still alive, then?'

'Snake,' he murmured, just over the top of my hair. 'I'll deal with you later.'

Well, blow me. I hadn't expected any therapy from this quarter, but if I wasn't mistaken there were flirty little undertones here. 'I thought she was *per*fectly nice,' I said, trying not to laugh.

He whispered into my right ear. 'She terrifies me.'

'Nick, you wimp. I thought you were a big boy.'

'I'm disappointed in you, Izzy.' With a hand on my elbow, he drew me a little aside. 'Grieved and disappointed,' he added, in a tone that might have fooled anyone who couldn't see his face. 'One miserable little favour and you let me down. Next time you come to me with zip trouble, I'll just let you wet yourself.'

Definite undertones. Still, at least he fulfilled the non-puking requirement. 'It was your own fault,' I said sweetly.

193

'If you'd wanted me to be "with" you, you should have done something about it before she pounced. Grabbed me and dribbled with uncontained lust or something.'

'Are you kidding? I've been having flashbacks to a certain terrifying little redhead on a beach. Dribbling lust might have been pushing my luck.'

'Oh, I'm used to a bit of dribbling,' I said, as if reassuring relatives of one of the more far-gone inmates of Mrs Denny's home. 'You should see Henry when he gets a whiff of tuna. And talking of food, it looks as if we're going to get fed at last.' Around us, people were moving towards tables.

We ended up at a round table for eight. With us were Chloe and her husband, who was called Simon and struck me as pompous. Still, the food was more promising. The buffet included everything from roast loin of pork to poached salmon.

I found myself between Rob and Simon. One of those people who've never learnt that conversation consists of listening as well as talking, Simon quickly told me he was an architect, a profession I'd always associated with Lively and Interesting. As he told me all about some civic complex he was engaged on, I did my best not to think that if he was anything to go by, it would have all the artistic pizazz of a row of Portaloos.

In any case, half my mind was on Felicity. Although it didn't hit you in the face, she was behaving differently. It was as if she'd made up her mind that every man present was going to see her as an object of desire, not just good old bouncy Felicity. I knew Ian had noticed. He was overcompensating with a lot of banter that sounded very slightly forced.

Chloe was talking about some friend who'd just got

engaged. '. . . and she said, well, if *that's* what it's going to cost to do it properly, she's going to slink off to the Seychelles and get hitched on the beach.'

Jane made a face of mock pain. '*Please* don't mention the Seychelles. Izzy and I are supposed to be off somewhere hot and tropical soon, on a little Club Val jolly, but my credit cards are looking a bit sick at the moment.'

'Club *Val*?' said Chloe. 'Is that like Club Med?'

'No, it's much more exclusive,' said Jane, who already looked as if she was on a half-pissed high. 'The Determinedly Solo Till After Valentine's Day Club. President and founder member, yours truly.'

'Oh, are you the one who just dumped her boyfriend?' Chloe asked.

'No, that was Izzy,' said Jane. With dance actions, she started singing in her seat about something biting the dust.

Beside her, Nick looked lazily tickled. 'Why Valentine's Day?'

Jane paused in her Freddie Mercury impression. 'It's a let-down limitation exercise. Don't you know the old saying: Blessed is she who expects nothing, because it's a bloody sight better than that wilted red rose he picked up at the last minute?'

'Oh, Christ,' said Ian. 'If this is turning into a Why We Hate Blokes session, I'm not here.'

A tiny Mexican wave of awareness ran round the table; the kind you only get when everybody's been pretending they haven't noticed simmering tension. 'Actually, I had a brilliant Valentine's Day last year,' I said quickly. 'Out of the blue I got a packet of Extremely Chocolatey Orange Mini-bites, and a whacking great card promising undying love and devotion.'

'Who from?' asked Jane, who knew perfectly well, but also knew I was trying to lighten things up.

'Guess,' I said. 'He's not very hot on writing, so I think he had some help with the biro, but he managed to sign it. I was quite overcome.'

Portaloo Simon, who'd been carefully picking every bit of mushroom out of whatever he was eating, gave me a look as if I were slightly deranged. 'Sorry, but are you saying you were overcome at getting a Valentine's card from someone functionally illiterate?'

'Well, yes. But when someone loves you that much, what's a little literacy?'

'A very great deal, I should have thought.'

Trying not to laugh, I caught Nick's eye and saw that he was having the same trouble. 'Did he sign it with a paw print?'

'However did you guess?'

'I'm telepathic.'

'It was Henry,' said Felicity to Simon. 'Izzy's dog, bless his furry little heart. Who held the biro in his paw?'

'The jokers I work with.'

'They would,' said Jane. 'They did a poster for her on a similar theme.'

'And what's that?' asked Nick.

I answered. 'Dogs are better than men, *because* . . .'

His mouth flickered. 'I don't think I'll ask why.'

'Better not,' I agreed. 'Most of it's not fit for polite company.'

'Like, dogs do not fart and blame it on the man,' said Jane blithely.

'At least no one can accuse me of that,' said Ian. 'Felicity can always tell, anyway. Shep's have a very distinctive bouquet.'

Felicity laughed, just a little too brightly. 'How about this one, Izzy? "Unlike men, it's perfectly socially acceptable for a woman to have two dogs at once." Or half a dozen, come to that.'

Shooting me a glance, Jane diverted this hint of gorillas to safer waters. 'Funny you should say that. When Izzy was at the height of her dogs-are-better-than-men stage, she was talking about having seven of them.'

I'd almost forgotten this. It had been a daft joke between us.

Chloe gave a little laugh. 'And plenty of air freshener, I hope.'

'It was just a thought,' I explained. 'A retirement option, if you like. I fancied myself as one of those alternative versions of a crazy old bag lady, pushing seven dogs in a pram.'

Rob started laughing, and so did Nick. 'I can't quite see it.'

'Oh, I can,' I said. 'Vintage Oxfam coat, string for a belt, ankle socks and lovely hairy legs . . .'

'Yes, and that's another thing.' Felicity shot another glance at Ian. 'Dogs do not say, "My God, Eff, you've got a lovely crop of bristles there." '

Ian sat back with an 'I give up' sigh. 'I didn't *mind*, all right? I was just passing comment.'

That was when I saw Felicity looking guilty, aware that she was creating an atmosphere. For a moment, as she glanced at Ian, I saw a stricken expression, as if she knew she was hurting him but somehow couldn't help it. At the same time, there was a gale of laughter from the next table.

Under cover of this, Rob murmured, 'Maybe we should get off dogs. Ian's already in the doghouse, by the looks of it.' To Jane he added, 'So are you and Izzy not off on your Club Val jolly, after all?'

'Oh, we are,' she said. 'But not on a hot-and-tropical. I don't think my Visa statements will stand it.' With a glance over her shoulder at the buffet, she added, 'Anyone coming for puddings? I need a major guts along, so I won't look like a pig. Come on, Rob – you'll do.'

'I'm not supposed to be gutsing,' he said, but got up anyway.

'Talking of hot and tropical,' said Chloe, as they went, 'it can be a very mixed blessing.' She started talking about getting bitten to death by sand flies on a recent holiday, and crunching massive cockroaches underfoot. Just as she was starting on the dire results of Simon eating something dodgy at the Local Flavour Barbecue Night, Rob and Jane came back, and I slipped off.

Since most of the pigs had fed by then, I was dithering almost solo over the goodies when Nick appeared. 'Couldn't let you come all alone,' he said. 'Far too dangerous for a woman in green. Luke Archer might mistake you for a lime jelly.'

I stifled a giggle. 'Nick, I'm touched.'

'Plus I had to escape the holiday from hell. Chloe just moved on to her bad case of heat rash. What's that you're having?'

'Lemon tart, but I'm thinking about some profiteroles as well.'

'Gross overindulgence,' he tutted, as I added two to my plate. 'But I'll let it pass if you'll promise to send me a signed photo of crazy Izzy, the dog lady.'

'No problem. I shall probably turn into a local *cause célèbre* and get my picture in the papers. And now who's overindulging?' I added, as he put five profiteroles on his plate.

'As you said, I'm a big boy. How are you going to get your picture in the papers?' he added, taking a grape from an arrangement of fruit and flowers that was supposed to be purely decorative.

'I'm planning on being a public nuisance.' The therapy was working. I almost felt properly flirty, right down to getting a tiny buzz from his sleeve brushing my bare right arm. 'And stop pinching those grapes,' I added, as he put another in his mouth. 'They're just supposed to look pretty.'

'Are they really? What a quaint idea.' He took a couple more. 'Exactly how are you planning to be a public nuisance, then?'

'Oh, you know.' I added a spoonful of raspberry meringue to my plate, but not so much that it was laden and I couldn't dither any longer. 'A house full of dog, general squalor . . . I thought it might be fun to have a running battle with the council. I shall barricade myself in and hurl missiles at the man from the Sanitary Department. Do you think that fruit salad looks nice?'

'It looks bloody awful. Too many melon balls.' He took one of those fat black grapes off his plate. 'Have some forbidden fruit, instead.'

I knew exactly what was coming next. It was straight out of a book I'd once idly thought of writing. Entitled *A Girl's Guide to Flirtation Techniques*, it had a section that went, 'NB. Do not open mouth so wide that he can pop whatever it is in without brushing your lips. This is the whole point of a subtle little exercise that should give you a piquant buzz.'

'No, thanks,' I said. Sleeves were one thing; erogenous zones were quite another.

'What missiles?' he said.

I'd almost forgotten what I was on about. 'Erm, I really hadn't thought. Cans of Ambrosia Devon Custard?'

He laughed, and a woman in a blue dress said brightly, 'Excuse me, could I just get at that raspberry meringue thing? Got to make the most of it – my diet starts first thing tomorrow.'

So we moved along, to the remaining flown-in strawberries and a severely depleted bowl of chocolate mousse. Nick dolloped some of this on his plate. Equally casually he asked, 'Was it his appalling diary management that got Leo the elbow, then?'

I might have been rehearsing my reply all day. 'Partly, but it was a bit like you and that seagull. When something's half dead already it's kinder to put it out of its misery. Do you think I'd be an utter pig if I had some of those strawberries as well?'

'That's a tough one. They look to me a bit like those all-looks-and-no-flavour jobs. Still, only one way to find out . . .' He picked one up.

He didn't give up, I'd say that for him. Still, if I couldn't enjoy a bit of erogenous stuff on New Year's Eve, I might as well be dead.

About to open my mouth like a baby bird, I thanked God I hadn't. He put it into his own mouth instead.

'Well?' I asked, as he pretended to reflect.

'Nothing to get excited about.' He looked me right in the eye. 'Aren't you glad I saved you that little disappointment?'

*OK, touché.* 'It's very bad manners to talk with your mouth full. Anyway, I'm really more of a cherry person, myself.'

I wasn't altogether sorry that Ian had chosen that moment to forage for puddings; right behind him were Chloe and Simon. Leaving them to it, I was halfway back when the lights dimmed and the wallpaper music ceased. 'Right, I want everybody on the floor *now*,' announced the DJ, 'and here's one to remind all you decrepit over-thirties of your misspent youths.' Suddenly the speakers were belting out 'YMCA', and within seconds at least half the revellers were on the floor.

At our table, Jane was saying about time too, she was beginning to think things were never going to warm up.

So much for your flirt-therapy, I thought. 'Little disappointment', indeed. As if I cared. However, after that pool-table episode I should have realized there were no flies on Nick. Still, it was all a bit of a turn-up. If anyone had asked, though, the most I'd have imagined him feeling was the vaguest sort of itch, the kind you can barely be bothered to scratch. A slightly itchier itch would partly explain his attitude to Leo. It shed a new light on his Tarzan wind-up, too. And it *had* wound Leo up. I could still see his face, the spark of jealousy at last.

What a joke.

Why did Sod's Law always foul up? If Nick had a little itch, why did he have to wait till now to show it? Why couldn't he have itched at Colditz? Why couldn't we have had that snog after all, a steamy, non-pretend one, and had Leo turn up in the middle of it? Oh, to have seen his face.

With that gnawing, empty ache, my stomach contracted. Bloody Leo – couldn't he stay in his cupboard just for tonight?

For distraction, I turned to Rob. 'What's the matter with Paula's mother?'

'A bad case of hypochondria and emotional blackmail, Paula thinks. She wanted her there for Christmas, but I was on call so she stayed here.' He lowered his voice. 'Is it just this diet making Felicity ratty, or have she and Ian had a row?'

I could hardly go into Luke Archer now. 'Looks like it. You didn't get called out over Christmas, did you?'

'Of course. A juicy case of pancreatitis, among other

201

things. I hope Henry isn't into stealing entire tubs of rum butter – he might not feel too clever afterwards.'

Ian and the others returned, a waiter came to light the candle lamp, and I turned back to Rob. 'I gather there are glitches over buying the practice. The son's planning to go over your heads.'

'He's got even more incentive now. The old man had another stroke on Boxing Day – it wouldn't surprise me if Markham junior was hoping it'd finish the poor old sod off. The last thing he'll want is to shell out nursing home fees.'

'Yes, Felicity told me he wasn't very nice.'

'He's desperate for money. Still, now he's got power of attorney he can help himself to the old man's investments. Maybe it actually suits him better if he's hanging on. If he died, he'd have to wait for probate.'

'How about your own place?' I asked, meaning the house he'd had in Bristol, before moving down here. It had been on the market for months, but he'd lost two buyers to collapsing chains.

'Looks as if it's moving at last, thank God.'

'Have you found anywhere round here?' I knew he'd been renting in the meantime.

'No, but I'll have to get a move on. The lease on my flat runs out next month. I might move in with Nick for a bit.'

Or with Paula, I thought. During the murder she'd told me about her little house with miles of views even from the bathroom. '*Honestly, it would have fetched half a million in Fulham.*'

Jane was getting restless. 'What do I have to do to get a dance round here? Nick, if you've finished stuffing your face, I'm dying for some action.'

So off they went, and Ian said it was high time Felicity got on her feet, and led her off, too. As Ian was neither the world's best nor most willing dancer, I knew he was making an effort. Had he seen her with Luke Archer after all?

These thoughts led me on to boring, comfortable ruts. Having known Ian from a child, Felicity had started seeing him in an item sense only weeks before her grandmother died, months after her grandfather. This had given them something in common, as Ian had lost both parents a couple of years previously. At twenty-two he'd been left to run the family business, which was in financial difficulties. On top of this he'd had the responsibility of younger brother Jack, who was still at school.

Before coming to Devon, Felicity had been living in Barnes, not far from me. If not for a sharer I couldn't very well kick out, she'd probably have been in my spare room. The change had come after a worrying visit to her grandparents. No longer able to cope, they'd refused point-blank to consider nursing homes. After some spectacularly unlucky investments there wasn't enough income to pay for anyone to live in, either. As for social services, Felicity might as well have told them she was asking Adolf Hitler to pop in and assess their needs. Interfering social workers, coming to patronize and pry? They'd push each other down the stairs first.

She'd stayed with them for fifteen months, found a part-time job and still been worn out most of the time, but her planned return to London had never come. Two days before the second funeral she'd moved in with Ian. She'd got on fine with Jack, and even enjoyed cooking tons of burgers for any friends he brought round. Within eighteen months she'd also acquired Shep, and had told me that for the first time in her life, she felt as if she had a proper family.

Until now, it had never once occurred to me that they might have got together for the wrong reasons.

While I was thinking all this, Rob brought me back. 'On your feet, Izzy. Time to show them what we're made of.'

Jane had been spot on about cheesy laughs. For the next twenty minutes I enjoyed the best exercise I'd had in months. Abba, Eddy Grant, Blondie: if it had an irresistible beat, that DJ played it. The room throbbed, and for a hefty bloke Rob was a pretty good dancer. I came off the floor flushed with silly laughter, my hair coming adrift. However, I'd barely grabbed a glass of water when Ian said come on, it was his turn.

After that, it was everyone with everyone else as the DJ dug out everything from 'Who Let The Dogs Out' to 'Waterloo' and 'One Love.' At one point I saw Felicity with Luke Archer, but since he wasn't actually clutching her bottom I relaxed. The only person I didn't dance with was Nick. I saw him with Felicity and Chloe, even with Tamara at one point. You'd better watch her during any smoochy ones, I thought. She'll be checking out your *glutei maximi* for staying power. Still, I had no doubt he'd do an Ian: stiffen his upper lip and take it like a man.

Soon there was a smoochy one, and I was back with Rob. With my cheek against his shirt, as he'd ditched his jacket by then, we got our breath back to 'Eternal Flame'.

It was odd, dancing like this with Rob, because I never had. He felt lovely: firm and reliable – and safe. If Paula had been with him now, she'd never have had the feeling that he was eyeing someone else over her shoulder, thinking, mmm, nice tits. It was a thousand pities there weren't more Robs around. The ad-people could write a lovely slogan: *You know where you are with a Rob*. Still, that would be the truth, which was not the purpose of advertisements. They'd have a lot more fun with a Leo: *Love a Luscious Leo*. Oh, shit . . .

Rob drew back a little. 'All right, Izz?'

'Fine.' *Get back in your cupboard, Leo.* 'Are you?'

'Mmm.' He came back close. 'Might take a break after this one, though. De-knacker myself.'

'Me, too.'

I went back to the table with Rob, feeling pleasantly shattered. After kicking my shoes off, I poured us glasses of water and Nick came up.

He'd worked up the kind of earthy glow a rugby player gets, only without the mud. His top two buttons were undone and the ends of his tie hung loose. 'Come on, Izzy,' he said. 'Work some of those overindulgent puddings off.'

'Crocodile Rock' had just started, a number guaranteed to make my feet itch, just when they needed a break. '*Now* he asks me,' I said to Rob. 'When I feel as if I've just done six straight hours in the gym.'

'Always was an awkward sod,' grinned Rob. 'You tell him, Izz.'

Nick's mouth flickered. 'Be fair, Izzy. After your rubbish-dancer remarks, I had to get in some practice first.' He knocked back half a glass of someone else's water. 'Anyway, every time I looked you were with someone else.'

'Which is why I'm just a teensy bit shattered.'

'Only a bit? Then you haven't been working hard enough.' Taking my wrist, he yanked me to my feet, and I can't say I protested. It would have been pathetic to hold that strawberry against him.

'I should warn you that I'm not exactly Izzy Travolta when it comes to this sort of thing,' I said, as he led my stockinged feet on to a packed floor.

'I'm not exactly John either, but who gives a toss?'

And he wasn't, but what he lacked in expertise he more

than made up for with rhythm and the kind of style that makes it look as if you know exactly what you're doing. I managed to twizzle in most of the right places, only crashing into other couples about three times, saying, 'ooh, sorry!' as you do, and laughing as Nick caught me briefly in his arms.

And then it was over. The music stopped.

Looking down at me, he undid another button. 'Stuff Travolta,' he said. 'I think we made a pretty good team.'

Probably pink-cheeked, I was still getting my breath back. 'Your tie's coming adrift.' I touched one loose end; the other was escaping over his left shoulder. 'Why don't you put it in your pocket?'

'Your up-sa-daisy hair's coming adrift.' He blew gently on a wisp that was getting in my eyes, but it wafted straight back.

'Nice try,' I said, because it was. Rather nice, I mean.

'Waste of breath,' he said, but his eyes said something else. In warm hazel they were saying, 'I know it was nice. That's why I did it.'

As if I didn't know. If I wasn't careful, this therapy would be getting seriously out of hand. Still, the music was starting again.

'Are you up for another?' he asked.

'Why not?' It was Queen, and I could almost have laughed at the DJ's choice.

During the first, slow bars of 'Old-Fashioned Lover Boy', Nick caught me in a sort of daft, *Dirty Dancing* send-up, but then it was fast and furious again. Right afterwards came another Queen number, back to back. By the end of 'Don't Stop Me Now', I might have taken some wild, intravenous drug. Everything glowed. Endorphins were whizzing in my blood, and Nick was looking down at me again.

'That should sort out the profiteroles,' he said.

'I only had two!'

He laughed. Slipping a light arm round my waist, he gave me a little squeeze. 'I meant mine.' Up close, he was assaulting my olfactory whatsits, too. It was quite a pleasant cocktail: warm, exercised male, clean shirt, plus a dash of some *Eau de Macheau* or other. Vaguely recognizing this, I sniffed more obviously than I'd intended.

'Christ, is it that bad?' With a wry expression, he sniffed at an underarm.

'No!' I laughed. 'Stop it, you dope. . .'

Just then a man a few yards away yelled, 'Come on, dozy! What happened to the music?'

There was a crackle at the mike. 'Sorry, folks, but I just had a special request. Anne Bridges would like to say Happy Birthday to her husband, Bob. Anne's asked me to play a very special number that means a great deal to both of them.'

Nick looked down at my stockinged feet. 'Can they cope with one more?'

'Just about.' I knew exactly what that special number was going to be. 'Unchained Melody' or 'Wind Beneath My Wings'. Slow, haunting, cheek-against-shoulder stuff. More minor-buzz material, and why not? Might as well get my money's worth. Ticket, petrol, drinks: by the time I'd finished the bill for this evening would be running at a hundred and fifty quid.

'So no prizes for guessing,' the DJ went on. 'Since we're talking about the one and only Bob Bridges here, of Bridges Builders and Contractors, don't let the bugger near your extension. . .'

Gales of laughter went up. I don't mind admitting I felt just a bit cheated.

Nick seemed only amused. 'Do you want to pass?'

207

'God, no. I'll try anything once.'

During the next few minutes a hundred adults cavorted to 'Bob the Builder', darling of infant popular culture. Stamping our feet, we gave raucous choruses. It gave my endorphins another whacking boost, but by the end I knew another slow one was coming up. Any DJ worth his salt knew people needed a cool-down session.

The mike crackled again. 'Right, we're going to take a little break now. Time to draw the raffle, and then we'll be warming up for Big Ben. More to the point, I need a beer.'

Just as well, I thought, as we returned to our table with Nick's hand on my hip. As if he'd read the instructions in these matters, it was light enough not to be oppressive, firm enough to make it quite clear what sort of animal you were dealing with. A smoochy one would have done nothing for my endorphins. Ten to one that look-alike would have drifted right under my nose with his hands on someone's bottom, and Leo would have been dragged out of his cupboard again.

Exactly where my thoughts had dragged him now.

In lights undimmed for the purpose, I delved in my bag for my raffle tickets. A waiter brought two ice buckets containing champagne, and Rob signed a chit. 'Reinforcements,' he explained. 'They'll only give us one miserable glass at midnight.'

After thanking local businesses for the prizes, Ms Ticket called winners. There was a case of wine, a manicure and pedicure, a mountain bike. Simon Portaloo won dinner for two at a Greek restaurant, which I thought grossly unfair when he'd only bought two tickets. Then there was a weekend at a health spa, a hundred pounds' worth of vouchers for the garden centre. After a further half dozen I could barely be bothered to check any more. It was taking for ever for people to go up and my hands were getting sore with clapping. My high was wearing off fast. I needed some fast and furious dancing to bring back that endorphin rush.

The first prize was a week for two on St James Beach, Barbados, and the dozy idiot who won it was too stupid to realize at first. Not that you could altogether blame her. She never won anything anyway, and when they called, 'Blue, forty-seven,' she thought there must be two types of blue. Light and dark, and she'd have the wrong one. It was only when Rob jabbed her, and said, 'Shit, Izzy, that's you. . .'

# Chapter 13

What a way to start the New Year. I probably kissed more people at midnight than the official world record. I drank oceans of champagne. After 'Auld Lang Syne' I danced my tights into holes with anyone who'd have me. By chucking-out time I was on a euphoric high, as if my blood had turned into champagne, and the evening had yet to end. Everybody was starving again, and Rob and Nick were coming back for bacon sandwiches.

After collecting coats, we stepped out into a night that had gone suddenly cold. In a clear sky, the stars were like frosted diamonds; our breath came out like clouds of dry ice. Our taxis were already there, and the men were waiting for us. Nick had put his jacket back on but his tie was still undone. He had one thumb in his trouser pocket and he was laughing with Rob about something. Suddenly I longed for a camera. I wanted a picture of them just like that, a memory of the night I was made of champagne.

'My God, my *feet*,' said Jane, who was as Moët-soaked as me, and very giggly. 'Oops, I forgot something – hang on a tick . . .'

She came back with a wicked expression and something concealed under her coat.

'Oh, God,' grinned Rob. 'I know that look.'

Jane opened her coat to reveal two small pineapples, last

seen in those purely decorative arrangements on the buffet table. 'Anyone feeling fruity?'

I started laughing.

So did Felicity. 'You nicked those! Honestly, you can't take her anywhere.'

With an even wickeder grin, Jane held the pineapples like extensions to her breasts, pointing the spiky bits at us like weapons. Making machine-gun noises, she moved from side to side as if massacring us all, and the hapless taxi-drivers, too.

I was seized with the kind of laughter you get once a year if you're lucky. I was doubled up, helpless, scarcely able to catch my breath. Vaguely, I was conscious of a grinning Rob and Nick half carrying me to the cab. 'Better have her in with us,' Rob said to Felicity. 'At this rate she'll need resuscitation.'

The cab must have been two hundred yards down the road before I finally regained control. Beside me in the back, Nick produced a proper handkerchief from his pocket and I wiped my eyes. 'Do I look like a panda?' I asked.

'Gruesome,' he assured me. 'I shall probably have nightmares.'

'And God knows what my hair looks like . . .'

'It's not so bad, for an ups-a-daisy haystack.' With the lightest of touches, he tucked an escaping wisp behind my ear.

Was he at it again? I wondered. With that 'I know it's nice . . .' stuff? Because it was, rather.

'God, what a pompous little dick that Simon was,' said Rob from the front seat.

'Too right,' said Nick. 'Jane could have found a cosy little home for one of those pineapples.'

That sent me into another fit.

211

'I hope Felicity's got plenty of bacon,' said Rob cheerfully. 'I could eat a horse.'

She did have plenty, because being Felicity, she'd anticipated this. It was all washed down with cups of tea and a vilely potent liqueur someone had given her. Ian said it was probably Wurzo-Slavinian brake fluid, but what the hell.

Jane whispered that Felicity seemed in a slightly better mood with Ian now. Maybe she'd gone off Luke Archer, close up. Maybe he had really hairy nostrils. That sent me into another fit, like a fourteen-year-old with the giggles.

Nick shot a grin at Rob. 'I'm not sure those two should be let loose on Barbados without an official warning to their government.'

'Highly dangerous,' said Rob. 'Maybe one of us should tag along to keep them in order.'

I was still wiping my eyes. 'Feel free. We could do with a slave along to fetch the drinks.'

'And for the sun cream,' said Jane. 'Any slave must be highly skilled at slapping on factor fifteen.'

'I've got a PhD in it,' said Rob.

'My hands are legend,' said Nick.

'Toss for it, then,' she said. 'And don't forget your swimmies. But none of those revolting male knickers, please. The ones that look as if you've got a milk bottle down the front.'

That set me off again.

'Has Izzy been sniffing something on the quiet?' said Ian. 'Because if so, I wish she'd give me a snort of it.'

'Just Barbados,' said Rob. 'Ten-quid Barbados, and a skinful of champagne.'

If Rob hadn't zonked out around three thirty we might

have started playing silly games, but he did, and Nick started making time-to-go noises. He called a couple of cab companies who said sorry, no chance till six. Felicity said never mind, they could sleep on the sofas. Ian brought down duvets and pillows and we tucked Rob in. It was nearly four when I finally staggered upstairs with Jane and Henry.

She came back from the bathroom just as I was about to get into bed. 'Izzy, what *have* you got on?'

'Alice's Christmas present. Not really me, but I thought I might as well christen it.'

'Hmm. Probably the sort of thing the kind of person who irons her knickers would wear for a ladylike dirty weekend.'

'Can you *have* a ladylike dirty weekend?' But I saw her point. An ankle-length nightie of cream satin, it was splashed with deep pink roses. Cut like a slinky dress, it had tiny straps on a V plunge top.

The next thing I remember, after the lights went off, was Henry, whining softly and nosing my face. The clock on the bedside table said one minute past six. 'Sshh!' But he went to the door and started pawing at it.

Oh, Lord. This was what came of letting him devour bacon sandwich crusts at a time when his stomach was normally asleep. I tiptoed down old-house stairs that creaked, like the kitchen door when I opened it. After Henry shot out I felt suddenly dehydrated. Running the cold tap, I filled my hands, splashing my face at the same time. Then I looked for something to wipe it on, caught the back of a kitchen chair with my thigh and winced as it made a scraping noise on the tiles.

From the open back door I called in an urgent whisper, 'Henry! Come on, good boy . . .'

That was when I heard a creak behind me.

213

I whirled around. 'Nick!' I put a hand to my heart in relief. 'My God, you gave me such a fright . . .'

'I gave *you*?' From pausing on the threshold, he came in and shut the door. 'Crashing around giving me heart failure – I was gearing myself up for a burglar with a sawn-off jemmy.'

He did a good line in fake hacked-off with a giveaway little smile. 'Henry woke me up.' I nodded at the back door. 'He was getting desperate.'

'That's no reason to stand there with the door open.' He went straight over and shut it. 'It's brass monkey stuff in here.'

'I know.' I gave my goosey arms a little rub. 'But I didn't want him doing his best let-me-in woof and waking everybody up.'

'Let him. You'll catch your death like that.'

'You can talk.' He was wearing nothing but a pair of boxers, only they weren't plain white like last time. They were black, emblazoned with Dennis the Menace. 'Were they a Christmas present?'

'Spot on. Go on, you can laugh,' he added with a smile.

A bit late, as I already was.

'I think Alex's mum does his Christmas shopping,' he added.

'Mums usually do, when you're six. Sorry I woke you,' I added.

'No problem. After that brake fluid, my radiator could do with a top-up.' Filling a glass from the tap, he nodded at my splashy roses. 'Was that a Christmas present?'

'However did you guess?'

He downed half the water. 'I had you down as more of a Tigger type.'

Un-flirty, unflattering, but undeniably true. 'You're dead right. The Tiggers don't need ironing.'

He laughed.

'And at least they're warm,' I went on. 'Oh, Lord, there's the animal . . .' As he was scratching at the door, I charged to open it before he barked.

'Oh, *Hen*ry! You vile animal!' Delighted to see me, he jumped up, planting two filthy paws on my ladylike satin. Having done that he charged to Shep's water bowl, leaving a trail of filthy paw prints.

'Well, that's christened this good and proper.' I looked down at my nightie. 'My sister would have a fit.'

But Nick was laughing, and that set me off, too. 'Trust him,' I added, as Henry slurped noisily. 'Just look at his feet!' They must have been two inches deep in mud. 'I can't take him upstairs like that. Excuse me, if I could just get to the cupboard under the sink . . .'

He moved aside and I found Felicity's dog-cloth, lurking among bleach and non-bio capsules. 'Right, come here, you horrible animal . . .'

Henry hated having his feet wiped. Either it tickled or he objected on principle. As I dealt with his back paws he did his best to escape.

'I'll hold him.' Nick took his collar while I did the other paw and took the cloth to the sink for a rinse.

'Up you get, Muttley.' As I came back Nick stood astride him, and lifted him by his front legs, so he was more or less upright with captive front paws dangling.

'How very practical,' I said. 'Thank you.'

'Don't mention it.'

I resumed wiping. 'At least it's just mud. He's been known to get into fox poo. You wouldn't believe how rank that can be.'

'I would. I've had a sick fox crap all over me.'

I got the giggles again. Either it was leftovers from Jane or all that Moët still coursing in my system, but it was a serious case. In fact, I was still at it when Henry was done. 'OK, you can take the handcuffs off . . .'

Over captive Henry I looked up at Nick, and my daft giggles died in my throat.

Something had sneaked up while I wasn't looking. As he released Henry and straightened up, there was only a foot between us. In his eyes I saw every hint of itch he'd shown all evening, magnified fifty-fold. The air between us crackled with it. Suddenly, I was acutely aware of my flimsy satin, and only me underneath. I might have been back at Colditz, only fifty-fold. I was on that bed, holding my hair up, tingling in anticipation of the kiss that had never come.

I swallowed, hard. 'Maybe I should, erm, do the floor . . .'

His answer was to take the cloth from my hand and sling it at the sink. Without a word he took me in a fierce, possessive embrace. His mouth was hard, hungry and melting all at once, and it melted me. As his lips and tongue searched and possessed, waves of desire coursed through me. Suddenly my arms were round him, my hands all over him as his were over my slippery satin. To put it bluntly, it was the kind of warm-up old Mother Nature must have had in mind when she started thinking that merely splitting yourself in half, like an amoeba, or laying half a million eggs, was actually a bit boring.

There was a moment when we came up for air. He was just holding me, his whole body tense as a hot, coiled spring. It was like a pause in a storm, between one clap of thunder and the massive one you knew was about to break directly overhead. Over the top of my hair he said, 'Do you still want to do that bloody floor?'

Roughened with desire, his voice electrified me almost as

much as hard evidence of storms about to break. 'I don't think there's any Mr Muscle in the cupboard.'

I felt a vibration of laughter in his chest. 'I'll give you Mr Muscle . . .'

*Oh, yes, please . . .*

And that was it. Within another couple of heartbeats, a savage beast was raising its ugly head, and I don't just mean Dennis the Menace. It was in the garden, and we'd never have known it was there if not for Henry.

It was the sharp, urgent bark I called his war cry. His whole body tense and quivering, he was pawing desperately at the back door.

'Shut *up*!' Jerking away from Nick, I charged over and grabbed his collar. Before he barked again, I clamped my hands around his jaws.

'Let him out,' said Nick.

'I can't!' I looked up to see a cocktail on his face: roughly equal parts of amusement, exasperation and frustration. 'He's heard a fox or something – he'll be off like a greased missile, woofing his head off.'

'Let him.'

'Are you kidding? He'll set Shep off and wake the whole house!'

He took Henry's collar himself, but when he was quivering with outrage Henry could be very single-minded. Some wild beast was out there, some upstart fox or badger that needed tearing apart. Even with my hands around his jaws, he was trying to bark.

'He's like this at home, when cats sit on the fence taunting him,' I said. 'He goes absolutely ape.'

'Then we'll take his mind off it.' Nick yanked the fridge open. 'Right,' he said, rifling the contents as I hung on to Henry. 'Yoghurt, bean sprouts, ah, this could be salami – oh, *fuck* . . .' Ransacking crammed shelves, he dislodged

Liz Young

something. A pottery dish containing something reddy-brown fell on the tiles and smashed.

'*Fuck*,' he said. 'Bolog-bloody-naise, by the looks of it.' He bent down and picked up a brown shard. 'Can't even get him to lick it up now.'

However, the smash jerked Henry from the door. He was now straining in the other direction, his nose quivering towards the lovely foody mess. 'For heaven's sake, clean it up!' I said. 'Before he gets his feet in that, too. Or hold him while I do it.'

'I'll do it.' With a handful of shards he headed for the bin, via me. Tilting my face up, he dropped a soft kiss on my lips. 'You should come with a warning. Explosive material, handle with care.'

He was back at the mess when the door opened.

It was Rob. Still in his dress shirt and trousers, he stood on the threshold, blinking away sleep. 'What's going on?' His eyes went to the mess, and thence to Nick and me.

'Sorry, Rob,' I said quickly. 'Did the racket wake you up?'

'Something did.' His eyes returned to Nick, and the first thought in my head was, please, let his erection have gone down, followed by, but Rob probably wouldn't notice it, anyway, while he's squatting on the floor like that.

'Nice one, Nick,' he grinned. 'Raiding the fridge, were you?'

'It's my fault, I woke *him* up,' I said brightly. 'Coming down to let Henry out. He's trodden half the garden in.'

'I can see that. Well done, Henry, my old son.'

Nick was still picking out bits of smashed dish. 'Go back to your pit, Rob. It's all under control.'

'Oh, I don't know.' Rob came right in and shut the

218

door. 'Now I'm up, I wouldn't mind a nibble myself. Any cornflakes, I wonder?'

Nick looked over his shoulder. 'What happened to the diet, you fat bastard?'

'Sod diets,' said Rob, already investigating cupboards. 'I'll be back on it tomorrow.'

Henry, meanwhile, was being cunning. He'd stopped straining in the hope that I'd forget and let him go, and he could get at that meaty mess after all. Only his quivering nose betrayed him.

As for me, someone might have chucked a bucket of cold water over me. Not for the first time in my life, I was finding out how overpowering desire could vanish faster than sausages down Henry's gullet. What had I been about to do? What if Rob had caught us on the kitchen table, my ladylike satin bunched around my waist? Or up against the fridge, with Felicity's British Wildlife magnets digging into my bottom? All right, it would have been nice for five minutes, but probably more like two. Fizz, bang, wake up in the morning with that 'oh shit, why did I do it?' feeling.

'Eureka,' said Rob, taking a packet of cornflakes out of a cupboard. 'I was beginning to think there weren't any.'

I'd heard of bedroom farces, but this was ridiculous.

With a handful of shards, Nick stood up and caught my eye.

Funny how the idea of washing floors can suddenly appeal. 'I'll give the floor a quick mop,' I said, like some demented TV ad housewife. 'Nick, you can get up most of that mess with kitchen roll. Rob, if you could just hold Henry to stop him getting his feet in it . . .'

Rob's brow creased. 'Go back to bed, Izzy – you look half frozen. Nick and I'll clean up. Go on,' he added firmly, as I opened my mouth. 'You're all goosey.'

I was. 'I had the door open. It's cold out.'

219

'Go on, off you go. You tell her, Nick.'

Nick looked at me, and a second was all it took. His expression barely changed, but something in his eyes said he knew exactly what had just been going through my head. His eyes went to my bare toes and back again. 'You shouldn't have come down like that, Izzy. You could have got a bad case of cold feet.'

If I'd still been prone to flushing I'd have gone hot pink, but his tone was so deceptively light, Rob picked up nothing.

'Pretty little nightie, though.' He patted my shoulder. 'Off you go, Izz. Night night.'

'Night, Rob. Thanks.' I kissed his cheek and headed for the door. 'Night, Nick.'

'It's morning,' he said. 'But I won't split hairs.'

It took me ages to get back to sleep. In the dark, with Henry snoring softly beside me, I thanked God for whatever British Wildlife he'd been determined to tear apart. My cheeks burned at the thought of Rob catching us, or indeed anyone else. It was six thirty, not the middle of the night. What if Shep had needed to go out? What if Jane had woken with a sudden desperate urge for a cup of tea? Then my cheeks burned again at his 'cold feet' taunt. What the hell was I supposed to do? Say, 'Actually, Rob, we were about to have a quick shag, so if you don't mind . . .' What kitchen ever had a lock, anyway? Was he planning to do it in the dining-room? In the downstairs loo? In the bloody garden?

Never again would I mix heartbreak with flirt-therapy and buckets of champagne. It was a classic recipe for making a tit of yourself. Or, at least, for making you susceptible to the first attractive man with an itch. And if it had got itchier during the evening, whose fault was that?

*Confucius he say, when woman joke to man about dribbling lust, man apt to think she maybe not joking.*

But it had been a joke.

*Confucius he also say, serve you right for making flirty joke, then, when you knew it was flirty at the time.*

I thought again of Colditz and Sod's Law's woeful timing. I even had a bitter little wish that we'd had a quickie after all. I could have sent Leo a nice little text message by now: '*Hi, just to let you know I just shagged Med Max aka Nick and v nice it was 2. Oh and he told me he let you beat him on purpose at pool because he thought you were a tosser. PS do hope you liked the prawns.*'

Yes. Brilliant. Very grown-up. What sort of pathetic wreck was I turning into? Why was I letting him do this to me?

Just before drifting off, I heard Jack and Pip come in, scuffles and muffled laughter as they crossed the landing. I heard Pip's giggly, 'Sshh!' and the door closing. Somehow that turned the knife worse than anything. Once again, aching pangs seized me, contracting the lonely void where my heart used to be. Turning over, I shed a few silent tears into my pillow.

I woke again feeling horrible, drugged and sticky-mouthed. Jane was up, in wet hair and a borrowed robe. 'What time is it?' I asked.

'Ten past eleven, you lazy cow. Everybody else is up.'

It was all coming back to me. 'Are Rob and Nick still here?'

'Of course.' She was running a wide-toothed comb through her hair. 'I'm going down for breakfast – are you coming?'

'I don't want any.' I turned my face into the pillow. 'I couldn't face it.'

'It's not a fry-up. Just fruit and yoghurt and stuff. You want to see Rob, don't you? He'll probably be off soon.'

I did want to see Rob. I just didn't want to see somebody else. 'He can come up and say goodbye. Ask him to bring me a cup of tea while he's at it.'

'Oh, all right.' After slapping on moisturizer she departed.

'What a way to start the New Year,' I said to Henry. 'Why didn't I quit while I was ahead?'

He licked my arm. 'Chill out. Could have been worse.'

After so long together, you'll gather that I could read Henry's thoughts like my own. 'I bet he's calling me all the names under the sun now.'

'No, just one. Two words, beginning with P and T.'

My eyes turned to the window. Jane had drawn the curtains. Outside I saw the intense blue sky that goes with crisp, bracing cold.

It braced me, anyway. Hiding up here was pathetic. I had to go down.

# Chapter 14

I was dying for a shower, but what if Nick had left by the time I'd finished? He'd think I was too chicken to face him. So after hygienic basics, I slipped on a robe evidently belonging to Ian and went down.

About to come up, dear old Rob had a cup of tea and a croissant on a little tray. 'I changed my mind,' I said. 'But thanks anyway.'

'Poor Izzy,' he said. 'Are you feeling rough?'

'Not really. I just slept too long.'

Ian speared some chopped pineapple on a fork. 'Have some of Jane's machine-guns. They taste even better for being nicked.'

'Thanks,' I said, as he popped some in my mouth. 'Yummy.'

As well as pineapple there was Greek yoghurt and honey, a nearly empty jug of orange juice, and croissants that smelt warm and fragrant from the oven. Wearing a smaller pair of jeans than I'd seen her in for ages, Felicity was putting more oranges through a juicer. Ian and Jane were at the table, both still in bathrobes. Nick was standing against the worktop with a coffee, one ankle crossed over the other. Like Rob, he was wearing last night's trousers with a different shirt: a navy rugby version with a white collar. 'Morning, Nick,' I said, nice and bright and casual. 'Have you been raiding Ian's shirts?'

If not for a tiny flicker in his eyes, I could almost have convinced myself I'd dreamt last night. 'Felicity did the raiding,' he said.

Felicity licked her orange-juicy fingers. 'I couldn't possibly let them put those sweaty shirts on again. How did you sleep, Izzy, after all the excitement?'

She could hardly have said anything more unfortunate. 'Apart from waking up to let the animal out, like a champagne-soaked baby.'

Rob was stirring runny honey into yoghurt. 'Considering how much you put away, you were remarkably well-behaved. I was half expecting some spectacular entertainment.'

*You very nearly got some.*

'No, she's past all that,' said Jane. 'Izzy's days of doing cartwheels with her tits out are done, I fear.'

'Pity,' said Nick. 'If you'd got half that lot last night to sponsor you, you could have raised another bomb for the hospice.'

His expression reminded me of that first night at the Coach and Horses. Detached, slightly cynical amusement. And that was the night he'd wanted to kick something, too.

'I should think they'd have sponsored me a hell of a lot more *not* to do it,' I said. 'And talking of last night, I think I'll just read the small print.'

On the worktop was a white envelope containing details of my prize. I'd only skimmed it last night, while Portaloo Simon had tried to take the edge off by telling me it would probably be hedged in with all sorts of restrictions, I'd be confined to a couple of weeks in November.

'Well?' said Jane.

'It seems straightforward. Subject to availability of flights and accommodation, standard rooms in a choice of

224

three hotels. But not school holidays, and it has to be used by mid-December.'

'Luke Archer told me last night that he goes to Barbados at least twice a year,' said Felicity. 'He stays at that really smart place. The Sandy Lane.'

'Well, good for Luke Archer,' said Ian, in a certain tone.

Felicity gave him a certain look. 'I don't know why you've got a thing about Luke Archer.'

'I haven't got a thing. I just don't like him.'

Felicity's only reply was to start tidying up in the way Mum used to when some aspect of Dad's behaviour was causing her simmering frustration. In Felicity's case, she'd virtually said it herself: Ian wouldn't notice if she went out topless with her nipples painted green. Luke Archer, on the other hand, would certainly notice that she'd turned almost overnight into an altogether sexier version of herself. Luke saw her as a woman, not as the fixture who made sure there was enough bacon last night and clean shirts for Rob and Nick to borrow. Over the years she'd turned herself into Ian's housekeeper, even a sort of replacement for his mother. She might have done it willingly, because she was one of nature's nurturers, but he'd come to take her for granted and she was sick of it. She wanted to be desired because she was desirable, not just because she was conveniently available in Ian's bed every night.

If it wasn't Luke Archer, I thought, it would be somebody else. And at this rate, before many more moons had passed.

Felicity put more warm croissants on the table. 'There. Nobody's going hungry, I hope. After Rob and Nick prowling for food last night, I wouldn't want anyone moaning that they're not being properly fed.'

There was a slightly awkward silence, which didn't

surprise me, because the remark had an edge that was quite unlike her.

'We were just being a pair of pigs,' said Nick. 'I'm sorry about your dish.'

'Nick, for heaven's sake.' I could tell she felt bad now. 'It was chipped anyway. I should have thrown it out ages ago.'

I stood under the shower half an hour later, letting hot water gush over my relief. Obviously, not even Jane had an inkling, but that didn't surprise me. It wasn't as if there had been anything overt at the ball. Knowing looks are bad enough at the best of times.

I came downstairs to find Nick coming out of the sitting-room with last night's jacket and shirt over his arm. The hall was otherwise empty and suddenly we were face to face. Again he wore that expression of elusive, faintly dry amusement. 'You've got that "oh, dear, what do I say?" look.'

*Lose it, then. Keep it light.* 'I'm sorry you got lumbered with washing floors at unsocial hours. Or did you get Rob to do it?'

He slung the shirt and jacket over his shoulder. 'He was too busy stuffing his face.'

'He always was addicted to nocturnal cornflakes.' With a glance at the closed kitchen door, I stepped just inside the sitting-room. As he followed, I almost closed the door behind him. 'Look, I'm sorry if, well . . .'

*If you were 'uncomfortable' afterwards. If you suffered the grinding balls-ache a long-ago boyfriend told me could turn into testicular cancer.*

But I could hardly say either of these. 'I just got a bit carried away.'

He gave a lopsided little smile. 'It takes two.'

226

Phew. No sulks, then. 'It was all the champagne.'

He raised his eyebrows in a 'well, that's life' manner. 'Don't forget the brake fluid.'

'I hardly had any.' In a rush I went on, 'The fact is, I didn't want to get into anything I was going to regret in the morning.'

I saw at once that I should have kept my stupid mouth shut. 'I gathered that,' he said, in those 'pleasant' tones that come out chilled at the edges. 'But I'm glad you're not regretting anything this morning. I wouldn't have wanted to foul up your New Year.'

I knew I'd asked for that, but it still hurt. 'I think I just did that myself.'

'Forget it, then.' He gave a perfectly 'pleasant' little smile that matched his tone exactly. 'I can promise you I will.'

This really felt like a slap in the face. Suddenly my eyes were pricking, but not for anything would I let him see. Deliberately flippant, I said, 'Still, at least I kept my first New Year's resolution: no quickies up against the fridge unless he's bought me at least a bag of chips first.'

'I think you'll find it's a kebab nowadays.' Then, just as I'd imagined before the ball, his eyes X-rayed into me after all. Hazel-green, all-seeing perception. 'What really happened with Leo?'

A wash of heat flooded me. 'It's none of your business!'

'I can guess.' The eyes were still at it like lasers. 'I know the type. Sixty per cent ego, forty per cent bullshit.'

Without conscious thought I raised my hand. My palm connected so hard with his cheek, it was a toss-up who felt it more. He made no attempt to stop me. He didn't turn his head or flinch. As I stood there, almost appalled at what I'd done, he said, 'Hurts, doesn't it?'

I turned and fled upstairs.

227

Whether he sloshed his cheek with cold water I don't know, but by the time he and Rob left half an hour later, there was no redness to explain away.

Since Nick was kissing Jane and Felicity goodbye, he could hardly leave me out. He did it perfectly: just a bare brushing of my cheek. 'Bye, Izzy. Enjoy Barbados.'

'Thanks. I will.' Then it was Rob, and the bear-hug I needed so badly.

'Be good, Izz,' he said. 'Come and see us again soon.' They drove off into a perfect, sunny day.

As Jane had a train to catch that evening, we left an hour later. For the first few miles she nattered practically non-stop: Luke Archer, for starters, and the depressing possibility of Ian and Felicity going down the pan. 'Still, it was a good laugh, wasn't it? Aren't you glad you came?'

'Yes, it was brilliant. Perked me up no end.'

As we zoomed past neatly ploughed fields with wintry sun on them, my mind replayed everything Nick had said.

Cold feet.

Kebabs.

Bastard. Cutting, smart-arse bastard. Grabbing me like that, too. I hadn't even seen it coming. How were you supposed to see anything coming from a man who's just been talking about fox crap? Pouncing on me like some rampant jungle ape . . .

Tarzan, indeed. He deserved the cannibal. I hoped she ate him alive, him and his bloody Dennis the Menace boxers. Leo wouldn't have been seen dead in Dennis the Menace boxers.

Bloody Leo.

Bloody men. Bloody, dick-centred, *homo-fornicatus* men.

Eventually it dawned on Jane that something else was

going on in my head. 'Look, Izzy, about Barbados – I don't want you to think you have to take me. You might want to hang on to it and go with somebody else.'

'I don't! For heaven's sake, it never even occurred to me!'

'Well, if you're sure . . .' She shot me a little glance, as if to check. 'You seemed a bit quiet, that's all.'

I lied. 'I was thinking about Felicity. I wish I'd had it out with her.'

'What for? If she'd said, "OK, I'm bored, I'm looking for somebody else," what would you have said? "Don't be silly, you've got a nice, sensible man there, count your blessings and hang on to him?" You'd have sounded like someone's mother. Nobody can ever tell anyone else how they ought to feel.'

She was absolutely right, of course, but they did it anyway. All the time. That was why I didn't tell her about Nick. She'd have said, oh stuff it. If that's all you have to worry about all year, I'll swap places now.

The crisp, sunny start to January was only to fool us. By Twelfth Night it had turned as miserable as all the denuded Christmas trees shoved out for the dustbin men to take away. There were two months of dreary winter to look forward to and everyone at work had another reason for being out of sorts. Moving On were taking over in mid-February, just in time for the spring rush, and nobody was ecstatic about it. Louise grumbled about the end of our flexible hours, by which she meant that a new manager might not be so happy about her taking two hours off to have her highlights done.

For Ralph, the worst disaster was the end of personal emails. 'I know someone who used to work for them,' he grumbled. 'One strike and your balls are in the bacon slicer.'

'You can kiss yours goodbye, then,' said Louise tartly. 'Considering you spend eighty per cent of your working life forwarding puerile jokes to your puerile little friends. And what the hell have you done with the keys for twenty-one Elm Grove?'

Ralph fished them out of his pocket and tossed them to her. 'You're always reading them over my shoulder,' he said, all hurt. 'You *asked* me to forward you that one about the school reunion!'

'That's because it was actually *funny*.'

'Now, now, you two,' said Barbara.

Ralph fed a corner of his tuna sandwich to Henry. 'Poor old boy. What will you do with him?'

'What do you think, dipstick?' said Louise. 'She'll have to leave him at home. He'll start eating doors out of boredom and have to go into therapy. Honestly, I could kill Anthea. She's got no consideration.'

Ralph fed a last morsel to Henry. 'I wouldn't eat doors, mate. You'll get splinters in your arse.'

Quite apart from Henry, I wasn't exactly ecstatic, either. Although I'd had a feeling Anthea might take a permanent back seat, I'd never imagined her selling out. I'd even thought she might make me official manager. Louise wouldn't mind; she'd often said she wouldn't want the responsibility. I certainly didn't want some new broom coming in when I could do it all perfectly well myself.

Still, I couldn't resent Anthea altogether. If not for her, I'd probably never have got into the market before prices rocketed. At the time, buying hadn't entered my head: I'd only come in with a long-ago boyfriend who was looking for a flat. Idly flicking through particulars, I'd remarked that Christmas Cottage was a lovely name and it seemed very cheap. Anthea had said that was probably the best bargain on the books. It was in a bit of a state, but she had a hunch that period cottages like that were about to become sought-after.

That was when my thoughts had become less idle. The boyfriend, who was a pilot and incredibly arrogant when I looked back on it, had scoffed. I didn't believe all that sought-after crap, did I? She was just looking for the first likely sucker to offload it on to.

It had been very sweet to prove him wrong. I'd bumped into Anthea once or twice after that. Shortly after being grounded for that ear trouble, I'd collided with her at the gym. She'd said, 'I don't suppose you'd be remotely interested, but I'm going mad in lettings.' A stopgap had turned into four congenial, reasonably paid years, and once Henry had entered the equation it had never really occurred to me to look for anything else.

But the cottage had been in a terrible state. I'd cleaned, painted and sanded until I was exhausted. Then there had been the garden. Only marginally bigger than one of those headscarves the Queen likes when she's not wearing a hat, it had been full of rubbish and waist-high weeds. Last summer it had been a little oasis: crammed with scented flowers and climbers. On long evenings, Leo and I had sat out there with a bottle of wine. Once we'd even heard a nightingale. He'd put some honeysuckle in my hair and said, 'Shall I make love to you out here under the stars and really give Craig something to bitch about?'

I still thought about him a lot, but the ache was moving into the distance. The worst moment was when I made up my mind to delete all the emails he'd ever sent me. I was stupid enough to open just one first. I'd only been seeing him for three weeks; he'd had to go to Scotland for a few days. It said, 'I'm in a soulless, crappy hotel room and I miss you like crazy. See you in my dreams.'

Glowing pink all day, I'd shown it to Louise, who'd grumbled that her Todd would never think of sending an email like that. All right, he'd probably lie down and die for her, he might even grout bathroom tiles, but he was hopeless at little things.

Leo was brilliant at little things. My eyes welled up as I read it again, but I hit 'delete' anyway. Empty trash, *finito*.

Besides, I had Barbados to focus on. It was booked for the second week in February, exactly the dates Jane had wanted. When I got back, the new broom would have moved in. No more walking Henry to work. I'd have to take the car and nip home at lunch-time to let him out. He'd gaze at me mournfully; I'd feel terrible, not being able to explain. And what about all those evenings when we were really busy and I stayed late? It wasn't going to be satisfactory at all.


Felicity phoned one evening, just as I was wondering whether I dared try on last summer's bikinis. Could I stand the sight of winter-white bulging over the edges?

'Rob and Paula have split up,' she said. 'I thought you'd want to know.'

'You're kidding!'

'No, and she finished it. Over New Year, when she was with her mother, she met up with an old flame. She was apparently crying her eyes out when she told Rob, she felt so bad.'

'Is he all right?'

'A lot better than he was after Juliet, but then it had only been a few months. Shell-shocked, though. He certainly hadn't expected it.'

My own wounds might have been torn open in sympathy. 'Poor old Rob – how dare she dump him?'

'Still, I'm glad it was now rather than later. Those two never quite seemed to "go", if you know what I mean. Anyway, I just spoke to Jane – I gather Barbados is finally booked.'

'Yes, I'm going to ring the kennels in the morning.'

'Oh, Izzy, don't put him in kennels! He'll hate it!'

I knew that. Allowing for dropping him off the day before, it would mean nine nights in doggy prison.

'Why don't you bring him down here?' she went on. 'He can have a nice little holiday of his own, with Shep. A couple of Jack and Pip's friends are coming to stay – a pair of Aussie backpackers they met in Thailand. Henry'll get loads of fuss – he'll have a great time. I could meet you halfway, at those services on the M5.'

'I don't want you driving all that way!'

'Oh, stuff it. I'll bring Shep – he loves the car.'

We were leaving on the Friday morning. On the Thursday afternoon I loaded Henry and his bed into the car.

The weather was so vile, I couldn't wait to get away. For several days there had been torrential rain and high winds in much of the country. On the motorway, the car was buffeted by wind and the wipers were going flat out. I met Felicity in the car park, in gusting wind and nearly horizontal rain. For once, Henry was reluctant to get out of the car, and I knew it wasn't the weather. He enjoyed a bit of wind and rain – it exhilarated him.

'Oh, dear,' said Felicity. 'I think he knows.'

The way Henry sometimes sensed things could be uncanny. Instead of showing his usual joy at seeing Shep, his tail curled between his legs. I practically had to push him in through the tailgate.

Before Felicity shut the door, I gave him a big kiss and cuddle. 'Be a good boy and have a lovely time with Shep. I'll be back very soon.'

The sky was so dense with pewter cloud, it was already getting dark when she left. I stood in the rain, waving. I watched Henry's funny, scruffy, mournful little face gazing at me from the back window until it was out of sight.

Just after take-off, I told Jane I'd left Dearling and Dearling for good. 'It seemed like a natural break. I know I'll probably resent any new broom, and if Henry's going to have to stay at home anyway, I might as well move on. I'm overdue for a change.'

'What will you do?'

'Temp for a bit and think about it. I might even retrain for something.'

'My God. Like what?'

'I don't know. Maybe a horticulture course. I really enjoyed doing my garden.'

'Yes, but you wouldn't be earning! What would you do for money?'

'Get a loan. I could even sell up and move somewhere cheaper. Prices are sky-high just now.'

'You're mad. Wheelbarrows full of muck, out in the rain mulching your organic oregano . . . I'd run a mile.'

'It's very trendy,' I said, tongue in cheek. 'Gardening is the new cool, you know.'

'Stuff that. Your nails'll look like nothing on earth. You'll get massive butch-lezzie shoulders from lugging paving slabs about. Yes, please,' she added to the stewardess with the drinks trolley. 'Vodka and tonic, double nibbles, please. And a little strait-jacket for my friend here. I think she's going mad.'

We arrived in heaven just in time for Happy Hour.

It was a little hotel, nestling in tropical gardens. The setting sun was like liquid gold on the sea. Our room was on the ground floor, twenty seconds' walk from the Caribbean. We probably broke the world record for getting into bikinis and into the sea.

Afterwards we sat in the sand with rum punches, watching the last of the sunset, listening to tree frogs and soft calypso from somewhere down the beach. 'Cheers, Felicity,' I said. 'If it hadn't been for you organizing us into that ball . . .'

It turned into one of those rare holidays on which nothing was wrong. You couldn't say, 'Yes, it was quite nice, but the food was awful,' or, 'Yes, the weather was brilliant but the mozzies were a nightmare.' Still on UK clocks, we woke before dawn and walked for miles down deserted beaches. We fed bananas to the monkeys that came in the early morning to the gardens. We lay on a raft, anchored just off the beach, gazing down at bright little fishes in crystal water. We had fresh aloe vera massages from a Rasta with dreads down to his waist, who sat with us at sunset and offered us friendly puffs of his spliff. We lay on the canvas deck of a Hobie Cat and sailed gently up the tree-lined coast, while the owner told us juicy stories of famous people who stayed at swankier hotels and expensive villas. He was funny and extraordinarily handsome, with a voice like lilting honey and a body that would put most male gym-rats to shame. Jane said she'd be seriously tempted, if not for the fact that she'd probably be the seventeenth since Christmas.

On the third day we saw a newspaper from another world, but only because someone had left it on a sunbed. 'I feel even smugger about being here, now,' said Jane.

So did I. You couldn't help it when you saw headlines

about gales, floods and rivers bursting their banks. The West Country had been particularly badly hit; there was a photo of mountainous seas at Westward Ho! 'Maybe I'll give Felicity a ring,' I said. 'Just to make sure they haven't been washed away.'

It was Ian who answered. Felicity was out, and I thought he sounded tense. 'Is everything OK?'

'Fine, except for a bloody tree crashing on to the roof. I should have had it felled before.'

'But everybody's all right?'

'Oh, yes. Absolutely fine.'

I worried for only three minutes about where Felicity might have gone; I was still in heaven. That night, as we sat on the beach listening to the tree frogs, I told Jane about Nick.

Initially stunned, she then started laughing. Echoing me at the murder, she said, 'Jane, how on earth can you fancy anything in that shirt?'

'It was the dinner jacket.'

'Yes, he did look rather tasty.'

Later she said, 'But to be fair, it could have been a bit hurtful to say you'd have regretted it in the morning. I don't suppose you'd be exactly over the moon if a man said that to you.'

I do hate this, when someone says exactly what you've been trying not to think. Sifting soft sand in my fingers, I felt an uneasy little pang. 'I know.'

'And maybe it was just a *bit* OTT to slap him,' she went on.

'He shouldn't have said that about Leo!'

'OK, I know. It was salt on the wound.'

But it was partly true, that was why it had stung. 'You're right, though.'

'Send him a postcard: "Sorry, Nick, no hard feelings?" '

'And sign it "The Slapper".'

She laughed. 'Go on, I dare you.'

'Maybe not. I know who I will send one to, though.'

'Who?'

'Rob. I'll send him one tonight.'

I did. On the back of a golden Caribbean sunset I wrote, *'Wish you were here – I really do. Jane says you can join her Club Val even though you're a bloke. Lots of love, Izzy XXX.'*

Underneath Jane wrote, *'Too idle to send one myself but love and Xs anyway, J.'*

The week went by on wings. We boarded the night flight with passable tans and bags full of presents. We took a cab from Heathrow, and as soon as we thought they'd be up, Jane phoned Devon. I was planning on driving down that afternoon.

But it wasn't Felicity who answered. 'Hi, Ian!' Jane said brightly. 'We're back, we're brown, and we've got lots of goodies. How's things?'

Making coffee, I was suddenly aware that she'd gone quiet.

I could see from her face that something was terribly wrong. I had a sudden vision of a car, crushed by a falling tree. 'Jane, for God's sake, what's happened?'

# Chapter 15

Under her tan her colour had drained away. 'Oh, Izzy . . .'

I went cold. Without a word I grabbed the phone. 'Ian?'

'It's Henry, Izzy. I'm so bloody sorry. He charged into a river. We've had so much rain, it was like a torrent. We've searched and searched, but there was no sign of him.'

'What river? What was he doing near a river?'

'He shouldn't have been near it. Felicity had him on the lead a good fifty yards away, but some kids were throwing a Frisbee – Henry was straining so hard, his collar broke. It just gave way. He shot off like a bat out of hell, but the Frisbee went into the river, and he went after it.'

I felt so sick. His collar. The collar I hadn't got around to replacing.

'We combed the banks,' he went on. 'Jack and his friends, too. We were all out there. I'm so bloody sorry.'

Then they hadn't looked hard enough. They hadn't called hard enough. 'I'm coming down. I'll come right now and go and look myself. He must be there somewhere – he can't just have—'

'Izzy, we've done everything. We've been on to every vet's, every rescue centre, ever since, but there's been nothing. I'm so sorry, but if he was going to turn up, he'd have done it by now.'

'What d'you mean, *by now*? When did it happen?'

'Last Sunday morning.'

Last *Sun*day? I felt so sick. 'Why didn't you tell me?'

'Izzy, what could you have done? We didn't want to wreck your holiday.'

An hour and a half later, I drove off in a bad dream. Or maybe it was a sick, cruel joke. I'd felt a bit like this on hearing that Princess Diana had died. It was some sort of sadistic April Fool: any minute someone was going to say, ha ha, had you there, didn't we?

No wonder Ian had sounded tense when I'd called. He'd been 'fielding' the calls in case it was me. Felicity had been too upset to bluff; she'd been in agonies of guilt ever since. But it wasn't her fault, was it? It was mine.

Whatever else he'd lied about, Ian hadn't lied about the roof. A blue tarpaulin hit me in the eye as I turned into the drive. The tree had fallen from the back, but even the front garden was littered with debris.

Almost the worst thing I had to bear that day was Felicity's guilt and anguish. For nearly a week she'd had to live with the thought of telling me. I felt terrible for putting her through this, all because I hadn't got around to buying a new collar.

Even Shep was subdued; a pall of gloom hung over the house. I briefly saw Jack and Pip and the Aussies. They mumbled about how sorry they were, he was a nice dog, it was a terrible shame. I thanked them for helping in the search; Jack said any time, and the Aussies said no worries, and they all went out, presumably to escape the atmosphere.

Because Felicity was so stricken, I had to cover just how bad I felt. She kept saying she'd never forgive herself; I kept telling her it was my fault. We tried to talk of other things; Ian said it was typical for the tree to fall on the fucking

239

roof now, he'd had a new roof put on last year, if it had happened then he could have got it on the insurance. And Felicity said how could he be thinking about fucking insurance at a time like this? Ian put on a closed-up face, as if he'd been putting up with this sort of thing for days.

Later, with the television talking to itself, she said, 'Why the hell didn't I take them to the beach? I was going to, but the sea was so rough. I was worried about them charging into the waves.'

'You mustn't blame yourself,' said Ian. 'It wasn't your fault.'

'Will you stop saying that?' she flared. 'It doesn't help!'

With a glance at me, as if to say, 'She can't help it,' he left us.

I felt dreadful. Whatever tensions existed between them, I was making them worse. I felt terrible for bringing this anguish on Felicity, but at the same time I almost began to be guiltily angry with her, for making me feel worse by taking it out on Ian. I had Henry's empty basket in the kitchen and his worn, broken collar in my hand. She had Shep, curled up at her feet.

As we were throwing supper together, she said, 'Scott and Sean can sleep on the sofas tonight. You can have their room.'

Scott and Sean were the Aussies. 'No, leave them. I can stay at Rob's.'

'They won't mind!'

'I don't want anyone sleeping on sofas on my account. It'll be a whole lot easier if I go to Rob's.'

'He's moved in with Nick. In any case, he's not there. He went to Bristol to clear the last of his stuff out of his house – it's finally changing hands on Tuesday.'

It was like a kick in the guts. Suddenly I wanted Rob so

badly. I needed to be with someone who wouldn't make me feel even worse than I already did.

'I'll go to the Coach and Horses,' I said. 'They've got a couple of rooms, haven't they?'

'You don't have to stay there! You could stay at Nick's anyway – I'll give him a call.'

'No! I don't really know him,' I added, seeing her face.

'For heaven's sake, you know him well enough!'

Exactly. 'Please don't argue – I'd really rather go to the Coach and Horses.' But they were inexplicably full, so I picked somewhere else out of the phone book: a pub I'd passed often, where I vaguely recalled an 'Accommodation' sign.

When I told Felicity she had a fit. 'Izzy, you can't stay there! It's a dump!'

'It's a bed. Anyway, it's done now.'

I left at nine, feeling bad because I was glad to get away. But Felicity was right. The place I'd picked wouldn't have won any roses from the English Tourist Board. They gave me a small double bed that smelt musty, in a room smelling as if someone had hastily squirted lavender polish around, to counteract the odour of stale beer and chips from downstairs.

I couldn't sleep. My head was tormented with horrible visions. When I put out my hand I could almost feel Henry beside me, almost hear his snuffly little sighs. In the lonely dark I almost thought his ghost had come to comfort me, like Mrs Denny's Ron.

I woke to a sky full of pearl-grey clouds being whipped by the wind. It was raining, but not in torrents. I went downstairs at half past nine, and found the owners busy and insisting on giving me the included breakfast.

I sat in the saloon bar with coffee, toast, and a

tortoiseshell cat so anxious to make friends, she jumped on to my lap. I was glad of the company, because I wasn't expecting any other until someone knocked on the locked door. The landlady grumbled as she opened it. 'We're closed.'

'I'm sorry, I realize that. I've come to see one of your guests.'

'We've only got one. She's having her breakfast.'

I probably looked a bit dumb as he walked across grubby red carpet that smelt of beer and fags.

There was no 'Good morning'. He sat opposite me. 'Izzy, this is silly,' he said, in a low voice. 'Why did you come to a place like this?'

'The Coach and Horses was full.'

'That was no reason to come to a dump. Why didn't you come to me?'

This told me he'd spoken to Felicity, and more or less what she'd said: 'I know, I told her you wouldn't mind but she wouldn't listen . . .'

I also knew what he was leaving unsaid: 'Yes, I realize why you might have felt awkward, but for crying out loud . . .'

I looked down at the cat, purring under my hand. 'I needed to be on my own.'

'I phoned Felicity on the off chance that there'd been any news.' He paused. 'I'm so sorry.'

'It was my own fault.' Suddenly my eyes were filling; I had a job to plug the leaks. 'He used to belong to a neighbour of mine. She used her old dog's collar – he was called Rusty. I knew it needed replacing, I just never got around to it.'

'You weren't to know it was going to give.'

The landlady came up. 'Will you be wanting breakfast?'

'Some coffee would be nice,' he said. 'Thank you.'

I watched her depart, in grubby pink slippers. 'It won't be nice,' I said, *sotto voce*. 'I think she makes it herself out of old beer mats and acorns.'

There was a fleeting smile. Then he looked down, seeming to deliberate, before raising his eyes again. 'Look, can we just get New Year out of the way? I said things I shouldn't have.' He paused. 'I'm sorry. I was out of order.'

I should have learnt by now that he could be very direct, but this was so unexpected it almost got my leaks going again. 'No more out of order than I was. I'm sorry I slapped you.'

'I'm a big boy.'

The landlady came back with a cup. 'Sure you don't want anything else?'

'I've already eaten, thanks.'

As she withdrew, it seemed a good time to draw a line under awkward topics. 'What a shame. I'm sure she's got a couple of six-week-old eggs thinking nobody loves them.'

He gave one of those little smiles that only extend to one side. 'That animal,' he said, nodding at Puss, 'is grossly overweight.'

'Cuddly, though. And probably the cleanest fixture in the whole place.'

For a moment there was one of those silences during which you don't quite know what to say.

He broke it. 'You've got a nice little tan.'

' "Little's" the word.' To think how chuffed I'd been with my dusting of gold.

'How was it?' he asked.

'Paradise, until we got back.' Again I was glad of Puss. Focusing on tortoiseshell fur is very helpful when you're feeling wobbly. 'It might sound morbid, but I want to go and see where it happened. I can't ask Felicity – she's in

243

enough of a state as it is.' I looked up at him. 'Do you know where this place is?'

'More or less. It's five or six miles.'

'Could you give me directions?'

'I'll take you, if you like.'

He took a sip of his coffee and made a face. 'Christ, I see what you mean.'

'You have to drink it all, or I'll make you eat some of this rubbery toast, too.'

With a little smile, he nodded towards the door. 'Come on, let's get out of here.'

Outside it was still raining slightly, from a wild and windy sky. I got into his car, realizing that I'd never have imagined this last night. However, the atmosphere was easier now that skeletons had been taken out of cupboards. After so many weeks, that episode felt unreal anyway.

He took a route I didn't know. Any flat land we passed looked sodden, pools of water lying on grass or between ploughed furrows. How could I have been sitting smugly in Barbados while this was happening? What was I doing while Henry was struggling for his life? Idly thinking about swimming to the raft? How could I not have known?

'How's Sasha?' I asked, just for something to say.

'Still pulling pints. She's applied for some theatrical job in Edinburgh.'

'A long way to go for an interview.'

'She found a cheap flight.' He glanced across at me. 'Did you know she used to be my cleaning lady?'

'You're kidding!'

'I'm not.' Slowing down, he frowned at one of those signposts partly obscured by trees. 'It was last summer. I was putting in a hell of a lot of hours and my place was turning into a bit of a tip when one of those little flyers came through the door. It said, "What do you really hate? Ironing? Cleaning out your fridge? Let me do it for you." I was expecting some middle-aged woman.'

'God.'

'I'd seen her before, at the Coach and Horses. She was still doing that, living with Mum and looking for anything else to help pay off her debts.'

'And has she?'

'No, but if this job comes off it's a case of *carpe diem*. Seize the day. I admire her, you know. I think she'd have shovelled muck for another tenner.'

I knew what he was saying underneath. 'I know what everybody thinks, but it isn't quite like that.'

All right, so maybe it wasn't. At any rate, it had taken my mind off Henry for all of a minute. 'I've jacked my job in,' I said, for the same reason.

'Why?'

'Chain reaction. There's a lot of it about.' I told him briefly about Moving On. It distracted me just until I said, '. . . and it was going to be the end of Henry in the office . . .'

As my voice tailed off, I felt sick. I saw Nick glance across at me, but he said nothing. You didn't know what to say. You just felt awful, like I'd felt awful after Mrs Denny's Ron. '*I keep forgetting, that's the awful thing. The back door goes, and I think, "Oh, that'll be him . . ."*'

And I'd said such stupid things. Like, 'Shall I make you a cup of tea?' A cup of tea after fifty-four years.

After a few miles' silence he slowed down for a couple of riders on horses with shaggy winter coats. 'You're not really terrified of horses, are you?'

'Of course not.' Recalling that incisive, 'Do you ride?' I went on, 'But I don't think my idea of riding would be quite the same as hers. I can apply brakes and accelerator, but I never had it down to a fine art.'

For several minutes he said nothing. I knew he was wondering whether to try to distract me from the empty sickness in my stomach, or to shut up.

He shut up.

The rain had died to a few fat spots by the time we got there, which was just as well, as I only had a fleece. On one side of the little curving road was a steep wooded hill. From the top, you'd be able to see for miles across rolling hills, but Felicity hadn't come for the views. She'd brought the dogs here because a hill would be drier underfoot than the usual walks. She'd have parked on the little road where Nick had just parked, but on the other side was a gentle slope of grass, running down to a river. It had happened as she was getting the dogs back into the car, and I could see exactly how. While unlocking the tailgate she'd have had them on leads, because of the road, but Henry would have seen the kids chucking the Frisbee. A game! Wow! Desperate to join in, he'd have strained on the leash and that would have been it. Off like a greased missile, and then it would have been only a matter of seconds. A throw too far, a gust of wind . . . Oops, it had gone into the river. Still, who cared? Even better fun. Take him to a lake and he'd fetch sticks out of it all day.

We walked about halfway down that grassy slope. It wasn't really much of a river, only about ten feet across. In summer it would be placid but just now it was almost overflowing. Before my eyes, millions of gallons of rushing brown water were hell-bent on the sea. Within seconds he'd have been out of sight.

'It must have been even worse last week,' I said. 'The river, I mean.'

He was standing a little apart from me, hands thrust in his jeans pockets. 'A lot worse, I'm afraid.'

'I don't suppose he'd have stood an earthly.' Unbelievably, as I said it, a large dirty white object was swept past on that rushing brown tide. It was gone incredibly fast, almost too fast to identify, but not quite.

A sheep. A dead, drowned sheep.

I turned away.

Nick touched my shoulder. 'Come on, let's go.' He said nothing else until we were back at the car. Instead of going straight to the driver's side, he unlocked the passenger door first. 'I'm so sorry.'

His voice was low and sympathetic, and if I'd flickered an eyelash I knew he'd have put his arms around me. It would have been entirely unconnected with any skeletons, merely because he felt sorry for me. But I knew it would make me dissolve, and I didn't want to. 'You never know, maybe "Whom the gods love . . ." applies to dogs, too.'

'Maybe.' With a little smile, he opened the door.

He drove off while I was still strapping myself in. 'He was on borrowed time anyway. Mrs Denny – that's my neighbour – found him running in a busy street. He'd only just missed being flattened.'

That was when it hit me. God help me, how was I going to tell Mrs Denny?

Something must have shown on my face. He said, 'It's a bit early to find anywhere that does stiff shots, but we might find a proper cup of coffee.'

'No, I'm fine.'

He didn't push it.

As we neared the pub, thoughts were taking shape in my mind. 'I know it's almost certainly a waste of time, I know Felicity's been on to all the vets and shelters already, but I'm going to do it again. Just in case.'

'You've got nothing to lose.'

Except time, and a sliver of hope refusing to be abandoned. 'I can't just do nothing. What if he somehow managed to scramble out and someone found him? With no collar, they'd have thought he'd been abandoned.'

'Was he microchipped?'

Why did he have to ask that? I looked out of the window at wet sheep in a field. 'That was something else I never got around to. I meant to ask when I took him to the vet for his last shots, but we started talking about Bedlington terriers and I forgot. You know, the ones that look a bit like little woolly sheep.'

'For God's sake, don't ever say that in the earshot of a certain Mrs Parks I see on a regular basis. At the last count she had five of them.'

'I hope she doesn't bring them all at once. That would make a big hole in your nice meaty chews.'

He gave a little chuckle. After a moment he went on, 'If you're going to check shelters, I take it you'll be staying a couple more days?'

'If that's what it takes. Just as well I haven't got a job to rush back to.'

'I hope you're not thinking of going back to that dump?'

'It wasn't that bad. I know it sounds awful, but I had to get away from Felicity. She feels so bad, it was making me feel terrible. In any case, she's already got a houseful, what with Jack and Pip and their mates from Oz.'

He turned left at a little crossroads with one of those old-fashioned pointy signposts that used to remind me of *Dick Whittington*. 'I'm surprised the Aussies are still here, and not hitting London.'

'Their grandparents came from around here, so they wanted to take a look. I said they'd certainly picked lovely

248

weather for it, and they said, well, it made a change from the fires round Sydney.'

'That's one way of looking at it.'

Having pulled in to the scruffy car park, he turned to me. 'I'm not going to push it, but I do have a reasonably comfortable single bed covered with scary green dinosaurs. Officially it's Alex's, so I can't guarantee there won't be any sticky sweet papers underneath, but it's there if you want it.'

All I saw in his eyes, or heard in his tone, was a kind, practical offer that nearly dissolved me after all. 'Thank you.' I got out quickly, before it did.

As I was unlocking my own car, he wound his window down. 'And if the dinosaurs get too scary, Alex has left a death-ray gun that Rob needs absolutely no excuse to play with.'

I don't think anything would have made me laugh that day, but that very nearly did. 'I bet he doesn't.'

'He'll be back tonight, by the way.'

I knew why he'd said it: in case I felt awkward about accepting his offer. 'I thought he might. Thanks so much for taking me.'

'I wish I could say my pleasure.'

As if she realized why I'd really left them Felicity seemed marginally less tense when I got back. At any rate, she'd stopped snapping at Ian. When I told them I was planning some last-ditch checking, neither of them said I'd be wasting my time, but I know they thought it.

Rob turned up around six, and Felicity naturally insisted on feeding us, so it was around nine before we left. Nick's place was only about four miles away, on the outskirts of the town. It was a pleasant, unremarkable, new-ish detached house, in the kind of quiet residential road popular with families.

'He calls it the Rabbit Hutch,' said Rob, as he unlocked the front door. 'He didn't give a toss when he moved here, except that he couldn't be arsed with decorating and he thought the garden would be good for Alex. But as he said, unless he's not actually taking him out, all the little sod wants to do is watch videos.'

Inside it was light and spacious, but still in that unfinished bachelor state in which as long as you've got a fridge and somewhere comfortable to sprawl, the rest doesn't much matter.

Rob slung his keys on a light-coloured wooden coffee-table. 'Now, what can I get you? Beer, vodka, or just a good old shoulder to cry on?'

As Nick was out, now would have been a pretty good time to dissolve, but having been turned back a few times, the flood had retreated. 'It's OK, I'm not going to soak your sweatshirt. I could use a vodka, though.'

We sat together on the squashy sofa and talked of anything but Henry. Pretty soon we got round to Paula, and I was relieved to find Rob hadn't been breaking his heart. 'She could be hard going,' he said. 'Very intense, and what I think they call "emotionally needy." But the fact is, when we got together she needed someone badly, and so did I.'

That didn't surprise me.

'She was running away from a miserable relationship when she came down here,' he went on. 'The classic married man who'd been telling her for two years his marriage was on the rocks. She thought distance was the only way she was going to put a stop to it.'

'She hasn't got back with him?'

'No, just someone else who messed her around. I think she's had more than her fair share of mess.'

'Poor Paula.' I knocked back the last of my vodka. 'She's probably one of those women who only really want men who treat them rotten. They crave the emotional roller-coaster. Still, I'm glad you're not upset. You've had enough lately in that department.'

After a pause he said, 'I suppose I knew she was restless. I just hadn't realized how much.'

I knew he wasn't talking about Paula. 'Didn't she take off shortly afterwards and go travelling?'

He nodded. 'She'd talked before about Vietnam and Cambodia. And Macchu Pichu, come to that. She could be anywhere.'

'Every other person you speak to nowadays is going travelling. It's not just gap-year kids any more.'

'I know. I think she felt she'd missed out.'

As Juliet had been an NHS physio, overworked and underpaid, I could imagine a bad case of sudden itchy feet. You'd wake up one morning and think, God, what am I doing? Life's too short – if I don't do it now, maybe I never will.

'I nearly sent her an email at Christmas,' he went on. 'Just to say, hi, hope you're all right . . .'

I turned to him. 'Then why didn't you?'

He gave a very Rob-ish, rueful little smile. 'I didn't want her thinking, oh, shit . . .'

This was so typical of Rob. 'You never know, maybe she's being eaten alive by mozzies, or staying in some dump with cockroaches the size of rats. She might be glad of a little message from home. When's her birthday?'

'Last week. I nearly sent her one then, too.'

'Just do it, Rob. Faint heart, and all that . . .'

251

But I wished at once I hadn't said it. I shouldn't be encouraging false hopes.

For a while neither of us said anything. Then he squeezed my hand. 'You can talk about him, you know. I can handle a wet shoulder.'

I knew he'd read my mind. I'd been gazing round the room, idly taking in a blown-up photo on the wall. Rooftops, masses of them, sprouting TV aerials with washing hanging on them. In the distance, by contrast, were soft green hills. It could have been Italy, a shot taken by a professional friend. Then my gaze had gone to untidily crammed book shelves and a couple of kids' videos by the VCR. It could do with a plant or two, I'd thought. A nice big one in the corner. And suddenly I'd looked at the carpet at my feet and wondered where Henry was. Always-there Henry, my furry shadow.

My stomach contracted. 'I'd rather talk about something else. What's the state of play with the Butchery?'

'The same. Little Markham's still negotiating with the big boys.'

'I can't believe he just went over your heads.'

'Izzy, he doesn't give a shit. And the fact is, he had a run-in with Nick when his father had the first stroke. He said, right, he was going to offload the whole lot, the old man should have done it years ago. Basically, Nick said perhaps he'd prefer his old man to cark it altogether, and little Markham told him to mind his own fucking business. He'd borrowed money off his old man before and lost the lot. And when he tried to borrow more, the old man asked Nick what he thought.'

'Oh. No minced words, I take it.'

'Hardly. And little Markham knew what had been going on. No love lost, in three words.'

'Still, it's not a total disaster, is it? You won't be out of your jobs?'

'No, they'll probably still be there, assuming we still want them.' He paused. 'It's not that we're dreamy-eyed idealists, we all have to make a living, but if we're going to have bean counters breathing down our necks, we'd rather they were our own.'

But talking of vets only made me think of the last time I'd taken Henry for his shots and how fearfully he'd trembled in the waiting-room. I couldn't understand why, as he'd never had any bad experiences. I could only think he was picking up vibes from a spaniel that was trembling even more.

Nick still wasn't back when I went to bed. I lay under a green-dinosaur duvet, haunted by that memory of Henry. I could still feel him trembling under my hand, and that led to far worse visions that wouldn't go away.

Both Rob and Nick had left when I got up. On the kitchen table, on top of the *Yellow Pages* and the phone book, Nick had left a key on a sheet of paper with a scrawl that said, 'Front door. Help yourself to anything – good luck.'

Armed with my road atlas, I phoned any establishment within a twenty-mile radius. My voice got worn out with saying brightly, 'Oh, good morning, I wonder if you can help me. I suppose you haven't had a large, rather scruffy mongrel brought in? He's got possible bits of Irish wolfhound and Bedlington terrier – well, some people think he looks a bit like a sheep – his fur's sort of greyish brown and he won't be wearing a collar . . . No? Well, thanks very much anyway.'

Just as I was beginning to wonder why I was putting myself through this, Mum phoned. 'I've been trying the house since yesterday morning, dear, and your mobile's been off. Where on earth are you?'

'In Devon, at Rob's.'

'Oh, lovely shaggy Rob? How nice. We got your postcard today – did you have a lovely holiday?'

'Brilliant. It was the getting back that wrecked it.' Of course I told her and she was dreadfully upset for me, but still the flood stayed back. Knowing Mum and Dad, they might get straight on a plane, just to show they cared, and I didn't need any proof.

Eventually she told me why she'd phoned. 'Marisa had her baby the other day – a little girl. I've sent some flowers, of course. I was going to ask you to buy me a nice little present if you were going to pop in, but it doesn't matter now.'

'No, I'll go. I should go home anyway. I don't know what the hell I'm doing here, tormenting myself with phone calls. Ian was right; he wouldn't have stood an earthly.'

'I'm so sorry, dear. Poor little Henry. But if it's any comfort, I don't suppose he'd have known much about it.'

I left shortly afterwards, leaving a note: 'No luck, but thanks for the bed anyway – I thought the dinosaurs looked quite cuddly.'

I got home early enough to head straight for shops that sold baby things. Again the parking was a nightmare, but at least it delayed my return to a house so painfully empty that I couldn't wait to get out of it. I phoned Marisa, who said, yes, come over, she'd love to see me.

En route to the car, it was just my luck to bump into Craig.

'Haven't seen you for a bit,' he said. 'Been away?'

'Yes, to Barbados.'

'Oh, *very* nice. The real-estate business is doing fine,

254

then, on all us poor mugs' one and a half per cents. I suppose you put the mutt in kennels? That would explain why I've seen fewer turds than usual.'

I began to understand those nice, normal people who suddenly go berserk with kitchen knives. 'He stayed with a friend, Craig. And while she was taking him for a walk he charged into a river and drowned. All right? Why don't you go and have a drink to celebrate?'

Leaving him speechless for once, I stormed to my car and slammed the door. Whatever was rising in me wasn't even a flood any more. It was a hot, wet volcano. Let loose, it would ravage my face, leaving it blotchy with red eyes that would take hours to go down. How could I go like that to someone who'd just had her first baby? So I lowered the window, took a few deep breaths, and turned the key in the ignition.

Marisa lived in a turn-of-the-century house that had been done up with elegant flair, but that was Marisa for you. You knew no interior designer had mixed that little rosewood desk with silk hangings from Kashmir and the latest in Italian sofas, or unearthed that vibrant curtain material from some little treasure house near Florence that nobody else had heard of. As for Marisa herself, apart from minor added poundage she might have just spent a week at Champneys.

'I don't think you've been reading the right articles,' I told her. 'According to current popular theory, you're supposed to be bursting with post-natal depression and bitterly resenting this Thing that's stopping you getting any sleep.'

'I know,' she laughed. 'Trust me to be awkward. Here's the Thing, anyway. Isn't she gorgeous? I just want to keep picking her up and cuddling her.'

I gazed into a pink-quilted Moses basket at a tiny,

perfect, fast-asleep little face. A minute hand was curled beside it and something in my heart twisted. 'She's beautiful. What are you going to call her?'

'Grace.'

And she'd fit her name, I could bet. 'Why did you keep it quiet?'

'I had a scare, at three months. I hardly told anyone till it was so obvious I didn't have to. But never mind that – have a cup of tea and tell me what you've been up to.'

'Nothing half as exciting as you. Was it hell?'

'Not exactly shelling peas, but worth it.' She started laughing. 'You're not still petrified at the mere thought?'

This went back years. When we were about eleven a friend and I had spent hours poring over some gynaecological manual of Mum's that had stuff about sex in it. We'd giggled over tasteful line drawings of erect organs and couples in various copulatory positions. Eeugh! Imagine your mum and dad doing that! We'd gone into hysterics at the thought. Then there had been The Miracle Within, and how The Miracle got out. One sentence had stuck for ever in my brain: '*The cut is made at the height of a contraction, so the pain is not felt.*'

Well, that was it, we'd decided. We were never, ever Doing It – willies were absolutely gross anyway. And I recalled telling Marisa exactly this, in much the same words.

'I suppose I still am,' I said. 'But don't tell anybody.'

After dishing out presents, I told her a little of what I'd been up to, after all. 'You'll never believe who I bumped into not so long ago.'

Of course she remembered; she laughed about it now. 'I was almost glad you'd kicked him afterwards. He promised to write to me, you know, and he never did. I was heartbroken for at least two days. How's he turned out?'

Funnily enough, it wasn't our kitchen fireworks that came to mind. I thought of the slap, and of what I'd said. Then I thought of the other day, and wondered whether I'd have been so kind to a man who'd told me he'd have regretted it in the morning. And an odd little pain pierced the huge lonely void called Henry. 'Oh, not bad,' I said. 'Quite nice, actually.'

'Weird, isn't it? I can barely remember his face now.'

Shortly afterwards her husband came home. At the wedding one of her friends had referred to him as 'boring Peter', which I'd thought unbelievably nasty but had guiltily agreed with at the same time. She'd specialized in such glamorous boyfriends before: film people or racing drivers. A few months after the wedding she'd said to me, 'I know what some people thought about Peter, but he was such a relief after the others. There were always a dozen women who'd have pinched them just like that if they could. And the only people men like that ever really love are themselves.'

Peter was quietly but extremely successful in the City. He was nice enough looking in a nondescript way, but anyone could see who he loved the instant he came in. It shone out of his eyes as he kissed her, and in a different way as he inspected the tiny face in the Moses basket. 'How's she been?' he asked. 'Can I pick her up?'

'Go on, then. I know you're dying to.' Marisa winked at me. 'He's a terrible softie. I know he's going to spoil her absolutely rotten, but I'll forgive him.'

I went home feeling so lonely I could die.

# Chapter 16

The house felt even emptier in the morning, and horribly quiet. In the past I'd cursed his frenzied barking at the postman, but now I'd have given anything to hear it. Only now that he wasn't there did I realize how much I'd talked to him: anything from, 'Nearly out of tea bags again,' to 'Do you think Craig's obnoxiousness could perhaps be related to lack of endowment in the dick department?' Any eavesdropper would have thought I was halfway to the crazy old dog lady already.

At ten to nine I called Louise. Before I could get a word in she said, 'Honestly, it's just not the same without you and Henry. Thanks for the postcard, by the way – we all really hate you. Are you sickeningly brown?'

'More like dirty cream. You couldn't meet me for lunch, could you?'

'I'd love to, but I've got a hell of a lot on today – how about Friday?'

If I was going to spill woes, the least I could do was buy her lunch first. 'Lovely, I'll give you a call.'

I thought of going to see Mrs Denny, but I couldn't face it. Not until I'd given it my best, last shot. For an hour I sat with my laptop, going through the cyber *Yellow Pages*. I phoned every rescue, every kennels, and every veterinary practice again. When they said, 'Sorry' I asked whether they knew of any minor rescues that wouldn't be able to afford *Yellow Pages* listing. I phoned everyone who might possibly know of some funny old dear who had eleven stray dogs at any given time and lived on economy baked beans. I phoned every possibility they came up with, saying, 'Oh, good morning, I wonder if you can help me . . .'

It wasn't long before a sort of paranoid suspicion seized me. What if they didn't recognize my description? What if the person who answered the phone had been away when he'd been brought in and couldn't be bothered to check? *'Oh, Lord, someone phoned about a dog like that earlier – I told her we didn't have him. Still, too late now. Bit funny looking, isn't he? Don't suppose anyone'll want him.'*

I knew I'd never rest until I'd checked for myself. By midday I was back in the car. I'd say I wanted to give a rescue dog a home. Oh, yes, someone would be at home all day, I'd just gone freelance. Journalism, if they asked. (Thank you, Paula.)

Of course, even in a twenty-five-mile radius there weren't that many places to check, which was just as well. It broke my heart looking in pen after pen, seeing the pathetic, excited little faces up at the wire, desperate for someone to love them. Worse still were the withdrawn ones, curled up in a corner with sad faces, too traumatized or depressed to respond at all. How did people do this? How could you choose just one? Choking back tears, I smiled brightly at the attendant, saying, thanks, I'd go away and think about it.

Wondering why the hell I'd put myself through it, I got back in the car. He was gone; I just had to accept it. Far worse things happened. I would go home now, be sensible and sort my life out. A good place to start would be something to eat. All I'd had since breakfast was a bar of Fruit & Nut. No wonder I was feeling wobbly.

At the first services I toyed with something that called itself lasagne. Surrounded by couples, families and groups of friends, I seemed to be the only lone eater in the entire place. It was raining again when I left. I drove in the dark to the next junction and did a U-turn.

When I was about two miles away I phoned Felicity, but there was no reply, and her mobile was off, too. I drove to the house anyway, but no lights glowed through curtains and neither car was in the drive.

I headed for Rob, and could have cried with relief when I saw a light on and his car outside. He answered the door in tracksuit bottoms and an old sweatshirt. 'Izzy! I didn't know you were coming down today!'

'I've been checking shelters. I couldn't bear going home alone. Is Nick in?'

'No, he's on call – there was an emergency.'

Thank God. I didn't want an audience.

Rob provided the mother and father of mopping-up operations that night. Entire rivers flooded out as I told him everything. Visions of Henry desperately struggling in the water, his lifeless body being swept into the estuary. His reluctance to get into Felicity's car, my last glimpse of his mournful little face. It was haunting me – had he somehow known? Rob held me close on the squashy sofa, passing me tissues. Of course he hadn't known, how could he?

He might have, I wept. Dogs sensed all sorts of things. And what if he *had* got out and been taken to one of those places where they only keep them seven days? With no collar, they'd have thought he'd been abandoned. They might have thought he was too funny-looking for anyone to want, and put him down.

They wouldn't, Rob soothed. But they might, I wept. He knew as well as I did that these things happened. There were just too many dogs and too few homes. I couldn't bear the house without him. He'd always been right beside me: when I woke up at night, when I was watching TV, even when I was in the shower he'd curl up on the mat. I felt as if I'd lost my best friend. And Rob held me, shushing me and stroking my hair, and saying yes, he knew, but he was my best friend, too. And I wept that I knew that, but he didn't curl up on the bath mat, oh, God, could he pass me another tissue . . .

Eventually I got on to Leo, and Rob held me close and said why the hell hadn't I told him? Because I couldn't, I sniffed, wiping a red nose. I'd felt such a fool. But deep down, I'd always known Leo would be over eventually, it was just a question of when. I'd never thought I'd lose Henry, not like this, not until he was old and his time had come. And Rob said, well, at least I'd been spared seeing him going downhill with arthritis, his legs packing up, maybe cancer, and having to decide it would be kinder to let him go.

That only made me think again of what some brisk, faceless person might have done to Henry, and set me off once more. Eventually, as the television talked quietly to itself in the background, we got off my woes and back to Juliet. Why hadn't he said anything? I asked. When she'd said it wasn't going anywhere, why hadn't he said, well, actually, he was hoping it was?

'I think she'd sensed that already,' he said. 'She already felt bad enough – I wasn't going to make her feel even worse.'

So, just like Rob, he'd made it easy for her. No scenes, no adding to the guilt she'd have felt anyway. By natural logic, this led us on to Ian and Felicity. 'Has he said anything to you?' I asked.

'Are you kidding? You know us blokes only talk about cars and football.'

As I disposed of about fifty soaked tissues in the bin, he disappeared to the kitchen and came back with a little glass and a mug. 'Get that down,' he said, passing me a shot of brandy. 'And here's the chaser.' It was hot chocolate.

Dear old Rob. Slumped together on the sofa, we talked about how brilliant we both were at getting it wrong. 'I hate being on my own,' I confessed. 'I know you're supposed to revel in the freedom, but I hate it. I get lonely.'

'So do I. I guess that was part of it with Paula. But I liked her, and whatever I had, she seemed to need it. And I don't mean sex.'

'I know you don't.' For a moment I gazed unseeing at the television. 'My trouble is, I always fall in lust.'

'Well, it's not a bad start.'

'I know, but I never seem to get the other bit afterwards. The best-friend bit added on.'

His encircling arm gave me a little squeeze. 'Maybe you and I should get a potion. We've got the best-friends bit down to a fine art – all we need is something to make us fall in lust.'

As he looked down at me, I knew what I'd often suspected: he'd once had a little spark for me, too. It was still there, if only just. If we'd wanted, we could probably have fanned it just then into a little flame. But we'd both know it would only be a comfort-flame, so that we could fall asleep in each other's arms and not be lonely. So that a warm someone would be there in the morning. If it could ever have been a fierce, real-thing flame, we'd have fanned it before. So I think we both knew the time was long gone. We'd been just-friends too long, and first-best friends was miles better than second-best something else.

'It would take some potion,' I said. 'Especially just now, when I'm looking like something out of a horror film.'

'Oh, come on. I don't know when I've seen such lovely pink eyes.' Giving me a little squeeze, he picked up the TV remote. 'Shall we see if there's any really good crap worth watching?'

I can't remember what crap he found, but I think it was some film with a lot of shooting. We didn't watch it, anyway. We somehow got on to adolescent angst, and he told me about psyching himself up for three weeks to ask some girl out, how she'd said, 'You are joking?' and it had taken him months to get over it. That led on to other things, and eventually I told him about Nick and the seagull. And he laughed, but startled me by revealing that Nick had told him years before. He'd joked that getting kicked in the balls and puked on by the same girl, in under a minute, was probably a national record.

Later, as I thought what a lovely friend he'd been in my hour of need, a thought struck me. 'Rob, about the Butchery. If it's a question of raising enough finance, if you wanted to outbid the Vets "R" Us lot, I mean, I could lend you some. The value of my house has shot up so much, I could probably unlock fifty grand in a couple of weeks.'

He stared at me.

'Don't look at me like that. I haven't a clue what an established practice would fetch but I know we're not talking peanuts. As for the premises, I've seen that house. Queen Anne, by the looks of it, and on a pretty prime site.'

'Izzy, I couldn't.'

'I don't see why not. Think of me as the more user-friendly kind of loan shark. A sort of loan goldfish.'

He laughed. 'It's very sweet of you, but no way. In any case, if little shit Markham wanted to give us the option we could probably raise enough.'

I knew it was no use pushing it. 'If you change your mind, I won't have.'

'I know.' Then we started watching some other film, and the next thing I remember is waking with his arm still around me. It was ten to one. I shook him gently awake, we crept upstairs and once again I slept under green dinosaurs.

I woke before six. For a moment I lay there with that horrible feeling that something awful has happened, but you can't remember what.

It soon hit me. No cold nose in my face, no full-of-beans tail wagging. My stomach contracted, and that empty ache came back. Once I heard movement, I got out of bed. Someone was already in the bathroom, so I went downstairs. In a bare, bachelor kitchen with blue cupboards, I put coffee on before finding there was no milk in the fridge.

On the fridge door, though, secured by a magnet, was that Caribbean sunset I'd sent Rob. As I reread my own words, the loss of Henry hit me afresh. Already, when I'd written that, lazily content in the sun, he'd been gone.

Also on the fridge was a Christmas card, or rather a child's felt-tip drawing on a folded A4 sheet. It depicted what was evidently supposed to be a reindeer, as he wore a coat saying 'Rudolph'. However, Rudolph's nose was blue and he looked miserable. Beside him was a man with dead straight parallel legs, a huge bottle saying 'RAINDEER MEDISIN' and a bag saying 'VET'. Inside was drawn another Rudolph, with a red nose and looking a lot perkier. Above this was written 'HAPPY CHRISMAS DADDY' and below it, 'love from Alex.'

I don't quite know why this made my eyes start filling, except that Daddy had kept it on his fridge for so long. When I'm feeling wobbly, it takes nothing to set me off.

I put it back just as Rob came down, in a towelling dressing-gown and with sleep-tousled hair. He slung an evidently just-arrived *Times* on the table. 'How are you feeling?'

'Better than I look, I hope.' The bedroom mirror had shown me vaguely blotchy skin and vestiges of pink-rimmed eyes – a lovely sight for anyone, first thing.

Nick came down right afterwards. Wet-haired, clad in only a towel, he was tactful enough not to gape at my face. 'Hi. I hadn't expected to find you up.'

'You'll gather that I took advantage of the dinosaurs again,' I said. 'I hope you don't mind.'

'Yes, I was going to have a little word with you about that,' he said, on his way to the coffee maker. 'I nearly woke you up last night and threw you out for falling asleep on the premises without written permission.' He grabbed a mug. 'Have you been helping yourself to my coffee, as well?'

Rob shot me a little wink, as if I might have taken his mock-stiff tone seriously.

'Not yet,' I said. 'I couldn't find any milk.'

He opened a cupboard and took out a carton of long-life. 'Will this do?'

With my face in the state it was, feeling unwashed and grotty, I was dying for a shower, but there was only one bathroom and Rob would need it first. And sure enough, once the coffees were poured Rob took his upstairs, saying he was going to make himself beautiful and sweet-smelling.

Left with Nick I suddenly felt awkward, and not just because of my face. However, the paper was lying there and Nick wasn't showing any interest.

'I'm afraid there's sod all to eat,' he said, leaning against the worktop with his mug. 'We're overdue for a supermarket run, but I could probably push the boat out with a piece of toast.'

I looked up from the riveting front page. 'I'm fine, thanks.'

'You'll fade away.'

'So will you and Rob.'

'No chance. We have standing orders at the bakery across the square. They do a pretty good bacon and tomato roll, delivered hot to the door.'

'Lovely.' I turned to the letters page, to take my mind off the eyes I knew were appraising me from a few feet away. Although my mind-set that morning was as far removed from such matters as it was ever going to get, the sight of him wearing very little in a kitchen had obvious connotations.

'What brought you down yesterday?' he asked.

'Last-ditch checking. Everywhere in a twenty-five-mile radius.'

He didn't need telling that it had been in vain. 'I'm sorry.'

'So am I. It was horrible. I wish I hadn't bothered.'

'Why didn't you just call them?'

'I thought they wouldn't check properly. I thought some dope who couldn't be bothered to find out would answer the phone.' I flicked to the Arts page. Goodness me, there was a lot going on in the way of dance and concerts. 'How's Alex?'

He gave a lopsided little smile. 'Still a little sod.'

'If he were a little angel, you'd probably think there was something wrong with him.'

'Probably.' Suddenly brisk, he put his mug on the draining-board. 'Right, I'm going to sling some clothes on.'

Only after he'd gone did I wish I'd said something nice, like, 'I like Alex's Rudolph.' But then he'd have known I'd looked inside what was obviously a Christmas card, just to be nosy. Even from a six-year-old, such things were personal. I'd never have nosed if he'd actually been there. So which was worse, having him think I was nosy, or feeling bad for not saying something nice? Or having him think I must have seen the card and not bothered to say, 'Oh, that's lovely – did Alex do it?'

Oh, hell, why was I worrying about something so trivial? The past few days had turned me into a quivering, emotional jelly. Like those marine invertebrates that lose their shells now and then, I'd have to find a new one, fast.

Rob and Nick left shortly afterwards. 'By the way, I saw Marisa the other day,' I said to Nick, on the doorstep. 'She said she was heartbroken for two whole days because you promised to write to her and never did.'

'Did I?' He gave a half-amused wince. 'Mind you, I might have just lost her address. I was pretty good at stuffing bits of paper in my shorts pockets and forgetting to take them out before my mother slung them in the wash.'

'You were just a callous little sod, you mean,' grinned Rob. 'Why didn't you tell me it was Izzy who nearly ruined you for life?'

'I was afraid of embarrassing her,' he said, tongue in cheek. 'I thought she might do it again. Bye, Izzy.' He brushed my cheek with his lips. 'Take care.'

'You, too. Is that Alex's Rudolph on the fridge, by the way? Brilliant artwork.'

He smiled. 'I'll tell him. When he passed it over he said, "I'm afraid I drew it rather craply but Mum wouldn't let me give you a shop one."'

I laughed. 'I hope he won't mind a *girl* sleeping under his dinosaurs. But thanks anyway.'

'Any time.'

Then it was Rob, and one of his classic hugs. 'Thanks, Rob,' I said, putting my arms around him. 'For the shoulder and everything.'

'It's always there. I'll give you a call later.'

At eight o'clock I rang Felicity.

'If only you'd called a bit earlier,' she lamented. 'I was at my slimming group, or Pork and Beans Club, as Ian calls it. God knows where Jack and his lot were – Ian was probably playing squash.'

Suddenly I knew that before I went home, I had to talk to her properly. 'Could you manage lunch before I go?'

She named a little place in the town square, but ten minutes before I was due to leave she called again. 'Could you come to the house, instead? That restaurant's very busy at lunch-time.' She paused, and her voice wobbled. 'I really need to talk to you.'

It was a very long lunch. 'Oh, buggeration, just look at me,' she despaired afterwards. 'Whatever am I going to tell Ian?'

'That I was upset, and you were coming out in sympathy. He'll believe it.'

'Yes, but it seems so awful, using poor Henry . . . If you dare tell him one word of this, I swear I'll never, ever speak to you again. I know you won't,' she added, with a wan little smile, 'but I had to say it anyway.'

When I eventually got home I phoned Jane. After last ditches, I got on to other things. 'We couldn't have got it more wrong. Do you remember that friend of hers from school? Caroline somebody?'

'Vaguely. What about her?'

'Just after the murder party she phoned Fliss in a terrible state. She'd been with the same bloke for nine years, perfectly happy, all hunky-dory. Until one day he turned round and said, "I'm sorry, I thought I loved you, but I've met someone else and she's blown me away. I hate to do this to you, but it's beyond my control. I'm moving in with her."'

'Oh, my God.'

'Exactly. Nine *years*. She was absolutely devastated. And Felicity started thinking, What if Ian did that to me?'

'Well, it doesn't altogether surprise me. I always thought she was insecure, underneath. Her parents virtually rejected her – it's bound to affect you.'

'OK, but it wasn't just Caroline. There was a magazine article, too. Something on the lines of, "Dare you give him the big U?" U as in Ultimatum, i.e. "Are we ever actually going to get married, because if I'm just OK until you find someone better I'll clear off now."'

'I'd never thought Fliss was that bothered about getting married!'

'I don't think she was, until Caroline put the wind up her. And the thing is, she thought that even if she did issue a big U he'd never say, "Actually, no." She thought he'd say, "Well, why not? Good excuse for a piss-up."'

'About as romantic as macaroni cheese.'

'Yes, but that's not the point. She wants it to come from him, and the fact that it hasn't makes her think that deep down, he doesn't want to commit. All that Luke Archer stuff was just to see if she could arouse a spark of jealousy. Poor Fliss, she wanted Ian to come over all macho and drag her away.'

'After the way she was having a go at him earlier? He was keeping out of her way.'

'Yes, but why do you think she was having a go? After

getting herself all tarted up like that she said, "Do I look
OK?" and he said, "Yes, you look gorgeous." Just like he
always does.'

'That's just Ian.'

'Try telling her that. She was desperate for him to say,
"Wow!" for once. And get this – just after she'd started
her diet he said, what for, he didn't mind a good old
armful of pork and beans.'

'Oh, Lord.' Jane gave a despairing little sigh. 'If only
we'd realized. We could have had a little word in his ear.'
She paused. 'Mind you . . .'

'Jane, don't you dare. If you drop one word, she'll know
it was us. I promised.'

'OK, OK.' She changed the subject. 'If you're feeling all
lonely and bereft at the weekend, you could always come
up here.'

For a moment I was seriously tempted. 'Thanks, but I've
got to get used to it. In any case, I've got things to do, like
sorting my life out.'

To keep me going I registered with a couple of agencies.
One offered two weeks' admin in a property company,
more or less up my street, except that it was in Central
London.

On the Friday, having put it off that long, I went to see
Mrs Denny. She was visibly upset, but I think it was as
much for me, because she knew I'd been afraid of
distressing her. 'Maybe it was meant, love,' she said
eventually.

Mrs Denny was very hot on things being Meant.

'He'd have been a tie to you,' she went on. 'It was all
very well when you could take him to work, but things
change. And he'd have hated being left alone at home all

day, bless him. Sometimes things happen for the best, though it might not seem like it at the time.'

As I was leaving she said, 'Don't upset yourself, love. Ron'll be looking after him.'

I think she really believed it. I almost envied her. 'Then I hope he's getting on with Rusty. If they're fighting like dog and dog, Ron'll be cursing me to high heaven.'

The job started on Monday. I joined ant-like hordes of commuters, grabbing my free *Metro* and take-away cappuccino. And apart from the fact that it was in a horrible basement office with no windows, it was congenial enough. My colleagues discussed the deliciously loathsome Jason out of *Footballers' Wives*, and invited me for drinks at the Punch and Judy. But when there was overtime, I took it. Returning at seven thirty to an empty house was still too soon.

On the following Tuesday, Felicity phoned. 'It's Rob's birthday next Monday – had you remembered?'

*Shit, I must get a card.*

'But Monday's a terrible night for a party, so we're all going to the Coach and Horses on Saturday night,' she went on. 'Why don't you come down?'

'I thought you were sick of the Coach and Horses.'

'I wasn't. I just didn't want to go there on New Year's Eve as well as ninety-three other eves during the year.'

'How are things with Ian?'

'Better.' She paused. 'I told him I was sorry for being a cow, it was just the diet.'

'Did he buy it?'

'I don't think so, but he pretended to. He went out at lunch-time and got me a prescription. He said it was a strictly controlled drug, one to be taken every day as a purely preventive measure.'

'What was it?'

'A bag of mini Mars bars.' She gave a guilty little laugh. 'Will you come down? Scott and Sean have gone, so there's no problem about beds.'

It wasn't a difficult decision, especially if those two were getting back to normal. 'After consulting my packed diary, I think I can just fit it in.'

'Great. Oh, and guess what? Rob and Nick are getting the Butchery after all. The chain pulled out. Markham junior apparently thought he could screw a bit more out of them and they pulled the plug.'

'Serve him right.' I couldn't have been more pleased.

I bought a hilarious and very rude card for Rob and ended up leaving it behind. While I was in the shower, the house phone rang. When I checked just before leaving, I found the message light flashing.

'Izzy, it's Leo.'

*What?*

'I didn't try your mobile, I thought you'd cut me off.' He paused. 'Look, I need to talk to you – I'll call back later.'

His tone lacked its usual verve. In fact, it was uncharacteristically sombre and the first thought that hit me was so horrible, I went cold.

*It can't be that.*

*Why not?*

*Because it just can't.*

*That's what everybody thinks until it happens.*

For a few minutes my skin crawled. How could I get through the weekend with this hanging over me?

I couldn't. I called him back.

Feeling sick, I barely waited for him to utter. 'What did you need to talk to me about? Have you got HIV?'

'*What?*' He actually laughed.

272

'It's not funny! How do I know you weren't playing around with anyone else? I was having visions of some horrible STD at the very least!'

'Vera, for God's sake . . .'

'Don't "Vera" me! Why the hell were you ringing, then?'

'Not to say, "nice one," for the prawns, anyway. Look—'

'No, you look, Leo. I don't want to talk to you, I don't want you ringing, I don't even want to think about you, OK? Just leave me alone.'

Bang.

What was he thinking? That I'd still be languishing? Thinking of the good times with nostalgic tears in my eyes? Was he imagining I'd be up for a couple of drinks for old times' sake, like he'd had with Laura?

*Bugger off, Leo. You might be at a loose end – I'm not.*

I pointed the car south-west on one of those days that make you realize summer isn't so far away. There was warmth in the sun, the first daffodils were nodding their heads in the breeze, and here and there one of those trees that blossom early wore a dress of hazy pink. And once I'd got over the shock, I was glad Leo had rung. Maybe it had taken Henry to put him in perspective. Once you can tell someone you don't want to talk to them and actually mean it, you know you're finally over them. If not for the sad shadow of Henry, I'd have been on top of the world.

It was only when I pulled into the services for a coffee that I realized Rob's card was still on my kitchen worktop. I thought about checking the shop, but their selection of cards wouldn't be brilliant. Still, I could stop somewhere closer to Felicity's; I wanted some flowers for her anyway.

I made a little diversion to her local town square. The

sun was warm enough for people having a mid-shopping coffee to sit at tables on the pavement. Tubs and horse troughs were a mass of crocuses in purple, yellow and white, with daffodils and narcissi beginning to take over. After finding a card, I looked across the square at that Queen Anne house. A man was coming down the steps with a dog that wore one of those anti-scratch lampshades round its neck, and Nick's car was parked outside.

Nick.

It was as if I'd pulled a curtain aside and found something I'd been telling myself wasn't really there. Something so suddenly heart-stopping I was almost afraid of it. As I gazed at that house with the stone dogs, I might have been fifteen again. I needn't have come here at all. I could have picked up some flowers at the services and probably a card, too, but I knew why I hadn't. Just like this, I'd made detours on my bike past Jamie Aldrich's house, on the off chance that I might see him. Just like this, my stomach had contracted with nervous anticipation. And just like this, I'd been telling myself I wasn't bothered, I really didn't care two hoots, it was all the same to me if I saw him snogging Sally Wilson at the bus-stop . . .

*Grow up, Izzy. It had damn all to do with dinner jackets. It wasn't just take-it-or-leave-it lust. You're not just 'over' Leo. He's been eclipsed..*

Why didn't I just give him a call? I could say, 'Look, you were right about Leo, but that mess has finally been washed down the sink and I've come to realize that I like you rather a lot. So if you fancy lunch, I'm just across the square.'

Yes. That would come across really well. In any case, I didn't have his number. I'd have to look up the business number and the receptionist would say brightly, 'Actually,

Mr Trent is with a patient at the moment – can I give him a message?'

I went flower-hunting, instead. After buying half a dozen bunches of scented narcissi I paused at the estate agent's I'd checked before. Again there was a queue at the bakery next door, and the scent of fresh bread made me think of Nick's standing order for bacon and tomato rolls. I could smell fresh doughnuts, too. It was very distracting when I was checking out relative property prices. That Devon-white version of Christmas Cottage was gone, but no wonder. This was second-home country.

'Hi,' said a voice at my shoulder. 'Is this purely professional interest?'

'Oh, hello, Nick.' I think I said this much as anyone else would have, and not as if I were suddenly all of a dither, as Mrs Denny would say. He was wearing chinos and an open-necked shirt in blue and green checks with the sleeves rolled up, and the sun was on his face. 'Yes, I'm afraid so.' For an instant I thought of making lunch noises, but he'd just come out of the bakery. In his hand, wrapped in a paper napkin, was a Cornish pasty that smelt warm and savoury. 'Is that a late breakfast?'

'More of an early lunch. My twelve o'clock just called to cancel.'

'Very considerate, if you were feeling peckish. I was just wondering whether to go mad with a doughnut.'

'You'd better get a move on – they sell out fast. I take it you've come down for Rob's birthday bash?'

'Yes, I made a detour to get him a card.'

We moved in slightly, as a couple with a twin buggy and several Safeway's bags came past. 'So how have you been?' he asked.

'Oh, fine. Commuting into central London every day, like a good little ant.'

He made a face. 'Sooner you than me. I'd rather shovel muck.'

Recalling those sun-starved suits I'd been crammed in the underground with, I believed it. By contrast, he might have just been for a run on the beach, in a wind that hadn't seen land for four thousand miles. His eyes looked as if they still had that open-space sun in them. 'Are you going to Rob's do?' I asked, as if I wasn't particularly bothered one way or the other, and no butterflies were adrift in my stomach.

'Probably, but I won't be making a heavy night of it.'

Dammit. The way Fate had it in for me lately, I was beginning to think I must have been thoroughly evil in a previous life.

'I've got an early start tomorrow,' he went on. 'I'm having Alex for the day.'

'Another NBK do?'

'In a manner of speaking. His mother's heavily pregnant, she's just moved house, and her husband's away. And Alex can be hard work.'

'A P&Q day, then.'

'Peace and quiet with packing cases.' He smiled. It was weird how a little smile from greeny-hazel eyes can give you a bitter-sweet pain in your stomach. And it was no use looking elsewhere, because every other bit of him was suddenly as bad. The V of neck and chest exposed by that shirt. His forearms. It only hit me that minute how a man's forearms could really do things to me: lovely hunky ones with the sleeves rolled up, a goodly fuzz of light brown and that open-air tan that never quite fades.

'I said I'd pick him up first thing,' he went on, 'and it's a good hour's drive.'

'I heard about the Butchery,' I said. 'Congratulations.'

'Thanks. I don't much care for putting money into mercenary little Markham pockets, but there you go.'

As a couple of teenage girls came past, we moved aside again. The epitome of fourteen-year-olds out to raid Boots' make-up counters, they were shiny-haired, giggly and oblivious. Although they made me feel ancient, I knew I wouldn't want to be back there. Homework hanging over you all weekend, spending three hours getting ready for a party, desperately hoping Tom Anderson would fancy you at last . . .

No, it was so much better being twenty-nine and a quarter, making pathetic detours in the hope of seeing a man I'd nearly had sex with: a man who was talking to me as if I were just a friend of a friend he'd pass five minutes with while his pasty cooled off . . .

He glanced at his watch. 'Better get back. My twelve-twenty'll be waiting, and you should get in the queue if you want that doughnut.'

I was about to say, 'Maybe see you later, then,' when his mobile buzzed in his breast pocket.

But I said it anyway. 'Maybe see you later, then.'

He acknowledged me with that, 'Yes, OK,' lift of the eyebrows, while saying, 'Oh, hi,' into his phone as he headed back across the square.

I didn't watch him go. I was too busy trying not to remember that daft saying we'd used at school. *'Too late!' she cried, and waved her wooden leg* . . .

Yes, a doughnut would be very good just now.

# Chapter 17

Felicity was looking perkier than the last time I'd seen her. Dusting off garden chairs, she was saying we might even have lunch outside.

'Where's Ian?' I asked, trying not to notice how Shep was looking round for the friend who always came with me.

'Playing squash, but he won't be long.'

I sat in the sun, in a garden that had been established fifty years. She and Ian had thrown some brilliant barbecues out here, the smell of steaks mingling with night-scented stocks. Somewhere a wren was trilling a song far too big for such a tiny bird. While Felicity sloshed me out a glass of wine, Shep put his head gently under my hand, as if he knew I was missing someone to fondle.

She put some hummus and mini pittas on the table. 'I've told him I won't be managing his office any more.'

'You're kidding!'

'I'm not. We're together practically twenty-four hours a day. It's not healthy for any relationship. I've already found someone to take over.'

I dipped a mini pitta in the hummus. 'Have you got another job lined up?'

'No, but it won't be difficult. Anyway, I've already got something part-time. Someone who used to live down the road has asked me to manage half a dozen holiday lets for the summer: checking in and out, organizing cleaning and maintenance, you know. Talking of which, I'm thinking of buying a place of my own.'

This gave me a jolt. 'You're not moving out?'

'No, but it's about time I had my own foot on the property ladder. Prices are shooting up here as well, you know, and I've still got some money from Granny and Grandpa. I could buy something cheapish to let and tart it up myself.'

This was a turn-up.

'And I'm going to learn Japanese,' she added.

'What?'

She laughed. 'Just kidding.'

We turned up at the Coach and Horses around half seven. It was Saturday-night packed, with twenty-odd purely for Rob's birthday. As usual, Felicity had organized this; she'd ordered a simple buffet in a corner of the bar: curry and chicken drumsticks and salads.

From the moment I arrived, I tried not to look around for the one head I'd been hoping to see. As I finished my second glass of wine, I tried not to care that it wasn't there. When Felicity said to Rob, 'What happened to Nick?' and he said, 'Oh, he had something to do, he might drop in later,' I tried not to notice that disappointed contraction in my stomach.

At ten to nine I told myself I would stop looking at my watch every two minutes, wondering what time 'later' could be, and whether 'might' actually meant 'probably not'. I told myself it was thoroughly ill-mannered of him to be so casual about it, when Felicity had gone to all this trouble and had certainly counted him in her 'mouths to be fed' order. In fact, with such a disgracefully cavalier attitude, I wasn't at all sure I wanted to see him anyway.

Who wanted a man with little-sod baggage, after all? A man who lived three and a half hours' drive away, even when there weren't any roadworks?

I went to talk to Sasha, who was behind the bar.

After she'd said how sorry she was about Henry, I asked about the job.

'I got it,' she said, with lit-up relish. 'Starting in three weeks. Just a backstage dogsbody, not much money, but you have to get a foot in the door.'

'And much closer to your boyfriend.'

'Yes, except that we split up. I wasn't that bothered,' she added, seeing my face. 'We were bitching at each other like mad over New Year. I'd have applied anyway, just because I loved Edinburgh last summer.'

'Good luck, then.' I looked around in a supposedly nonchalant way. 'I thought Nick was supposed to be coming tonight.'

'Might have changed his mind. He's having Alex tomorrow.'

'Yes, I gather he's doing his ex a favour.' It came out casually, but I knew exactly what I was doing. Suddenly obsessed with someone, all you want to talk about is him, while trying to pretend he might be Tom, Dick or Lancelot Wetherington-Smythe. You nurture crazy hopes that the other person might say, 'Oh, he mentioned you the other day, something about thinking you were the most unbelievably gorgeous woman he'd ever laid eyes on.' You know this might turn dangerous, as the other person might tell you he's just fallen for someone called Heidi: supermodel, concert pianist and *really lovely girl*, too. But you still do it, even when the other person's just been asked for two pints of John Smith's. 'It's nice that they get on,' I added, as she wielded the pump.

'Well, they do *now*.'

The supposedly-casual bit was getting harder. 'A bit fraught, was it?'

'You could say that. Three pounds forty, please.'

After ringing up the money she lowered her voice. 'She wasn't sure Alex was Nick's until he was *nearly two*! Imagine! She only told him when Alex got ill and they sent him for tests. She was in a total panic, thinking he might need a bone-marrow donor. It turned out to be nothing serious after all, but she was so terrified she blurted it out, thinking he'd find out the hard way.'

No wonder Felicity had said it was 'messy'. 'Bit of a turn-up.' (Nicely casual, I thought.) 'Were they still together at the time?' *Please, don't tell me he's still holding candles.*

'Oh, no. They'd actually split up just before she found out she was pregnant, but he'd had no idea she'd been seeing an old flame. He'd gone to work in New York – she hadn't got the nerve to tell either of them.' Suddenly she wore a vaguely awkward expression. 'But don't go blabbing it, will you? He never said it was a secret, but . . .'

'Look, it's OK. I won't say a word.' I put my empty glass on the bar. 'Must have been upsetting for him, though.'

'You could say that. In one breath she told him his little kid might have some life-threatening disease – in the next she told him he might not be his at all. He said he was absolutely poleaxed. D'you know what a poleaxe actually *is*, by the way? I looked it up afterwards – it's a thing they used to use for killing pigs. Oh my God – what's going on?' she added, nodding towards the door. 'Have you lot organized a little birthday surprise for Rob?'

'Not that I know of.' Around the entrance was a little huddle of bodies and a tell-tale buzz had gone up. 'God, I hope Felicity hasn't organized a stripagram. I wouldn't altogether put it past her.'

'Probably a policewoman,' she grinned. 'Coming to tell him he's being arrested for gross indecency with an Afghan hound.'

'Oh, Lord. Rob'll hate it. He's just not the type to relish random boobs shoved in his face. Where is he, anyway?'

I was looking around for him when I heard the bark. That quick, excited bark I'd heard so often lately, but only in my dreams. Just as I was surely dreaming now. As I turned towards it, the sea of bodies melted away. He was on the leash, straining to get to me until Nick let him go.

A missile of greyish-brown fur nearly knocked me off my bar stool, and I don't think I'll ever forget the minutes that followed. Anyone who thinks dogs can't talk is way out. As I knelt on the floor with him, choked with disbelieving tears, he poured it all out. In between licking my face and arms, anywhere he could reach, it streamed out in a hoarse, frantic frenzy: 'Oh, I'm so happy to see you – you'll never believe what happened – there was this Frisbee and I went for a swim – only everything went a bit wrong – I was trying so hard to find you – I thought I'd never see you again –'

Behind all this was a cacophony of cheers and 'aahs', someone saying, 'Well, I think we can take it they're pleased to see each other,' and everybody laughing. And then there was Nick, looking down at the wreck with swimming eyes, too choked to speak. 'He was barking like that virtually all the way,' he said. 'Nearly fifty miles, right in my bloody ear.'

But it was Felicity I spoke to. 'Why didn't you tell me?'

She was in tears herself. 'I didn't know, Izzy, I swear. Not until just now.'

Vaguely I remember standing up, putting my arms

A Girl's Best Friend

round Nick and hugging him, but I was still too choked to say much. That came a little later, when I was more or less coherent again.

'I just don't know what to say,' I said. ' "Thank you" seems so inadequate.'

'To be honest, I didn't think there was much of a chance,' he said. 'But it was worth a try. *If* he'd managed to get out, I thought, what would his canine logic tell him? As far as he knew, you weren't in Barbados. You were back in London, and that's where his nose would take him. I drew a straight line on the map and took it from there.'

I looked down at Henry, now flaked out at my feet. 'I wish I understood how on earth he knew which way to go.'

'Dogs have a built-in compass. They've been known to go a lot further than him.'

'Yes, but even across country he must have had to cross busy roads!'

'He's an urban animal. An urban dog with brains soon picks up a certain amount of road sense. He was still very lucky, though.'

I was probably going soft in the head, but I almost began to think Mrs Denny's Ron must have been watching over him. 'Yes, but fifty miles! And virtually nothing to eat, from the look of him.' Picked up only four days ago, he was still terribly thin.

'I guess he's not much cop at catching rabbits. They didn't think he'd have got much further without a square meal.'

He went on to say Henry had been found on a country road, wet and bedraggled, limping from a little stone lodged between his pads, and obviously exhausted. Just as I'd feared, the couple who'd found him had thought he'd

283

been abandoned. Saying very rude things about callous owners who should be strung up, they'd taken him to a little shelter run on dedication and car-boot sales.

'They told me to read you the riot act,' he went on. 'First for the collar, second for failing to have him microchipped. So consider yourself duly tongue-lashed.'

'You must let me have the address – I'll send them a donation.'

'I already did that on your behalf, but I'm sure they wouldn't argue if you sent some more.'

'How much did you give them?'

He hesitated.

'Nick, please!'

'All right, a hundred quid.'

'I'll pay you back tomorrow. And what about his collar?' He wore a new one, in bright tan leather.

'Have that on me.' He looked down at Henry, still curled up peacefully. 'He'd been fed before I picked him up, but if you ordered another plate of sausages I don't think you'd have much trouble finding a more deserving dustbin than I was.'

As he said it, something in his expression quickened my pulse, but one of the nurses from the practice chose that moment to come up. 'I can't believe what perfect timing it was,' she said. 'They could easily have left it till tomorrow to ring you back.'

The story emerged throughout the evening. After mulling it over for days, Nick had started his search barely a week ago. Just like me he'd phoned umpteen places, but further afield. One place where he'd left a message had left him one in return that afternoon. But Nick had been busy: it had been nearly six before he'd got it. Yes, they had a dog fitting that description. Yes, he responded to 'Henry'.

So Nick had left shortly afterwards, driven fifty cross-country miles, and come straight here.

Then Felicity came up. 'Nick, there's masses of food left – aren't you hungry?'

'Starving.' He crisped up, as if she'd flicked a switch. 'Point me at the trough.'

It was only then that I thought of ringing Mrs Denny. They went to bed early in the home, but it was worth a try.

I hung on while they checked before putting me through.

'I couldn't wait till tomorrow to tell you,' I said. 'Henry's been found, and he's fine.'

'Oh, love . . .' On the other end I heard her voice start to wobble.

Before hanging up she said, 'Will you bring him to see me?'

'I'll be there tomorrow evening, so save him a couple of biscuits. Sleep well.'


Before I knew it, it was twenty to eleven and Nick was leaving.

'You have to feel sorry for him, really,' said Sasha mischievously. 'He can't help turning old and boring.'

He aimed a mock cuff at her head. 'I've got a six-year-old to cope with tomorrow – I need my wits about me.'

'Thanks again times about a million,' I said. 'I'll be over tomorrow with your cash.'

'And the interest. Don't forget the interest.' He brushed my cheek. 'Sleep well.'

I didn't sleep very well, as it happened. I dreamt that Henry had come back, woke up thinking it had been a dream, and for a moment thought I was still dreaming when I found him beside me.


It was around twelve when I set off for Nick's, after a

detour to the cash machine. It was sunny again; the forecast had said it might even hit seventeen degrees. Beside me, Henry sat with his head out of the window, catching smells.

I found Nick a hundred yards from his house. On the pavement he was running beside a little cyclist, his hand on the saddle.

I parked outside the house. Hanging on to Henry, I watched them approach. Alex was pedalling hard, his face under the helmet creased with anxiety. 'Don't let go, Daddy – don't let go . . .'

'I won't, just keep going – look straight ahead . . .'

He stopped when he saw me, and I felt bad for interrupting the lesson. 'You took the little wheels off, then,' I said.

'About time, too,' he said, in an undertone.

'Hi, Alex,' I said. 'I like your bike.'

He gave Nick a look as if to say, 'Please, not *girls*.'

'Say hello to Izzy,' said Nick firmly.

'Hello, *Izzy*.' With his feet safely back on terra firma, his anxiety had evidently disappeared. 'It's a weird name.'

'It's short for Isabel. And this is Henry.'

He was looking dubious. 'He's very big. Does he bite?'

'No, but I won't let him near you if you don't want.'

Nick shot me a very wry look. 'His mum isn't mad keen on dogs,' he murmured, but not quietly enough.

'Well, she can't *help* it,' said Alex. 'She got bitten when she was little.' Impatiently he added, 'Come on, Dad, will you stop just *talk*ing?'

'We'll go inside if you're going to talk like that.' He raised his eyebrows at me. 'Can you hang on for a bit?'

'Don't mind me. I'll hang out here and watch.'

Leaning against my sun-warmed bonnet, I observed a

master class in instilling confidence. Despite his lippiness, Alex was terrified of Nick letting go. More than once as Nick ran beside him I heard that, 'Don't let go . . .' But as I warmed up enough to peel my cardie off, he did just that, continuing to run beside him until Alex realized he was going it alone. As disbelief on his face turned to exultation, I almost wished I had a camcorder.

Eventually Nick said right, that was it for now, we were going inside.

'Oh, *Dad* . . .'

'Alex, I'm shattered. We'll go again later.'

As Alex ran inside, Nick turned to me. 'Serves me right for going against instructions – I'll be at this all day unless I can rope Rob in.'

'Where is he?'

'Still asleep, the lazy sod.'

It was almost hot in the sun. As we went inside I got a whiff of warmed-up male, mingling with the clean-laundry smell of a white polo shirt. Honestly, someone should bottle it.

'Can I watch a video?' Alex demanded.

'Go on, then.'

As he disappeared, Nick was inspecting the contents of his fridge. 'What can I get you?'

I could have murdered a lager but even a legal half would make me drowsy in the car. 'Anything soft.'

'Apple juice?'

'Lovely.'

Within seconds Alex was back, casting a wary eye on Henry, demanding a drink, and announcing that he was starving. He was a good-looking little boy, with quick, intelligent blue eyes, and I wondered whether his father had been a little sod at the same age.

As Nick was pouring him some juice, Rob came down,

yawning in a towelling dressing-gown. 'About time, too, you idle bastard,' said Nick.

'Well, it's not often. Hi, Izzy. I hadn't expected to see you here.'

'Repaying debts.' I took the cash from the pocket of my un-tatty jeans. With them I wore a pale pink scoop-neck top and matching little cardie, and suddenly felt it was obvious I'd made an effort. As it seemed awkward giving cash directly to Nick, I put it on the table, under a pepper-mill.

He glanced, but made no comment. 'Right, I'd better feed that little tyke. Anyone else hungry?'

'No, thanks,' I said. 'Felicity's feeding me.'

'I wouldn't say no,' said Rob, fondling Henry. 'What are you cooking?'

'Since I made a rash promise last time, junk.' Fishing a bag of oven chips out of the freezer, Nick slung it on the table, followed by a packet of breaded chicken shaped like dinosaurs. 'He's never allowed any at home.'

While he put the oven on and read the backs of the packets, Rob and I talked about last night. Alex came back, gave Henry another dubious look, and asked Rob if he wanted to come and watch *A Bug's Life*.

Rob was only too pleased, which left me alone with Nick. With his back to me, he was putting chips and dinosaurs on baking trays. 'You'll gather that his mother's made him nervous of dogs.'

'It's probably better than being overconfident,' I said, although I didn't quite think it. 'I used to go up to absolutely any dog. It's a wonder I never got bitten.'

'All right, but they smell fear, and it makes them think there's something to be afraid of. Alex!' he called to the sitting-room. 'Do you want peas or baked beans?'

'Peas,' Alex called back.

'Both,' called Rob. 'Thanks, Nigella. I'll give you a kiss later.'

With a wry grin Nick made an obscene gesture towards the sitting-room.

I laughed, but only on the outside. I was thinking of all the trouble he'd taken, that might so easily have been for nothing. If it had been for nothing, I'd probably never have known he'd taken it. 'I was probably too dazed to say it properly last night, but I can't thank you enough.'

'Put it down to my awkward-cuss streak. I always look on long odds as a challenge.'

'If you ever need a really massive favour, you only have to ask.'

He took a can of beans from the cupboard. 'Anything particular in mind?'

'Oh, I don't know,' I said lightly. 'Stitching the odd button on a shirt – I bet you hate that even more than I do.'

His mouth flickered. 'Don't go mad. I might just take you up on it.'

That was when Alex came back. 'I'm *star*ving. Can I have some crisps?'

'No, your junk's nearly ready, and in any case I forgot to buy any.'

'Oh, *Dad*. You're *use*less.' As he grumped off, I couldn't help laughing.

Nick's eyebrows gave a little lift. 'No respect. Give him time and he might even turn into a total little tyke like I was.'

As he took plates and cutlery from the dishwasher, I began to feel like a spare part. 'Anything I can do?'

'No, it's all under control.' With a hiss, he opened a can

of beer. 'So what's this job you're commuting like an ant to?'

'Oh, just a stopgap while I look around. Admin, for a massive property company.'

'Should be halfway up your street, then.'

'I'm not sure where my street is any more. Still, the people are nice. There's one girl who's starting to drive me mad by saying, "What am I like?" six times a day, but you always get one of those. I probably drive her mad, too.'

Leaning against the counter, he eyed that wodge of cash under the pepper-mill. 'You didn't need to do that. It looks too much, anyway.'

'Of course I needed to. I added a bit for your petrol money.'

'For crying out loud, Izzy—'

'Give it to charity, then.' As hoots of laughter were coming from the sitting-room, I added, 'Or buy something for Alex.'

'He's already got everything.'

His phone rang in his pocket. Within seconds I gathered that it was an anxious pet owner, and began to feel even more like a spare part. Should I mouth, 'I'll be off, then,' and slip out? Would he mouth back, 'OK, see you,' and that would be it?

*Carpe diem,* Izzy. Show a little initiative, can't you?

It wasn't difficult. With the phone clamped between his ear and his shoulder, he took a can-opener from a drawer and started trying to open that can of beans.

So like a useful little person I mouthed, 'Let me,' and took it from him. And lo, he mouthed, 'Thanks,' and smiled. I will admit here that as I took the can I touched his fingers on purpose, and it was very nice. I tipped the beans into a pan, just as if this was the sole purpose of the exercise, and found another for the peas.

During all this he was saying things like, 'Not to worry, it was normal, just keep an eye on her . . . yes, OK, then . . . no, better not give her milk, stick to water for now . . . try wrapping her in a towel, you must get the antibiotics down her, it's no use if she's just spitting them out . . .' At the same time, he was digging ice-cream out of the freezer and emptying the dishwasher. It had never occurred to me before how attractive a man could be with a phone clamped to his shoulder, but life is full of little surprises.

When at last he hung up, the beans and peas were bubbling.

'Jesus H,' he said, putting his phone back in his pocket. 'Mrs Riley has the noble art of getting her drawers in a twist off to a T.'

I laughed. 'Over her cat, I take it?'

He nodded. 'Fluffy Riley, and Fluffy hates me. Mind you, I guess I'd hate anyone who poked me about and cut half my guts out.'

'I'm surprised you dish out your mobile number.'

'I don't usually. But it was a major op, and old Mother Riley gets herself in a right old tizz.'

His dry tones fooled me not at all. I saw some old dear worried sick about poor, cut-up Fluffy. I saw Nick, knowing she'd be worried sick, saying, 'Look, she'll be fine, but here's my number just in case . . .' I saw a nice man trying to pretend he wasn't soft, and a gooey feeling washed over me, as if someone were filling me with warm, pink jelly. 'It was nice of you. A lot of people would let her tizz until tomorrow morning.'

'Don't be fooled.' Picking up his beer again he shot me a tiny wink. 'I'm still a nockshus bastard underneath.'

The jelly was filling me so fast, I was heart-deep in it already. Unfortunately, it was suddenly overpowered by something wafting from the oven.

'*Shit*, that food . . .' Suddenly galvanized, he yanked it open.

It was only very slightly overdone. 'Right, peas and beans,' he said briskly. 'Could you grab a colander out of that cupboard?'

The next minute made me think of breaks in the middle of TV dramas. Just as you're coming up to a really good bit, they're advertising ocean-fresh fabric conditioner and everybody charges out to make a cup of tea. As we drained and dished, another of life's little surprises struck me. It was amazing how attractive a man could look while ladling out baked beans with an oven glove over his shoulder. He didn't even curse at Henry, who was getting excited at chicken smells and doing his best to trip us up.

'Alex!' he called, once chips and dinosaurs were dished up. 'Come and get it.'

Alex was giggling hysterically as he came in, probably because Rob was holding him upside down by the ankles, pretending to devour his calves. 'About time, too,' said Rob. 'Alex tastes appalling with no ketchup.'

Why ever had I turned down lunch? Having said Felicity was expecting me, I couldn't hang around much longer.

'Ooh, yummy junk . . .' His eyes lighting up, Alex speared a ketchup-covered dinosaur. 'My mum doesn't hardly *ever* let me have stuff like this,' he said to Rob. 'She says it's full of ees or something.'

'Better not let on you've had any here, then,' said Rob.

'Too right,' said Nick. 'Or I'll be in—'

'—deep shit,' said Alex, through a mouthful of dinosaur.

As one, Rob and I choked back laughter.

'I was going to say "trouble",' said Nick, with a trying-not-to-crack-up expression. 'Who's been teaching you stuff like that?'

'Mike,' he said, still with his mouth full. 'And Mum said, "*Michael*!" '

We all laughed, which probably only encouraged him, but it was just tough. Once the cackles had died down, though, I thought I should make a move. I was about to say so when Rob said, 'Have some of these chips, Izzy. I don't want to turn into a fat git all over again.'

So I took a couple, while formulating a Devious Plan. At the other end of the table, on the seat of a chair, was my pink cardigan. If I conveniently 'forgot' it, I could come back later, on my way home. For a horribly guilty moment I wished I hadn't promised to see Mrs Denny tonight. They went to bed very early in that home.

'Can I ride my bike again after lunch?' asked Alex.

'Certainly not,' said Nick. 'I only wanted you to learn to ride it by yourself so I could say you couldn't ride it ever again.'

Alex found this hysterical. 'Oh, *Dad* . . .'

Nick speared a couple of chips. 'I'm going to make you ride it all afternoon.'

'Not *all* afternoon! Rob and me are going to watch *Toy Story*, aren't we, Rob?'

'Yep,' said Rob. 'Great stuff.'

Alex turned to me. 'You can stay and watch it, too, if you like,' he said graciously. 'It's very good, you know.'

'I know, and it's really very kind of you, but I should be off now.' I glanced at my watch. 'Heavens, look at the time. Felicity'll be thinking a flock of man-eating sheep have got us.'

This set Alex off again, but I was already making a move. 'No, don't get up,' I said quickly, as Nick was doing just that. 'I can see myself out. Bye, Rob.' Bending to kiss him, I pinched another of his chips. 'Bye, Alex.'

But Nick saw me to the door anyway. 'What time are you off home?' he asked.

'Four-ish. I've promised to take Henry to see his old owner.'

'That's a shame.' He paused. 'You could have come and shared Alex's non-junk tea. He'll just about eat a stir-fry if it hasn't got any ginger in it.'

'What time are you taking him home, then?'

'Seven-ish.'

'*Dad!*' Alex came running from the kitchen, in fits. 'Rob's trying to steal my dinosaurs!'

'OK, I'll come and beat him up, just hang on a tick . . .'

'*Now*, Dad!'

As his overexcited son tried to drag him away, I said quickly, 'Don't let your lunch go cold. I could pop in for a cup of tea on my way home, if you're going to be in.'

With Alex dragging at his arm, his smile was eighty per cent comic resignation. 'We'll be in.'

'See you later, then.' After an instant's hesitation, I brushed his cheek with my lips. 'Bye-bye.'

As I went down the path I heard Alex say, 'Yuck! She *kissed* you!'

'I'll give you yuck,' said Nick, and the door closed behind them.

I drove off feeling as if I'd had a shot of speed. A man doesn't offer theoretical stir-fries without it meaning more than food. I could see that in his eyes as he'd said it. Still, I could probably stretch that cup of tea to forty minutes. The stir-fry wouldn't have been much of a Part Two anyway, not if he had to shoot off to take Alex home. At any rate, my cardie plan was redundant after all. Brilliant ruse, though. *Carpe diem* stuff if ever there was.

With the window down, the air smelt of warm, damp

294

earth and spring. On the right was a gently rising field of sheep; the hedge was already showing green buds, and in the bank underneath, primroses were coming out. On the left was the kind of wood that would be full of sun-dappled shade in summer, springy with leaf-mould and a carpet of bluebells by May.

I couldn't have gone more than a mile when déjà vu caught up with me. Just like before, someone was behind me, flashing their lights. My heart beating faster, I waved to show I'd seen him, and as soon as we hit a straight stretch I pulled in.

He overtook and pulled in about ten yards down. Just like before, I got out and stood in front of my own blue bonnet.

He came up to me with my pink cardie in his hand. 'You forgot this.'

'Did I?' I gave a daft little laugh. 'What an idiot.'

'And I forgot to say something to you.'

'Did you?' I swallowed hard. 'What was that?'

His eyes were as warm as the sun on my face. 'I wouldn't have regretted it in the morning.'

# Chapter 18

All I could hear was the birds, and time standing still. It was one of those moments when all the corny lines you've ever heard don't seem quite so corny any more.

'Can this be happening to me?' (*The Sound of Music*.)

'Oh, Nick, I've been such a fool . . .' (Just about any corny old black and white film you care to name.)

'I think this was meant to be.' (Mrs Denny.)

Of course I said none of them. My brain was having difficulty connecting with my vocal cords; I think my heart had somehow got in the way. 'I left my cardigan on purpose. I wanted an excuse to come back.'

The next few minutes were some of the best I've ever had on a Sunday morning. I think we gazed at each other a moment, and he brushed a wisp of hair from my cheek. After that it was serious mouth-to-mouth, as we made up for lost time.

Eventually we came up for air. 'I wish you didn't have to go,' he said.

'So do I, but there's work tomorrow, and Mrs Denny would be so disappointed . . .'

'I know.' He kissed my hair, and I kissed his shoulder.

As a car went past, our eyes went together to the woods behind us, but in the distance was a strolling couple, and on a day like this there would probably be more.

Neither of us said what I knew he was thinking, too. We

could have driven somewhere else, found a more secluded spot, but it wasn't on. Alex would wonder where he was. Even if it were just Rob, we wouldn't go back to the house. It wouldn't have felt right, charging upstairs like a couple of adolescents. We'd want privacy anyway, just to talk.

'Why do you have to live so bloody far away?' he asked.

'Why do you?'

'I asked first,' he said, like a kid in a playground, and I laughed.

He caught me to him again. 'What are you doing next weekend?'

'Oh, masses of exciting things.' His shoulder smelt warm and male; his arms around me felt like tender steel. Together they were almost making me come over all girlie. 'But I might cancel if something even better came up.'

'Not much use my driving up, then?'

'Oh, I don't know. If you actually managed to find somewhere to park, I don't think I'd turn you away.'

He drew back. 'I haven't even got your phone number.'

That was easily fixed. Then we kissed again but less desperately, as if we'd tacitly agreed that there was no point stirring up hungers that would only have to wait. When at last we drew apart he said, 'I hope you're coming back for that cup of tea, anyway. Alex might even let you have one of his chocolate biscuits.'

That was an offer I couldn't possibly refuse.

I said nothing to Felicity; it seemed too private a thing to share just yet. In any case, she and Ian put my glow entirely down to Henry.

That cup of tea lasted three-quarters of an hour. I think Rob had sussed out what was going on by then, because while I was with Nick in the kitchen there was a lot of horseplay noise coming from the sitting-room. When I went to say goodbye, I found Rob and Alex chucking cushions at each other. Rob said sorry, he couldn't possibly come to see me off, he was in the middle of a very serious war.

Dear old Rob. I kissed his cheek and left him.

We kissed goodbye at the front door. 'Unless we're suddenly inundated, I could probably leave by six thirty on Friday,' Nick said.

'But if you are?'

'Then I'll leave later. Or come in the morning.'

'Leave later,' I said. 'But drive carefully.'

'You, too. I'll call you tonight.'

I drove back feeling as if my heart had sprouted wings. I went straight to Mrs Denny, where Henry was greeted with much joy by everybody. They all wanted to know how he'd been found and there was a lot of aahing at our happy ending.

I was finally alone with Mrs Denny. 'He sounds a nice sort of fellow, this Nick.'

'Yes, he is.'

She gave me a quizzical little look. 'A little bit special, is he?'

'I think he just might be.'

'I thought so.' She gave a satisfied little sigh, before casting an eye at my jeans. 'Take my advice, love, and buy yourself something pretty. Those things are all very well, but you can't beat a really pretty dress and a pair of stockings.' Leaning forward, she patted my knee. 'And don't be too eager. Keep them guessing, that's the way.'

He called at ten past ten, to say it was just as well I'd passed on the stir-fry. Alex had jumped on his back just as he was about to dish up, and he'd dropped the whole lot on the floor. Then he'd forgotten himself, and Alex had said he was going to tell Mum he'd said that, it was an ex*treme*ly rude word that meant making babies, and by the way, how did you make them, exactly?

I laughed. 'How did you get out of that one?'

'I said you plant a seed, if he ever jumped on me like that again there'd be big trouble, and did he want fish fingers instead?'

After we'd talked about a dozen more silly things he said, 'Shit, it's starting to rain.'

'Where are you?'

'Officially getting some fresh air.'

So then I knew he'd come out just so he could talk to me in private. 'Go back, before you get soaked.'

'It's not much. Just a half-hearted downpour.'

Only when I finally hung up did I realize that it was ten to eleven. We'd been talking about nothing for forty minutes.


That whole week was a new experience for me. I'd never started a relationship quite like this: barely begun, followed by several days apart, followed by a planned weekend together. The anticipatory buzz it gave me should be on prescription. I'd have been on top of the world, anyway, because of Henry; this was the cream and the icing.

My house didn't know what had hit it. It wasn't that I imagined him giving a toss about a bit of dust; I just wanted everything as nice as I could make it.

On the Wednesday night, just as I was wondering whether to bath Henry and the house plants, he rang. At least, I thought it was him.

'Izzy, it's me. Please don't hang up.'

*Leo. For God's sake.* 'I'm busy.'

'Izzy, please. I just want to explain.'

I couldn't believe he was doing this. 'Explain *what*, Leo? That you can't help it if desperate thirty-five-year-olds find you irresistible? That it's not your fault, your mummy wouldn't let you take your sucky thing to bed? I'm sorry, I haven't got time for this. Ring again in about seventy-three years.'

Bang.

On the Thursday night I blitzed myself. Waxing, exfoliating, eyebrow-plucking: you name it, I did it. During my Friday lunch-hour I bought three matching sets of bras and pants; the prettiest, filmiest ones I could find.

He phoned as he was leaving, just before seven on Friday night. 'If you can wait that long, I'll have something to eat,' I said.

'I had a sandwich half an hour ago. Don't go to any trouble – I'll see you soon.'

I wasn't planning on 'trouble': just fresh pasta (four minutes), fresh tomato and basil sauce (made earlier and ready except for slivers of mozzarella), and baby leaf salad.

Showered, moisturized and scented, I put on one of those filmy new sets. Like transparent white gossamer with tiny blue embroidered flowers, it was a thoroughly girlie contrast to slim black trousers and a sweater of softest black angora.

The doorbell rang at ten to eleven, and I don't think even a five-year-old waiting for Father Christmas had ever been in such a state of buzz.

I hadn't realized it was raining until I opened the door. As Henry charged to do greeting duty, he was standing on the step with raindrops on his hair. 'You were right about the parking. I had to leave the car in the next street.'

'I know, it's a nightmare,' I said, as he came in. 'Did my directions make sense?'

'Spot on. Hi, Muttley.' He was fondling Henry, who was very pleased to see him.

Then he straightened up and looked at me, and I looked at him, and thought never had anybody been so worth waiting for. 'Are you hungry?'

'Starving.'

'I've got some pasta.'

'Only if you let me do the starters.'

They were delicious starters: hot and tender, with enough passion quivering just under the surface to power the National Grid. At the same time, I knew there was going to be no frantic shedding of clothing just yet. As if we were out for dinner, we'd sit over one of the two ten-pound bottles of red Bordeaux I'd lashed out on. We'd look into each other's eyes, getting tinglier by the minute, until the hunger for a third course got bigger than both of us.

While I put a pan on for the pasta, he looked at the poster on my fridge and started laughing. 'Did anyone ever actually tell you his ex had really nice tits?'

I took a couple of plates from the cupboard. 'I'm afraid so.'

'What did you say?'

'I'm not telling you, but he took it very personally.'

This tickled him again, but as our eyes met, he wasn't laughing any more. When he spoke, his voice was warm and rough at once, a bit like Henry's fur. 'Why don't you turn that bloody pan off?'

It's very odd how words like that can make some buried organ lurch for England. 'I thought you were hungry.'

'I am.'

And they do say hunger is the best sauce . . .

During the next minute or so, I really thanked God I hadn't been born an amoeba. Or one of those hermaphrodite

301

snails that do it with themselves, so to speak. Say what you like, I maintain that one of the sublime pleasures of a girl's life is when her beloved's hands first steal under the back of her sweater and undo her bra. As for a moment later, when your flimsy gossamer cups are replaced by those same hands . . .

A few heartbeats later, in a husky sort of voice, he said, 'This is a lovely fluffy little jumper, but I'm afraid it's got to go.'

'Well, if you insist . . .'

It was tossed I know not where.

'And this is a very pretty little bra, but it's getting in the way.'

'Oh, dear. Better ditch it, then . . .'

As we came together again I was rapidly turning into hot, rampant jelly. 'Are you wearing your Dennis the Menace boxers?'

His laugh was warm and rough and lovely. 'No, my Nick the Menace ones.'

I put a hand down, just to check. It was indeed Nick the Menace, and a fine, upstanding young fellow he was, too. 'He feels awfully hot in there. Do you think we should let him out?'

'Oh, Christ, Izzy . . .'

En route to the beanbag sofa, further garments were flung aside with reckless abandon. Henry retired to a safe distance, and within two minutes we were rubbishing that old saying about lost opportunities being like spent arrows, never coming back. As quickies go, I'd call it a top-of-the-range version: sound effects, flashing lights – and an arrow Robin Hood would have been proud of. Hard as Ye Oake of Olde England, trusty and true, it certainly hit the bull's-eye.

*

We had our candlelit dinner after all. My ten-quid Bordeaux went down very well, though Nick nearly choked on it when I mentioned Tamara the cannibal. He said – choke, splutter – that he'd never been 'seeing' her – pause for cracking up – whatever had given me that idea?

'Somebody said something about riding stables. And it's very dangerous to crack up with a mouthful of red – you should be more careful.'

'It was one of her employees. I told you Tamara terrified me – it'd be riding boots and a whip, lashing me to a flat-out gallop.'

Well, it was nice to know. I was dying to ask whether the employee neighed and smelt of horse, but didn't push my luck. He might say, no, she was Anna Kournikova in jodhpurs.

Later, as we sprawled on the beanbag, he told me Rob had spilled the beans about Leo. I wouldn't get mad with him, would I?

I thought back to my flood-stained face after that evening with Rob. I imagined Nick saying later, 'I gather you were mopping up last night?'

'No, I thought he might have.' I paused. 'He phoned the other night. Leo, I mean.'

'Oh, did he.' It was a grim statement, not a question. As he turned to me, I felt a guilty little thrill. I almost felt his hackles rising, a surge of antler-clashing testosterone. 'What did he want?'

Then I knew I'd said it to get precisely this reaction. I hadn't been conscious of the thought process, but as I'd have hated him doing the same to me, I wished I'd kept quiet. 'To "explain". I told him to bugger off.'

'I should hope so.' He relaxed, and it was a relief to realize he didn't think I'd said it just to make him jealous, like some manipulative neurotic. 'If he phones again, pass him to me.'

I will admit I was enjoying this. 'That sounds ominous.'

'God, no. I'll ask him very politely to go away.'

I laughed, and he kissed me, and I wondered how much better life could get. We sprawled on that sofa for ages, talking lovely rubbish, until it dawned on us that it was gone two o'clock. 'I think it's high time I took you upstairs,' he said.

'I'm not so sure about that. Upstairs has Connotations, you know, and Mrs Denny says you should keep them guessing.'

'Oh, yes?' His eyes were glinting with laughter. 'What else does Mrs Denny say?'

'That I should invest in a pair of stockings. To inflame your wild lusts before I keep you guessing. But since I ironed my duvet cover specially, what the hell.'

One of the old dears in Mrs Denny's home once told me that she couldn't face another man after she lost her Eric because, to be honest, she never did quite take to the upstairs work. I dare say that was Eric's fault, but I'm happy to say here that Nick's upstairs work was masterly. To put it delicately, he didn't need any instruction in the use of tongue and fingertips. He didn't need telling that applying them with tantalizing artistry could bring someone like me to a state of delicious wantonness, to use a quaint old-fashioned word. In fact, I turned into the filthiest little hussy I'd been in a long time, and he didn't complain at all.

Well, not precisely. At one point, in a sort of strangled, death-by-pleasure tone, he said, 'Izzy, you are a very bad girl.'

Emerald would have been proud of me.

*

I awoke in his arms, still feeling like the cat that had got the extra thick double cream. It was nine thirty and Nick was still out for the count. I lay still, trying to fool Henry into thinking I was still asleep.

However, as Henry's sixth sense was in perfect working order, the next thing I knew was a nose in my face.

'Sshh!' I lifted Nick's lovely encircling arm gently enough not to wake him, and slipped into my dressing-gown and downstairs. I didn't altogether mind being dragged from bed. Once he'd been out and had a couple of Bonios, Henry would go back to sleep, and I could brush my teeth and so on, all nice and fresh to slip back into bed with Nick.

What I hadn't banked on was the doorbell ringing. Bloody postman, I thought, as Henry charged at full bark, all ready to see him off.

Hanging on to his collar, I opened the door.

*Oh my God* . . . 'Leo, why are you doing this?'

'You wouldn't talk to me on the phone. Please, just give me ten minutes.'

Once or twice in the dark days, I'd imagined this. But now he was here, I couldn't even despise him. I just saw a man who hadn't measured up. Who'd been rubbed out, totally eclipsed by someone else. 'Leo, there's no earthly point. I've moved on, I don't want to know any more. Please, will you just—'

'Five minutes, then. I'm not going away. Hi, Henry.' He actually stepped inside and shut the door.

His nerve took my breath away. 'What do you think you're doing? Don't you understand English?'

'What's going on?'

Nick was on the stairs. Still fastening a towel round his waist, he'd paused halfway, and his face and tone said it was a rhetorical question.

'He won't listen! He just barged in . . .' I turned back to
Leo, and his expression gave me a certain satisfaction.
He'd never imagined this. The Tarzan wind-up merchant.
The one he'd put in his place over the pool table.

'Oh,' he said, in a tone that said it all. 'I see.'

'Good,' said Nick, in dangerously pleasant tones. 'That's
a start.' In a bijou residence like mine, it's only about four
strides from the middle of the stairs to the front door, and
he covered them in two seconds. 'So now you've seen, clear
off.'

I'm sorry to say I was loving this. Physically, he just had
the edge on Leo; he exuded the more subtle kind of don't-
fuck-with-me intimidation.

'Look, calm down.' In that supposedly soothing manner
that just winds you up even more, Leo held up his hands. 'I
only want to talk to her – there's no need to come over
all—'

'Heavy?' From Nick's tone as he said this, I almost
thought he was going to come over exceedingly heavy
indeed. Again, I could almost scent the antler-clashing
testosterone. 'Don't tempt me,' he went on. 'Unless you
want me to kick your two-timing little arse out of that
door, clear off now.'

Oh, how I wished he would. 'Got that? So sorry not to
invite you for breakfast, but we'll probably be having it in
bed.'

I yanked the door open myself. 'Bye bye, Leo. And just
for the record, I wouldn't want you back if the only other
man on earth had just turned into a toad.'

'I never thought you would. I just came to say you were
right. About Joanne.'


Leo left half an hour later. With coffee on, I was putting
oranges through the juicer. 'Typical,' I said, in a pretend

A Girl's Best Friend

huff. 'The one time in my romantically deprived life I actually thought two blokes might be going to fight over me, the other bugger didn't even want me.'

Half laughing, Nick slipped his arm around me. 'I wish I'd punched him anyway. I felt like it, I can tell you.'

Well, it's the thought that counts. But I just hope they make a go of it this time. For the kids' sake.'

This was what Leo had spent half an hour explaining: that my instincts had been right. He was getting back together with Joanne. For over a year he'd been trying to ignore a voice that told him they should have made more of an effort to make it work. And after finally splitting with Desperate Dan, she'd said she felt the same. All right, the Laura thing had been unforgivable, he'd been an arse, he didn't mind admitting it. He just didn't want me to think of him for ever more as a shag-happy, total waste of space.

Nick had tactfully retreated as he told me all this. When I'd related it he'd said, 'OK, maybe I got it wrong. Only thirty per cent bullshit.'

While Nick hit the shower, I realized why Leo had come to Colditz. It made a lot more sense now. Increasingly resentful of Desperate Dan, he'd hated the thought of him spending the day with *his* wife, *his* kids. The prospect of a cosy family evening, with Mum talking about Uncle Bert and Angie's lovely salmon patties ('You must give me the recipe, dear') was more than his restless state could handle. He had to get out, and a long drive wasn't a bad escape route. Especially when someone at the end of it would be over the moon to see him. Someone who'd give him her sole, flattering attention. He just hadn't reckoned on some smart-arse murderer muscling in.

I took the smart-arse murderer into London. Starting with

the London Eye, we did the tourist bit. We stood in a pod holding hands as it rose slowly over the spreading panorama, and oohed and aahed over the Tower set in jewel-green grass, and the Queen's whacking great back garden. We picked out the Serpentine and the Globe, and Nick wondered *sotto voce* how often pigeons crapped on the audience's heads, and I started laughing so hysterically our fellow tourists gave us some very funny looks.

Later we walked along the river to the Tate Modern, and had lunch in the café that looked across to St Paul's. Then we walked over the wobbly Millennium Bridge, only it wasn't wobbling any more.

I was, though. Halfway across he said, 'It wasn't you that woke me, that night after the ball. I was already awake. I couldn't stop thinking about you.'

My heart lurched like a drunken parrot about to fall off its perch.

'I cursed myself afterwards,' he went on. 'Grabbing you like that, with all the finesse of a rugby ball in the guts . . .'

'I'd call it pouncing. But I *liked* it, that was the trouble. Any time you get the urge to pounce again, feel free.'

He pounced right there on the bridge, and I swear it wobbled after all.

Then he told me how he'd felt on finding Leo with me at Colditz, how it had only started hitting him then. How he'd wanted to shove that pool cue up his arse. (I did laugh here.) How he'd tried to stop thinking about me afterwards, until Rob had told him Leo was history and Jane and I might be coming to that ball.

Then, as we strolled on arm in arm, he told me about the aftermath of Henry. He'd begun to think it wasn't the ghost of Leo in his way at all, but Rob. The way he'd found us cuddled up together fast asleep, my offer of money, even that postcard I'd sent, once Paula was off the scene: '*Wish you were here, I really do* . . .' Rob had actually shown him. He'd said, 'Christ, poor Izzy,' because by then of course they'd thought Henry was gone for ever.

I said nothing about my former little thing. It was history, from that other country called Long Ago. Maybe I'd tell him one day, but not now. 'Rob's just a friend,' I said. 'One of the best.'

'That's what he said about you, too.'

With glinting sun on the water and gulls crying overhead, we ambled back along the river and he told me about Alex's mother.

I said nothing about Sasha's spilt beans. I wanted it from him, and he gave me a lot more than she had. Her name was Francesca. He told me how furious he'd been when she'd told him she'd missed a few pills, but it was largely fury with himself, for leaving precautions up to her. He told me how guilty he'd often felt afterwards, for assuming she'd take the easy way out. How unprepared he'd been for what he felt when Alex was actually born.

As people strolled past, he told me more. The sun was warm, but there was a cool breeze that smelt of the river, with a whiff of the sea. At our feet strutted plump and busy pigeons, looking for anything to scavenge. An inflatable craft was making a little wake on the water, and over the hum of traffic Big Ben was chiming the half hour. He told me how Francesca had suffered terrible post-natal depression that had made a lot more sense afterwards. She'd thought she'd somehow know at once who the father was, that some instinct would tell her. But even as Alex had grown, the only person he'd really resembled was her own father.

All along, of course, she'd been hoping the old flame was the father. She'd hoped to get back together with him. He told me how miserable she'd been when she heard he was marrying someone else. He told me how her revelation had stunned him; how he'd thought of trying for custody, but had known he'd almost certainly lose and in any case it would only unsettle Alex. How relieved he'd been when Francesca had finally found Mike, as he got on with him and he was good with Alex. By the time he told me this we were nearing the Globe, where a couple of tourists asked us to take a shot of them with the theatre as a backdrop.

As I handed the camera back, Nick took this as a natural break. 'I think that's enough of my lurid past,' he said. 'Let's have a bit of yours now. Can I buy you a drink?'

We stopped at the Dr Johnson not far away, where there were tables in the sun. Over a beer we shared a packet of cheese and onion crisps, which can be a very romantic sort of nibble when you're in the right mood.


He didn't leave until nine on Sunday night, and only when he was about to go did we talk properly about next time. I could go down, but it wasn't ideal as he was going to be on call.

'I don't mind,' I said, as we held each other close by the front door.

'You will, when I have a mashed-up cat on the line just as you've arrived.'

'I can live with that.' There was a long, lovely kiss goodbye. 'Ring me when you get back,' I said, and waved him off in the dark.

He phoned exactly an hour later. 'That was quick,' I said. 'You didn't tell me your car could fly.'

'Didn't I? It's got this clever little gizmo on the dash. One push and it turns into a helicopter.'

'You're driving with your mobile at your ear, you mean. I hope you're watching the road. I don't want a mashed-up you on the line, either.'

'I won't be mashed. I just stopped for petrol.' He paused. 'I was thinking on the way. About weekends, and all that driving.'

'What about them?'

'They're not enough. If I take a week's leave next month, will you come away with me?'

# Chapter 19

On a sultry August Saturday eighteen months later, Felicity was throwing another party, only this time it was the biggest do of all.

We were back at the Tawton House Hotel, out on green lawns where you could see for miles over undulating summery fields. The air was heavy with heat and the scent of thousands of roses. It would have been a perfect day, apart from a bad case of inner turmoil that was only going to get worse.

I was listening to some aunt of Ian's telling me what a terrible drive they'd had from Market Harborough, when Jane came up. In a short-sleeved suit of eau-de-Nil linen she looked cooler than almost anyone else. 'Izzy, you and Nick haven't had a row, have you?' she asked, as Market Harborough aunt moved on.

'What on earth makes you say that?'

'Oh, come on. I saw the pair of you a couple of minutes ago. I might not be brilliant at lip-reading, but even I can make out "Bugger off, will you?" '

Oh, Lord. 'He was just being a bit of a pain.'

'Why?'

We were interrupted by a woman who really strained my false smile to its limits. Very thin, very tanned, with an air of ravaged elegance, she wore something extremely expensive-looking in brightly patterned silk. She looked me up and down as if I were a faintly weird species. 'Are you the one who's gone into business with Felicity?'

'That's what we like to call it. Isn't she looking gorgeous?'

The woman, whose name was Madeleine, turned in that direction. Felicity's dress was pale cream silk, strapless and very simple. She looked just as a bride should an hour into her own reception: glowing with happiness and champagne.

'Yes, I must say I'm pleasantly surprised,' said Madeleine. 'She was such an unpromising child. Always verging on the podgy.' She turned to me again. 'Which is your husband?'

'We're not married,' I said. 'But he's over there. With the girl in the pink dress.'

Detailed for usher duty, Nick was wearing a morning suit, but had ditched the jacket because of the heat. The girl was laughing up at him and as I watched my stomach contracted like never before.

'Oh,' said Madeleine. 'Yes, I think you did introduce me. Excuse me, I'm going to see if anyone in this place can make me some iced tea.'

'Iced bourbon, more like,' Jane whispered, as she made her carefully elegant way to the marquee. 'Dreadful old hag, isn't she?'

'Who's an old hag?' said a voice at her shoulder.

It was Guy, who was Jane's latest and reminded me in the nicest possible way of Leo. 'Oh, hi, darling,' said Jane. 'Felicity's mother. I can't think why she invited her. She's hardly seen her for years.'

'You have to invite your mother to your wedding,' I pointed out. 'Anyway, she never thought she'd actually come.'

'Still, at least all her proper family's here,' Jane said.

'That's us lot, Guy, in case you hadn't worked it out. The mob. Alastair and Ellie and Rob – doesn't he look great?'

With Juliet on his arm, Rob did look great. He'd sent that email in the end, and for the next few weeks there had been friendly toings and froings courtesy of cyberspace, until eventually Juliet had sent one that said, *'If you'd like to meet up for a couple of drinks when I get back . . .'*

She'd had a bit of a shock at first. What was with the haircut? No, she wasn't at all sure she liked it. Well, OK, she did, but he might have warned her. It was like going home and finding that your mother's had *Changing Rooms* in to tart up your old bedroom. She wanted her dog-eared old posters back, and the carpet with the Coke stain that never quite came out.

It hadn't taken long after that. Rob hadn't told me much, but reading between the lines she'd started missing him like mad. At the same time, though, she knew she'd needed to get away. Maybe it was a case of not knowing what you want until you've thrown it away, or think you have. At any rate, any fool could see they were happy.

If only I could have said the same for me. Keeping a smile glued on was increasingly difficult. Nick was still talking to that girl, not that I cared. As far as I was concerned, he could chat up every sickeningly slim, gorgeous girl present until chucking-out time. In fact, I wished he would. He'd been a total pain since the organist struck up *'Love divine, all loves excelling'* in the church.

*'Joy of heav'n to earth come down . . .'*

'Are you listening to me?' (This was Nick, muttering.)

*'Fix in us Thy humble dwelling . . .'*

'No! Just shut up, will you?' (Me, in hissy whisper.)

*'All Thy faithful mercies crown.'*

'Don't you tell me to shut up.'

He hadn't exactly endeared himself to me first thing,

314

either. When you step on the scales and scream with anguish because you've put on another pound and a half, you'd like a little sympathy. You don't want a man saying, 'Calm down, Piglet – when you start putting me off my breakfast I'll soon tell you.'

Piglet! Though I grudgingly had to concede that it could have been worse, when a short-sighted pig farmer might easily have mistaken me for a great fat sow. A hot fat sow, now. God, it was boiling. Why was everybody out here, instead of under the marquee? Why were there no slaves laid on, to fan us with palm leaves? All I had was the order of service from the church.

Rob frowned at me. 'Izzy, are you all right?'

*Oh, just fine and dandy.* 'Fine! Just hot.'

'Roasting, isn't it?' said Jane. She nodded to the far side of the gardens, where you could just see a small turquoise pool. 'As soon as they're gone, I'm falling into that water.'

'With your clothes on, I hope,' said Rob. 'I've still got half a roll of film.'

That was when I caught Nick's eye. Seeing him head for me with a purposeful expression, I said, 'Just off to the loo,' and scarpered.

He caught me up, just as I was going in. 'Come on, I'm going to take you home.'

'That's what you think,' I said, thankful to be in the cooler inside.

'Do you want me to come over all heavy and put my foot down?'

'If you put your foot down anywhere near me, I'll step on it, OK?'

He couldn't come any further, as I'd just reached the door that said 'Ladies'. 'Go and chat up that girl in the pink dress,' I added, as a parting shot. 'Drool into her cleavage if you like – I won't say a word.'

He was still there when I came out, having splashed my face.

'Come on,' he said, more gently. 'And don't give me any more guff about Braxton Hicks contractions – you've started. You started even before we hit the church.'

He really did go on sometimes. Left to him, I'd have been whipped into hospital there and then. I'd told him it was just textbook uterine practice, but he hadn't bought it any more than he was buying it now. 'All right, maybe I have, but it'll be hours yet.'

'How do you know? How often are they coming?'

'Nick, will you stop fussing? Every single book says the first stage lasts for ever. Stop being such an old woman, will you?'

'Don't you "old woman" me. You'll be exhausted even before you start. This heat's a killer. Just look at you.'

'Oh, that's right – make me feel like a hot pink hippopotamus. I'll go when they go, all right? Felicity'll probably cancel the honeymoon and they're only having three days as it is.' She'd already cancelled a longer one, because we couldn't both be away for any length of time.

He gave in, but didn't leave my side for the next two hours. And despite what I'd said, I began to wonder whether I should have gone home after all. No wonder they'd called them 'pains' in the old days. It was a good deal more honest; at least you wouldn't feel it was down to your own pathetic mismanagement if they hurt. Not that I could 'manage' anything just now; shallow panting would rather have given the game away. While my stomach went rock hard, I just grinned a frozen grin and prayed that my waters wouldn't break. This was Felicity's day, and Ian's, and I didn't want to be a sideshow.

After that lunch we'd had together, I'd promised her faithfully not to say a word to Ian, and I hadn't. However, she'd said nothing about words to anyone else. I'd had a little word with Rob, who'd told me that Ian had eventually confided in him one night when Felicity was out. She'd gone through a very twitchy patch lately – did Rob think all this 'new image' stuff meant she was on the lookout for somebody else?

As Rob had said, you felt like banging their heads together. So when Felicity told me Ian was taking her away for her birthday, for a couple of days in Paris, I'd managed to say, 'Oh, that'll be nice,' as if I'd had no inklings of anything afoot. Privately, I'd thought he could have exercised a little more imagination. Felicity had been to Paris loads of times. 'It's just a bit clichéd,' I'd said to Jane – and had to eat my words afterwards.

She'd only found out when they'd headed for the Istanbul check-in, instead. She'd phoned me when she'd got back, crying her eyes out, and not because she'd been slightly short of hot-weather clothes. On the night of her birthday Ian had taken her to some gorgeous little restaurant and asked her to marry him. Poor Ian, he'd been worried that she was going off him. She'd felt so bad ... But imagine him organizing this! Who'd ever have thought he could be so romantic?

Not even me, I had to confess. Still, Ian's Pork and Beans was only his way of saying Beloved Jewel of my Heart, but like most men, he'd feel a prat.

They left more or less on time for a flight to Jersey. 'What a shame they're only having three nights,' said the Market Harborough aunt, as we waved them off.

'They're going away for longer in October,' I explained. 'It's my fault, really. She couldn't be away too long in case I was out of action for a bit.'

'Oh, yes.' She looked down at my bump, which would

have made a prize-winning pumpkin come Hallowe'en. 'When are you due?'

I was about to say, 'Officially in ten days,' when Nick cut in.

'Probably tonight,' he said. 'Excuse me, but I'm taking her home.'

I only told Jane, and left her to pass it on. 'Brilliant timing,' I said to Nick, as we drove off. 'Serves me right for getting a mad fit of broodiness.'

'You weren't to know it was only going to take two months.'

Personally, I blamed the media. Everywhere I'd looked there were suddenly articles about plummeting post-thirty fertility; I'd imagined it taking a year at the very least. 'That was your fault,' I retorted anyway. 'If you'd been a bit more lackadaisical about it, instead of applying yourself at every opportunity, I'd probably be obsessed with ovulation charts by now.' I glanced across at him. 'I'm sure it was that time you waylaid me in the bath, when all I wanted was a lovely soak in the Radox.'

'What do you expect?' He turned in to a lane like a green tunnel, the leaves thick overhead. 'If you will lie there, all pink and wet with bubbles on your nipples . . .'

'You could have stuck with blowing them off, and not started talking about dirty little trollops who could do with a good soaping . . .' As another contraction hit me, I breathed through it.

He held my hand. 'All right?' he asked, as it faded.

'Fine. And I know I've said this before, but I don't want you telling me you forgot. You're to stay at my head and shoulders throughout. No gawping at the sharp end. I'd like to keep a little mystery in this relationship. And don't start telling me about that mastiff bitch that was having problems, or yanking lambs out when you were a student doing your farm animals.'

'No, dear,' he said, deadpan.

The house was only four miles away. Initially we'd wanted a pretty, Devon-white house, maybe sixteenth century, with four or five bedrooms. But however pretty they'd been, there had always been two things wrong with them. One, old houses ate money, and two, the windows were too small. So we'd ended up with this: a twenty-year-old house designed by an architect who wasn't just thinking of his fee. On top of a gentle rise, it was full of light and space.

And chaos, however, because we'd only got the keys five days previously. There were still tea chests everywhere, but getting straight hadn't been a priority. In the past fifteen months I'd never worked so hard in my life.

Jane was dead right about the horticulture course; I'd soon realized I'd want to come in whenever it rained. For a while, I'd thought of being a student again, but a proper one this time. I'd thought of psychology or business studies, but that would mean being broke for three years, essays and exams – and feeling about a hundred among a load of eighteen-year-olds.

No, thanks. I was past all that.

Still temping and 'thinking about it', I was working for a particularly irritating and inefficient boss when it hit me. I could do her job so much better. My organizational/people/everything skills were a damn sight better than most of the people I'd been working for. Why was I slaving my backside off for them, when I could be working for myself?

It was so simple, except for one minor point. While

reading half a dozen books on the subject, I racked my brains for the next niche nobody else had thought of.

In the end, I didn't need a new one. All the time a well-worn one was sitting on Felicity's doorstep.

A couple of months after Nick and I became an item, she'd told me that those half dozen holiday cottages had turned into a more scattered ten. What's more, it had got around that she was doing this. Second-home owners who didn't want upkeep hassles had been on the phone; Ian had even joked that she should go into it full-time.

'Well, why don't you?' I'd echoed, half-seriously. 'Eff's Property Management, for that extra-special personal touch.'

'God, no. I don't think I've got the entrepreneurial thing.'

That was when I knew I had.

'Someone even asked if I'd like to manage six flats in Westward Ho!' she went on. 'I'd need my own office. I'd have to pay someone else to muck in, and get mad if they phoned in sick when I knew they weren't, and be too chicken to sack them. And you know me – the minute anyone got stroppy, I'd be taking ten per cent off the bill.'

*I wouldn't.* A little thread of excitement was stirring in me, but I sat on it. 'In any case, there must be lots of competition.'

'Yes, and largely from Luke Archer's outfit. But I know for a fact that his lot slip in extra charges for this and that, and they take ages to get things done. Are you coming down at the weekend? I've found a sweet little house at Appledore – it'd let like a shot. I'm dying for you to come and tell me what you think.'

After she'd hung up, I mulled it over for three hours before ringing her back. That weekend, pretending I was house-hunting with Felicity, I spent half the morning looking at possible premises and once we'd seen number three, Candle-makers' Yard, I think that was it. Ten minutes' walk from the town square, it hadn't seen any candle-makers for about three hundred years. It had a bow-fronted window like an old-fashioned sweetshop, but as the last tenant was a now upsizing accountant it was wired for computers. Apart from a lick of paint, nothing needed doing. When I saw the little flat upstairs, my mind began racing.

'You could sublet that,' said Felicity. 'As a matter of fact, I know someone it would just do for.'

Felicity always did know someone.

'And that little yard at the back even gets some sun,' she went on, peering out. 'Lovely for Henry.'

'And Shep.'

'What?'

'You and me, Fliss. Oh, come on,' I urged, seeing her face. 'I've got the background, you've got the contacts. You said yourself it'd take two.'

She looked down at the sheaf of house particulars in her hand. The Appledore house was already under offer, but she had her eye on a couple more.

'You can still buy something, Fliss. I'll put up the cash.'

Until then, I don't think she'd quite realized I was serious. 'Izzy, you could lose thousands just starting up!'

'I know,' I said. 'But nothing ventured . . .'

Perversely, just as she began to get excited, my own feet started going cold. Still seeing Nick only at weekends, I was commuting like an ant. Left at home, Henry was let out every lunch-time by someone from Furry Friends. Parking was getting worse by the week. With all this in mind, part of me was saying, *Yes! Go for it!*

On the other hand, what if we didn't get the business? What if all my capital drained away on rent and rates and unpaid invoices, and everything else that so often killed the fragile little creature called Small Business?

And what about Nick? He knew nothing of this, yet already Felicity was assuming I'd move in with him. No way. That mini-flat would do fine for now, but even so, would suddenly living round the corner smack of being 'too eager'? What if he started cooling off?

The answer had soon come to me. 'If he does, isn't it better to find out now?'

In the event, Nick's reaction had been the least of my worries. He'd said thank God for that, it'd be nice to see me on a Wednesday for a change, but if I thought I was moving into some poky little flat designed for midget fifteenth-century candle-makers, I had another think coming.

I had moved into it, though. For the first two months I'd lain awake at night, wondering whether it was all a terrible mistake. I'd dreamt of that rushing brown river, sweeping all my assets away on a tide of cash-flow deficit. Even when we were making enough of a go of it to take on someone else, I'd still had the odd such dream, as if my brain were trying to tell me this couldn't last.

When I'd found out I was pregnant, I'd had the worst nightmare of all. Nick was on the beach, holding some nameless little bundle in his arms. I was up on a cliff and he was laughing and calling to me, but behind him a massive tidal wave was roaring in. I was screaming at him to run, but he couldn't hear me. I'd woken in a terrified panic, Nick trying to soothe me. 'Oh, just the usual,' I'd said, when he asked. 'A German lit exam and I haven't read any of the books.'

But all that had passed. The worst dream I'd had in ages was of going into labour in Safeway's. Surrounded by Saturday shoppers, Nick delivered me on the checkout, in a pair of Marigold household gloves. 'Well, fuck me,' he said, gaping at the sharp end. 'She said she was having kittens, but I never really thought she meant it.'

Having already packed a bag, I only had to grab it and go to the loo for the fourteenth time that day while Nick fed Henry. It was a twenty-minute drive to the hospital, and the closer we got, the more my stomach went into knots. In the car park Nick yanked the handbrake on and turned to me. 'All right?'

'No,' I said. 'I'm scared. Pathetic, isn't it?'

'No.' His eyes softened, and he leant over and kissed me. 'I'd do it for you if I could.'

I don't think I disgraced myself too much, though I grunted to Nick at one point that if he ever came near me again, he'd be peeing sitting down in future. She was born at two minutes to ten, pink and slippery, with none of the dark hair I'd expected. As they put her in my arms, I wondered how on earth anything so new and tiny and perfect could also look like my great-granny when she was about ninety-three and hadn't got her teeth in, but then she hadn't any teeth, and my great-granny had been quite a stunner when she was young.

I'll never forget Nick's face. Before the event, I'd thought I might mind that it wasn't his first, that he might be blasé about it. All that vanished like mist. When they left us alone together, I watched him cradling her in his arms. She was awake, looking around with a sort of sleepy, blue-eyed wonder. Goodness me, where am I? Who's this looking at me and sticking his little finger in my hand? Still, it feels quite nice – I might as well hang on to it.

'Hi, little one,' he said. 'Was it a pig of a journey? I'm

going to have to call you Mini for now, because we haven't quite hit on a name.'

I stroked her cheek with a fingertip. 'This is your daddy,' I told her. 'I was very careful to find you a specially nice one. In fact, I think I can safely say he's the best.'

They let us go home at lunch-time the next day. We'd only been back an hour when the phone rang, just as I'd finished feeding Mini. As I stuffed myself back into a Jersey-cow bra, Nick took her. In her little bunny-covered sleepsuit, miles too big even though the label said 'New-born', I thought she looked very sweet up at his shoulder. Very weeny, too: his left hand practically covered her little bunnies.

He answered the phone with his other hand. 'Hi, Jenny. Yes, they're fine. Yes, as beautiful as her mother. Hang on, I'll pass you over.'

It was Mum. Beside herself with excitement, she was about to book tickets home. No, they would absolutely *not* stay with us, I could do without house guests. They'd rent a car at the airport and go to a hotel. No, dear, absolutely *not*. Well, all right, if I really in*si*sted . . . They'd try to make themselves useful. Cooking, shopping, dog-walking . . . *do get plenty of rest* – oh, and here's Daddy, he'd like a little word . . .

'That's it, the house'll be vacuumed to death,' I said, once they'd finally hung up. 'You should get Dad on to the garden – he'll be only too willing. And a certain little baby's going to be cuddled non-stop. I hope you won't feel left out,' I added, stroking Henry, who was sitting at my feet. Delighted to see me back, he'd sniffed with waggly interest at Mini, but had refrained from slurping, which was a relief. She'd have to get used to it sooner or later, but just now her little immune system might not be up to it.

Later, when Mini was tucked up in her little basket, Nick sat beside me on the sofa. 'Are you sure you're up for Alex tomorrow?'

'Of course!' His stepfather was due to bring him for a quick visit in the afternoon. Francesca wasn't coming; her second son was at the terrible-handful stage and she'd said she couldn't possibly inflict him on me. Rather to my surprise Alex hadn't said, 'Yuck! Not a *girl*!' when Nick had called to tell him he had a baby sister. He'd said, oh, well, at least she probably wouldn't bash him up, like James – when could he come and see her? 'Don't forget to make a big fuss of him,' I added. 'You don't want him feeling left out.'

'Don't worry, he won't.' He took my hand. 'You know something? Given our new co-parenting status, I think it's high time I made an honest woman of you.'

I'd been half expecting this. 'I can't be thinking about weddings now. The mere thought makes me feel exhausted. Can't we just stay partners?'

'Rob's my partner. I don't need another.'

'Lovers, then?'

'Sounds as if all we do is cavort under ceiling mirrors, instead of arguing the toss about what colour to paint the bathroom.'

I pretended to consider. 'How about co-parenting co-mortgagees?'

He choked back a laugh. 'Bit of a mouthful if I ever have to introduce you after a few beers.' With a sigh, he sat back. 'I suppose I'll have to do an Ian – cart you off and pop the question on top of the Taj Mahal or something.'

With some difficulty I remained deadpan. 'I know what's brought all this on. Yesterday's gone to your head. Just because you look pretty damn good in a morning suit, there's no reason to get carried away.'

'Oh, come on. I was thinking of far more serious matters. A new sandwich toaster, for starters. Ours is useless – it doesn't seal the edges. All the cheese gunges out and makes a bloody mess.'

I bit my lip. 'Anything else?'

'Yes, while I'm at it. You keep saying you'd like one of those gizmos that make frothy coffee. Oh, and there's one other little thing . . .' Delving in his trouser pocket, he brought out a tiny box covered in blue velvet.

As he put it in my hand, my throat constricted.

'I expect I've cocked up on the size,' he said. 'And the style. So feel free to say so.'

I opened it to see a diamond solitaire that caught the sunlight streaming from the window. It flashed blue and green fire.

My eyes were pricking. I could not utter a word.

'We could still do the Taj Mahal,' he said. 'But it's a hell of a long way to go to say, "I love you."'

I knew he did. He didn't have to say it. With my eyes welling up, my voice came out appallingly wobbly. 'Making me cry, now, and I haven't even got a tissue . . .'

'Oh, come here,' he said.

If you enjoyed *A Girl's Best Friend* why not try
Liz Young's first two novels,
*Asking for Trouble* and *Fair Game*

Read on for extracts ...

# Asking for Trouble

## It was only a little white lie . . .

Sophy's single and happy about it. She does, however, have an imaginary boyfriend, Dominic, a little white lie designed to keep Sophy's mother off her back.

Which is fine, until his presence is demanded at a family wedding. So does Sophy admit Dominic is a fantasy? Oh no. Sophy hires an escort.

But when the distinctly delicious Josh Carmichael arrives on her doorstep, Sophy can tell things are going to get tricky. And the wedding is only the beginning . . .

## Praise for Liz Young:

'Perfect comic timing and wickedly funny moments'
*Cosmopolitan*

'A lively Lisa Jewell-esque debut novel with a bit more bite than you might imagine'  *Daily Mirror*

# Prologue

The invitation came on a Saturday morning, just in time to wreck my weekend. On stiff, crinkly edged card it read:

Mr and Mrs Edward Metcalfe
request the pleasure of the company of
Sophy and Dominic
at the wedding of their daughter
Belinda Anne
To Mr Paul Fairfax
At
The Inn by the Beck
On Saturday, 11th May, at 1.00 p.m.
RSVP

It wasn't that it came as a shock. When your sister's wedding date's been set, you don't have to wait for the invitation to arrive to find out. If you have a mother like mine, BT lines are buzzing instantly. She'd probably announced it in the *Telegraph*, the *Manchester Evening News*, and very possibly the *South China Morning Post*, too. For all I knew she might even have announced it on the Internet. Not to be outdone by an arch-rival neighbour, Mum had recently acquired a Toshiba laptop.

There had been an engagement bash back in January, but three months had whizzed by since then, and if ever a party had been thrown from mixed motives, it was Belinda's. You only had to listen to my mother.

To Maggie Freeman, the arch-rival neighbour, there was a barely concealed hint of up-yours: 'Oh, yes, he whisked her off to Florence just last week – proposed right on the Ponte Vecchio – I suppose you've seen her ring?'

To neighbours she actually liked it was: 'Well, of course, Ted and I are delighted – he's doing terribly well and obviously besotted . . .'

To me, while we were whipping satay sticks from the oven, it was a whispered, '. . . and I feel he'll be *good* for Belinda – nothing *wishy-washy* about him, if you know what I mean. Don't ever tell her I told you, but I always thought she'd end up with one of those wishy-washy boys she could never say no to. Daddy was afraid it might be that Tim – a nice enough boy, of course, but not much use in a crisis, if you ask me. I won't tell you what Daddy called him – it was terribly rude.'

There must have been forty-odd guests at Belinda's party, which wasn't bad at short notice. Two-thirds were specifically her friends; the rest assorted family and friends, all milling pleasantly in my folks' party-sized sitting room and spilling into hall and kitchen, as they do. As always at any bash thrown by my folks, foody-drinky warmth hit you the instant you walked in the door, which was just as well, given the sub-zero frost outside.

In case you're a normally nosy person (like me) let me share some more eavesdroppings. From assorted friends of Belinda's I heard this:

'He bought her that dress, you know. In Florence. She won't say, but it looks like Versace to me. Mind you, Belinda could almost make British Home Stores look like Versace.'

'Makes you sick, doesn't it? The most Ian's ever bought me is a satin teddy from Knickerbox.'

'Mind you, I'm not sure I'd actually *want* a bloke like Paul. I'd never relax for a second – there'd always be half a dozen bitches trying to pinch him.'

Belinda, as you may have gathered, was floating on a euphoric pink cloud. The dress was little, black, and possessed that simple yet out-of-the-ordinary something that screams megabucks. And if Paul's arm scarcely left her waist all evening, you could hardly blame him.

Nobody ever believes we're sisters. She modelled for a bit, among other things (cookery course, secretarial stuff) but wasn't tall enough to make the grade. I have the inches, at five foot eight, but Belinda has the rest. A perfect size ten, the kind of creamy-honey skin that never goes pink and pasty even in the depths of winter, a luxuriant mane of dark-honey hair, and hazel eyes with lashes you would swear came from Boots Over-The-Top range. And a face, well . . . A friend of hers once confided to me, 'I hate to say it, but when someone looks like that you almost wish she was an utter cow so you could hate her with a clear conscience.'

I'm not an Ugly Sister, exactly, but with competition like that you can't help feeling like one. I'm a perfect size thirteen and three-quarters: 36C top, 37D bottom, skin of cream without the honey, and a luxuriant-ish mane of common-or-garden dark brown hair like Mum's. I have Mum's eyes, too: big, navy-blue jobs which I may modestly say are my best feature.

I'd only met Paul a couple of times before, and since he'd fit right into a mail-order catalogue of Grade A men, it had been a relief to find I didn't actually fancy him. About six foot one, he had the lithe build of a tennis pro, with that medium olive skin that looks brilliant against

7

white. He had dark brown eyes to match and hair the colour of very old, polished mahogany. At thirty-one, four years older than Belinda, he was a meteorically rising star in some management consultancy.

'Great to see you again – how's London treating you?' he asked, when I finally made it to the happy couple. 'Hope the traffic wasn't a complete bitch.'

'Fairly bitchy, but never mind.' I'd driven up and been a bit late. 'Well, what can I say? Congratulations, and all that . . . I think you should have warned us all to wear sunglasses before looking at that ring.'

It was a mega-watt diamond cluster, not so huge as to be knuckle-dusterish – her fingers wouldn't take it – but the stones flashed a blue fire that made you blink.

Belinda gave a guiltily pleased little laugh. 'I'm sure it was horribly extravagant . . .'

His hand was still on her waist in that *she's mine* fashion. 'Sweetheart, you should know me by now. If a thing's worth doing . . .'

'You did the whole thing properly.' I said. 'Right out of the romantic rule book. Men like you are an extinct species in London.'

'Sophy, how can you say that?' Belinda tutted. 'Didn't Dominic whisk you off from some boring party to some flash restaurant right after you met?'

'Yes, he has potential,' I said lightly. 'As long as he doesn't start asking me to sew buttons on his shirts I might tolerate him till Valentine's day.'

Belinda gave another little laugh. 'Sure sign she's mad about him,' she stage-whispered to Paul. 'Any madder and she'd be saying she was going right off him already, just so as not to tempt Fate.'

'Sweetheart, Fate is for losers,' Paul said crisply. 'If you want something, you go out and *make* it happen.'

8

When I caught her alone for a minute, later on, free-flowing alcohol had only heightened her glow. 'I just couldn't believe it,' she gushed happily. 'I mean, we'd only just arrived and he took me straight to the bridge, and there we were at sunset, and suddenly he took this little box out of his pocket – it was like a dream. And later, back at the hotel . . .' She drew me aside and whispered, 'All I wore for practically the next twenty-four hours was the ring.'

'And a big fat grin, I bet.'

'You bet.' She went on in a giggly whisper, 'I've never met anyone who turns me on like he does. I never have to say "left hand down a bit" – he just seems to *know*, if you get what I mean.'

'Trollop,' I said severely, thinking: Lucky old you. 'No wonder you're walking like Clint Eastwood.'

During the next hour I did plenty more eavesdropping – I couldn't avoid it, not that I actually tried. From a couple of Mum's friends from the golf club I heard, '. . . mind you, I always think it's a shame when the younger sister gets married first. Sophy must be coming up to thirty and it's so hard for girls these days. Half the chaps are raging poofs.'

'Trudi, you're not supposed to say that word nowadays. Anyway, Sophy *is* seeing someone, Sue told me: a merchant banker, apparently. She was hoping she'd bring him tonight but it's probably a bit soon for family dos.'

From another knot of Belinda's friends I heard: 'Does that Paul ever let go of her? He's had a proprietary arm around her all bloody night.'

'She probably likes it. By all accounts they hardly got out of bed their first four weekends – I'm only surprised she hasn't moved in with him already. Mind you, all that

9

rampant non-stop bonking gave her cystitis. It bruises your tissues.'

'Christ. Still, if you'd like a dose of that from rampant non-stop bonking, I'm willing and able.'

'Oh, grow up. And stop gawping at her legs, will you? If you start sticking a rifle in my back at three o'clock in the morning I'll know who you've been dreaming about.'

Around half-nine I opened the door to a latecomer. 'Tamara! We'd just about given you up.'

'Hi, ratbag,' she grinned. 'Long time no see. Quick, let me in, it's freezing – I walked all the way from The Bear. I got waylaid by Dave Doodah earlier and he dragged me off for a quick one, only it turned into three and a game of pool. I'm a bit pissed already, actually.'

'So am I,' I replied happily. The Bear was half a mile up the road. Tamara Dixon, an old schoolfriend of mine, lived four doors away. She'd been abroad for three years on and off, so I hadn't seen much of her lately, and at Christmas she'd been skiing, so I hadn't even seen her then. Under a halo of red-gold curls and the kind of innocent-angel face you see in sentimental Victorian paintings, Tamara possessed a blithely wicked streak. She could be on the dippy side, too, but she was a good laugh.

'Glad to be back?' I asked, once she'd warmed up.

'Not sure yet, but Mum's so chuffed to have me home, she's even doing my ironing. So how's this Dominic?' she added, with a grin. 'Belinda's told me all about him.'

'I'm surprised she had to. Mum's already told half of north-west England.'

She laughed. 'Did you meet him through Posh Whatsit?'

'Are you kidding? We don't quite deal in big-league stuff.'

By 'Posh Whatsit' she meant Aristos Recruitment, who had twenty branches in London and the south-east, of

10

which I was supposed to manage one. 'Aristos' wasn't meant to have 'posh' connotations, exactly. Pronounced 'Aristoss', it apparently means 'best' in ancient Greek, which is a laugh if you could see some of the people taking our literacy and numeracy tests.

'I gather Paul's big-league,' she said, nodding towards the star guests. 'Or well on his way. No wonder your mum's looking like the cat that got the goldfish.'

Later, as people were drifting off, I heard someone say, 'So when's the wedding?'

You should have seen Mum's face. Radiant glory, wreathed in beaming smiles. 'They haven't *quite* fixed a date yet, but I'm sure it won't be long . . .'

Which brings me neatly back to that invitation hitting the matt. With it came a note:

It's all going to be a terrible rush – barely six weeks to organise everything – I really must lose a few pounds before I even *think* about looking for something to wear – but they were very lucky to get a cancellation. I do hope Dominic'll be able to come. We're so looking forward to meeting him. Much love in haste,

M x

And a x from D, of course.

I stuck the invitation on the mantelpiece, where it glared balefully at me. 'Well?' it seemed to say. 'Are you going to sort this out, or what?'

Mum phoned that same evening. 'You will bring him, won't you, dear? I've told absolutely everybody about him and you do want to keep your end up – Zoe Freeman's still seeing that Oliver – I had to invite him, of course – he looks a bit chinless to me but that's all the more reason for you to indulge in a little bit of flaunting—'

'Mum—'

'Yes, I know it sounds bitchy, dear, but Maggie's on and on about Oliver this and Oliver that – I really will murder that woman one day – you'd think a corporate lawyer was a cross between God and Mel Hudson to hear her carry on—'

'*Gibson*, Mum. Mel Gibson.'

'You know what I mean. Please do tell Dominic we'd love to see him – he surely can't be booked up six weeks in advance – if he thinks enough of you I'm sure he'll be only too pleased . . .'

After another minute of this I said weakly that yes, I was sure he'd love to come, yes, I was fine, everything was fine, give my love to Dad and Belinda, see you soon, and hung up.

'She wants me to keep *my* end up,' I said. 'Permit me a hollow little laugh.'

Alix, my friend, flatmate and unpaid counsellor was giving me her *God, You're hopeless* look. 'God, you're hopeless,' she said. 'Why can't you just dump him and be done with it?'

'I can't just *do* it! I've got to psych myself up first – think of an utterly unarguable reason why we're no longer compatible.'

'I can think of a brilliant one,' she said. 'Death is generally considered the perfect grounds for ending an inconvenient relationship. Have him mugged to death for his gold cards.'

I don't mind telling you, such callousness appalled me. 'Wouldn't it seem just a bit ungrateful, after I've used him so shamelessly?'

'Stuff that. Have it done next week – quick, clean, and no chance of a reconciliation. You can't take a corpse to a wedding.'

12

'A messy murder would cast a bit of a cloud over the wedding,' I pointed out. 'I don't want to be a killjoy, with everyone feeling sorry for me. And how on earth would I look heartbroken when I was actually thinking: Thank God for that – pass me another large vodka and the best man, please?'

'You think of something, then!' She gave an up-to-here sigh. 'I hate to say I told you so, but I *did*. If you will invent some perfect, pain-in-the-arse bloke just to get your mum off your back—'

'He wasn't *entirely* invented,' I pointed out.

'Don't split hairs.' She sloshed me out a third glass of Jackdaw Ridge. 'You made him up, you get shot of him.'

# Chapter 1

I blame it entirely on pressure of work, but for the next couple of weeks Dominic and I were still officially an item at the bottom of my in-tray. Every time it rose to the surface, saying, 'Well?' I told it to bugger off, I was far too busy and important to deal with it just now.

After a lull we were suddenly inundated. IT, marketing, accounts: you name it, they wanted it, and that was without the temps. We were trawling old candidate files and advertising everywhere but the backs of cornflake packets. There was barely even time to discuss really crucial stuff, like the previous night's *Friends*, or that irritating woman in the sandwich shop.

I didn't tackle Dominic properly until Sunday morning, nineteen days before the wedding. Having *him* dump *me* would have been the simplest way out, but that wouldn't keep anybody's end up, least of all mine. I suppose I'd been hoping my imagination would suddenly whack me on the head with the perfect way out. It had been very creative once. I'd had brilliant fantasies about being in the Famous Five (instead of that wet Anne with her dolls) or plotting against the Sheriff with Robin Hood (instead of that wet Maid Marian).

Mind you, I hadn't exercised it much lately, except with the kind of fantasies you don't tell your mother, about, so since all it had come up with was 'Abduction by Aliens', I was still dithering over alternatives.

Nobody was helping me, either. Alix was still asleep, and although a vaguely human body was sprawled on the sofa, it was absorbed in the football pages. Its beloved Tossers United had screwed up yet again so it was serious stuff. I was up against a bad case of TMD, a.k.a. Temporary Male Deafness.

The body belonged to Alix's 'little' brother Ace, all five foot eleven of him. He was twenty-six, quite nice-looking under the scruff, and his light-brown ponytail was in vibrant condition, thanks to my Pantene 2 in 1, which he pinched constantly. With it he wore one gold earring and, except when Tossers had screwed up, a chilled-out air I defy anyone to beat.

'You might make *some* suggestion, even if it's completely brainless,' I muttered. 'You could at least show *willing*.'

Not so much as a primeval grunt.

Currently occupying the cupboard that passed as a third bedroom in this flat, Ace had moved in for a week a couple of months back, and had stayed because he preferred paying cupboard-sized rent to the room-sized variety. Despite nicking Pantene and everything else, Ace had his uses. If you had a sudden craving for Jaffa Cakes just before *EastEnders*, he'd nip to the Pop-In News 'n' Grocery if you asked him very nicely.

After a thirty-second time lapse, something got through the footie fog. 'I'd make him a perv, if I were you,' he announced. 'Tell your mum you went round one night and found him poncing around in high heels and one of your bras, all upset because he couldn't find enough socks to stuff it with.'

'Dominic's not like you,' I said testily. 'He doesn't have

to hunt under the bed every morning for any putrid socks that haven't actually walked to the washing machine by themselves. He's got whole drawers full, all neatly rolled up and colour-coded.'

'S&M, then.' The little toad was grinning his face off. 'What if he suddenly asked you to do the Miss Bumwhack bit?' He put on a lecherous, grasp-and-pant voice. 'I've been a really, *really* bad boy – I was playing with my winkle all night—'

'For God's sake, he'd never call it a *winkle*. Anyway, I refuse to have a relationship with a perv.'

'Suit yourself. Sling me a couple of those chocolate fingers, will you?'

I slung. There were four left in the packet on the coffee table. *Four*, and I'd bought them only an hour previously, while picking up the papers at the Pop-In.

Ace bit half off both of them and continued with his mouth full. 'Your mum was bound to resort to emotional blackmail in the end. It's a mum's favourite weapon and if you haven't sussed that out by now, then quite frankly, I despair of you.'

I could almost have written a dissertation on Emotional Blackmail, Maternal Variety Of. Before phoning home an hour and a half previously I'd been psyching myself up for a hefty dose of precisely that. I'd decided to be strong, harden my heart, not give in to it. I'd worked out exactly what I was going to say.

I'd started all brisk and non-nonsense, as you do. I was very sorry but I didn't think Dominic was going to be able to make it, after all. He was terribly busy.

Cue for, 'Oh, Sophy, *really*! I knew you'd let me down again, just when everybody's dying to meet him. I told wretched Maggie he was almost definitely coming and you know what that woman's like . . .' She went on a bit.

16

Eventually Mum'd gone all plaintive on me: 'Sometimes I wonder whether you're ashamed of me and Daddy. Every single time you've promised to bring him home . . .' Etc.

To distract myself from the memory of Mum's soulful voice and Ace's demolition of the biscuits, I leafed through the *Mag on Sunday*; the lovelorn small ads are always good for a laugh. As usual they were crawling with slim, attractive, bubbly women who WLTM unmarried, un-sad, un-ugly blokes for caring and sharing. You had to admire their optimism.

'Maybe I should put an ad in,' I said now. '"Daft cow, 30, needs passable blokes for one day only. No polyester shirts, no creeps, positively no sex, fifty quid."'

'I'll do it for fifty quid,' the little toad grinned. 'Only you'll have to buy me a flash suit first.'

'Brilliant. You look *exactly* like Mum's idea of a thirty-five-year-old merchant banker.'

I mooched to the window. This corner of south-west London could occasionally look quite passable; for once there wasn't so much as a crisp packet dancing in the breeze. The sun was pointing shining fingers at our grubby Edwardian sashes, making sanctimonious observations about lazy cows and Mr Muscle.

I ignored it. 'I'll just have to say I've dumped him. Maybe he's turning horrendously jealous and possessive.'

'That'll never wash with your old lady. She'll only think it shows how keen he is.'

True.

'Course you could always do what I usually do when up to my nuts in hassle,' he went on, turning the pages noisily. 'Leg it. Or wing it. I'll take a quick look in the cheap flights bit . . .'

Constructive suggestions from Ace had always come

under the heading of 'Forlorn Hope'. Working on autopilot, my hand conveyed another chocolate finger to my mouth. The previous fifteen or so were making me vaguely sick, but what the hell?

'The basic problem is that old hag Maggie Freeman,' I explained. 'Mum's bragged to her about him, so if I don't produce this hot favourite in the perfect-potential-son-in-law stakes, she stands to lose about three million points.'

Maggie Freeman had been my mother's 'friend' and neighbour for nearly twenty-five years. Neither could stand the other really, but they pretended for the sake of form. It all stemmed from them each having two daughters of similar ages. Arch-rivalry, in other words, from the time we were old enough to do anything to brag about.

Take our first ballet exam, when Sarah Freeman and I were six. At the end of a doorstep conversation Maggie had dropped a casual, 'Oh, by the way, Sue, did I tell you Sarah got a Highly Commended?' This had been uttered in the smug knowledge that I'd only got a Fairy-Elephant Pass, and the neighbourly rot had started there, so to speak. But Mum had got her own back later, when I got my Junior Dolphin swimming badge a whole term before Sarah. Fifty points to the Freemans, fifty to the Metcalfes. And so it had gone on: me *versus* Sarah, Belinda *versus* Zoe.

The scores had been relatively even until three years ago, when Maggie had notched up fifty trillion points in one go. Sarah Freeman had Got Engaged. And not to just anybody: to some minor landowner with a country house and a second cousin who was a *Sir*.

Maggie's smugness had known no bounds. For months she'd popped round every other day with pictures of pageboys' outfits, saying, 'What do you think, Sue? We're still dithering over transport – can't decide between the white vintage Rolls and the horse-drawn carriage. Such a pity you can't rely on the weather.'

At first Mum had smiled nicely and made her a cup of tea. Later she'd smiled through clenched teeth and made her a cup of tea. Later still she'd smiled through clenched teeth, made her a cup of tea, and wished to God she had some arsenic to put in it.

So Belinda's wedding, to my mother, was the rough equivalent of a rollover lottery jackpot. There were no ancestral acres or Sir-type cousins to brag about, but in one respect at least, she could outdo Maggie. While Sarah, Zoe and I are what you might call passably attractive – at least nobody's ever asked us to stick a bag over our heads – Belinda, as I said before, is Something Else. Mum's hour of glorious getting-her-own-back was about to come. All she needed to ice her perfect wedding cake was one thing: to cap Zoe Freeman's chinless Oliver with my tall, suave, handsome, witty, I-think-he-must-be-getting-serious Dominic Walsh, merchant banker.

Ace had gone quiet. I thought he was back with the Tossers until he jabbed his finger at the paper. 'Blimey, I'm a genius. Take a look at that.'

Half expecting a one-way cheapie to Outer Mongolia, I humoured him and cast it a glance. And another.

'Ace, this is an escort agency!'

He gave me that noble patience look blokes do so well. 'I'd hardly be showing you an ad for a male impotence clinic.'

'There's no way I'm going to an escort agency! They'd think I was desperate. The *bloke*'d think I was desperate.'

'You *are* desperate.'

'You know what I mean. What kind of man does that, anyway?'

He considered. 'OK, a bloke who fancies himself and wants money for old rope. Still, worth a try.'

I scanned the blurb. It was worded to persuade cynics like me that hiring an escort was no iffier than hiring a carpet shampooer, and a lot more fun.

Nice try, I thought, but Ace was giving me a *Well?* look.

'I'd feel a prat, explaining the situation,' I protested. 'They'd crack up.'

'Course they wouldn't.'

'I bet they would.' The woman in the advertisement looked as if 'desperate' had never entered her vocabulary. Cool. Classy. In control. The type who hasn't done anything stupid or embarrassing since she was three and half and knows she never will again. 'I'd have to check the small print, but I have a feeling that paying a man for his company is against my principles.'

'Look at it this way, Sophe. If you hadn't got a car for the day, you'd hire one. You haven't got a bloke for the day, so hire one.'

'Ace, hiring a Dominic is not precisely the same as hiring a Ford Escort with airbag. The men are bound to think you're dying to inspect their credentials.'

'You could always say you're a lezzie but you haven't got the nerve to tell your folks.'

'Any more helpful suggestions?' Still eyeing the smug, skinny blonde in the ad, I consoled myself with the thought that she probably had no boobs to speak of, unless they were silicone implants. 'I bet they charge an arm and a leg.'

'Probably. You wouldn't want some cheap bloke, would you?'

Well, no.

At this point Alix staggered in, yawning as if she'd been up half the night. Which she had, if the crawling-in noises

I'd heard at roughly four fifteen were anything to go by. Actually, I was surprised she'd crawled in at all. As her current bloke was turning out better than expected, I didn't see much of her lately. I missed her, especially when there was someone particularly annoying on the television and I had no one to have a friendly bitch with. Alix and I always found precisely the same people annoying, which was one of the reasons we got on. She was five foot six, a grey-eyed natural blonde, 34A top and bottom, but since she envied my cleavage bitterly I had to love her.

Wrapped in a long, fleecy dressing gown patterned with teddies, she flopped into an armchair and yawned. 'Ace, if you make me a cup of tea I'll give you two quid.'

'Bugger off,' he said.

'Three quid,' she pleaded. 'Before I quietly die of dehydration.'

'You'll have to die, then. I'm trying to talk Sophe into giving this a go.'

He passed her the paper. 'See? Perfect answer to her little problem, or what?' He really looked unbelievably pleased with himself.

Alix's sleep-fogged eye slowly de-misted. 'Ace, this is an escort agency!'

He raised his eyes to the ceiling. 'I know, thicko! She needs a bloke for the wedding! Only she's got this idea that the bloke'd think she's panting for it.'

'He probably would,' she yawned. 'Most blokes think all women are panting for it anyway.'

'No, we just hope. It's what you call eternal optimism.'

'It's what you call eternal obsession with your dangly bits,' she retorted.

'Can we please get back to the *subject*?' With a pained expression, he pointed at the ad again. 'I mean, I'm a bloke

21

and I don't think most other blokes'd think old Sophe's that desperate for a Melvyn.'

Dear little boy. I felt my self-esteem positively soaring.

Poor Alix wasn't quite with it. 'It's a Dominic she's desperate for, not a bloody Melvyn.'

I reached for the last chocolate finger. 'A Melvyn *Bragg*, dopey.'

Alix made the *might-have-known* face that often followed Ace's utterances. 'He really is a bit much first thing in the morning. I've told Mum often enough he should have been drowned at birth but she just says, "I know, dear, but at least I cut his tail off."'

Inured to this sort of thing, Ace was gaping at the empty packet. 'She's eaten the whole lot!' He waved it at Alix. 'Look at that! She'll be moaning next week that her knickers have shrunk!'

'She's stressed!' she snapped. 'Go and do something useful, will you? Like sticking a tea bag in a cup.'

'Why can't your regular slave do it?' he demanded.

'He's still asleep and you're not. If you do me some toast and Marmite as well, I'll make it five quid.'

'OK.' He departed for the kitchen.

While Alix re-bent her head over the paper, I thought about toast and Marmite. Even better, one of Ace's Marlboro Lights. After months of worthy abstinence I could suddenly have killed for one really good nicotine hit. As a bonus it would probably taste vile and make me throw up all those chocolate fingers.

Alix was reading the ad. 'You're not actually going to do this, are you? I thought you were going to phone your mum this morning and say he couldn't make it.'

'I tried. She gave me a load of emotional blackmail about being ashamed of them, then, to ensure she had the last word, made an excuse about being busy, and hung up. So yes, I might just clutch the odd straw.'

'Sophy, you can't *pay* for a man! It goes right against the grain.'

I'd almost known her first, instinctive reaction would be the same as mine. Alix and I went back a long way, to our third day at university, where we'd had rooms in the same hall. We'd both been desperately homesick, while pretending to be the height of cool as we downed gallons of beer at Freshers' Night. After getting drunk enough to throw up in adjacent loos, we'd confessed to each other how we wished we were dead and were terrified of lectures starting, in case everybody else was cleverer than us and made us look thick. From then on, things had improved no end.

Maybe it was desperation, maybe it was the thought of that conversation with Mum, but although we were invariably right about absolutely everything else, I was beginning to think Alix and I were both overreacting on this one. 'It's a service, like any other,' I said tentatively. 'After all, what if you fancied a civilized evening of *La Bohème* and wanted someone else to fight their way to the bar in the interval?'

'Oh, come on! What kind of "service" are they going to think you're after? I saw a chat show about escorts not so long ago. You should have seen them – all bragging about how much they made on the optional extras and how the poor desperate women were so grateful. And believe me, none of them looked remotely like a Dominic.'

'Perhaps this place isn't like that. Surely there's no harm trying. If they haven't got anyone suitable, I'll forget it.'

'You should have forgotten it weeks ago. You should have dumped him before your mother started hoping it was Getting Serious.'

23

Exactly. So why hadn't I? Because it was easier not to, that's why. I'd have been back to square one.

Square one had started like this. About eight months back I'd split up with Kit. Kit and I had been an item for ages, until he'd told me he was terribly sorry, he was still very fond of me, but to be honest, he thought we'd turned into a *comfortable habit*.

Unlike me, Kit would barely have scraped a GCSE in fibbing. He'd delivered his dump-line in the awkward, stumbling tones of a hopeless liar and I'd known at once what was behind it.

Or rather, *who*. I'd met her at a do thrown by a colleague of his a couple of weeks previously. She'd given me that poisoned-honey smile such women always give you when they fancy your man like mad and are hoping you'll conveniently get run over on the way home. I'd poison-honeyed back (as you do) and hoped she'd come out in nipple warts for her pains.

On the way home afterwards Kit had said reproachfully, 'I thought you were just a bit off with Jocasta.'

*Jocasta*. I ask you. 'Of course I was!' I'd retorted. 'She fancies the pants off you! She was giving you the eye half the night, only you're too thick to see it!'

'She was doing nothing of the sort,' he'd said irritably. 'God, women can be so unbelievably *bitchy*. She's a really nice girl.'

Bloke-speak for, *I wouldn't kick her out of bed, either*.

So when we'd come to that hideous, 'Sophy, we need to talk,' bit, I don't know how he could have imagined I was too thick to put two and two together. Too devastated to be dignified, I'd screamed it through a throatful of tears. The word 'cow' had figured prominently, I'm not ashamed to say, and faced with that, he'd admitted it. He was terribly sorry but you didn't choose these things, they just happened.

If Belinda hadn't been occupying our cupboard at the time, my loving mother would never have known the extent of my misery. But as it was, Belinda was doing a sort of foreign correspondent of the love-war zone, reporting back with messages like, 'Emergency supplies of vodka and tissues are being rushed in but the situation is frankly desperate.'

Which naturally resulted in worried maternal phone calls every other day, to check that any overdoses were only of the Nutella variety: 'Are you *sure* you're all right, dear?' etc. Eventually these had progressed to anxious variations on, 'You really must get out more, dear, and find somebody else,' so one night, just to keep her happy (all right, to shut her up) I'd lied. Dominic had just slipped out, perfectly formed, but as I said before, he wasn't *entirely* plucked out of thin air.

Four nights before the fateful phone call, I'd gone to a party. I hadn't been in the mood, but the hostess was Jess, my number two at Aristos, who was thirty-six and even more blokeless than me (not so much as a damp squib in eighteen months). Jess was what my mother called 'a worrier', she'd been worrying about this do for days: what if hardly anyone turned up and she was left among her M&S nibbles like a female version of Mrs Merton's Malcolm?

So I'd taken along a duty-free bottle of Stolichnaya and prepared to be a party animal. I'd even put on a little black dress with a tiny bit of fluff just above my left nipple, as I'd read somewhere that it's a foolproof way of pulling; blokes are irresistibly drawn to said fluff and itch to brush it off. Nobody had told Jess this, however, as two minutes after I'd got there she said, 'Oh, look, there's a bit of fluff on your dress,' and flicked it off herself. Well, that's the last time I donate my duty-free booze to her.

At first it had looked as if her nightmare was coming true. Guests were thin, conversation strained, and people were starting to give their watches furtive glances. Knowing I could hardly desert a sinking do, I just carried on hitting the vodka, grinning fatuously and trying to break awkward silences with stupid jokes.

But lo, suddenly there arrived a raucous horde, courtesy of Luke and Neil from the estate agent's next door to Aristos. (I quite fancied Luke but he was a serial three-night-stand man.) They had a dozen friends in tow, most of whom Jess knew not at all, but who cared?

And there he was, across a crowded room, dressed from some previous do in a dinner jacket and dress shirt, open at the neck, his bow-tie wrenched undone. In short, the type to make your worst female enemy hate you even more if you had him on your arm. So I charged off to Jess's loo to look for another bit of fluff, but since she's one of those irritating houseworky types I couldn't find any. Not that it would have made any difference if I had.

For the next three hours, Dominic Walsh (for it was he) had assorted size-ten women hanging on to him. After an initial, perfunctory introduction I only managed to catch his eye twice and my alluring smile (perfected in bathroom mirror at age sixteen) had sod-all effect. So I carried on hitting the vodka and let some bloke called Clive chat me up. I phone a taxi about one fifteen, and would you believe, just as I was about to leave, Dominic came up, eyed my cleavage and said, 'Not off already?'

Story of my life.

If I'd been sensible and switched to Evian an hour previously, I might have said, 'Well, maybe not,' while metaphorically punching the air and yelling, 'Yes! Yes!

Yes!' However, since I was Sophy Metcalfe, with incipient hiccups and a horrible feeling I might actually throw up within the next twenty minutes, I gave an enigmatic (drunken) smile, said, 'Afraid so,' and thought: Shit.

But then (I've only ever done this when really far gone) I grabbed a pen from Jess's side table and took his arm in what I imagined was a seductively inviting manner. In a huskily inviting tone (thank God no hiccups came out) I said, 'But feel free to give me a call,' and wrote my number on his wrist. I smiled again, floated out without falling over, and threw up the minute I got home.

Needless to say the bastard never phoned, but he served my devious purpose. I embroidered him nicely and he went down like a dream. I never told Belinda he was merely a Mum-pacifying concoction. She'd gone home by then and had seemed so pleased for me, I hadn't liked to disillusion her.

Back to our unhoovered living room, however, and still tea-less Alix.

'My mother was going on just as much as yours, and I didn't invent anybody. And I was in just as bad a state as you were. Worse, if anything. I mean, Simon just told me straight out that there was somebody else.'

Shortly after Kit had given me the elbow, Alix had suffered exactly the same. 'You always knew he was basically a reptile,' I pointed out. 'You always used to fall for reptiles.'

'So did you. Kit was too "nice", if you ask me. You'd only have got bored with him in the end.'

'I was nowhere near bored with him! He was the first decent bloke I'd had in ages!' However, I have to confess that she'd uttered a crumb of truth. Just occasionally his 'niceness' had made me guiltily irritated; for example, he'd always refused to bitch about anybody, no matter how bitchy or bastardy they were. I'd almost wished he'd show a normal, human, bloke-ish crack.

And of course, I'd got my wish.

'Couldn't you ask that Luke bloke to do the honours?' she asked. 'I mean, I know he's an estate agent but he looks the part, at least.'

'Are you kidding? The real Dominic's a friend of his, or at least an acquaintance. I'd never tell him I'd invented a bloke, anyway. He'd crack up.' I hadn't even told Jess about Dominic, in case she let it out. More than once I'd nearly told Harriet, who was new and much more on my wavelength than Jess, but there'd always been an interruption.

'What about that Adam bloke at the gym?' she said. 'You used to quite fancy him.'

'I went off him. He's besotted with someone else.'

'Who?'

'Himself.' I hadn't been to the gym for weeks anyway – my sub had run out.

'Belinda's never met Calum,' she mused. 'I suppose you could ask him.'

Calum was the slumbering 'slave'. Alix had met him one freezing afternoon a couple of months back, after 'accidentally' spraying him with foam at the car wash. 'He looked marginally less primeval-slime-ish than the average,' she'd explained, 'so I thought, sod it, live dangerously.' Lately Alix, for her, was going right over the complimentary top, e.g. 'He looks quite sweet when he's asleep.'

Much as I appreciated the offer, I wouldn't have dreamt of inflicting my entire family on Calum for the day. I wasn't sure his relationship with Alix was on a firm enough footing to stand it. Besides which, Calum wasn't exactly how I pictured Dominic. He reminded me of a big, shaggy dog – very loveable, but not quite groomed enough. And very slightly portly about the tummy, if you want the truth.

'I couldn't possibly ask, if only because he's far too nice to say no,' I extemporised.

She didn't persist, 'I still think this agency business is mad. They'll all be slimeballs, you mark my words.'

'There's no harm in giving them a ring. I would like to keep Mum's end up, if only for a day.'

'You mean she'll be "off" with you for six months if you don't,' Alix corrected me sharply. She glanced over her shoulder towards the kitchen, whence came merry banging and crashing. 'God, he can't even make a cup of tea without creating a racket. If he wakes Calum up, I'll kill him. He looks really sweet when he's asleep.'

You see?

Ace's return, with sustenance, restored her humour. 'Thanks, *mon angre*. There should be a fiver in my bag, if you can find it.'

'Nah,' he said. 'You can iron me a couple of T-shirts.'

This was intended as a wind-up. Alix was supposed to echo, '*Iron? What the hell do you think I am?*' whereupon Ace would grin, 'A woman.'

Ignoring this bait, she made a face at her toast. 'You've put far too much Marmite on. How many times do I have tell you to scrape it?'

'God, I can't do anything right.' Ace shot me a hurt look that was rather spoilt by the wicked little wink he added. 'Bitch, bitch, bitch – moan, moan, moan – she's getting just like dear old Mum.'

'I'll tell her you said that!' Alix threw a cushion at him, Ace threw it back and a fight ensued. I didn't care whether it ended with Alix's tea going all over the carpet, but I retrieved the paper before it got torn or tea-soaked, or both.

*We know the feeling,* the blurb said. *We are Sally and Julia and we started Just For Tonight because we know exactly what it's like to be missing that one vital accessory for important occasions. If you've got the perfect dress, the perfect jewellery, the perfect shoes, why not choose the perfect man to complement them?*

Just too easy for words.

# Fair Game

## Let the best woman win . . .

Up to her eyes with her friends' dramas, Harriet Grey has no time for her own. Let alone getting entangled with John Mackenzie. He might be the most gorgeous man she's met for ages. But he's entangled with someone else. Nina.

Glamorous Nina wasn't exactly Harriet's best friend at school, but Harriet has principles. Still, surely one innocent little drink to repay a favour wouldn't hurt? Her friends aren't so sure.

Harriet tries to be strict, but John Mackenzie won't stay out of her life. When she finds herself alone at Christmas, she'd have to be a saint to walk away. And halos never did suit Harriet . . .

### Praise for Liz Young:

'Feel-good romance'   *Marie Claire*

'A warm, sunny read that is as astute as it is humorous'
*Good Housekeeping*

# Prologue

My sins caught up with me outside the deli, on one of those January afternoons we hardly ever get in London. It was arctic, ear-biting cold; the air smelt of coming snow.

Not that I cared; my personal central heating was on Dangerously High. Next door to the deli the travel agent's window was offering long-weekend cheapies to the Gambia, but even they couldn't tempt me. I was popping in for some fresh pasta when I almost collided with Rosie, coming out. 'Harriet! I was just on my way to see you! I hope you weren't after any of that tomatoey salady stuff, because I've just had the last of it.'

'No – why were you coming to see me?'

I don't know why I asked. Rosie was a lovely person but if she'd had a website the address would have been *don'ttellanyoneItoldyoubut.com*. She had round brown eyes, full of what I can only describe as guilty relish. 'I just *had* to tell you the latest in the Nina/Helicopter saga.'

Rosie, Nina and I had all been at school together. 'Helicopter' was what Rosie called Nina's ex, and since he *was* ex, and had been for about a week, I didn't quite follow. 'What do you mean, the latest? He dumped her!'

'Yes, but she was just a teensy bit put out, remember?'

I hadn't witnessed the scene but Rosie had heard about it and passed on every gruesome detail. Nina had ranted and screamed and demanded to know if there was

5

someone else, and he'd said no, there wasn't, and she'd shrieked that he was a lying bastard, she knew he'd been seeing someone else, and who was she, the bitch?

'Of course, she never believed there *was*n't anybody else,' Rosie went on. 'So no prizes for guessing what she's been up to now.'

I have special sensory equipment for occasions like this: antennae finely tuned to pick up 'oh shit' situations. 'What?'

'She's put a private dick on to him!'

'*What?*'

'Yes, that's what I thought. Bit OTT, isn't it? It's not as if they were engaged or anything.'

Maybe the Gambia wasn't a bad idea, after all. 'Since when? Since when did she put the dick on him, I mean?'

'Since right after he dumped her. I mean, what's the use now? Except that she'll know who to make wax images of and stick pins into.'

Forget the Gambia – maybe a cheapie to Ulan Bator?

'It's costing a bomb but she said she had to know,' Rosie went on. 'The bloke said it might take a while to catch him at it – well, not exactly *at* it, perhaps, but *with* whoever she is.'

'They'll see him. Some furtive bloke in a grubby raincoat . . .'

'Oh, come on! He's a *pro*! Mega-zoom paparazzi lenses, you name it. I hope they keep their curtains drawn, that's all.'

They most certainly would.

'She's got a fair idea who it is, you know,' she went on. 'Some dopey blonde she sacked a few weeks back – mind you, Nina'd call any blonde dopey – she had to introduce them at some do and Dopey was eyeing him up even then. She's done it to get her own back, Nina says.'

I moistened my lips. 'How would she know? The girl's no dopier than the average, either.'

Rosie's eyes popped wide. 'Are you telling me you actually know her?'

'I do, actually,' I said. 'Intimately.'

'You're kidding!'

'I'm not. I've known her for as long as I can remember.'

'You're *kidding*! Why the hell didn't you tell me before?'

Actually, Rosie's not that thick. As she gaped at me I saw her brain furiously working back, going whirr whiz bang, and so on. When it finally went 'click' her eyes popped wider still, if such a thing were possible.

Just across the road was the Drunken Dragon. 'Fancy a drink?' I asked. 'You look as if you could do with it.'

Rosie found her voice. '*Me*? What about you? You do realize she's going to kill you?'

# Chapter 1

I don't quite know why I said 'sins' back there. I never set out to pinch anyone's bloke, let alone Nina's. The day it all started, picking up a bloke was the last thing on my mind. Even I don't go out on the pull in manky old combats, a sweater that's seen better days, and hair sorely in need of Frizz-Ease.

All I was thinking of, that drizzly afternoon, was calling it a day and finding a cab home. Since it was early December I was laden with what was supposed to be highly organized Christmas shopping. I'd made a methodical list saying *Mum, Bill, Sally, Tom, Jacko* . . . so I could go round the shops briskly and efficiently ticking them all off.

With customary efficiency I'd only ticked off Tom. My bags were full of impulse buys for the house; having come late to the nesting bit I was making up for lost time. There were also two bottles of ready-mulled wine. I buy stuff like that when Christmas is coming and I need something to put me in the mood – the weather certainly wasn't. Mild and damp, it felt more like October.

Having started off in mist-like fashion, the drizzle had moved up a gear, as if it were thinking about turning to proper rain, instead. At this point I was just up the road from Covent Garden, with drizzled-on hair, arms coming out of their sockets, and a jumper starting to smell of wet

Shetland sheep. That was when I saw Nina, coming out of some smart little restaurant, with a bloke on her arm.

If I can misquote Jane Austen here, it is a truth universally acknowledged that if you are fated to bump into someone like Nina when you haven't seen her for four years and don't particularly want to ever again, you'll be looking like a pig's breakfast.

While she'll be looking like, well, like Nina.

Like a *Sunday Times* fashion shoot of some taupey thing in silk and cashmere, a snip at only £799. That dark-haired bob as sleek and glossy as ever. A face like an airbrushed L'Oréal ad.

Only about six paces away, she was talking and laughing in her silver-tinkle way to the bloke, who was holding her umbrella up to stop her getting drizzled on.

If she'd seen me, and recognized me, she'd have been over before you could say 'sick as a pig', with a delighted smile (delighted to make me sick as a pig, I mean) and a '*Harry*! How *are* you!' Then there'd be a couple of *mwah-mwah* kisses, and a 'This is Gorgeous Bloke – Gorgeous Bloke, this is Harriet – we were at school together and I used to be terribly nice to her on the surface but laugh behind her back because she had size eight feet and looked like a scarecrow.'

So before any such daymare actually occurred, I turned around and pretended to be riveted by a shop window. For maybe half a minute longer I heard tinkly laughter with stuff like, '. . . and don't you *dare* be late – tinkle tinkle,' a kissy noise, and the sound of a car door slamming.

Of course I'd never intended to lurk there, eavesdropping. I'd have been fifty yards back down the road by then, telling myself I was pathetic, when was I going to grow up, etc., if something in that window hadn't detained me. To be frank, it had given me a bit of a jolt. When you're hiding from the Ninas of this world you don't expect to find yourself gaping at a massive wooden willy.

No, it wasn't a sex shop; the window was full of ethnic art. And the pride of the display was a six-foot-ish twisty chunk of tree, carved into a misshapen man with a crown thing on his head and an outstretched hand with what looked like an egg in it. The carved whopper wasn't half as riveting as his face, though. It was such a powerful mix of noble suffering and raw masculinity, he looked like a primitive Jesus and fertility god combined. I was just searching for a price tag when someone beside me said, 'Different, isn't it?'

And lo, there he was. Standing quite casually about three feet away, hands shoved in his trouser pockets. They were grey trousers, if you're interested: the bottom half of a quietly pricey suit. There was a black polo shirt, I think, only I wasn't really looking at his clothes.

It took me a second to get over the shock, but I said, casually enough. 'That's one way of putting it. I suppose you can't see a price tag?'

He peered a bit closer, straightened up, and turned to me. 'Fifteen hundred quid.'

And I took my first, proper, full-face look.

My first thought was: well, might have known, just the sort of bloke I'd expect to see attached to Nina, followed swiftly by: on the other hand, maybe not.

The last time I'd seen her (at a wedding four years back) she'd had some tall, dark specimen in tow, of the type generally described as classically good-looking, with an eligibility rating of eleven and a half out of ten. I say 'generally' because although everything about him was theoretically perfect, personally I hadn't been particularly impressed. OK, maybe it was sour grapes, but to me he'd seemed just a bit *plastic*, somehow. It had been quite a

10

boost to my ego to realize I didn't actually fancy him, especially when everybody else was saying, 'Trust Nina to get a bloke like that.'

I don't quite know what it was with this one – he wasn't classically good-looking, exactly, but there was definitely no plastic and the spark hit me at once. His eyes were greeny-blue, his hair the colour of old, polished oak. He was taller than me by half a head (and I'm five foot nine) and marginally heftier than is currently fashionable.

I said, 'Oh, well, I suppose it's a bit steep for a cat-scratching post,' and he laughed.

Well.

His spark had practically turned into a fire hazard, most of it coming from those greeny-blue eyes. For some reason I thought of those corny old films in which the hapless Lady Arabella's carriage is held up on the Great North Road. '*I will never part with my jewels!*' she says hotly to the horrid, rough-looking fellow in the mask. '*I would sooner part with my virtue!*' And the rough-looking fellow drawls, '*Then I will have your virtue, my lady,*' and she suddenly sees the wicked glint in the eyes behind the mask, and thinks, '*Well, actually . . .*'

Thinking, trust bloody Nina to get a bloke like this, I said hastily, 'Well, better hit the road, if I can find a cab,' and readjusted my shopping. In addition to five carrier bags, my bag was slung over my shoulder, and I suddenly realized the zip was open and my purse wasn't in it.

If you've never done anything so stupid as to leave your bag open when you've just been shoving your way through Christmas-shopping crushes you won't know the feeling, so I'll tell you. I went all cold and frozen and gaped at my bag. I said, 'My purse has gone,' like an idiot, and he said, 'Christ – are you sure?' and I hunted through my bag again, as you do, but I knew it wasn't there.

11

I said, 'Yes, God, what a *fool* – there wasn't much cash, but all the other stuff . . .'

He said, 'When did you last have it?' and I thought back, and realized it was twenty minutes ago, in some shop called Expensive Useless Stuff That Seems Like A Good Idea At The Time.

Twenty minutes! The thieving scum could have bought himself three Paul Smith suits by now. In a frozen panic I said, 'My credit cards – I must ring and cancel them . . . God, I didn't even bring my mobile . . .'

'Use mine, then. And let's get out of this weather.' In the relative shelter of the shop doorway, he handed me his mobile.

Of course I hadn't a clue what numbers to ring, so I phoned Sally at home, asked her to dig out credit-card statements and cancel for me. Then I said, 'If Jacko's in, ask him how much cash he's got. I'm laden with shopping – I want to bum a cab fare.'

'He's just gone out, wouldn't you know it. And I've only got about six quid.'

'Never mind. See you later.'

I handed the phone back. 'Thanks so much. If I had any money, I'd buy you a drink.' I only said this as a throwaway line because I'd just noticed a little wine bar two doors away. I certainly wasn't expecting the reply I got.

'Look, I can let you have a cab fare.'

I was appalled. If he thought I'd been dropping hints . . . 'No, really, I don't need a cab.' From the thigh pocket of my tatty old combats, I dug out my One-Day Travelcard. 'See? I'll take the tube.'

He glanced down at all my bags. 'With that lot? How far have you got to go?'

'Putney, but it won't kill me.'

12

'Christ, that's miles!' Almost before I'd blinked he'd whipped his wallet out and extracted a couple of notes.

I gaped at the proffered thirty quid. 'Look, it's very kind of you, but I really couldn't.'

'Why not?' He sort of smiled and added, 'It's Christmas.'

And I sort of looked at him, and he looked back at me, and I thought: God, it's not *fair* – I could fancy you rotten. But since I hadn't fancied anyone even half rotten for months, I decided I might as well make the most of it. Waste not, want not, as my Great-Aunt Dorothy used to say when she was saving the oval tops off Kleenex boxes. (Handy for shopping lists, you see.)

Besides which, a cab beat the tube any day, especially with four tons of shopping and a ten-minute walk the other end. 'I'll only take it if you let me pay you back. Give me your address and I'll send you a cheque.'

'It's really not necessary.'

Great. I could see I'd put the wind up him. If you dished out your address to drizzled-on messes, they might turn up on your doorstep.

'But you could maybe buy me that drink sometime.'

*Er, sorry?* I waited for him to grin, 'Only kidding – my girlfriend would kill me,' but there was just a raised eyebrow and a little half-smile.

Well, I can be as cool as the next drizzled-on mess. 'Do you actually know anywhere that does thirty-quid drinks?'

'A couple of drinks, then.' The smile turned into three-quarters. 'And a packet of pork scratchings?'

I have to say, a wicked little *frisson* went through me. All I could think was: God, if Nina could see this, she'd go ape. 'Give me your number, then, and I'll give you a call.' I scrabbled in my bag for my organizer, only I was so organized I'd left it at home. All I could find was a Tesco's receipt, so I gave him that.

It was while he was scribbling that I went all frozen again. In fact, I felt as if I'd just been nicked for criminal deception. Because in a sudden flash I knew exactly where my purse was.

I'd bought a cast-iron warthog in that Expensive Useless shop (because he looked cute and it seemed like a good idea at the time) but after paying I'd ended up with my hands full of shopping and my purse tucked under my arm. And because I couldn't be bothered to put all those bags down again and put my purse away properly, I'd let it drop in a carefully aimed manner into the Expensive Useless carrier bag, with the warthog.

Only just as he'd stopped scribbling, and I was about to open my mouth to tell him, he opened his first.

'Right, let's find you a cab – before this rain really gets going.' And Sod's Law being what it is, one hove into view even as he uttered this, while I was still trying to work up to telling him my purse was cuddling up to a warthog.

Two seconds later he'd not only grabbed the cab but put that thirty quid and the receipt into my hand, and I just didn't know how to come clean. I'll admit I didn't altogether want to, either. He might have put me down as a worrying case of pre-senile dementia.

In any case, there wasn't time. The taxi driver was saying, 'Where to, love?' the rain was beginning to show downpour ambitions, and my saviour was getting wetter by the minute. All I said was, 'Thanks again – bye bye.'

'Bye.'

I waved, and once he was out of sight peered sheepishly into the Expensive Useless carrier bag. There it was, battered brown calf, saying, are you mad, or what? Credit

14

cards cancelled all for nothing, all that hassle, just for a ride home and a drink with a bloke of Nina's?

Sally said much the same, moments after I was in the door. 'You dope! After I'd gone mad unearthing Visa numbers, too.'

However, I hadn't got to the best bit. Once we were in the kitchen I tipped one of those bottles of mulled wine into a pan. 'Remember Rosie? Ex-school Rosie who came round the other week?'

'Yes, she was nice. She had two helpings of my gone-wrong veggie lasagne and pretended it was lovely.'

'Well, she was talking about someone called Nina, remember?'

'You were both talking about her. She always had everything, except spots and bad-hair days, and you both loved her to bits.'

OK, I'll admit we were having a little bitch.

'What about her, anyway?' she went on.

I turned just enough to see her face. It was almost an act of charity to drop such morsels in Sally's lap. She got so few lately, except courtesy of TV soaps. 'Her bloke just gave me his phone number.'

A couple of minutes later, after I'd related every juicy detail, she said, 'So what's his name?'

I realized I hadn't a clue.

'Had a good day, dear?' said Sally, when I made it home two days later after my nightly game of District Line Sardines. 'It's been so exciting here, I can't tell you. The milkman said would we like a free bottle of apple juice to try and there were terrible ructions on *Home and Away* – I needed a good strong cup of PG to settle my nerves.'

Sally was 'unwaged', as they like to put it, and had been for months. She didn't feel any more brain-dead or useless than the rest of us, but was sensitive about other people thinking she was brain-dead and useless.

While spooning coffee into the filter I started telling her about my day, to perk her up. I left out anything to do with work, however, especially the bit about making a fat commission on an IT placement, as it would only make her feel more financially challenged than she already was. 'I gave Rosie a call this morning and we met for a sandwich. I told her about Mr Cab Fare and she's met him.'

Sally's green eyes widened instantly. 'And?'

'At least, I suppose it's him,' I went on. 'Nina's been seeing him for a couple of months and thinks he's the *cojones del perro*.' This had a more sophisticated ring than 'the dog's bollocks'; we'd used it almost since we'd met, which was eight years ago now, on a bus from Malaga airport.

Having clicked immediately, Sally and I had never seriously unclicked since. She could be unbelievably pig-headed but so could I, so I didn't hold that against her. We'd had masses in common. Both heading for English-teaching jobs in Granada, we were also both recent graduates with no idea what we wanted to do, except that we didn't want to do it in England, and both thought teaching English would be a brilliant way to travel and get paid at the same time.

We'd soon discovered even more similarities. Both only children, we had the kind of parents who'd made tutting noises about offspring who were putting off getting 'proper' jobs. Why hadn't we applied for a graduate traineeship with Price Waterhouse, like Louise Bradshaw down the road ('*That girl'll go right to the top, you see if she doesn't*') who'd always kept her bedroom tidy, too.

Actually it was my mother who'd said stuff like this.

16

Dad had said, 'Do what you want – I wish I had,' and slipped me a cheque, bless him.

I'd done the TEFL bit for five years, since when I'd had more jobs than you could shake a P45 at. Frequently I'd had two at once, while frantically saving for six weeks' scuba-diving in Sulawesi or whatever.

Back to Nina and Mr Cab Fare, though. Rosie had met him at Nina's flat-warming only last week, having been dragged there by Suzanne, another old contemporary from school. Having only recently moved to London, Rosie was staying with her on a temporary basis while Suzanne's co-sharer was 'doing' India.

Rosie had talked about Nina's do all through our lunch. 'She was up to here with Nina even before they went,' I told Sally. 'Even Suzanne was, and she's supposed to be best buddies with Nina. Nina had been swanking on about this bloke's five-star gorgeousness, his corporate high-flying-ness and all that. She'd even chucked in a snippet about some flight the other week being forty minutes late, which would have been a disaster had it not been for his personal helicopter waiting to whisk him off to an urgent meeting with God.'

'Well, I suppose God gets a bit hacked off if people are late.'

'Sally, you've missed the *point*,' I said patiently. 'God was about to get a right old bollocking about getting his act together and running a more cost-efficient universe.'

'Oh, right.' Sally poured two coffees and came to join me at the battered pine table. It was antique and might have been worth a bit if not riddled with squillions of worm holes.

'Even Suzanne was browned off with all this helicopter swank,' I went on. 'So by the time they left for Nina's do,

17

Rosie was hoping this Helicopter'd turn out to be a pompous prat, at least.'

'Can't blame her.' Sally rubbed at what looked like dried sick down the front of a grey sweatshirt. It was one of Jacko's cast-offs and already manky, quite apart from having LIVERPOOL FC emblazoned on the front. She had exhausted circles under her eyes and her chin-length, natural blonde hair had that mind-of-its-own look, telling me she'd let it dry itself again.

'But she had to admit that he was at least four-star gorgeous and seemed really nice, too,' I continued. 'Not only that, but the flat was a state-of-the-art loft conversion with acres of blond wood floors, and the goats' cheese tartlets were ambrosial. In short, there was nothing to pick even a minor, bitchy little hole in. Rosie said it was enough to take away all your faith in natural justice. She had to have two helpings of tiramisu to cheer herself up.'

'And this helicopter bloke's the one who gave you his phone number?'

'Looks like it, doesn't it?'

'So what's his name?'

'John,' I said, tasting it on the way out. 'I rather like "John". Conjures up a sort of what-you-see-is-what-you-get nice-bloke-ish-ness.'

'Harriet, nice-bloke-ish-ness doesn't exactly tie in with kissing your girlfriend goodbye and chatting up someone else the minute she's gone.'

'You could hardly call it a chat-up. I've got a horrible feeling he *was* just being a nice bloke. Sort of humouring me. He wasn't bothered about the money, but he didn't want me feeling bad about taking it. Anyway, I was looking like a pig's breakfast.'

'OK, but if she's always that perfect, maybe he's sick of perfection.'

18

This was a gratifying notion and I won't pretend it hadn't occurred to me already.

'Or maybe he just likes pigs' breakfasts,' she added.

Great. She'd be saying maybe he fancied a bit of rough, next.

'Especially if they've got legs up to their tonsils,' she went on. 'But are you sure your bloke *is* Helicopter? Maybe he and Nina are just old mates.'

Before talking to Rosie, I'd been exploring this minute possibility, too. And not only 'old mates' but 'old exes', fourteenth cousins twice removed – anything that would mean he was potentially available.

But even without the evidence of my own eyes, everything Rosie had told me fitted. 'Sally, I think I know "old mate" behaviour when I see it. She was all tinkly and flirty like she always was, and Rosie said she's obviously obsessed with him. When she wasn't hanging onto him at that do she was watching him like a hawk, in case anyone else got ideas.'

Sally fetched the jug and poured me another coffee. 'So when are you going to phone him? You are *going* to phone him?'

'Of course! There's the little matter of that thirty quid, isn't there?' There was also a weird little flutter in my stomach. It was a cocktail of guilt and that *frisson* you get when you're even thinking about a brand new object of prime fanciability. Which explains the guilt, of course, because he was Nina's object of PF, damn it.

'I wish someone'd give me thirty quid,' she grumbled. 'There's some mail for you, by the way.' From the debris at the end of the table she retrieved a small pile.

There were two credit-card statements, which I didn't open, and five Christmas cards, which I did. The first four

19

were from Mum and an assortment of my widely scattered friends. It was the fifth that gave me a jolt.

I gaped at Sally. 'Nina's sent me a Christmas card! Rosie must have got pissed enough to give her my address.'

The card was a glossy, fine-art thing. Inside was written, in arty, flamboyant script, 'Much love, Nina.'

I was seriously spooked, I don't mind admitting it. The last card I'd had from her, about four years back, had included one of those round-robin photocopies that ought to be banned on the grounds that they arouse unseasonal feelings of loathing for the sender. You know the kind of thing: *'Hi, fans! Yes, it's me – I'm far too busy to write to you individually, but I'm sure you'll all be thrilled to know my life is even more stunningly successful and deliriously happy than it was a year ago.'* I mean, you absolutely never get one of these that says the sender's been made redundant, her bloke's been banged up for GBH, and she's lost all her hair from the stress. A letter like that might just cheer you up a bit, if it was from Nina.

This time, however, she'd added a paragraph. 'I saw Rosie the other week at my flat-warming. I gather you're only a couple of miles up the road – maybe I'll pop in sometime!'

I thought, God, I hope not, she'd be sure to pop in on a Sunday morning when the place was a complete tip.

I showed Sally. '"Much love"! It's a bit weird, when we were never even third-best friends.'

'Some people send much gushy love to everybody,' Sally yawned. 'It's a good old Christmas tradition, like rowing with your entire family and pretending you like Brussels sprouts.'

Talking of family . . . I re-read the card from my mother, who was no longer married to my father. Under 'Lots of love Mum and Bill,' she'd written, 'I do understand about

20

Christmas, but I'm sure Sally's parents will be very hurt if she doesn't go home, even if they don't show it. If you change your mind we'll be very pleased to see you, of course.'

I handed this to Sally too.

'Why does everybody have to make me feel guilty?' she groaned. 'OK, they might be a bit hurt but they'll be relieved, too, even if they won't admit it. All their loathsome friends'll be popping in and out non-stop for drinks; I'll just be rubbing their noses in it.'

Sally's relationship with her folks had been a mite strained since the minor bombshell she'd dropped in May. I should explain here that Sally's parents are somewhat 'proper'; having married late they produced Sally when they'd just about given up. In fact a much less 'proper' aunt had once confided to Sally that she thought they'd never quite got to grips with that messy conjugal stuff in the first place. She'd said something like, 'If you ask me, they were on the point of saying, "Well, we tried," and ordering single beds. They met through bridge and married for bridge – Penelope always said if you find a good bridge partner, you hang onto him.'

Back to that bombshell, though. Unlike me, Sally had continued to capitalize on the global English explosion and was by then working in Muscat on the Arabian Gulf. Home on leave for a couple of weeks, she'd been staying with me, trawling the London shops for new summer stuff to take back and trying it all on in my bedroom.

It was the black bikini that did it.

With a frown she'd said, 'Maybe I should get a couple of one-pieces. I know I've never exactly had a wasp waist, but I'm getting positively lumpy around the middle. Look at this!'

I'd seen only a marginally thickened version of the usual

Sally. She had one of those figures they call apple-shaped – lovely slim legs, but a bit of a tummy she was endlessly wittering on about. I was about to make my usual soothing noises when she'd added, 'Anyone would think I was pregnant!'

'I almost wish you were,' I'd retorted. 'Then at least you'd really have a massive gut to bitch about.'

'It's not funny! I could hardly do my jeans up yesterday! My tits have got bigger, too!'

'I wish mine would,' I'd grumbled, until I'd seen her face. It had gone all weird and frozen.

And suddenly, so had mine.

In a weird, frozen voice she'd said, 'They were tingling the other day, too – is that a sign?' Putting her hands to her stomach, she'd said in a panic 'I *can't* be. Please, let me wake up . . .'

She'd gone on hoping to wake up until four and a half months later, when eight-pound Tom put in an appearance. The clinic had said it was nothing unusual to overlook the signs, especially when your usual signs were highly erratic anyway, but if she was going for a coil again added precautions might be a good idea.

She'd known at once who the proud daddy was: a certain Steve she'd met at an overnight beach party on Bandar Khayam, a little island half an hour by speedboat from Muscat Yacht Club. I know this because I'd been a reveller at that party, too. My feet had been itching badly at the time, so I'd got a cheap ticket and invited myself to stay with Sally for a fortnight.

There had been around twenty of us at that beach party, and the lethal setting had nothing to do with the bar some joker had erected on the beach out of a few bits of plywood and his kitchen curtains. The stars were like

22

diamonds on black velvet, the sea lit with silvery phosphorescence. As Sally had said, when you've just met someone you fancy rotten it certainly beat Bognor, and who could sleep anyway, on a beach towel with hermit crabs crawling over you half the night? The thought of sharks had only increased the buzz as they'd swum round the rocks to a secluded little beach in the small hours.

This Steve had not been one of her usual crowd. Working in Singapore, he'd been on an en route visit to friends of Sally's. Barely twelve hours after their little twosome (once in the sand, once in the sea) he'd carried on to Singapore and the wife he'd somehow forgotten to tell her about. Sally had only given her folks the blunt details a couple of months ago, when they'd demanded for the thirty-eighth time that she contact the father and make him 'face up to his responsibilities'.

Catatonic shock had ensued. 'You'd known him *how* long?'

Going back to Muscat had been out of the question, as expat single mothers in Muslim countries can be a mite embarrassing to the institution that arranged their visas. After spinning them some line about 'family problems' she'd stayed with me from then on. Nobody in Muscat even knew about the baby, let alone who the father was.

Tom was now six months old, with Father Christmas scheduled to make his first visit down a London chimney, rather than his grandparents' one in Chester. Apart from Sally and Tom, the other residents of our house these days were Frida, a Swedish girl who was hardly ever in, Jacko, who usually was, and Widdles, a geriatric cat of dubious personal hygiene.

'Where's Jacko?' I asked.

'God knows. He had a physio appointment at three, so he's probably crawling home via half a dozen pubs.'

23

Just as she said it a faraway bang announced the front door. Seconds later the kitchen door opened and Jacko hobbled in.

Sally said, 'Shut the door, Ape-Face, it's blowing a gale from the hall.'

He gave the door a whack-bang with his crutch and flopped noisily into a chair at the kitchen table. He had short, sandy-brown hair, non-designer stubble to match, and a Scouse accent that had been thicker than Cilla's when I'd first met him, although he'd toned it down now. We'd both been nineteen then, sharing a grotty student house with five others. At the time he'd been the most outrageous, foul-mouthed and instantly likeable boy I'd ever met. He'd inhabited one of my best soft spots ever since.

'How's the itching?' I asked, looking at his right leg which was in plaster.

'Murder,' he said pathetically, turning hazel eyes on me. They were quite nice when he'd had a full complement of sleep. 'I'm dehydrated from drinking myself to death last night, to get some sleep. Harry, my angel, for fuck's sake stick that kettle on, would you?'

I obliged, if only because of said plaster and an arm that was similarly recovering from a fair old mashing. Jacko was still based in Liverpool but since I'd been in London he'd come down often, usually for some football match. On the last occasion, ten minutes after leaving, he'd collided with a joyrider. It had been the umpteenth accident of his driving life and by far the worst, but one of the few that wasn't his fault. He'd been in hospital for three weeks; his mother had stayed with me much of the time and been constantly frantic. Once he'd been discharged she'd been desperate to get him home. Not to his

24

own place but back to the nest, so she could fuss him to death.

Still too weak and wobbly to manage alone, Jacko had nevertheless amazed me by putting his foot down. He told her he wanted to stay if I'd have him, and would go for his follow-up to the hospital that had sorted him out. Sorry, Mum, but her fussing would do his head in.

While I made him a cup of tea, Jacko was inspecting my mail. 'Who's Nina, then?'

'An old friend she can't stand,' Sally said. 'Her bloke tried to pick Harry up on Saturday – even gave her his phone number.'

He put on his hurt-puppy look. 'You never told me!'

'I was looking like nothing on earth! It wasn't *exactly* a pick-up, either.' I explained briefly, playing it right down.

'Why can't you stand this Nina, then?'

'She was a little cow,' Sally said.

You will gather that I'd been having another quiet bitch about Nina. 'That's a slight exaggeration. She just used to make me feel like one of those *Blue Peter* things built from bog-roll tubes that's supposed to be a dinosaur, but just looks like bog-roll tubes falling apart.'

'Why?' he asked.

Well, if he really wanted to know . . . 'Because she was five foot five and perfect, with silk-curtain hair and size three feet. And I was all awkward and gangly, with a mouth full of braces and feet I hadn't grown into, tripping over everything and blushing like the Revenge of the Killer Tomato and feeling a prat. And even when I was past the killer-tomato stage, she *still* made me feel like a bog-roll dinosaur, OK?'

'Plus she was a little cow,' Sally said. 'One of those little cows who pretend they're not, which is even worse.'

'How can you tell, then?' he demanded.

I was wishing Sally had kept her mouth shut. Blokes never understood these things – at that age they simply thump each other. 'You just can. They give you sweetly patronizing smiles and say, "Oh, your hair looks really nice," but the second your back's turned you know they're saying, "My God, her *hair*!" and cracking up.'

'What's wrong with your hair?' he asked, as if he'd only just noticed it after ten years, which wouldn't have surprised me.

'Nothing,' I said. 'I've come to terms with it.' It was just fine if you liked bunny-coloured clouds, but it'd never, ever shine, no matter how much I spent on hot-oil conditioners.

Apparently satisfied, he went back to inspecting my mail. 'So are you two off home for your turkey after all?' he added, scanning Mum's card.

'No way – I'm staying put,' Sally said. 'But I wish Harriet would. Her mother's going to blame me for depriving her.'

'She won't,' I said. 'She'll be too busy to miss me and I'm not sure I can face those kids again, anyway.' I got on fine with Mum now, though all had not invariably been pink and cosy in earlier years. Bill was great, too, and the picture-postcard Devon longhouse was lovely, but it would also be full of Bill's son, plus son's wife and three kids, two of whom were whiny little pains. After a couple of weekends in their company I wasn't sure I could stand a repeat without Prozac.

'Maybe I'll stay too, then,' he said. 'The mistletoe between two prickly bits of holly, scattering little baby sunbeams when you're fighting over what crappy Christmas telly to watch.'

'God help us,' said Sally.

As Frida had already booked her ticket home, I'd been hoping he'd stay. He'd be gone for good soon enough, and

26

more was always merrier. 'Won't your folks be put out if you don't go home?'

'Probably, but you don't know Christmas in our house – Auntie X bitching about what Auntie Y said thirty years ago, Granddad snoring with his mouth open, and Uncle Dick putting a grape in it for a laugh and nearly choking him to death, and Mum wishing she and Dad could just piss off to Barbados for once.'

'Then why don't they?' Sally asked. 'They're not exactly skint.'

'They're going in February,' he said. 'So they have to suffer first. It's the rules.'

Just as he said it, a faint whimpering came from the baby alarm on the sideboard. 'Oh, God, not *again*,' Sally groaned, heaving herself to the door.

'She's knackered,' Jacko said, as she departed.

'She's been knackered for a week.' Tom wasn't usually so exhausting but he was teething on top of a bad cold; poor Sally had hardly slept for several nights.

Jacko was rereading Nina's card. 'So you're going to see this bloke of hers?'

'It's not exactly "seeing", is it? Just a little thank-you drink.'

'Sounds like "seeing" to me. Speaking from the enemy camp, I can tell you that dishing out emergency dosh is one thing. Dishing out phone numbers is something else.'

'Jacko, he was just being nice.' I said this largely to fool Fate, who was bound to be listening. Privately I was wallowing in the piquant possibility that he wasn't just being 'nice'. Even more piquant was the off-chance that he was also, after all, a fourteenth cousin of Nina's who had a phobia about silk-curtain hair.

I started tidying up, though the kitchen never looked tidy even when it was. The house was one of those six-bedroomed Edwardian jobs that fetch bombs when done up, and lesser bombs even when they're not. This still possessed 'a wealth of original features', including prehistoric chain-pull loo and built-in, wall-to-wall draughts. It had been the family home of my father's old Auntie Dorothy, who'd spent virtually nothing on it since circa 1937, unless you counted a brief mad impulse circa 1962, courtesy of the kind of builders who love old ladies on toast for breakfast. Besides what passed for central heating, they'd knocked an old-fashioned pantry and scullery into the breakfast room to make a big kitchen, and added a few 'modern' units. These had been falling to bits ever since, which was why three of the cupboards had possessed no doors for fifteen years.

Poor old Dorothy was still there, tucked up in an urn on the dining-room mantelpiece. I felt bad leaving her there, especially as she'd left half the house to me, but she was waiting to be scattered off a particular cliff in Dorset. Only Dad knew where it was and he was in Turkey, according to the latest phone call.

Sally came back, with Tom on her hip. He was pale, poor little sausage, but he gave us a dribbly grin. 'Hi, stinker,' I said. 'Keep Mummy at it, there's a good boy.'

Jacko said, 'Start the way you mean to go on, mate. Treat 'em mean. And when you've got it sussed, give your Uncle Jacko a few pointers.'

Sally shifted a pile of washing, flopped onto the sofa, and yanked up her sweatshirt to give Tom his comfort food. I'd made the kitchen into a living room with a Tulley's sofa (it's amazing what you can find in charity shops) and a 14″ all-in-one TV and video on the sideboard. Since October we'd hardly used the sitting room, because although it would soon be described by estate agents as an 'elegant and well-proportioned drawing room', it was perhaps best suited to defrosting a chicken over six weeks or so. It contained the only truly modern item Dorothy had ever lashed out on: a massive Sony television, as her main pleasure in life had been the racing and her eyesight had been getting dodgy.

As always when Sally was feeding Tom, Jacko watched in unashamed fascination. If any other bloke had been gawping like that, Sally would have uttered a tart 'Have you never seen boobs before?' or at least felt uncomfortable. With Jacko it was impossible to feel uncomfortable; even in his worst excesses there'd always been a certain disarming innocence about him.

Tom soon drifted off, and Sally crept away to put him down.

'It's enough to make you wish you were six months old again,' Jacko sighed, after the door had shut behind her. 'Trouble is, at that age you don't appreciate what you're getting. Life's so sodding perverse.'

As this was normal rambling, rather than new and original thought, I made no comment.

He then picked up Nina's card again. 'My bog-roll dinosaurs always fell to bits, too. Or was it egg boxes? I once made a really great stegosaurus out of egg boxes.'

My mind was elsewhere.

'So when are you going to phone this bloke?' he went on.

This was where my mind had been, of course. Saying, 'Just get on and *do* it, Harriet. Nice bloke, fourteenth cousin or even wrong number on purpose, there's only one way to find out.'

Further titles available in Arrow . . .

Also available in Arrow

# Running in Heels

Anna Maxted

'To say that Babs is my closest friend is rather like
saying that Einstein was good at sums. And if you've
ever had a best friend, you'll know what I mean. Babs
and I had such a beautiful relationship, no man could
better it. And then she met Simon.'

Now Babs, noisy, funny Babs, is getting married. And
Natalie, 27, is panicking. What happens when your best
friend pledges everlasting love to someone else?

As the confetti flutters, Nat feels her good-girl veneer
crack. She teeters into an alluringly unsuitable affair that
spins her crazily out of control and into trouble – with her
boss, Matt, and with Babs.

Caught up in the thrill of bad behaviour, Nat blithely
ignores the truth – about her new boyfriend, her best
friend's marriage, her mother's cooking and the wisdom of
inviting Babs's brother Andy – slippers and all – to be her
lodger. But perhaps what Nat really needs to face is the
mirror – and herself . . .

# The Marrying Game

Kate Saunders

**They set out to Marry for Money ... But ended up falling in love**

With a batty Mother, a crumbling house and no education to speak of, the four Hasty girls aren't best equipped for the modern world. And when the death of their father leaves them nothing but mountains of debt, drastic action is called for.

Luckily, the eldest, Rufa – already an expert at making ends meet – has a Plan. If their sole inheritance is their ravishing good looks then she and her sisters must put all thoughts of love out of their minds and Marry Money. And so, with her outrageously sexy sister Nancy, she sets off to blaze a trail through London society.

The Marrying Game has begun ... .

# Virtue

Serena Mackesy

**Saints, sinners and the mere mortals in between**

What do you need to be a saint these days? Ambition, determination and good PR. But what do you do if your mother's a saint and you just want to be human?

Anna and Harriet share a burden: hellishly saintly mothers. So armed with a wicked sense of humour, they set out to paint the town red. And for a while life goes swimmingly. But when they tread on one toe too many, they find that they have only their worst instincts – and each other – to rely on.

Be good. And if you can't be good, be careful . . .

Order further *Arrow* titles from your local
bookshop, or have them delivered direct
to your door by Bookpost